PRAISE FOR KARIN CATHER

"Cather effectively blends a police procedural with a thrilling space odyssey, with all of the darkness and death that can occur in both genres doubly amplified."
— Kirkus Reviews

A MILLION MONKEYS

A MILLION MONKEYS

KARIN CATHER

Betelgeuse Books

Copyright © 2025 by Betelgeuse Books LLC

Book design by Katherine Kirk

Cover design by AuthorsHQ.com

ISBN 979-8-9986785-0-9 (paperback)

ISBN 979-8-9986785-1-6 (ebook)

betelgeusebooks.com

To my mom, Sally Horwatt Brodsky, who taught me that books are important.

PART ONE

PART ONE

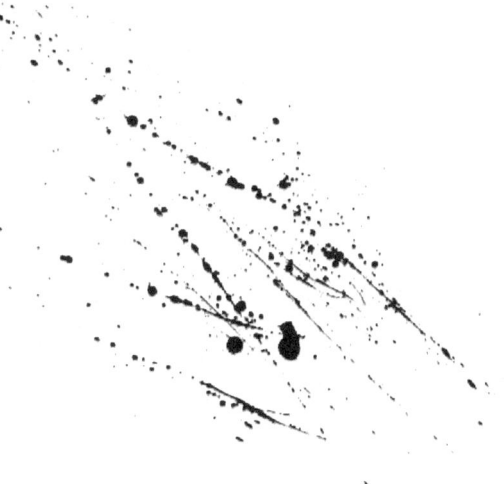

HIS BODY WAS in the whirlpool tub in the master bathroom.

Eliza had just finished listening to a recording of the 911 call on her way to the scene. Kelly Chatworth told the dispatcher that her husband, Glenn Sommars, had been shot. The dispatcher told Kelly to shelter in place. Kelly had had the hollow, shaky voice of a person inches from full-on panic.

When Eliza arrived, one of the patrol officers at the scene told Eliza that Glenn Sommars was fifty-eight years old and a software engineering manager for a major airline, and Kelly Chatworth was fifty years old and a stay-at-home mom. Neither had criminal histories.

Eliza went to speak with Kelly, who was sitting in a police cruiser. "I'm Detective Eliza Benveniste. I'm so, so sorry for your loss."

Kelly had been crying hard. "They didn't stay long," she said.

"Who didn't stay long?"

"The paramedics. I lost it a little at first. I asked the paramedics why they weren't doing anything. I'd just finished telling the dispatcher what I saw—" and she covered her eyes, then rubbed them. "Then I said to them, 'I'm sorry' at the same time one of them said, 'There's nothing we can do.' Then they asked me if they could call anyone for me. Only there's no one to call."

"No one?" Eliza asked.

Kelly looked down at her lap. "I should call the kids and tell them."

"Where are they?"

"With my parents. They're with my parents. I should call them."

"Kelly, I will do the best I can to find out who murdered your husband." She paused. "It's a lot cooler back at our office."

Kelly started. "Am—am I under arrest?"

"What? No! But we'd—"

"Well, it's better than sitting in this car. But can Officer"— and Kelly peered at his badge—"Officer Swift run me by Earthquake Coffee on the way?" She looked at him. "Would that be okay?"

"They're open?" Eliza asked.

"Twenty-four hours," Swift said. "Sure."

"Can we go in? I know this sounds strange, with my husband dead. I guess I keep expecting him to show up." At "show up," Kelly's voice broke. "But I worked out for two hours before I got home, and I'm hungry."

"Did you shower in the house?" Eliza asked.

"What? Next to the body of my husband? No! At the— where I work out."

"Sure, he can go in with you," Eliza said. She knew that Kyle Swift wouldn't try to interview Kelly and spook her into invoking Miranda.

Eliza decided that she had time to go through the house briefly before going to the office. She handed Kelly a copy of the search warrant, telling her that it was just protocol. Kelly put the search warrant in her lap without reading it. The car pulled away.

Eliza walked back to the driveway. Her partner, Detective Jamie Cloud, was staring at the house. Then they looked at each other.

"This would be my definition of hell," Eliza said.

The house was a Northern Virginia colonial-style cookie-cutter model in the interior of the development, four houses up from the cul-de-sac.

"This street looks like a meth pipe," Jamie said, "cut lengthwise."

Most of the other houses had pastel blue or yellow siding. Some had bright white siding. The fake shutters were black or white. They had basketball hoops in the driveway and flowers planted around the trees in their yards. The porches had rockers or swings, garden boxes of more flowers, hanging plants.

The siding at the Sommars house was beige, and the fake shutters were tan. The front lawn looked sickly, mowed to HOA-regulation height, but faded. There was a wraparound porch with no furniture, just an ugly, undersized black doormat.

Now the house had yellow crime scene tape around it, beginning in the driveway and running all the way around to the back fence. Eliza noted with approval that Officer Joe Costa had placed red crime scene tape across the door.

"Gives it a needed splash of color, don't you think?" Eliza said to Jamie.

Jamie laughed. "You're dark, Eliza."

She walked up to the street cop. "I see security cameras, Joe. Did they get anything?"

"Oh," Joe said, rolling his eyes, "the wife says they have a state-of-the-art security system and lots of cameras. But they were off."

"State-of-the-art? What the hell does that mean?"

"A state-of-the-art security system is the same amount of cameras as a peon security system, only with more cloud storage. Probably. Maybe it makes their coffee for them. Fuck, I dunno. But it was off. The wife says they only turned the security system on at night."

"Fantastic."

Joe handed Eliza a clipboard with the entry/exit log. She saw that only Joe, Officer Ezra Sams, and three paramedics had been in the house so far.

Eliza and Jamie printed and signed their names, then documented time of entry.

Ezra Sams walked up, twentysomething and eager.

"Paramedics came, saw, and went," Joe said.

"This time," Jamie said, looking at Ezra. "I had a case where EMS responded to an ice-cold subject found dead in a freezer, and a noob started chest compressions. Dead guy was in total rigor. Also, his throat had been slit from ear to ear."

It had been Eliza's case too.

"You're bullshitting me," Ezra said.

"You didn't hear about this?" Eliza said.

"I'm not bullshitting you," Jamie said. "I asked the paramedic what he thought he was doing, and he said, 'They're not dead until they're warm and dead.' I dunno, maybe he missed arm day at the gym. I told him that if he could bring back a guy in rigor, he could start a new religion."

"Well at least it didn't work," Joe said. "That would've been worse."

"It was his first day on the job!" Eliza said. "Give the guy a break!"

"Did he notice the man's blood volume decorating the freezer floor?" Joe asked.

"Is ... is your body camera on?" Eliza asked Joe.

Joe pushed a button. "Now it is."

The interior of the house was sweltering.

Eliza entered with Jamie and two CSIs.

Right past the front door was a little wooden hanging rack for keys. Eliza noted five pegs, one set of keys hanging from one peg. Hanging from another was an ID badge on a lanyard, which upon inspection turned out to be Glenn's. A third peg showed wear and tear, but Kelly would have had her keys with her. The other two pegs had no such wear and tear.

Below the key rack on the spotless dark wood floor squatted a small shelving unit for shoes. It had one pair of shoes on it, which Eliza decided belonged to Glenn. Next was a thin composite-wood sideboard with a tiny vase full of fake daisies. Anyone walking in saw it edge-on, not lengthwise.

Eliza confirmed that the coat closet across from key rack contained no murder weapons, suspects, or additional bodies.

Then Eliza searched the sideboard. The shallow drawers contained nothing but a pen with no cap and some batteries. The larger sections beneath should have contained china that no one ever used. Instead, they contained nothing.

To the left was the living room. It was huge, because of course it was. In it was a gigantic faux-leather beige couch that matched the washed-out siding. At ninety degrees to this couch, its back to Eliza, was a recliner. It too was beige. On the seat was the remote for the eighty-five-inch flat-screen TV.

The TV had been placed oddly, so people on the couch would have to sit slantwise to watch it, even though the wall in front of the couch was bare and more than big enough for the TV. Anyone who sat in the chair, on the other hand, had a perfect view of the TV. Eliza decided that Glenn sat in that chair and speculated that he had been murdered by someone who lived with him.

The thermostat was at the entrance to the dining room, and Eliza saw that it was set to ninety degrees—despite the fact that it was July and the temperature outside approached a hundred degrees. As always in Northern Virginia during the summer, it had rained in the afternoon, which merely made the heat afterward even more stifling.

The kitchen had faux-country cabinets and a breakfast bar with two barstools. The breakfast nook had no table or chairs. The sink was as spotless as the rest of the kitchen.

The refrigerator had nothing stuck to it—no pictures, no magnets, no grocery lists.

"They spared every expense," Jamie said. "This place is depressing." He looked like he'd walked into his own apartment and found an unzipped body bag on his living room floor. "And it's hot in here!"

"Agreed." She looked at him sharply. "You okay? We respond to outdoor crime scenes in the summer all the time. Pretend we're outside."

Jamie looked at her as if he was about to say something but stopped himself, then settled on, "Yeah. Whoever set this thermostat was an asshole."

At six-five and 210 pounds, Jamie towered over thirty-two-year-old Eliza, who was five-two and 110 pounds. Jamie was pushing forty. He was slightly stooped in the way that some middle-aged men are before they eventually look like a question mark in old age. The two had been partners for five years and friends for almost that long.

"I guess if the house setup is all Glenn's idea, there could be many suspects," Eliza said.

They soon determined that there was no sign of forced entry on the main floor.

Eliza wondered whether they were house poor. If they'd bought more house than they could afford, maybe they couldn't afford better furniture or any wall art.

Nothing explained the TV setup.

Back in the living room, Jamie asked, "Whose chair is that, do you think?"

"Glenn's," Eliza said immediately.

"How do you know?"

"Because he's the one who's dead."

Jamie laughed.

She spotted a den off the living room and pointed Jamie toward it.

"Look, a man cave," Eliza said as they went in. "And it's cool in here. Why is that?"

"Separate heating/cooling system?" Jamie gave a low whistle. "That cost extra."

"Of course he did."

"Did what?"

"A guy who could make everyone else watch TV sideways could also pull this shit with the AC and the heat. It's miserably hot and stuffy out there, and it's nice and cool in here. Turn a fan on and you could have a little thunderstorm in the doorway."

The den had nothing but a desk, a laptop, an office chair, and another TV.

"It's almost like all of the things in the house are just ... props!" Eliza said, looking around the room. "The sideboard? Almost nothing in it. There's"—she opened the desk's drawer —"nothing in the drawer here. Nothing on the desk itself other than the laptop."

"I wonder what Forensics will find on that laptop."

"Nothing? Because it's a prop?"

"You keep saying that. Maybe they're just obsessively tidy."

The window in the den was closed and locked, Eliza saw, and there was dust on the windowsill.

The detectives were following department protocol, starting the farthest away from the body and working inward, spiral fashion. This reduced the chance of missing crucial evidence. Afterward, they would reverse the process, inward to outward—or Jamie would. Eliza would be back at the office, interviewing Kelly.

The stairs to the basement were covered with beige carpeting. At the bottom, there was what looked exactly like a well-equipped commercial gym.

"Put a receptionist at the bottom of the stairs and they could sell memberships," Eliza said. "This place has everything."

"They had more than enough money for upstairs furniture and any goddamn thing on the walls. Must have cost thousands to put this together."

"I'd guess probably twenty thousand." She gestured at the equipment. "And a lot of it is redundant. Why do you need a power rack *and* a squat rack?"

But Jamie was looking around. "Notice that all the weights

are too heavy for the wife? Eliza, can you lift anything in the room?"

"Are there thirty-five-pound dumbbells?" She looked more closely. The rows of dumbbells reminded Eliza of rows of coffins. "Nope. Then no."

The weight room looked immaculate, nothing out of place. No weights covered with blood, no broken mirrors. There was disinfectant and—

"Ohhh, look!" Eliza said. "Lookee who has his very own TV set!" Eliza saw that Glenn could watch himself in the mirror or turn around and use an elliptical machine or exercise bike and watch TV. "Still think the wife gets to sit in the chair?"

Jamie barked out a laugh. "Maybe she gets the chair because he's got the gym?"

At the far end of the gym was a sliding glass door. On the other side of the sliding glass door, there was a gigantic spider web with a giant orb weaver in the middle—the very poster child of huge spiders and huge spiderwebs. The bar on the sliding glass door was locked in place. Eliza imagined the photograph of this spider on its web being sent out for discovery to defense counsel, and she smiled. She put her hand on a CSI's shoulder and pointed at the web with an evil grin. The CSI took a prizewinning photograph of the whole thing, the spider remaining cooperatively immobile.

Eliza knew that it took an orb weaver close to an hour to spin a web, and the bar was down. The killer was highly unlikely to have made entry here.

Jamie was at her elbow. "Ugh," he said, looking at the spider. "Kill it with fire."

"That's a female *Argiope aurantia*," she said without

looking at him. "See how she's got those yellow and white markings? The males are smaller and all brown."

"I'm not even going to try to pronounce that. How do you always know this shit?"

"They're everywhere, and I got curious."

"Well, how else are we supposed to get through that door?"

"By going upstairs and through the gate. Don't bother the spider, or I'm going to lose my temper. Killing animals you don't like is reprehensible."

They went back upstairs and out the front door and walked around the house. There was nothing remarkable other than a tree next to a bedroom window.

Eliza saw that the gate was unlocked. In the backyard, there was nothing but an ill-tended lawn interspersed with crabgrass and boxed in with a cheap wooden six-foot privacy fence.

They went back in and up to the second floor. At the top of the stairs, they turned right and found a home office. In it was a chair and a plain desk with a laptop sitting on it—no desk lamp or even a cup full of pens. By the window was an exercise bike with a pink headband hanging from it, never worn. The window was intact, locked from the inside, with dust on the windowsill.

The closet had nothing in it. There were no drawers to the desk, and there was no trash in the wastebasket.

"It's hers," Eliza said, pointing at the bike. "He gets the home gym, she gets an exercise bike—and it's not even as good as his. I'll bet he was an absolute tyrant."

"I don't think Denny would let you testify to that," Jamie said, "over a TV setup, a thermostat, and a gym." Denny was the most experienced homicide prosecutor in Tauxenent County. And an absolute legend.

"But here again," Eliza went on, "pieces of furniture in

rooms no one uses—and no wear and tear on the carpet to show that anyone sits in this chair at all!"

They left the home office and entered the next room down the hall. It was a bedroom, which was furnished for a teenager or young adult and looked unused. The room had a fusty smell. The bed was made with military precision, with a thin gray bedspread and a single pillow with a black pillowcase. There was nothing under the bed.

Eliza gestured at the room. "What teenager or young adult wants to make a bed like that?"

"It smells like no one has lived here for a while. Maybe someone else made the bed."

When they looked in the closet, they saw that it was empty but for some wire hangers. There was nothing under the bed.

The window showed no signs of forced entry.

"They'd have to rappel down from the roof," Eliza said, "or use a ladder or maybe climb that tree." But there was dust on this windowsill too.

The bed in the next bedroom had hospital corners at the foot of the bed, but at the head, someone had taken the bedspread and sheet and yanked them into disarray, leaving the lone pillow on the floor. Science fiction posters covered most of the walls, including from the Star Trek franchise, from the show *The Orville*, and one from the movie *Metropolis*. On the wall across from the bed hung a collection of fan-made posters from the science fiction book *Rebellion at Broken Oar*. There was a small shelf of books. Science fiction, speculative fiction, fantasy. Eliza recognized most of the titles, including the *Broken Oar* book, which was sitting in her to-be-read pile.

When Jamie saw the posters, he whispered, "Ffffuck."

"What?"

"It's the book *Rebellion at Broken Oar*. Glenn Sommars

was a bad guy in the book." As if he had seen something horrifying, Jamie turned on his heel and walked out of the room.

Eliza looked in the closet and found utilitarian clothing that she speculated was worn by a girl. On the floor was one pair of shoes.

In the doorway of the master bedroom, she smelled the familiar iron smell of blood—and the separate metallic smell that signaled gunfire.

The bed was the lone piece of furniture in the room. It had no headboard. It was also made to military precision, the corners pointed somehow, with a white comforter that must have been a bear to sleep under in the heat. There was no TV on the wall and no artwork. No nothing. Just a bed.

Beneath it was only carpeting.

Jamie stood just inside the doorway, waiting for her, and Eliza knew that she was going to have a pointed discussion with him later about his strange behavior.

"California king," Eliza said. "At least she didn't have to touch him."

The walk-in closet was to the left. The dead guy wore nothing but polo shirts, with the occasional business suit. Lots of khaki. Kelly had three pairs of shoes in the closet.

The master bathroom was on the same side as the door to the bedroom. Eliza noted wet footprints leading from the master bathroom to the carpeted bedroom, and they ended at the bed. There was a depression on the bedspread.

She walked to the entrance of the bathroom. She saw a trail of water that led from the threshold of the bathroom to the shower. In the stifling humidity of a Virginia summer in a home with virtually no air conditioning, this could have happened a minute ago or an hour ago.

"Whoever it was didn't want to get dressed in front of Glenn," Eliza said.

Jamie walked into the bathroom.

She caught up with him. The smell of blood was powerful here. "Jamie, I know something's wrong."

Jamie put his hand on her shoulder, but he did not answer.

The shower and the whirlpool tub were to their left. The clear-glass shower door was designed to open outward, but it was closed. A 9mm handgun rested on the floor of the shower. Eliza noted that there was no blood on the floor of the bathroom or in the shower.

The near end of the tub abutted the shower and extended to the left corner.

There was a window in front of them and a window over the tub. The glass was frosted.

Jamie looked closely at the window at the far end of the bathroom. "Soundproof glass," he said.

"How do you know it's soundproof glass?"

"It's triple-paned laminated glass."

"You'd think that after Dyson, people'd stop soundproofing their homes." Eliza shuddered.

A double vanity was to their right, with a cheap oval mirror over each sink.

The toilet seat was up.

Eliza turned her attention to the whirlpool tub. Glenn lay fully clothed in the empty tub as if he had backed up against it and fallen backward, his calves resting over the side. The body was slightly aslant relative to the feet. The back of his head rested against the far wall of the tub, with his chin resting almost on his chest, and he lay in a large pool of blood, which was clotting to brown.

He'd been shot multiple times. Eliza looked at the tub and

then at the shower. *No way could he have shot himself and then tossed the weapon there.*

From where she stood, she could see a smallish gunshot wound between his eyes, one through his throat, and another one in his muscular forearm. There was brain matter spattered on the bottom of the tub and the wall behind his head. Blood spatter on the wall and on the ceiling. Eliza thought that the back of Glenn's head probably looked like a smashed pumpkin. The blond hair on his forearm caught the light. There were multiple gunshot wounds to his torso—one of them to his heart. She stared at that wound. *Contact gunshot wound to the heart?* She looked at the throat shot and all of the other bullet holes in Glenn, trying to imagine the state of mind of the shooter.

"Did someone bring him upstairs at gunpoint or accost him here?" Jamie said, looking down at her. "Swift said there were two kids. Would either of them or the wife be cold enough to walk the shithead up here at gunpoint? Because that's a long time to think about shooting Daddy or Hubby."

"You mean because he might take it from them on the way up the stairs?"

"Nah, he's a desk jockey. Because someone would have to be pretty coldhearted to force their dad or husband at gunpoint to his death. Really cold."

"He had time to take off his shoes and hang up his lanyard." Eliza was grateful that EMS recognized that he was dead and hadn't started rescue protocol, or this crime scene would've been a mess. "But it looks like he didn't even try to get out of the tub at all!"

"How would he? He was shot!"

"Some people keep fighting after they're shot, Jamie.

That's why they teach us to use empty-hand tactics at close range."

"Point taken."

"Plus, if that bullet wound to the throat severed his spine," Eliza said, "maybe he couldn't. Or he dropped like a sack of groceries and lay there stunned. That would also explain why the shooter hit him with every round. Most of the time, people miss some."

"At this range?"

"Yes, at this range. Particularly if the subject is moving."

"No way."

"Want to see the FBI statistics? Even trained shooters miss at close range. Very close range. Like in a single room or even a walk-in closet. This shooter either lucked out or has a heart of ice. Or both."

Neither of them had ever fired their own weapon, although they'd come close a few times.

Glenn's mouth was open. His ice-blue eyes were open, but the corneas were cloudy in death. He had the typical facial expression of the dead, as if they'd answered the door and been greeted by their ex.

His features were sharp. He had a dirty-blond Hitler Youth haircut, graying at the temples. His polo shirt was tucked in his pressed khaki pants, and he wore a narrow black leather belt. He had long, thin fingers and clean, short nails. He was in excellent shape, except for being so dead.

Someone had emptied their gun into Glenn Sommars, then gotten in the shower with it and washed it off.

On Glenn's left inner wrist, which was face-up in the tub and resting in blood, was a tattoo about the size of the man's thumb. It was a black kraken with red eyes. The contrast of black and red against the wax of corpse flesh made the thing look even more evil.

Next to her, Jamie froze.

"What is it?" Eliza asked.

"*Rebellion at Broken Oar*. One ship, the markings had a black kraken with red eyes. It was a symbol the bad guys used." Jamie looked like he wanted to be sick. After a moment, he said, "Her name's Kelly."

"What? What are you talking about—and who's 'her'?"

"There's a Glenn Sommars who's shot to death in the book, and Glenn's wife in the book is Kelly too, and ... Jesus, he was shot exactly the same way." He looked down at Eliza. "How does that happen?"

"You mean in *Rebellion at Broken Oar*?"

Jamie was silent.

"Jamie? You mean in the book?"

"The one."

"That's really spooky. *Twilight Zone* spooky. Maybe we need a list of the characters to make sure that the killer doesn't treat it like a contacts list."

Jamie walked out.

The fuck?

When Jamie walked out, a CSI watched him leave, looked at Eliza, and shrugged.

Eliza saw no signs of a struggle, but then there wasn't really anything in the bathroom to put in disarray. The countertops were as empty as the desktops.

There was a hand soap dispenser beside the sink—but no hand towels. These were store-brand products, she saw, which was interesting given how affluent the family had to be to live in this house and pay for that gym.

Eliza wiped the sweat off her face with a handkerchief and

individually loathed every single dumbbell and piece of equipment in Glenn's goddamned gym. And Glenn Sommars. It was July in Tauxenent County, Virginia, it was ninety-eight degrees outside, the humidity was probably close to 98 percent, and the thermostat was set at ninety fucking degrees.

She looked at the water pooled at the bottom of the shower. She saw that there was no soap of any kind and wondered if the killer had taken it.

As Jamie continued working in the master bedroom, Eliza walked downstairs, stopping to sign out on the clipboard. Jamie would remain to direct further evidence collection, which could take over six hours, and uniformed police officers would remain at both entrances to make sure that the scene was preserved, as it might need to be for days. They might have to go back in to collect further evidence, and they did not want the scene corrupted.

Only when CSI was done would Glenn's body be released to the medical examiner's office. The ME wasn't coming, because Richmond had directed that MEs not go to the scene unless specifically requested by the detective or according to a thick policy manual in an unexamined three-ring binder in a random administrator's office. It mystified Eliza, because Tauxenent County for one reason or another was willing to match state funds and pay its own medical examiner when others normally covered more than one county.

Neither Eliza nor Jamie would have any reason to go back into the Sommars-Chatworth house.

KELLY SAT in the interview room, and Eliza stood at the observation window and watched her for a moment. She had a lanky build, with shoulder-length, silky blond hair that Eliza felt sure was her natural color. Her skin was that golden color that some people with blue eyes and blond hair have in the summer. Kelly was beautiful.

She wore pale blue denim jeans and a long-sleeved pink linen shirt with loose, cuffless sleeves. The shirt was too hot for the weather. She was also wearing a black cotton scarf with tassels. It was very fashionable, but also not appropriate for the weather. It covered her neck, and the bottom edge of it fell below her collarbone. She had black ankle boots on and a very small gold ring on her left hand. No other jewelry.

Eliza watched as Kelly looked around the room nervously. The space had been made deliberately comfortable, but the table was nevertheless bolted to the floor and shaped so that a suspect could be handcuffed to it. This was the interview room used for witnesses who could turn into suspects and who might otherwise get up and leave if the room screamed "police interrogation."

Kelly was still crying.

Eliza saw a travel tumbler on the table in front of Kelly, so she went and poured herself a mug of coffee. Then she walked into the room and sat down at the table as if the two women were about to have a confidential chat.

As soon as Eliza sat down, Kelly wiped her eyes and looked at Eliza's coffee mug, then said, "I'm not under arrest?" She was gripping the side of the table with one delicate hand.

Kelly's eyes were startling, a blue the color of very faded denim, the ring around the edge of her iris not much darker.

"What? No!" Eliza said. "Can I get you anything?"

Kelly relaxed slightly, but she looked around the room again and scanned the ceiling and corners. Eliza realized she was looking for cameras.

"No, thanks." Kelly held up her travel mug. "I got a sandwich at Earthquake Coffee. And used the bathroom." Then she said, "Middle-aged bladders. Just you wait." She looked at Eliza's mug again. "You drink it black?"

"Everyone asks me that," Eliza said, smiling a little. "You?"

"Almond milk and sugar."

"Oh! Like my sister!"

Eliza's sister drank green tea.

Kelly studied her. "But we're not here to talk about coffee," she said, eyes welling up.

"No, we're not. But you've had a terrible shock today, and coffee is a food group, no?"

Kelly laughed. "I'd never heard it put like that, but that sounds about right. I almost put wine in it. But I didn't. Wanna look?"

"I believe you. Wine in a coffee tumbler is a terrible way to drink it."

"How can I help you?" Kelly said.

"Do you want anything to eat or to use the restroom before we start? I could come back with some cookies."

"No, thanks. Officer Swift was very kind. He made sure that I got what I needed."

"Okay, but anytime you need to use the restroom, or you get hungry or thirsty, let me know."

"I will."

Eliza meant to start with the basics—Kelly's occupation, who lived in the home with her, and similar—and ease her into talking about what she'd seen.

Nothing doing.

Kelly said, "I was late coming home today. I wonder what would've happened if I had come home on time."

"You were late?"

"Yes, I was. I'm usually home before 5:30 on Fridays. Today I was home late because I had a flat tire." She held out her smartphone. "Here's the receipt." As Eliza studied it, Kelly said, "I guess ... I guess it's a good thing I was home late."

"Did you try to call your husband to tell him you were running late?"

"I did, but he didn't answer. I thought he must be angry at me."

"Why?"

"He didn't like for people to be late."

"When did you try to call him?"

Kelly looked at her and let out a long breath. "After working out, I went to the Tauxenent County Central Library because I'd left a jacket behind, and I left here right at 5:00." The library and station were both at the Civic Complex, diagonally opposite, with the library on the southeast corner. "When I got to the car, the front driver's side tire was flat. Just completely flat."

Later, Eliza would pull the library video. It would show Kelly rushing out of the library at 12:37 p.m., leaving a pink jacket on the back of the chair, and rushing back into the library at 4:56 p.m. Kelly had gone back to the seat, looked at the chair, looked under the table, and then hurried up to the front desk, where a librarian eventually handed her the jacket, neatly folded. Kelly was standing by her car at 5:06 p.m.

In the interview room, however, Kelly was either telling the truth or getting caught in a verifiable lie.

Kelly showed Eliza a photo on her smartphone. Eliza saw that, in fact, this photo was taken in front of the library and the tire was, in fact, flat. The car in the photo matched the car in the garage of the Sommars-Chatworth home, right down to the license plate. Eliza looked at the time stamp. She noted that there was an app on her phone that prevented alteration of time stamps and thought of Glenn. The time stamp showed 5:07 p.m.

Just as Eliza wondered why Glenn hadn't also put a simple tracker app on the phone, Kelly said, "I put the spare on and drove it to replace the tire. Of course, you can never replace just one."

Eliza studied the photo, then looked up. "That must have been really frustrating!" She took a sip of coffee.

"It was."

"You took a photo of the tire. Why?"

Kelly shifted in her seat. Then she showed Eliza the call list on her smartphone. It showed two phone calls to Glenn—at 5:06 and 5:15 p.m.

Eliza thought about the home gym, the TV setup, and the time-stamp app and realized that Kelly was a woman who was used to having to account for her whereabouts. She wondered if that was why Kelly had been looking around for cameras.

Eliza also noted that, at least on paper, Kelly had expected Glenn to answer the phone.

"So I was late." Kelly stared at the coffee tumbler and toyed with it, turning it back and forth. Then she looked up. "I got home at 5:50 p.m. Normally, at that time of the day, Glenn would be working out downstairs. But he wasn't in the gym. So I went upstairs and that's ... that's when I found him. I realized that he was dead." She covered her face with her hands and took a gasping breath. "I mean, parts of his brain were in the tub. And ... and all that blood." Kelly broke out into a cold sweat. "I called 911, and police and ambulance came, and then you came."

"I'm so sorry," Eliza said. "That must have been a terrible shock."

"My husband's body was in the bathtub in a pool of blood, and his brains were in the bottom," she said. "How would that *not* be a shock?"

Eliza ignored this and asked Kelly about how her day had started and then worked forward to the moment when she made the 911 call. Then she asked, "Do you go to the library a lot?"

"Yes. I got my master's in linguistics, and now I'm working with my dissertation supervisor to finish my PhD. And I'm a teacher's assistant."

"You didn't want to take courses at GMU?"

"I'm taking courses from UVA remotely ... behind Glenn's back. You can imagine why." Kelly turned the tumbler around so the writing on it faced her again. "When I'm teaching, I use one of the library's booths. They're set up to not make noise."

"Are you working on your dissertation yet?"

"Yes, I am."

Eliza took down the contact information for Kelly's dissertation supervisor. Then she smiled. "I'd ask you what it's about, but I know I wouldn't understand it."

Kelly told her anyway.

"That's way over my head."

"You don't have a degree?"

"I do. Cognitive anthropology."

"What you have to learn and think in order to belong in a culture. And yet you're a cop. And if you understand cognitive anthropology, you understand the topic of my dissertation, so there's no need to play dumb."

Eliza shook her head. "Not enough of an overlap. I have a little knowledge about your topic, enough to get it wrong with bigger words."

Kelly smiled briefly.

"And yeah, I became a cop. It's amazing how much my background comes in handy. And you chose to stay home with your kids. I'll bet you took some flak for that."

Kelly uncrossed her arms and clasped her hands in her lap. "I did take some crap for that. And I'm sure you got some crap from people about being a cop."

"Yes. I did. It seems that fundamentally, neither of us take direction well."

Eliza expected Kelly to laugh at this, but she turned pale. "In the end, I guess you're right."

Eliza sensed she was hitting a sore spot, so she changed the subject. "Who lives in the house with you? Is it just the two of you?"

"No, my daughter Maura lives with us. Glenn kicked Cody out when he was sixteen and Maura was twelve. Cody lives with my parents."

"Why?"

Kelly looked down.

"Was there a problem?"

"Please leave my son out of this. He didn't do anything wrong!"

"No," Eliza said in a soothing voice. "Just getting some background information."

"Cody's first name is Glenn. Too. His father called him Junior. We all did. Cody's his middle name. Then in his freshman year of high school, he started calling himself Cody. That's what teenagers do, right? But Glenn had a meltdown. And as Cody got older, they started butting heads even more. Cody started practicing martial arts in his freshman year of high school. I saw the shirts—they had to wear shirts with their logo on them. Glenn didn't see them. I made sure of that."

"Why is that?"

"Glenn was ..." Kelly sunk down in her chair again and tensed, "upset a lot."

"What upset your husband?"

"A lot."

"What do you mean by 'upset'? Do you mean abuse?"

"Cody was always standing between him and me or Maura."

"Did he ever tell you he wanted to hurt your husband?"

"No. And if you saw what Glenn did to him over the years, you'd stop thinking my son is a time bomb. When Cody came home, he normally climbed up the tree—you know, the one outside our house—and went into his bedroom through the window instead of walking through the door. He didn't the day he got kicked out. I didn't know why."

"I just want to understand. When Glenn kicked Cody out, how old was he?"

Kelly looked down, crying silently. "Sixteen."

"How old is he now?" Eliza slid a box of tissues across the table.

Kelly wiped her face roughly, then brushed a stray hair behind her ear and Eliza noted a bruise on her wrist, as if someone had grabbed it.

"He's twenty now. Cody ... Cody just made Glenn ... really upset. About nothing. You never knew when Glenn would get upset or about what. And then Cody came home one Saturday morning after being out all night." Kelly gripped the coffee tumbler so tightly her arm was shaking and the skin underneath her fingernails turned white. "He walked up on the porch, and Glenn was standing in the doorway. Cody just said, 'Hi, Dad.' Glenn said, 'Get inside! Now!' And Cody said ... Cody said, 'Jesus, you are such a miserable cocksucker, aren't you?' He'd never talked to his father like that before. And Glenn started toward him, and Cody yelled, 'Get *over* yourself, why don't you? Just get the fuck *over* yourself!'" Kelly stared off at a point over Eliza's shoulder, tears running down her cheeks.

"He hit him?" Eliza noted that Kelly's delivery was understated, but Eliza imagined the argument and knew that *it* hadn't been.

"He tried to."

"How did you feel about that?"

"He hit him all the time, Detective. All his life. This time, Cody blocked it. Twice." She grabbed a tissue and wiped her face roughly with it. "Glenn just laughed at him and told him he fights like a girl. And that was the end of it."

"Did any of the neighbors see this?"

Kelly went white. "You're saying it didn't happen?"

"No, I believe you! I'm just wondering whether the neighbors—"

"I don't know. My—Glenn was kicking Cody out of the house." Kelly was shaking, as if she might as well have been on that porch. "And I let him. *I let him.* I knew that my parents would take him in. And I knew that he was safer there. I went to his school the next day and told him that, and he said, 'Why don't you just take Maura and go too?' And I told him the truth. That Maura was too young for a judge to listen to her. That I couldn't pay a divorce lawyer. That I had nowhere to move to. That I would have lost custody of both of them because Glenn had convinced everyone that I was crazy.

"I went to see Cody a couple of times at school. But then I saw Glenn's car. I saw Glenn's car in the school parking lot. He was just sitting there. So I turned around and went home before he saw me."

"How did you feel about that?"

"About what? That my son did not live with me or that Glenn was trying to stop me from seeing him?"

"Either," Eliza said softly.

"Terrified." Kelly said this in a dull voice.

"Why didn't you visit Cody at your parents' house?"

"My mother would have called Glenn to ask him why I was upset. Even if I had told her not to. She was convinced he was a good man, and nothing I said would change her mind."

"Your mother wasn't supportive?"

"She likes to believe that everything is perfect. She liked Glenn. I was supposed to be a wife she could brag about, and I couldn't be that." She studied Eliza. "Mom refused to believe me. And ... I guess you'd expect my parents to protect me, but not all parents do."

"No," Eliza said. "Not all parents do. I'm sure your family's relationship dynamics didn't start with your marriage. Which is how even brilliant, educated women like you can end up in a marriage like yours. Were your parents abusive?"

"No," Kelly said immediately. "And Glenn didn't escalate until Cody was born."

Eliza knew she'd come back to that. "How often would Cody stay out all night?"

"A lot. He never got in any trouble with the law, nothing like that."

Eliza already knew that.

"He ... he stayed with friends. They were ... they played a lot of role-playing games, and one had one of those home weather stations, and another one liked to talk about his telescope. Bookish types. I met them once."

"When Cody would stay out all night, did you worry?"

"I worried a lot, but there wasn't anything I could do. You can't chain a teenager to a radiator, you know? And ... I had an idea that he needed to escape the house for a while. He never came back drunk or high. I worried all night. But what could I have done?"

Thinking back to when she was that age, Eliza said, "Not much. Except make it worse. It sounds like you didn't."

Kelly relaxed and took a deep drink of coffee. "I'm glad you see it that way. Not so many people would."

"We've all been teenagers, Kelly."

Kelly laughed. "I might as well have never been one."

Eliza was silent for a moment. "How ... how did Glenn convince your friends you were crazy?"

Kelly once more gripped the side of the table and looked at the floor. "I ... he told them in front of me that I ... dropped out of university after a semester because of my mental health, so I went to get my transcript and my diploma to show them ... but they were gone. I got so angry."

"What happened when you got angry?"

"I started sobbing. I asked them how they could believe my husband instead of coming to me directly. We'd been friends for twenty-five years. I told them I would have been glad to have official transcripts sent to them. I was crying at the same time, and one of them said, "You're getting hysterical." Another said, "Glenn said he asked for them, and there weren't any. You need help, Kelly." At that point, I hit my breaking point. I screamed at him, and then I screamed at them. Glenn told them I was having an episode, and they left. Of course, he'd recorded the whole thing. It would have been used against me in family court. And ... I would never have dared scream at him in private." Involuntarily, she reached for her throat.

"That's horrible," Eliza said. "I'm so sorry. These friends, surely they knew you when you were an undergraduate, no?"

"No, from after I graduated. I never figured out why my college friends stopped talking to me. Now I wonder what Glenn told them." Kelly was quiet.

After a moment, Eliza said, "Do you see Cody?"

"We practice martial arts at the same place. While Glenn is at work. You see, Glenn initially checked up on me so often that I never knew where he would turn up."

"He didn't put a tracker app on your phone or a tracker on your car?"

"No. Where would I go? I had no friends, and he knew it. The phones were in his name, so he could see every number I called or texted. He knew Cody's schedule, so he sat in the school parking lot during his lunch break. But then he let up. And ... it would never occur to him that I would practice martial arts. He underestimated me." She raised her head at that point, toasted herself, and took a drink out of her travel tumbler.

Eliza heard the ice cubes rattle around in the mug and thought of bones.

"Did you see Cody today?"

Kelly shook her head. "I didn't. And I can't imagine him wanting to see the inside of that house."

"Why not?"

"Well, would you go into a place where you were walking on eggshells every minute of the day every day of your life until you escaped?"

"I guess I wouldn't." Then she asked, "Does Cody have a key?"

"Yes. I gave him a key at school after his father kicked him out. That was four years ago. He's had a key for four years—but he's never used it that I know of."

"When was the last time that Cody saw Glenn?"

"I don't know. Why would Cody want to? After four years, why the hell would he?" She ran her hands through her hair and crossed her arms as if she were suddenly cold.

"Did you and Glenn argue that day he kicked Cody out?"

"I wouldn't dare argue with Glenn. It was an ordinary day, with me not seeing my son for more than an hour or two at martial arts classes, my daughter out of the house as long as humanly possible, with me in the library as long as humanly possible. It was an ordinary, miserable day with everyone keeping their head down and trying to stay out of his way. Just as it has been forever."

"Does Cody work now?"

"He just graduated from GW. Studying biomedical engineering."

"At twenty?"

This was the only time in the interview that Kelly looked

happy. "He skipped a grade in elementary school and then finished high school in three years."

"Who paid the tuition? That's an expensive—"

"My parents."

"Did Glenn know?"

"Yes."

"Who told him?"

"My parents. They came over to ... Cody told me they came over to placate Glenn. Cody was a little more graphic. In the course of that conversation, they told him."

"How did your husband take that?"

"He wouldn't let my parents into the house. He told me to stop talking to them until they supported his decision-making."

"And did you?"

Kelly suddenly grew very small in her seat. "Well ... I didn't want to upset him."

"So he cut you off from your parents. How did you feel about that?"

Kelly shrugged. "My mother had always said that I should build Glenn up, that it would strengthen our marriage. Going behind Glenn's back? I don't think my mother would have taken that well."

"She wouldn't have let you move in with the kids?"

Kelly started crying quietly and Eliza pushed the box of tissues closer to her.

"No," Kelly finally said. "She was very concerned about being fair to Glenn." She took a sip of coffee and said, "Thank you for not asking me why I couldn't just get a job and move out. You understand the logistics with that—first with young kids, then a suspicious husband ... and then the gap in my resume and my age."

"I've seen what can go wrong at every stage of that process," Eliza said quietly. She waited for Kelly to speak.

"She misses her brother, but Glenn said that if he caught her talking to him, he'd pull her out of school and make me homeschool her."

"How old is ..."

"Maura. She's sixteen. Just finished her sophomore year. A few days after he kicked Cody out, I told Glenn in front of her that she should have a tutor and study in the library. Then I told him she had to go to summer school because she flunked some classes. In reality, it gave Maura time out of the house. And I know she doesn't have a tutor. She takes an enrichment class remotely—from GMU."

"How does Maura get home from the library?"

"She takes the bus. Glenn felt it was important to teach the kids independence."

"She didn't get a car when she was old enough?"

"Glenn would never have allowed that."

Eliza let it go. "I noticed it was hot in the house."

"Yes, Glenn said that it was important to save money."

"Was money a problem?"

"Well, no. But he felt that he didn't want to coddle the kids, and he said the school of hard knocks never hurt anybody." She took a drink of coffee, put the tumbler down with a *thunk*. "Or so he said. And I wasn't in a position to argue."

Eliza likewise took a sip of coffee. "It sounds like a hard way to live."

"It was. For all of us, with the exception of my mother, that is."

"You must have felt trapped."

Kelly tilted her head and studied Eliza. "This is the part

where you conclude that because life was hell for me and the kids, I murdered Glenn."

"Not at all. This is the part where I try to get to know Glenn better—and you, in order to figure out who killed him. Based on what I'm hearing from you—and indeed what I saw of your house—it would be a bad idea to jump to a conclusion like that."

"My house?"

"Who sat in the chair?"

Kelly looked blank for a moment. Then it came to her. "Oh, that was Glenn's chair. And I guess I see what you mean."

"Whose idea was it to have so few chairs at the breakfast bar?"

"Glenn's."

"And the TV layout?"

"Glenn."

"The gym versus your exercise bike in your office?"

"Glenn."

"The man cave with a separate heating/cooling system. Was that standard in the house?"

"No. Glenn had it added on."

"Glenn wasn't having an affair?"

"I can't even imagine how he would even have the time."

"I want to explore the possibility that Glenn might have ... gotten in over his head about something. Could his salary cover the mortgage?"

"I think so. It was his idea to move there."

"Do you know how much he made?"

"He told me that was none of my concern. On the other hand, he was a software engineering manager, and I looked up how much those make. So I think so, yes."

"Did he have any unusual spending habits?"

"No. You basically know his entire life."

"Friends?"

Kelly took another sip of coffee and put the tumbler down on the table without a sound this time. "A guy like Glenn, do you see him having friends?"

"No," Eliza said. "I don't. Associates, then. Pickup basketball at a county facility? Pickleball? Anything?"

"No. Glenn goes to work, comes home, works out, eats dinner, and we watch TV and go to bed."

"No disagreements with family?"

"One sister, Gemma, in Australia, ghosted everyone. Glenn won't talk about her. His brother, Gary, is in federal prison for healthcare fraud and Medicaid fraud in Florida. Plus some drug charges. He's five years into a fifteen-year prison sentence and then he's going to the state penitentiary to serve a ten-year sentence for manslaughter. Glenn was pretty upset. He said Gary accused him of setting him up." Kelly started turning the tumbler back and forth.

"Setting him up how?"

"Glenn was in an airport on the way to a conference. He said he was just talking to Gary, discussing his crimes with him —but on speakerphone. Gary didn't know he was on speakerphone, but Glenn said he did this all the time because it was easier for him to be able to hear. So it wasn't his fault if just this one time, coincidentally, there was a State Police special agent waiting for a flight next to him."

"Do you think that Glenn set him up?"

Kelly thought for a moment, putting her hands between her knees. "It's hard to tell ... whether he was just accidentally on purpose careless or if he had been working with law enforcement. I mean, why would he?" Kelly sat back and crossed her arms again, thinking. "All I know is that Glenn came home upset because Gary was blaming him for just having a phone call, and that yes, sometimes Glenn's voice can be loud. I suppose it's possible ... I'm assuming that's something you can follow up on. Given life in our house, I didn't really have much ability to ... you know, analyze Glenn's relationships with others."

"I can understand that. Do you think Gary is still angry at Glenn about this?"

"Wouldn't you be? Gary ran an urgent care facility, and one of the other things he did was sell opiates to his patients. They tied two overdoses to Gary, plus there's a voluntary manslaughter sentence waiting for him when he gets out of federal prison because a confidential informant wearing a wire came in with what eventually turned out to be a heart attack, and instead of calling 911, Gary wasted time pushing painkillers on her. The State Police heard the whole thing. They're the ones who called 911, not Gary. She died. And Gary was submitting claims for patients he never saw."

"Do you think that Gary could have put a hit out on Glenn?"

"After all of this time? I don't know. Why now? And if Glenn were working with law enforcement, isn't that something you can find out?"

"What do you think happened to Glenn?"

Kelly looked at her, confused. "Someone shot him. If I knew who did, I would tell you." Kelly turned the tumbler around so that the writing was facing her. "He was a terrible man. We weren't the only people in his life. Have you tried talking to his subordinates?"

Eliza studied Kelly. She was wearing a scarf and long sleeves in the stifling heat of a Virginia summer. Her nose looked as if it had been broken in the past. "Did ... did he hit you?"

"And then he was killed," Kelly said, as if Eliza had not spoken. "Nothing was taken from the house, I don't think. Not that there was really much of anything *to* take."

"Did you find the gun?"

"No! I didn't even look for it."

"It was in the shower."

Kelly made a sound of disgust. "Okay ..."

"Does anyone in your house own a gun?"

Kelly looked at her as if she had just said the dumbest thing in the world.

Eliza relaxed and took a sip of coffee. Kelly had just gotten comfortable.

"With how mad Glenn could get?" Kelly said. "How Cody was poking him with a stick all the time toward the end?"

"Do you think Cody would have—"

"Cody is not a killer."

"But Glenn could be?"

Kelly was furious. "You've read the statistics, right? You mean that in your job, you don't know? When someone in a house gets angry a lot, the last thing you need is to add a gun to the mix. He got so ... *angry* at little stuff. You never knew what would get him mad. And when he was angry, he'd keep me up all night talking about it. There was no gun. In our house."

"Did you touch anything?"

"What? No! You know what?" Kelly stood up, and her scarf fell, and Eliza saw an ugly bruise on her throat.

"What's that?" she asked, pointing to her own throat.

"Nothing! I just—I don't know, pulled a shirt off too fast. I was mad at Glenn." Kelly caught herself. "Look, I haven't told the kids yet. I have to go home and call my kids. And—" Kelly dropped back down into her chair and started sobbing.

"How did I let us live that way?" Kelly was nearly howling. "I let him throw my son out of the house! How did I do that?"

"I don't think you hurt your husband."

"I wish I had," Kelly said, taking a wad of tissues and cleaning herself up. Shaking, she looked Eliza straight in the eye. "That's a terrible thing to say, I know. I didn't. But I wish I had. I know I shouldn't say it to you, but it's the truth. He's gone, and I'm so relieved." She ran her hands through her hair, which fell right back into place. "I was terrified of him, Detective Benveniste. Shooting him would have meant going out of my way to be close to him."

"Kelly? We'll have someone from Victim-Witness contact you, and—"

"I'm not under arrest?"

"For what?"

"I don't know. I guess I'm not really good about testing reality with regard to people's responses to me. Life with Glenn would do that to you."

"I could see that."

"Yeah, I don't ever want to look at a man again as long as I live. I'm going to sell that ... hulk of a house, buy a town house and a pair of nice, gentle mutts. Maybe even a cat. And a room for each of my kids. And turn ... turn the AC on in the summer and the heat in the winter." Her voice broke at "kids." She looked at Eliza strangely. After a moment, she said, "He wanted more kids, but I would have had to put a book on the ceiling."

Eliza tried to think of something to say to that and decided it would have been nothing good. "Buy a town house?"

"That house has gone up in value in the past ten years. And he did have life insurance. I can afford to buy a town house."

"You'll be able to survive on the life insurance?"

"If I'm careful, which I plan to be. I might even be able to go back to work. But I still didn't kill Glenn."

"What were you doing for a living when you met Glenn?"

"I was a reporter at a small-town newspaper when I met him. Nothing exciting. The crime writing, but it was local."

"Which one?"

Kelly told her. Eliza had never heard of it.

"A hell of a thing to do with a bachelor's in linguistics, but ... " Kelly shrugged. "Paid the bills."

"Just out of curiosity, had either you or your husband read the book *Rebellion at Broken Oar*?"

Kelly's eyes went flat. Eliza broke out in gooseflesh.

"My daughter was into that stuff," Kelly said. "So was Cody. Glenn, no. He was furious with the kids for even touching sci-fi. He thought it was for idiots."

"But the tattoo—"

"What tattoo?"

"He had a tattoo on his wrist."

Kelly looked at her blankly. "No ..."

Eliza said, "Hold on," and texted Jamie.

> Dead guy has a tattoo on his wrist, right?

She waited.

Kelly started to stand up again and then sat back down and said, "Why did you say he had a tattoo? He would have killed—*killed*—anyone in our family who got a tattoo!"

> I just looked through my photos. It's there all right.

> But the wife insists he didn't have one and said he'd have killed her or their kids if they got one!

Hold on.

"What are you doing?" Kelly demanded.

"My partner says he definitely had a tattoo—it's from the book I just mentioned ... *Rebellion at Broken Oar*."

"I told you. My kids read those books. Science fiction, fantasy. With the way Glenn felt about it, Maura hid her books under her bed."

"Kelly, the books were in a bookcase, and there were science fiction posters on the wall."

Kelly shot to her feet, holding on to the table for support.

"Where are you going?" Eliza asked, seeing how pale Kelly looked.

Then Eliza's phone vibrated again:

> Badri says the tattoo is temporary. Fake.

> I think we know who killed Glenn.

"Kelly, I'd like to talk to your kids, just to—"

"*You leave them out of this! You will not talk to them! You won't!*" Kelly grabbed her purse and tried to pick up her coffee tumbler but knocked it over by mistake and ran to the door without it. "Let me out of here!" she said, sobbing.

Eliza did. When she went back to the table to retrieve her own mug, she saw that the lid had fallen off Kelly's tumbler, and her coffee was staining the carpet the color of clotted blood.

After she watched Kelly get in the elevator, she called Jamie and asked him to dust the books and posters for prints.

Jamie was sitting at his desk looking sick and mangling a paper clip. "Do you think the wife did it?"

"No, not at all," Eliza said. "I think it was Cody."

"That coup de grâce—close-up gunshot to the heart ... sweet, really." He stood up. "I'm gonna get some more coffee. Want some?"

Wordlessly, Eliza handed him her cup.

Looking at the two detectives side by side, the difference between them was stark, height aside. Jamie had neatly cut, short blond hair, green eyes, and a ruddy complexion, while Eliza had abundant long black hair, large black eyes, olive skin, and an aquiline nose. Jamie had the body of a man who'd stopped exercising after he graduated high school, and she had the body of a trained martial artist.

Eliza also had scars on her outer left forearm between the wrist and elbow from blocking a knife attack by a suspect when she was a street cop. She had blocked the blade and punched the knifer repeatedly in the face until he dropped the knife. Then she'd elbowed him in the face.

"I don't think she did it, Jamie," she said after he came back. "She was crying pretty hard. She knew the exact time that she got back from the library—but like a woman whose husband tries to control her every move, not like someone searching for an alibi. I wonder if she knows who did it."

Jamie took a sip of coffee. "I wonder if the shot to the heart was postmortem."

"I guess Badri will tell us for sure."

He sat and reached for another paper clip.

She set her mug down and sat across from him. "What's wrong? And don't bullshit me this time."

Jamie reached out and took her by the arm, his green eyes bright. "All four of them ... characters in *Rebellion at Broken Oar*. And Cody in the book killed his father, Glenn Sommars."

"What the actual—"

"Weird coincidence, right?" Jamie said. "Sorry about the spoiler. Happens first thing anyway."

"Maybe we need a list of characters who get killed. And who'd have thought that reading a science fiction book could be required as part of a homicide investigation?"

"You mean the Human ones," Jamie said.

"Funny. But maybe it's one of those really weird coincidences. Or maybe the author—"

"Put Glenn's name in the book and then murdered him? I guess that could be an idea. I'll just call him and ask him. I'm sure he'll confess."

Eliza waited for him to speak again, but he knew that trick and didn't. So she said, "Well, we should probably try to talk to him. What if it's a publicity stunt? Puts the family in the book, Glenn gets killed, and—"

"And the book is already a best seller."

"But how would he know that when he wrote it?"

"I'll call him."

Eliza watched him for a moment, wondering what was happening to her normally affable partner.

*

Cody sat in the interview room calmly, as if it was the most natural thing in the world to be in a small room in a homicide bureau's office waiting to be interviewed about the murder of his father.

"What do you make of that?" Jamie asked, standing next to Eliza at the observation window.

Cody was lanky like his mother. His eyes were not the piercing, pale blue of his father's, but a cooler blue, with indigo specks in them. His expression was intelligent, and his features held none of his father's harshness. His hair was shaggy and straight, with a shiny blond forelock that he kept brushing out of his eyes. He wore faded blue jeans, a black T-shirt, and tactical boots. He was leaning back, feet shoulder-width apart.

"I think he knows that we have nothing on him," Eliza said. "Has he read the book?"

"I guess we'll find out." Jamie took a sip of coffee. "If he has, it hasn't fazed him, clearly."

Jamie walked into the interview room.

Cody immediately stood up and shook his hand. "Cody Chatworth."

"Chatworth?"

Cody sat down and leaned back in his chair just as Kelly had and crossed his arms over his chest. Then he pushed his yellow forelock out of his eyes and recrossed his arms. "Now that that bastard's dead, I'm changing my name to my mother's. Maura wants to do the same thing, and Mom said yes. She's calling a lawyer on Monday."

Jamie sat down. "Can I get you anything?"

"Look, you want to know if I killed my father," Cody said. "So forget about the dog treats."

Jamie excused himself and left the room. He walked over to Eliza and said, "You need to take this one."

"What's going on?" Eliza asked, taking a sip of coffee.

"Nothing." Jamie poured himself another cup of coffee and went back in.

After Jamie sat back down, Cody said, "You didn't want to talk to me, and your partner sent you back in, right? That's the brunette who was standing next to you? Why?"

Jamie took a sip of coffee. "Tell me about your father."

"You walked in here, and you recognized me from somewhere," Cody said. "You're wrong, but—"

"Have you read *Rebellion at Broken Oar*?"

"That I have," Cody said.

"The parallels don't strike you?"

"What's the saying? A million monkeys with a million laptops for a million years, one of them's gonna write Shakespeare? It's a coincidence. Weird, definitely, but a coincidence."

"Have you talked to your grandparents?"

"Since you surely know who I live with, I'm assuming you mean *his* parents. They cut him off." Cody brushed his forelock off his face again, then sat back in the chair, feet shoulder-width apart again.

"Why did they do that?"

"When Gary was arrested, they blamed Glenn. Which they should have, because he might as well have had those conversations in a police station lobby. On the other hand, they sided with a murderer."

Jamie waited for a moment, but Cody had nothing to add. "Do you have any aunts or uncles?"

"Dad's brother is in federal prison for some kind of fraud. And homicide. His sister moved to Australia and won't talk to anyone. Mom was an only child."

"When did the abuse start?"

Cody flinched. "Right after I was born."

"That's why they're paying your tuition."

"Fuck no. Grandma was convinced that I could make Glenn proud and then he'd've let me move back in. They wanted to talk to Mom, but Dad must have blocked their number on her phone, and the one time they came over, he threatened to have them arrested."

"Lovely," Jamie said. "Why did he throw you out?"

Cody sat up and leaned forward. "I didn't kill him. Maura didn't either. She was with me at the time. We were at our grandparents' place. They'll tell you that. None of us killed him. You already figured out that Mom was scared to death of him. Why don't you ask the people who worked for him? What do you think it'd be like to have him for a boss? I peg him as a brown-nosing, two-faced monster, don't you? Lots of people hated Glenn Sommars. Not just us. And dude, nothing would have made me happier than to blow his ass away, but none of us want to go to prison over that prick." He sat back and crossed his arms.

"How would you go about that if you were—"

"I wouldn't."

"But if you were going to—"

"If I were going to go to Lake Anne, tie a cinder block to my feet, jump off that observation tower, hold my breath all night, cut myself loose, swim to the surface, and go get breakfast, you mean? I'm just as capable of doing that."

"That's not physically possible. Shooting your father—"

"Requires parts of my brain to be broken that are working just fine."

"How often did you imagine doing it?"

"Whenever there was a new bruise on Maura. But keeping that thought in my head long enough to buy a gun, drive to that house, wait for Glenn, and ... no. I don't know anyone who could do that. None of us know anyone who could do that, not even Glenn."

"Did he ever hit your mother—"

"Detective Cloud, I did not kill my father. Neither did my sister or my mother or my grandparents. My father beat us all up. The house was always hot as fuck in the summer and freezing in the winter except in his hole because," Cody made air quotes, "'paying the bills has its privileges.' We could never have desserts or treats. We always had to watch TV sideways. He always picked the programs, if he let us watch at all. We still didn't kill him. Can I go now?"

Jamie ignored him. "Anyone in the neighborhood know the routine of your family? Who comes home when?"

Cody relaxed. "Glenn cut Mom off from everyone. Glenn had very successfully convinced her parents that she was crazy. Our social life was totally behind his back. No one ever came to the house. If the neighbors knew anything about us, we would have no way of knowing."

"Who had keys to the house?" Jamie asked. "Maid service—"

Cody let out an obnoxious laugh. "You think Glenn would allow Mom a—Jesus Christ, have you been paying attention? And why didn't you just ask me if I had a key? Of course I have a key. Glenn collected mine at the door the day he kicked me out, but Mom met me at school and gave me one. Took me to lunch a couple of times during school hours, but Glenn had anticipated that, so she stopped."

"If Glenn had put you out of the house, why did you need a key?"

Cody brushed his forelock out of his eyes and shrugged. "I took it in case Mom or Maura needed help. I think she gave it to me ... so I knew that she wasn't kicking me out, he was."

"When did she give you the key?"

Cody looked nearly through him. "Right after Glenn kicked me out."

"When did he do that?"

"Four years ago. When I was sixteen. I stayed out all night playing D&D and messing around with my friend's telescope. I came home in the morning, and the fucker was standing there in the doorway about to drag me inside and scream at me, maybe throw me around a little, and I told him off. He tried to punch me, then took my key, then told me never to come back again."

"Wow. Over that? I wonder how many kids your age would be sleeping in alleys if that was enough."

Cody relaxed. "Plenty. And before you ask, no one got drunk or high. I was too interested in getting into GW to fry my brains."

"I believe that," Jamie said, meaning it. "What are you studying?"

"I graduated from GW with a BS in biomedical engineering."

"What comes next?"

"What do you mean what comes next?"

"Grad school or job search?"

"I hadn't figured that part out yet."

"And now you have?"

"I'm still considering my options," he said impatiently. "I don't want to talk about it. My grandparents keep asking too. What does that have to do with who offed Glenn?"

"When was the last time you saw your dad?"

"You mean other than when he stalked my mother? Four years ago."

"Did your mother and Maura have a routine?"

Cody leaned his elbows on his thighs. "Glenn is home at 7:00 p.m. sharp every weekday except Fridays, when he's home by 5:30. Was. Mom went to martial arts practice down the street when Glenn was at work, same place I go. Real gritty kind of place. Showers there so she doesn't look like she's been. I keep her equipment. I bring it for her when I go. But I think she's gone all day. She's always home before Glenn gets there."

"Where is the training center?"

Cody told him. Jamie made a mental note to talk to the martial arts school.

"Do they do firearms training?" Jamie asked.

"They don't use live rounds in a martial arts training center full of cops and first responders, no. They use SIRT pistols and simulated ammunition for parts of the curriculum."

"A SIRT pistol?" Jamie asked, confused.

"A SIRT pistol has the shape and weight of a Glock, but it shoots laser-pointer lasers instead. Simulated ammunition is exactly what it sounds like."

"So your mom and you know how to shoot?"

Cody sat back and crossed his legs, this time one ankle over a knee. "Mom and I know how to use a SIRT pistol and fire guns with simulated ammunition. Those aren't handguns. But Glenn would never permit a firearm in the house. Probably afraid one of us would use it to defend Mom. I wouldn't want a gun in that house because of what he might do to Mom. I don't carry a gun either."

Jamie sensed Cody getting ready to walk out. So he changed the subject. "Didn't Glenn see the dues coming out every month?"

Cody uncrossed his legs. "Mom does—did—the thing where she gets cash back at the grocery store. Pays the martial arts dues in cash. Hands the rest of the cash over to me, and I put it in a separate savings account for her. And after I moved out, she took a loan out for school, and the invoices are emailed to my school address. If the student loan industry was what it used to be, there would have been no way. But she's got a master's now."

"Glenn didn't miss the money?"

"You think he has the slightest idea? He just knows she goes to the grocery store. He wants to know where she's going, not how much she spends on groceries. Besides, what he's really interested in is keeping her isolated. There's no point in her trying to make friends. Glenn calls them, then they ghost her."

"So your mother wouldn't get home until right before your father?"

"Stays out as long as she can."

"What did she do?"

"Takes her classes online at the library. Glenn has a keystroke logger on her computer. I gave her my old laptop. She has to keep it in a safety deposit box at the bank across the street from the library. She practices martial arts with me. She doesn't dare make any friends because Glenn will end up talking to them about her 'episodes.' Then there'd be yet more people who are convinced that she is crazy."

"And your sister? Does she have a routine?"

Cody brushed his forelock back. Then he told him, finishing with, "Mom actually makes sure to tell Glenn that Maura's grades are poor, so naturally, she needs a 'tutor.'" Cody made air quotes again. "And summer school. Gives Maura an alibi so she can stay out of the house. Maura has a 4.3 GPA."

"So what about yesterday? I thought she was with your grandparents."

"She was. I picked her up at her boyfriend's after school. She and I talked on Independence Day of having her move in with my grandparents too and asking Mom to come with her. The four of us sat down and talked about it. Grandpa grilled steaks, and that's what we had."

"What had you decided?"

Cody crossed his leg, ankle over knee, then crossed his arms. "We convinced Grandma and Grandpa that Maura *and* Mom had to move in with them. It took forever to convince Grandma. She made excuse after excuse. Finally, Grandpa put his foot down. All three of us would have been living there by Monday regardless of whether Glenn was around or not. Even if Glenn tried to go after Mom about it, Maura's old enough to tell him to go fuck himself in court, and a judge would listen."

"Were your grandparents abusive toward you or your mother?"

Cody let out a laugh. "No. Grandma just had a weird affection for Glenn."

"It must have been a relief—to finally have a second adult in your corner for a change."

"It was about fucking time."

"Can I make an observation?"

Cody pushed his forelock out of his eyes and made a "go ahead" gesture.

"Most of the time, in a household like that—"

"What would you know about a household like that?"

Jamie put his badge on the table.

Cody said, "Fair."

"In a household like that, a woman as educated as your mother has a way out and refuses to take it. Why did your mother stay? Did she love him?"

"What way out? She didn't work. Grandma wouldn't let

her move in. I don't know what Grandma's problem was. Mom had no money to pay a divorce lawyer. Glenn convinced everyone in Mom's life that she was crazy. If she testified that Glenn beat us up, he'd claim parental alienation or something. Accuse her of doing it. He'd get custody. Assuming he didn't corner her somewhere and beat her up."

"How do you know about parental alienation?"

"TikTok," Cody said.

"It sounds like hell. Did your mom ever get angry at him?"

Cody looked like he was counting slowly backward from ten. "Wouldn't you? Yeah, sometimes she yelled at him. She actually did. Interestingly, he recorded it one time and played it for Grandma, and that's one of the reasons Grandma believes him that she's crazy."

"Did your mother ever hit him?"

"No. She was terrified of him. Messed with her head. He told her things like, oh, that she never learned how to use the hot water in the tub—didn't she remember that she never knew how? He had turned off the water heater downstairs. I checked. And then her own mother agreed with Glenn that there must be something wrong with her. So in the face of this and more, imagine this: you're gonna get angry sometimes. And she did. But Mom was always on the other side of the room from him whenever she could help it. I didn't murder him. Like I told you, everyone would have been living with Grandma and Grandpa by Monday."

"What changed?"

Cody looked at the wall over Jamie's shoulder.

Jamie waited for him to answer and finally said, "When did you find out that your father had died?"

"Murdered. Glenn was murdered. Mom called us as soon as she left here."

"Who do you think could have killed your father?"

"Anyone. Anyone in the universe."

Maura sat as calmly as her brother. She took after Kelly too, but her eyes were steel blue, and she had short-cropped, shiny, silky blond hair. Eliza was struck with the fact that Maura was dressed exactly like her brother, except she had a lot of bracelets on both wrists, all of which looked homemade.

Eliza was also grateful that Kelly had finally agreed to allow Maura to be interviewed and had not insisted on being present.

"Do you want anything to eat or drink? Do you need to use the restroom?"

"Cody says you want to find out if I killed Glenn in between my biology homework and my D&D playing?" Maura popped her gum. "Also, I brought this," she held up a water bottle, "so, no, I don't need any cookies in order to perform."

"He was not the most well-liked guy in the world, your dad."

"That's an understatement. See how short my hair is?" She put her fingers through her hair and held it up. It was barely three inches long. "I could never grow it long. Glenn said I— I'd look like a whore and attract the wrong kind of guys."

"Glenn?"

"I don't have to refer to that prick as *Dad* or *sir* or anything else now. He goes by Glenn now."

"Why?"

Maura popped her gum again. She leaned on both elbows across the table and mock whispered, "I'll bet the neighbors will tell you that Glenn was quiet, polite, kept to himself mostly."

"That bad?" Eliza said gently.

Maura stood up, turned around, and lifted up her shirt. On her shoulder blade was a fresh bruise the size of a man's fist. She dropped her shirt and then she pushed down the waistband of her jeans. On her flank was an older bruise. "The lower one was where he shoved me into the kitchen counter." She readjusted her clothing and sat back down. Tears were flowing down her cheeks, and she was sniffling. Eliza passed her a box of tissues, grateful that Maura's bruises would be captured on camera. Maura took a tissue.

"We should have a doctor look you over. We have a pediatrician who works with crime victims."

Maura shook her head. "I'm fine. No. Can we talk about something else?"

Eliza opened her mouth, but Maura said, "No. I'm not talking about this."

"Then I won't. Can you tell me what happened yesterday?"

"Someone killed Glenn. I don't know when. I was at summer school. Then I went to Jack's—my boyfriend's—and then Cody picked me up and took me to Grandma and Grandpa's to talk about me and Mom living there too. Usually, Jack drops me off at the bus stop down the street, and I get home right after Glenn does."

"What did you do when you were at Jack's house?"

"Oh," Maura said, "play video games. D&D with our friends. Visit with Cody. Talk. Fuck." She studied Eliza.

"I was sixteen too once, Maura," Eliza said gently. "Does Jack treat you okay?"

"Yes." Then she leaned forward and said, "Don't worry. Mom got me fitted for a diaphragm. Jack never rides bareback either."

"That's good," Eliza said. "She's a good mom. How does Jack feel about the way Glenn treated you?"

"About what you'd think. But the president of the Science Club and the D&D Club at school is not going to take on my father."

Eliza waited for her to say more.

"If we told Jack's parents, they'd call Glenn, then Glenn would find out where I was. It would be my word against Glenn's, and he might even blame Mom."

"Do any of your other friends know about your situation?"

"Sure, but," she rolled her eyes, "I'm absolutely certain that a plucky group of very distinctive-looking nerds could absolutely walk into my house in broad daylight and lie in wait for Glenn. The lady across the street is always gardening or sitting on the porch, and then sometimes the lady next door to her comes over and sits on her porch with her. I'm pretty sure they run the HOA. Better get them right in here."

Eliza knew that those women had seen nothing, except they corroborated Kelly's and Maura's descriptions of their schedule.

"But I told you, we were at my grandparents' house trying to convince them to let me and Mom move there."

"Who cooked?"

"Grandpa grilled steaks. Grandma cooked the rest."

"Are they good cooks?"

"Oh, Jesus Christ, stop it," Maura said. "Just stop. No, not particularly. Grandpa always overcooks the steaks, and Grandma makes iceberg lettuce and ranch dressing. Stale cookies for dessert. But none of us killed Mom's sperm donor."

"I talked to your mother. Now you. I get the idea that your father was a tyrannical bully who treated his family so badly they don't even mourn him."

Maura started to cry, and Eliza handed her a tissue. Maura full-on sobbed.

After another hour, Eliza walked Maura to the elevator with her brother and went to talk to Jamie.

She sat down and powered down her computer. Then she swiveled her chair and saw that Jamie was already done. She said, "It's time to go home. We've been working straight through since Friday. If I have to write another affidavit for Denny, I'll drop."

Jamie massaged the back of his neck. "Tell me about what Maura said."

After Eliza told him, Jamie said, "Well, they're a bright crew. They could have compared notes."

"We should talk to people at that training center."

"What do you mean?"

"I mean," Eliza said, "that if Kelly showered there, maybe someone saw those bruises and got mad on her behalf."

"Agreed. But I still think it's gonna be Cody."

"Because of the book?"

"Not because of that goddamned book," he said through gritted teeth. "Because Cody had keys to the house, and he hated his father's guts. Because he's applying for jobs or to grad schools or looking at years of playing bodyguard to his sister. Or maybe Glenn found out about Maura's boyfriend, who we should bring in. Then we have a reason for why now, after all this time, Cody filled Glenn full of lead."

"Jamie, you look like absolute shit. Maybe the author—"

"The author didn't do it, Eliza. Why would some author with no ties to Virginia at all write a real person as a character, publish the book six months ago, and then murder the person? Maybe someone suggested the names. I still think it's a coincidence, but okay, I'll contact him."

"How do we know that he has no ties to Virginia at all?"

"The bio says he lives in New York."

"So?"

"So do you think he wrote a three-hundred-and-fifty-page confession?"

Eliza decided to let it pass for now. "Okay. We still need to get some sleep."

They took the elevator together and got in their cars, which they'd parked side by side.

"Text me when you get home," Jamie said, as he always did.

"You too," Eliza said, as she always did.

CHAPTER
THREE

ELIZA DROVE past the steak place where a victim had been pulled out of the freezer at 4:00 a.m. years back. She passed the house where she had her first case. The body had been on the back deck—a lover's quarrel. She passed the convenience store where the clerk had leaned against the cigarette case and looked stunned to be dead.

Eliza dropped her keys in a bowl by the front door and texted Jamie, who had already texted her.

After changing out of her work clothes and taking a shower, she ladled some stew into a bowl from her slow cooker, poured herself a glass of wine, and walked outside.

Taking a sip of wine, she opened her copy of *Rebellion at Broken Oar*. She had been a third of the way through *The Sizzling Scar*, historical fiction about the Second Pandemic and the Second American Revolution, and it had been good, but now she had to put it down to read this one. And she wished she'd never heard of it.

Rebellion at Broken Oar
Chapter 1
Ursinus b: Spring Equinox 50–9:30 a.m.

Captain Dina Baines of the SS *Kestrel* stared at Ursinus b through the ship's massive viewscreen. It looked like Earth—if Earth were a little larger. She saw clouds and ... *Is that an ocean?* The planet had two small moons. Sensors indicated that one of them was smaller than Illinois and shaped about the same. Not for the first time, she wondered why astronomers identified stars as *a*.

It had been two years since she and her colonist crew of Space Force personnel and civilians had left Earth, although they hadn't been awake for most of it. *I can't believe we made it.*

"Kinkead, do we have a breathable atmosphere?" Baines asked. "Because if we don't, we're fucked."

The astrophysicist studied his instruments.

Baines's stomach clutched.

"Seventy-seven percent nitrogen, twenty-two percent oxygen, some water vapor, carbon dioxide, and some inert gases. Like most computer models predicted."

Baines relaxed. "Some computer models gave us a—"

"Methane atmosphere," Kinkead said. "I know. But they picked Ursinus b for a reason. And here we all are. And it's not tidally locked either, which was another thing some of us were worried about."

"Star Service never notified us about that factoid,"

Gino said, shaken. He looked at Baines. "A tidally locked planet usually has a light side hot enough to fry lead and a dark side cold enough to have a snowball fight with nitrogen. And no liquid water. As a bonus, insane winds. Wanna go?"

"And about that," Baines asked, "why isn't it? Around a K-type star?"

"Ursinus is on the brighter side," Kinkead said. "And the planet's larger than Earth."

Baines grinned. "Gino," she said to her navigator, "let's land this thing."

"Aye, sir," he said.

Suddenly, Baines felt the ship lurch.

"*What the fuck!*" Gino yelled.

The planet's surface was getting bigger on the viewscreen.

"Gino, report!"

But the ship was on the ground, the pressure dampers keeping the ship from breaking itself, and them, into pieces. "*Report*, Gino!"

"I now know what my last words will be," Gino said. Bleeding from his nose, he said, "We seemed to have landed pretty hard, Captain. We might be able to get the ship fixed, but—"

The captain's comm buzzed, followed by "Sommars here."

Baines pushed a button on the arm of her chair. "Report."

"We've got power," Sommars replied from Engineering, "but for some reason, we don't have lift."

"Figure it out, Glenn."

She pushed another button on the arm of her chair. "Banner, report!"

"Right now only a few cuts and bruises," said the doctor.

Baines sighed and looked around the bridge. Gino was cleaning up after himself. Kinkead, the astrophysicist, was looking at his instruments and shaking his head. Commander Tony Polichek, her first officer, had already left to supervise repairs.

She hit a button again and asked, "What's wrong with the ship, Sommars?"

"Let me talk to Kinkead or Accardi, Dina," Sommars said.

Through gritted teeth, Captain Baines said, "This is the last time you will fail to call me 'captain.'"

"As you wish ... *Captain*. I'll try to make it simple—"

"The gravitational detection system has failed, sir," Gino said. "And the propulsion system. We can try to repair the damage, but—"

"It means," Baines said, "the ship doesn't know which way is up. And even if it did, it doesn't know how to reach escape velocity. Does the rest of it work?"

"Can you be more specific?" Sommars asked.

From his own console, Gino said, "The ship can do everything but fly."

"We need to rename this crate the *Broken Oar*, Captain." Cody said.

Baines looked at the viewscreen again. They had landed on the surface of Ursinus b, on the opposite side of the galaxy from Earth. Mission accomplished. Sort of.

Eliza texted Jamie.

> Were you able to reach David Dove?

Eliza had time to finish her wine and pour herself another before Jamie replied.

> No.

Then,

> I still think it's going to be the kids. But everyone's lawyered up. Grandma and Grandpa too.

Rebellion at Broken Oar
Chapter 2
Ursinus b: Spring Equinox 50–10:00 a.m.

Baines stepped onto Ursinus b with the rest of the colonists. Everyone cheered.

It was well after dawn, Baines knew. Ursinus was closer to Ursinus b than Sol was to Earth, so the sun was slightly, almost imperceptibly, larger in the dusky blue sky. The yellow sunlight had a slightly orange tint. Low on the horizon was a bright spot. She knew this was

Ursinus c, a great tourist destination if you always wished you could visit Pluto.

The civilian colonists were dressed in waterproof black jumpsuits with utility pockets. The four Space Force officers wore rank insignia and the emblem of the Space Force: a disk of the Milky Way in a blue field.

They all carried lasepistols.

Baines shifted her stance, and something crunched. The ground was covered with what looked like coiled tree roots, pale gray, which ranged from the thickness of a broomstick to the thickness of her pinkie. They were covered here and there with a kind of dark green lichen, creating a sort of thicket. There were patches of thin purple blades of grass or fungus poking out. Some of them were rolled up like ferns. *I'll ask Cody.* She wondered what animals lived within the thicket and made sure not to step on the purple things.

The breeze had a slightly tannic smell, like fallen leaves.

They were on a low hill beside an orange-pink wash.

Baines was 1.8 meters tall, with long muscular legs and unruly red hair she usually wore in a bun when she was on duty. It came down to her waist after hours, when there used to be such a thing as "after hours." Her eyes were amber. She was forty years old and had waited her entire life for just this moment.

"I wonder if the *Peregrine* and the *Archer* will catch up with us, Captain."

"I don't love that 'if,' Gino."

"We had some near misses when we were under, sir."

Lt. Gino Accardi was on the tall side, broad-shouldered, muscular, a little soft around the middle, balding and hairy, with warm black eyes. But there was an edge to Gino's tone that Baines could not interpret.

Maura Sommars—Glenn's daughter—walked up to her. "Captain," she said, running one hand nervously through her shiny blond hair, "we should wake up the dogs. It's not fair to leave them under."

Captain Baines looked into her steel-blue eyes and said, "We will, ASAP."

"See this?" Cody said. "The plants on the ground would be really hard to blow away or wash away. Those shrubs over there, next to that pond at the bottom of the wash? They're low to the ground too. See?"

"And?" Baines said, liking him.

"Perfect if it gets really windy. See those washes?" He pointed out places with exposed orange-pink dirt. "No moss, or whatever this is we're standing on, and the washes all lead right to those ponds. Flash floods. Right?"

"Well, some of the computer models back home predicted some nasty storms," Baines said. "But it's warm now. Let's keep an eye out for clouds." She looked at the clear dusky sky for a moment. "I wish our computer had time to take more readings before we crashed. We don't even know what life we're going to find here."

Suddenly, Maura grabbed her arm. "Look!" she whispered.

Everyone did. About six meters away, lining the washes, some things telescoped upward from the ground. They pulsed as they rose, with motion underneath the skin, like peristalsis. But they didn't make a sound. When they grew to about three meters tall, they stopped pulsing. There had to have been fifty of them. Baines's heart started beating wildly. This was why she was here!

She could not tell whether they were plant or animal. They were fleshy looking, purplish pink, and tinged with red. An adult Human could barely wrap their arms around one. As she stared at them, a crown of slick white fibers suddenly emerged from the tops of each one. At the top, each one was forked. They writhed together, but there was order to this too. Were they tongues?

Just like that, the white fibers withdrew.

Baines decided that these were animals.

Maura laughed. "Oh! Can we please call them dickweeds?"

Several people laughed.

"*Weedius dickus?*" Gino said. "What do you think, Cody?"

Cody laughed. "We must have startled them when the ship landed, which is why they retracted. I wonder if those white tendrils were sense organs."

"We'll have plenty of time to find out," Baines said.

Glenn Sommars appeared. "They were already like that when we got here," he said to Baines. "Look at them! They've been sticking up like that since we landed."

Baines suddenly understood the source of six months of ship politics. "Sommars, we all watched them pop up."

Glenn turned to her and said gently, "You're very

emotional right now, which is understandable, but they were definitely already like that."

"That won't work here, Dad. And it's even on video," Cody said, pointing to the SciCamera clipped to his shoulder.

"That's *sir* to you," he said to Cody.

"It won't matter, Cody, and you know it," Maura said. "He'd tell you the video showed that they were already there. Did *you* break the ship, Dad?"

Every time Cody or Maura called Glenn "Dad," his face grew redder, Baines saw.

Glenn reached out to grab Maura and then caught himself.

"Yeah, *Dad*. Hey, Dad?" Maura said, trembling. "Are you gonna stop beating me and Mom now that we're here?"

The colonists stared at the three of them in shock.

Glenn was so enraged his hands were shaking. "Baines, I'm sorry that these kids are out of control like this. Maura, get back to the ship, *right now* and—"

"That's *Captain* Baines, and I decide who's going back to the ship, right now. You may be a civilian, Sommars, but when you signed on to this mission, you agreed to follow my orders. Pack up your shit and move it to the shed. Those are your quarters now. I'm done with you." She turned to her first officer. "Commander, can you do a diagnostic to make sure that Sommars here didn't fuck up?"

Sommars's face was red all the way up to his Hitler Youth haircut, and a vein showed on his forehead.

"Aye, sir," Polichek said grimly.

Baines turned to the rest of the crew. "For some

unfathomable reason, the powers that be decided to send civilians on this mission. You may be the bestest, fanciest professionals in your respective fields, and you may not be Space Force. That doesn't mean I don't run this ship, and when you signed on, you agreed to obey my orders. Any questions?"

There were no questions.

The shed was a small empty compartment in the back of the ship, with bare metal walls and a bedroll. Glenn would have to stoop to move around the poorly lit compartment, and he'd have to walk down a long corridor to get to a bathroom and a shower.

Lt. Cmdr. Kelly Chatworth, head of security, walked up to Glenn. She adjusted her tactical belt. "Enjoy the shed. I'm staying where I am." She was shaking. Then she looked at Baines.

Baines was always surprised by the faded blue, nearly white, color of Kelly's eyes. "It's Sommars I'm sending to the shed, not you, Lieutenant Commander."

Glenn nearly emitted gentleness. "Kelly, are you having another episode? Because—"

"*Enough*, Glenn!" Baines said. She went face-to-face with him, in a manner of speaking, since his eyes were even with the bridge of her nose. "You play any more head games with this crew, you can sit out this mission in the brig. Is that clear?" She turned to the group and said, "We're going exploring."

"Captain," Polichek said, "don't we want to send up some drones first?"

"Seconded," Gino said. "We didn't come all this way to end up on a plaque at Space Force headquarters."

"Commander, Lieutenant," Baines said, "if we

wanted to explore this planet by drone, Space Force could just have sent probes."

"With respect, Captain," Dr. John Bynum said, "there is something to what Commander Polichek said. We are going to be here for at least two years. Surely we do not want to be precipitous."

"Noted," Baines said. "Commander, I want you and Kinkead to see what you can do about the ship. We need to set up the ecofarms too. Rodgers, Simms, analyze the soils and see what grows. We didn't travel two years from home to sit around the ship looking at instruments."

"Aye, sir," Polichek said.

Baines decided to take Lt. Cmdr. Kelly Chatworth, Lt. Gino Accardi, xenobiologist Cody Sommars, Maura Sommars (just because), botanist Chloe Jackman, and Dr. Banner Colson. Then she thought for a moment and decided to bring Glenn. She wanted him away from the ship while they tried to make repairs—if the ship *could* be repaired.

Baines took lead. Next was Kelly, and behind her, Chloe, then Cody, Maura, Banner, and Glenn. Gino brought up the rear. Baines saw that the group had insulated Glenn from his family.

Glenn had started the mission as one of the best there was, well-liked and pleasant, if a little flirtatious. And then ... a problem here, a problem there, his criticisms of crew performance that no one else ever saw.

Now he was violent. But Star Service hadn't devised a protocol for that. And the creatures that had telescoped upward ... well, the crew was there to do research, and Glenn turned a discovery into a head game.

She realized that she had her hand on the grip of her lasepistol.

Chapter 3
Ursinus b: Spring Equinox 50–10:08 a.m.

After walking a hundred meters or so, Baines's group found themselves in front of a forest of tall, turmeric-colored reeds. Most of these ranged from about three to eight centimeters in diameter and were at least four meters high. There were also fallen reeds and small shoots.

The forest extended as far as they could see in each direction, so to avoid it, they would have had to turn around and go back. When they turned around, they could just see the ship.

The warm breeze had picked up a little, and the reeds occasionally collided, making a dull wind chime sound.

"Captain, why don't we just turn around?" Gino asked. "Send up a drone?"

"We're going in," Baines said through gritted teeth. "Drop it."

"Yes, sir." Then he said, "I think this is a bad idea."

"Noted." Then she said, "We aren't sending up drones. We're here in person for a reason."

The group walked in single file. Since they had no

idea what they would find, everyone was as wary as they were entranced.

"Shhh!" Banner said, pointing to a reed about a meter and a half away.

A turmeric-colored, feathered animal the size of a squirrel was crawling busily up the reed in a slight side-to-side motion. The creature had eight short, feathered legs ending in long black claws. Out of its doglike head, moth-like antennae, but no visible ears. Out of its doglike muzzle, long whiskers. The creature sniffed the air, pink nostrils quivering. Its eyes were large and black. Right now, the creature had moon eyes like an anxious dog. The feathery tail was almost as long as the body and ended in two more antennae. The creature looked at Banner, yawned, showing carnivore teeth, and scurried up the reed.

"The tongue was red," Cody whispered. "I'll bet the tail is to fool predators. I wonder if the yawn was to display those teeth."

The creature's tail started twitching.

"The animal's afraid, I'll bet," he said, stepping backward.

"You think the tail is a decoy," Banner said.

"Yep. I wonder if it drops off and regenerates, like a gecko's," Cody said. "Eventually, I'll have enough data to create a taxonomy, but informally, I think we should name them Banner's geckos."

Banner laughed quietly, slapping Cody on the back. "You're okay."

Dr. Banner Colson was a compactly built, dark-skinned Black man with close-cropped hair. He had been tapped from Shock Trauma in Maryland to join the colony. Some of the higher-ups in the Space Force had wanted to bring someone from Walter Reed instead, but Banner's experience with the most severe trauma cases was well known. So instead, the Space Force recruited Banner, who insisted that the colonists have their appendixes and gallbladders removed before the mission started.

The group saw several more Banner's geckos crawling up and down the reeds. Without warning, one lunged and sank its teeth into an indigo arachnid about three-quarters its size. The indigo bug had eight jointed legs that were relatively thick and a narrow, jointed abdomen that tapered to a stinger. The bug writhed and tried to sting the gecko. The gecko yanked and then shook its prey, and Baines realized that the bug's proboscis had been deep into the reed, and it had taken too long to break free. Everyone heard the crunching as the prey struggled. The gecko's tail was wagging up and down again, then came a rhythmic chirping from the indigo creature's wings.

Maura said, "The little guy makes that bug sound so good."

"It looks disgusting," Gino said.

The gecko finished the indigo bug—all but one leg, which had dropped to the ground—and was already stalking another one.

The group resumed walking.

The sun shed dim orange light through the dark green tufts at the top. The soil beneath them was pinkish orange. People began to speak quietly, almost reverently.

Ahead, Kelly yelled, "*Hey!*"

Baines ran ahead. People stepped out of her way.

Glenn had taken advantage of the fact that the group was focused on the animals and jumped out of the reeds at Kelly.

"What's your problem?" Glenn demanded. "Why can't you handle yourself?"

Gino grabbed him by the collar and went nose to nose with him. "Don't ever pull that shit again."

"All I did was walk toward her. It's not my fault she—"

Baines put him in an armlock so that he was sandwiched between herself and Gino. "You do that again, someone might shoot you," she said through gritted teeth.

"Don't be hysterical, it was a joke!"

"I should break your arm."

"Ow! Calm down! Gino, maybe you should take over—"

Gino shoved him back into Baines, putting pressure on his shoulder, and Glenn flinched. "Fuck you. You take orders from the captain."

"Don't do that again, Glenn," Kelly said, hand on the grip of her lasepistol. Then she turned her back to him and moved ahead.

Glenn shrugged at her, laughing slightly. "Ma'am, this is a Wendy's."

"My God," Chloe slipped beside Kelly after they'd resumed walking. "What just happened? He was so pleasant and reasonable until we left the solar system. Kind of a flirt, honestly."

"That's him," Kelly said bitterly.

"What's that smell?" Chloe whispered. "It smells like an unflushed toilet!"

Baines signaled the group to stop. The group stopped.

They heard chaotic footfalls and reeds bumping into reeds. About three meters from the group, two humanoids emerged from the reed forest. They were naked, over two meters tall, sturdily built, long-limbed, and bowlegged. Their scalps had patchy white hair punctuated with circles of baldness. Their skin was slick, the color of skim milk, with the same blue tinge. Their eight black eyeballs protruded like a crown of concord grapes, but when the eyes closed, they sank back into the skull. No noses, just nostrils. Their thin blue lips were pulled back from canine teeth. Their groins were thickly covered in wiry white-blond hair, and neither had visible external genitalia. One had two small, deflated breasts. The other had an open sore on its chest that was weeping pus. It was the size of a dinner plate.

One humanoid charged the group and grabbed Chloe. Glenn pushed Kelly into the path of the other one. The other humanoid gave Kelly a hard shove and tried to take Chloe by the legs. Chloe kicked its midsection, aiming for the sore. The second humanoid stopped dead in its tracks. The humanoid with Chloe wrapped its arm beneath Chloe's shoulders and trotted backward.

Chloe was screaming, tried to reach the humanoid's eyes, hammered its abdomen behind her with a series of sickening thuds, tried to stomp on its instep.

Banner tried to fire on it, but Glenn stood in the

way, hands clasped behind his back, rocking on his heels, looking at nothing ninety degrees to the group.

Gino cursed and used Glenn's shoulder as a launchpad and tried to tackle it, but it moved too fast. The group could shoot at the humanoids, but they'd risk shooting Kelly or Glenn.

Kelly changed her angle and shot the immobile one, bumping into Glenn, and it cried out in a grotesquely high voice before it died. Or looked like it died. Kelly shot it one more time, between its front eyes. The skull opened, and thick, milky, viscous fluid poured out with the brains.

The other one had already disappeared with Chloe.

Kelly and Banner ran after Chloe, and the crew heard, in the distance, Chloe's screams turn guttural.

About ten minutes later, the two colonists came back, shaking. "There were more of them," Banner said in a terrible voice. "Chloe's dead."

Baines turned on Glenn. "She's dead because of you! If you hadn't pushed Kelly in front of them, we could have shot them both!"

"You stood in front of them, you piece of shit!" Banner yelled. *"She didn't have to die! I would have had a clear shot!"*

"When?" Glenn said. "Your eyes were on those things, and your memory's just filling in missing details. I was standing right *there* the whole time. Kelly tripped. You're—"

"You tried to murder Mom," Cody said, strangely calm, "and you killed Chloe."

"I was looking for more of them. Your mother is clumsy and can't shoot, so don't blame me for that."

"You pushed Mom toward one," Cody said, voice still cold and calm, "and you stood in the way so no one could shoot them."

"Things happened so fast you don't know what you saw. That—"

Cody drew his lasepistol and shot him in the throat.

Glenn dropped like a sack of groceries, head leaning against a reed, chin nearly touching his chest.

Cody shot him in the gut. Shot him again and again.

Baines smelled roasting meat and the iron smell of blood.

Glenn looked at Baines for help and tried to speak, but Cody squatted and shot him between the eyes, then shot him in the heart.

Eliza put the book down, shaking, and texted Jamie.

> Shit

It gets worse.

> How the hell can it possibly get worse?

There's an aunt in Australia.

Rebellion at Broken Oar
Chapter 3 (continued)

Ursinus b: Spring Equinox 50–10:15 a.m.

"I alerted Commander Polichek, Captain," Gino said. "They're back on the—the *Broken Oar*."

Baines turned to the group. "We're going after her."

Kelly bent over with her hands on her thighs, stared at the ground, and tried to collect herself.

"Captain," Banner said, shaking, "she is dead and beyond help."

Everyone started crying.

"You examined her?" Baines demanded.

With tears running down his face, Banner said, "There was no need. Based on the condition of her body ..."

Chapter 4

Two years before, the SS *Kestrel* had left Earth for the Ursinus system, located on the Perseus Arm of the galaxy 40,000 light-years from Earth. The ship had traveled at spacetime 9 until it had found the wormhole where astronomers thought it would. At least, the astronomers had been pretty sure it was a wormhole.

On the ship at launch: Captain Dina Baines, Commander Tony Polichek (engineer), Lt. Cmdr. Kelly Chatworth (linguist and chief of security), Lt. Gino Accardi, Dr. Banner Colson (trauma surgeon), Dr. John Bynum (trauma expert), Jonathan Greenbaum (anthropologist), Chloe Jackman (botanist), John Kinkead

(astrophysicist), Yossi Mizrahi (climatologist), Shannon
Rodgers (botanist), Christian Dodd (veterinarian),
Jennifer Simms (farmer), Cody Sommars (xenobiologist), Glenn Sommars (engineer), and Maura Sommars,
because Maura's family had insisted that she be brought
along, and after much argument, the Space Force caved.

Along with the Human crew were three service
dogs, trained to assist with trauma and to prevent the
disorientation that might occur from living in an alien
environment. All of the colonists had been taught the
rudiments of farming, and for the laypeople, trained in
basic first aid.

After the faster-than-light ST drive had been devel-
oped, it had taken twelve years to build the *Enterprise*.

The *Enterprise*, the first starship, had made a test
run of the new spacetime drive and gone to Kepler
442B, where the crew found lichen and microbes on the
freezing planet. The air had been almost breathable, but
the winds were not survivable. At least the *Enterprise*
had been close enough to turn around and return to
Earth after a year's research.

After the *Enterprise* left for Kepler 442B, it took
another three years to build the trio of ships headed to
the Ursinus system. The crew had trained on the ships
for a year, and in simulated landscapes.

The plan was that after the *Kestrel* left for Ursinus
b, the *Peregrine* would follow, and then a few months
later, the *Archer* would. At least one of those ships was
predicted to reach Ursinus b.

Even at ST-9 and with the help of the wormhole,
the trip from Earth still took two years. The technology

had been discovered eighteen years before the moment that Baines's ship landed on Ursinus b.

At the time of the *Kestrel*'s departure, the *Enterprise* was still being refitted so that it could resupply the *Kestrel*, the *Archer*, and the *Peregrine*.

Astronomers had been searching the sky for decades, finally sending probes and finding the wormhole and identifying Ursinus b as one of the few planets likely to support Human life. The other genuinely earthlike planets were as yet too far, unless someone found another wormhole, which no one had. So when the trio of ships had been built, everyone agreed on where to send them.

It had taken six months for the *Kestrel* to get to the wormhole. During that time, the crew collected data to send back to Earth. Then, just before the ship entered the wormhole, the ship put them under and went into automatic pilot mode.

Astronomers had been fairly confident that Ursinus b had an earthlike atmosphere. Probably. They also knew that Ursinus was a K-type star and that Ursinus b was the only inhabitable planet in the two-planet Ursinus system.

Now the *Kestrel* had come out the other end and crashed before it had time to take any data about the life forms on the planet, frying those sensors in the process. The mission was a one-way trip, because the colonists were supposed to settle there, so Star Service didn't want to spend more money on added power, environmentals, or supplies, but the crew was now stuck where the ship had crashed.

CHAPTER
FOUR

ELIZA AND JAMIE sat in Dr. Badri Trivedi's office. The forensic pathologist sat back in his chair and said to Eliza, "Today you have brought your partner with you. The case is this challenging? Under ordinary circumstances, you speak with me alone."

"What ordinary circumstances?" Jamie demanded. "We could've just read your report. That's the ordinary circumstance. Eliza insisted on coming here. I think it's a waste of time."

"Evidently," Dr. Trivedi said.

Jamie was nonplussed. "Okay. Then why are we here? You're supposed to be independent of our department." He turned to Eliza. "You were already at the autopsy. You didn't discuss this then?"

"Do you want to participate in the investigation at all?" Eliza demanded.

"Eliza makes these discussions the subject of a report," Dr. Trivedi responded. "To the extent that she supplies information that is relevant to my findings, I include it in mine. How have you not discovered this?"

"Dunno. I just keep my eye on the ball, I guess."

"Tell me what is unusual about this case," Dr. Trivedi said to Eliza and took a sip of tea.

"All four family members have the same names as four characters in a science fiction book called *Rebellion at Broken Oar*."

"Never heard of it," Dr. Trivedi said impatiently. "So, a coincidence, unless you think the author decided to call attention to himself by naming his victim in his own book. How many people have read this thing?"

"It's a best seller," Jamie said.

"It is possible that the author heard the names somewhere and they somehow remained in his mind. Or the suspect found the coincidence humorous. Had anyone in the family read this book?"

Eliza put her travel mug down. "Both of the kids. In the book—"

"The son kills the father," Jamie said.

"Why would the victim's son kill his father?"

"He was a total bastard," Jamie said.

"This is not information."

"He was a control freak and abusive, and the family is glad he's dead," Eliza said.

"And the fictional Glenn Sommars?"

"Same."

"This is interesting," Dr. Trivedi said.

"No sign of forced entry," Eliza said. "The security system is always down in the daytime, no sign of a struggle anywhere in the house, and—"

"No blood anywhere but in the tub," Jamie cut in. "His shoes—"

"Were off," Dr. Trivedi interrupted. "Yes, yes, I received the body, remember?"

"And something else," Eliza said. "The wife said that the victim would not let anyone in the family read science fiction. That the sixteen-year-old daughter hid those books under the bed. But when Jamie and I went to the scene, there were science fiction posters on the wall from *Broken Oar* and other science fiction franchises, and there were science fiction books on a small bookshelf. And you know about the tattoo."

"You have my attention," Dr. Trivedi said.

"That tattoo was an insignia in the book," Jamie said. "Of the bad guys."

"And as I already told you, the tattoo was temporary," Dr. Trivedi said. "And in good condition. These tattoos are not very durable. They start to break down from the oils on the skin. These start to show wear and tear within a few days. Did you find any wrappers or like that?"

"No," Jamie said. "Forensics did a trash pull, and they didn't find a thing."

Eliza said, "The son in the book—"

"Cody—"

"Yes, yes," Dr. Trivedi said impatiently. "I don't care. The son in the book, was he an adult?"

"About the same age as our victim's son," Jamie said. "Twenty."

"He's a xenobiologist, and he's a kid?" Eliza asked.

"Cody in the book is a prodigy," Jamie said. "Our Cody's a senior at GW studying biomedical engineering, but that doesn't make him a prodigy or everyone in his class would be one."

"He graduated already," Eliza said quietly. "Remember?"

Dr. Trivedi was typing on his laptop.

Eliza and Jamie looked at each other.

The doctor turned his laptop around.

"His name is Glenn Cody Sommars?"

"No way," Jamie said, with a look of horror.

"He's second author on three papers," Dr. Trivedi said. "Fourth author on two. The impact factors are quite high. I'd say he's a prodigy."

Jamie sat back in his seat. He'd broken out in a cold sweat. Eliza studied him out of the corner of her eye, wondering what the hell was wrong with him.

"How long does it take to apply a temporary tattoo?" Jamie asked Dr. Trivedi, shaken.

"Based on my research, between two and fifteen minutes."

"Someone wasn't in an extreme hurry," Eliza said. "You'd expect someone to get out of there as soon as they could. Someone stuck around to apply a tattoo and take a shower."

"Did the family always enter and exit the house at the same time of day?"

"They did," Eliza replied.

"Then the killer could be anyone who knows their routine, although the parallels to the book are ... interesting. And even without legal training, I know that motive and opportunity alone are not sufficient, if motive is relevant at all."

"And we can't even prove whose gun it was," Jamie said, "let alone who pulled the trigger. Serial number was filed off."

"Are you certain that any of the rounds in the victim came from this particular weapon?" Dr. Trivedi asked impatiently. "At this point, that is a hypothesis."

"Still waiting on Ballistics," Jamie said.

Eliza saw that Jamie was fidgeting, one knee bouncing up and down.

"The connection between the book and this murder," Dr. Trivedi said to Jamie. "This has upset you?"

"It doesn't strike *you* as eerie?"

"Your response is enough to concern your partner. Which means that it is out of character. Indeed, the death is not a particularly tragic one."

Jamie went white.

"You will need to sort this out with him," Dr. Trivedi said to Eliza. "His response is peculiar."

"I dunno what you're talking about," Jamie said. "And I'm right here."

Trading looks with Dr. Trivedi, Eliza nodded slightly, then asked him, "Tell me more about how the victim died."

"You were at the autopsy," Jamie said angrily.

"Tell Jamie more about how the victim died," Eliza said without looking at him.

Dr. Trivedi opened the autopsy file on his laptop.

"I will state my findings informally. My report is much more precise, of course. He had a perforating gunshot wound to the head that entered between the eyes and exited the back of the head. The track of the bullet was a downward trajectory. The round, informally speaking, shattered his skull. There was brain matter on the floor of the tub. There was a perforating wound to the trachea. He also suffered exsanguination due to multiple gunshot wounds. Each of these independently could have caused his death. The manner of death is homicide. He was shot fifteen times. Thirteen of these gunshot wounds were distant to medium range, consistent with his killer shooting him from within the room.

"The rounds were 115-grain full metal jacket. Our ballistics expert made this remark as I was removing these from the body. According to the literature, these rounds cause more catastrophic injuries than more commonly used rounds, and one would want to know how the suspect acquired these.

"I state the location of these wounds informally, in an arbitrary fashion, which is not meant to communicate the order in which these wounds were inflicted. The round that perforated his trachea severed his spinal cord at C6. This injury would have prevented him from using his extremities. The remainder of his injuries were almost entirely in the abdomen and the chest. Several of these were perforating wounds. Some were penetrating wounds. Once again, the locations and nature of each of these wounds are described more precisely in my report. The tracks of some of these rounds also caused skeletal damage to the ribs. Finally, he had a perforating gunshot wound to the right forearm, which shattered the radius. This gunshot wound would not have caused his death. The final gunshot was postmortem but would have been quickly fatal if it were not, since it penetrated the heart. I speculate that the shot to the heart was, how do I want to put it? Insurance."

Jamie looked at Eliza and said, "Someone—"

"Hated his guts," she said.

"The body's position in the bathtub is not significant to you?" Dr. Trivedi demanded. "It is possible that this is a business murder. The bathtub symbolizing the removal of dirt. While the idea that the events in this case mirror the events in the book may be an attractive one, it would be useful to consider further evaluation of the victim's social and business circumstances."

"He doesn't have any social life," Eliza said. "The wife reports that he goes to work, comes home, works out in his twenty-thousand-dollar gym, terrorizes the family, and goes to bed. One way or another, he's responsible for his brother's serving a lengthy prison sentence, whether because he cooperated or by accident. But the brother was incarcerated five years ago."

"The neighbors?" Dr. Trivedi asked. "How old were these homes?"

"New construction," Eliza said. "Soundproof. The neighbors didn't see or hear a thing. Previously, that was good for Glenn, given that he beat up the whole family."

"While it is tempting to suspect a member of this family, this is a hypothesis at this point that needs more data. If the victim has been cruel to the family throughout the life of the family, one would wish to know what changed."

"Well, right now, we couldn't charge any of the three," Jamie said. "Even though they all had keys. None of them have criminal histories. There are no records in dispatch that law enforcement or EMS ever went to the house."

"The wife couldn't have done it," Eliza said. "Absolutely terrorized. And the grandparents provide an alibi for the kids, who will provide an alibi for the grandparents."

"You historically mistrust those whom you interview," Dr. Trivedi said. "Like the rest of your colleagues. How is it that you believe the wife?"

"She could have made a credible self-defense claim, but she didn't. She came in wearing long sleeves and a black scarf around her neck. Her sleeve shifted when she moved. The scarf fell off her neck. She had bruises around her wrist and her neck, yet she did not show them to me. I saw them by accident. She claimed that the bruises on her neck happened when she pulled off a shirt too roughly—"

"Absolutely not," Dr. Trivedi said.

"In fact, my guess is she was covered with bruises. She did say something weird. At one point, she said, 'He wanted more kids, but I would have had to put a book on the ceiling.'"

Jamie laughed.

"I brought up her statement because it's a reflection of how she felt about him. She thought to share that on camera with a stranger."

"This could be an indicator of candor, could it not?" Dr. Trivedi asked.

"It was. She was open and blunt throughout the interview."

"Did she work outside the home?"

"No. She was also, according to the kids, completely isolated, even from her parents. Her lawyer could have showed photos of those bruises at trial, and at least one juror would have let her walk. She spoke freely about how she feared and hated him, how he sabotaged her friendships, and that she was glad that he was dead, but ... how did she put it? 'I was terrified of him, Detective Benveniste. Shooting him would have meant going out of my way to be close to him.'" Eliza took a sip of coffee. "But she was protective of the kids, who, as far as I can tell, were protective of her. The entire family was terrorized."

"I note that you continue to recite statements of this length from memory. When you have testified at trial, this ability has been confirmed."

"You watch her testify?" Jamie looked him in the eye.

Dr. Trivedi looked back at him impassively. "When my duties permit this. It is beneficial to see what issues surface on cross-examination. Obviously, like all witnesses, I may not observe these proceedings until my testimony is complete. It is interesting to see how the trial proceeds rather than simply returning to my office after a time on the witness stand. When I am released as a witness, I remain. With regard to the evidence in this case, I trust that Forensics did a thorough job looking for trace evidence from the bedspread. One might be able to dismiss this if the hair belonged to the daughter, but not if the hair belonged to the son. I nevertheless caution you not to treat this case as an extension of the book. You may miss something. Now I really must return to work. But it was very nice to chat with you."

As Eliza followed Jamie out, Dr. Trivedi said, "Eliza."

She stopped, letting Jamie go on ahead.

"You should determine what is upsetting your partner about this case."

Eliza and Jamie waited at the end of the corridor to be buzzed into the sally port and thence out of the building.

"What's taking them so long?" Jamie said. "Are they afraid the bodies are going to go shambling down the corridor? What the hell?"

"Oh, sometimes it can take ten minutes."

"That's a fucking fire hazard, is what that is."

"Well, we could go back through the morgue, down the stairs, and into the parking garage if you want."

"Yeah, I'll pass. But wow, you and Badri. Are you a thing?"

She turned to face him. "Go fuck yourself. Since we caught this case, you've been squirrely as fuck. Everything, and I mean everything, is setting you off at random. You're storming out of rooms, you're holding something back, and before we crossed paths with Glenn Sommars's perforated corpse, it would not have occurred to you to ask me a question like that. But I've raised the issue more than once that we need to get the author into our interview room, and you've been irrational about this since day one. And I need to know why."

"Any reason you need to talk to him at all? Any reason he's

watching you testify? Because shagging the ME would be a bad idea. That's why I'm asking if you are."

"It helps to process a complicated case with someone, and Dr. Trivedi is not only brilliant, but I can count on his absolute objectivity. You and I could do that instead, but you're a paint-by-number kind of a guy, aren't you?"

"So you're telling me that if you had met him at a bar, and you worked in separate jurisdictions, you wouldn't go out with him? Or is it that he's from India?"

"Do you ever pay attention to your surroundings? His diplomas are on the wall. He got his BS in the UAE, Jamie. Medical school at Johns Hopkins. Neither of those universities are located in India. If you don't believe me, I'm sure we can find you a globe at the toy store. I never asked him more, because it's fucking crass."

"Tell me to my face you wouldn't fuck him if you had a chance."

Eliza almost slapped him. "Can you hit the buzzer again before I lose it?"

"But you won't tell me whether you're attracted to him."

"Tell me that this isn't a distraction from the fact that David Dove is looking awfully good for the death of Glenn Sommars."

"This corridor has a hell of an echo, doesn't it?" Jamie said.

"When did you turn into a shit, Jamie?"

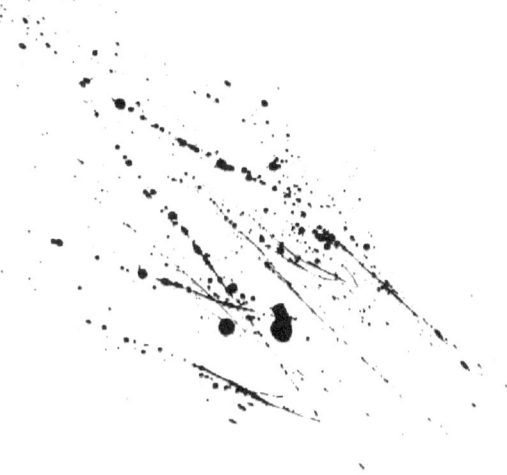

JAMIE AND ELIZA stood in a studio apartment leased to one Ira Smallwood. The apartment was located in a seedy area of Tauxenent County. Two police officers had responded to the apartment on a check-the-welfare by a sister, who said that Smallwood had no-showed for his birthday party the night before and that he had a history of substance abuse. She had insisted that this was out of character and that he always answered the phone when she called, but he hadn't been answering. She added that he owed someone a lot of money and he'd been vague about the circumstances.

The uniformed officers had reached the landlord, who lived on premises, and they subsequently found Ira's body at his computer desk.

The doorway was yellow-taped when Eliza and Jamie arrived, and the two detectives signed the clipboard and went in. CSIs followed them. The responding officers had already verified that Ira was the only name on the lease.

There was a slight scent of blood. The apartment still had boxes in the doorway.

"Do you want to get a search warrant?" Jamie asked sarcastically.

"I already got one."

"The dead guy's the lone tenant. You think he's filing a motion to suppress?"

"I don't want a fight with the landlord, do you? I mean, maybe it's overkill, but Denny hates litigating things that don't have to be litigated."

"It was overkill, but, you know, whatever."

After they glanced around, Jamie said, "A recent move?"

"Sister said his wife had just kicked him out and there were two young kids. Remember? I told you this on the way over. I wonder who he owed money to."

"Well, thank God he had the AC on. Otherwise, this place would stink to high heaven."

The AC was as loud as a tour bus.

The kitchen was filthy. The kitchen trash can was overflowing, the clamshell lid only partially closed, and there was a pizza box resting on the lid and propped up by the wall behind it. The countertops were covered with empty soda and beer cans and an overturned Solo cup.

From beside the coffee table, Jamie said, "Here we go."

There was a small baggie of pills, some of which had been crushed, and Eliza saw powder residue and a straw on the table, which was also cluttered with another pizza box and a half-eaten bag of cheese puffs.

"Well, a drug debt would explain some things," Eliza said. "Those can be fatal."

Jamie looked at one of the CSIs, turned to Eliza, and said, "Do we really need them? It kinda looks like overkill."

"I didn't think you were lazy, Jamie." Eliza definitely thought he was lazy.

"I'm not. I just don't want to waste time."

"Oh? On what? Got somewhere to be? The Board of Supervisors pays for six homicide cops in a jurisdiction with twenty homicides a year. There's a whole big story behind that if you want to read it in the *Washington Post*—if you were asleep for that whole thing. They took a shitload of flak for that until all those bodies piled up in Montgomery County last year. Everyone in Rockville was up in arms, and our Board of Supervisors said, 'Hey, see? We have enough murder cops to have handled that.' So, Jamie, what?"

A CSI looked at Eliza from behind Jamie, jerked her chin toward him, and rolled her eyes.

A set of narrow French doors led to the bathroom and bedroom. One of the doors had been pulled off the hinges.

Straight ahead was the bedroom. The bathroom was to the left. Eliza stepped in and made a sound of disgust.

"Oh," Jamie said, looking at the bathroom sink. "He had pizza last night." He walked out.

With a gloved hand, Eliza opened up the medicine cabinet and found three prescription bottles.

"Nothing in the fridge but a couple of beers!" Jamie called out.

A CSI was already at her elbow and took photos of the bottles.

After he took a series of photographs and videos of the bathroom, Eliza carefully took out the bottles one at a time and inspected them. "Quetiapine and divalproex sodium," she said. She recorded the name of the psychiatrist and his phone number. She saw that the quetiapine prescription was 200 mg twice daily, issued twenty-eight days prior, but the bottle was nearly full. The divalproex sodium prescription was for one 500 mg daily and one 250 mg daily, issued twenty-eight days prior, and these bottles were also nearly full.

The CSI placed the bottles in an evidence container, noting the case information, location seized, time and date of seizure, and name. Then he sealed it and signed across the seal.

The body was at a desk situated against a wall to their left, across from the lone twin bed. A handgun lay on the floor directly below his left hand. There was an exit wound in his forehead, a contact gunshot wound to the temple, and two near contact gunshot wounds between the back of his head and his left ear.

"Well, that doesn't look good," Jamie said.

Between the desk and the doorjamb, someone had punched holes in the walls.

On the desk in front of the body was a document and an open envelope.

"Nastygram from his boss," Eliza said. "Certified, return receipt requested."

"Drug debt. He stole from his job. His wife kicked him out," Jamie said. "We have three classes of suspect."

Eliza was at her desk doing paperwork when Jamie stood over her with a document. "What the fuck?" he said. "What the actual airborne fuck? Was Badri high when he wrote this thing?"

Eliza inspected the document. "Okay, Ira's autopsy report. And?"

"Check the manner of death."

Eliza did. Then she looked up at Jamie. She flipped

through the pages to make sure the last page wasn't stapled to the wrong report.

Nothing doing.

"Suicide?" she said, looking up at Jamie.

"I know! What's he on?"

"Well, let's go ask him."

"*You* go ask him. I think he's full of shit."

"I'll spot you that he didn't give an opinion on manner of death during the autopsy, but he must have had a reason."

Eliza sent an email.

After Eliza settled in, Dr. Trivedi said, "You are here to quarrel with my findings in the Smallwood matter."

"I hoped you knew me better than that by now. Me second-guessing a forensic pathologist is like a passenger back-seat-driving the pilot of a commercial jet."

Dr. Trivedi laughed. "This is the first time that our conclusions have differed."

"And if you weren't completely objective, I would never seek your advice in the first place. And I'm not arguing, I'm just confused. He's got three gunshot wounds to the head, but you say it's suicide. I'm here so you can tell me what your reasoning was, not to argue with it."

"You are not aware of the peer-reviewed literature concerning death by suicide due to two or more self-inflicted gunshot wounds to the head. This is not surprising. I nevertheless have had unfortunate experiences with homicide detectives who quarreled with my findings. I should have anticipated that you were not one of those."

"We hadn't pulled Ira's boss into our interview room yet.

You have no idea how relieved I am that we didn't. And I can guess who you're talking about, but I'm not here to gossip."

Dr. Trivedi relaxed. "I was able to base my findings on your thorough report. The decedent was prescribed quetiapine and divalproex sodium. Quetiapine is an antipsychotic commonly prescribed for bipolar depression, and divalproex is a mood stabilizer. You noted the date that the prescription was filled and the number of tablets remaining. One could easily determine that he had stopped taking his medication, and the toxicology report confirms this. Thus, his bipolar depression remained untreated. The decedent had a comorbid substance abuse issue. The drug report indicates that the substance seized from a coffee table contained fentanyl and alprazolam, and the toxicology report also shows that he had consumed these substances just prior to his death, and the metabolites present indicate that he had used them the previous day also. Among other effects, these can exacerbate depression. The body had no other injuries that would have been indicative of a struggle.

"You also seized a demand letter from an employer threatening criminal prosecution if the decedent did not repay a sum of nearly twenty thousand dollars. The decedent's sister indicated that there was a recent separation and the existence of an unspecified debt. The crime scene photographs depict a filthy apartment but no signs of a struggle, since the furniture was not in disarray. There were five holes in the wall beside the desk near the doorjamb, which are consistent with having been made with a fist, indicative of emotional dysregulation. You noted no signs of forced entry.

"I state the location of the bullet wounds more precisely in my report, and my statement of their location here is arbitrary, not meant to reflect the order that they were inflicted. There was a contact gunshot wound to the anterior portion of the left temporal bone. There were two near contact wounds to the left parietal bone: one perforating and one penetrating. These were all .22-caliber rounds, and according to Ballistics, these rounds were fired from the weapon that you seized. It is possible for an individual to remain alert enough to do this. These wounds were lethal.

"I formed this hypothesis during the autopsy, but it was necessary to conduct research to determine whether there were new findings. There were none. Based on the nature of the wounds and the surrounding circumstances, I made my finding of suicide."

"Thank you for explaining this, Dr. Trivedi—"

"Badri, please."

"I'll try," she said. "I can't promise. I'm grateful for your time. I can now go back to my office and talk my partner off the proverbial ledge."

"He was not so accepting of my findings."

"He said, 'What the fuck? What the actual airborne fuck? Was Badri high when he wrote this thing?' I'm not happy that he's not here with me so you could tell him what your reasoning is. I find this frustrating. In complex cases, it's important to be able to process the state of the evidence with one's partner, and given his working style, I can't do that with him. At first, this case didn't seem complex: dead guy, three lines of inquiry. Then it was complex even though it wasn't murder. Jamie was incurious."

"You have consulted with me on two prior cases. You may continue to do this with future ones."

"Thank you. Although most homicide cases are not complex. I doubt I'll be taking up much of your time."

Dr. Trivedi hesitated for a moment. Then he typed on his laptop and printed off a document. He retrieved it and handed

it to her. "This is a three-day conference sponsored by an asso-
ciation of forensic pathology. It is scheduled for August in
Baltimore. I recommend that you attend this conference. I will
be attending. I will be staying with a cousin, but the conference
has made an arrangement for local hotels."

Eliza studied the brochure. "This is incredible! Thank you!
Will they let a homicide detective attend this conference?"

"I will make a few calls," Dr. Trivedi said, "with great
pleasure."

When he looked into her eyes, Eliza felt unaccountably shy.

From the hallway, she heard him say sadly, "Absolutely
not."

When Eliza got back to the office, she went straight to
Sergeant Roth's office to request funding for the trip.

CHAPTER
SIX
TWO YEARS AGO

ELIZA SAT ACROSS FROM DR. Trivedi with a stack of crime scene photographs. She was pale and her hands were shaking. "Thank you so much for taking the time to meet with me." She looked down at the photographs in her file and said, "I don't know."

"What don't you know?"

"I've never heard of a serial killer of mothers, babies, and dogs. Third time in a row. So far, one a month. Which means there will be more until we stop him. I've seen murdered children, but—"

"I know this," he said quietly.

"Sometimes the family pet is killed too. It's awful, but I signed on for that. But *this*?"

She handed him the photographs.

"I received these bodies."

"I know. There are so many injuries inflicted here. He doesn't even seem to have a pattern. Except ... everything. We're cross-referencing their entire lives to see if there's any overlap and trying to find consistent bystanders. Our investigation already fills a banker's box. In fact, we've even got literally every business these people frequent in a rapidly lengthening spreadsheet. But maybe there's more information here."

"I have notified Richmond that I intend to respond to these scenes, if there are more. I concur that there will likely be further victims until the murderer is apprehended."

"I'm relieved you'll be there, but I'm also sorry."

"The crime scene photographs, do you have hard copies with you?"

"Yes. All of them."

"Come with me."

He led her down the hall to a conference room. Together, they laid out the crime scene photos and scene diagrams, and he put the autopsy reports beside them.

After about fifteen minutes, she said, "Am I intruding on your time?"

"No. I calendared an hour for our meeting."

"You did? We usually don't consult for that long."

"This is not a typical case. And the more rapidly this case is solved, the fewer similar bodies I have to receive."

The Tauxenent Strangler would go on to kill sixteen women, sixteen children, and sixteen dogs.

DYSON'S last known address was at the far south end of Tauxenent County. It turned out to be a nondescript, ill-maintained house at the end of a cul-de-sac. SWAT had surrounded it, although the underbrush was nearly touching the back door.

The Virginia State Police had appeared with their bomb dogs and their bots, but the Tauxenent Strangler, Lonnie Dyson, had not booby-trapped his own house.

Sergeant Roth and Eliza's lieutenant were at the command post. To her abject gratitude, the chief stayed out of it and kept the media at bay at the end of the street.

SWAT went in first.

The house was cleared, but SWAT found no one.

Officers were muttering that he had gotten away, that it was the wrong address.

No one, though, could have gotten through that underbrush.

Eliza nodded at Jamie, and they entered the house. CSI, who'd been waiting for the signal from them that it was safe to go in, followed.

Dr. Trivedi had been waiting by the front door, but out of the corner of her eye, Eliza saw him push past the patrol officers standing on the crumbling sidewalk and on the weeds poking between the cracks.

Eliza looked around. There was no TV. There was no couch. There was a kitchen table with a single chair. Nothing in the greasy bathroom. Clothes in piles, possessions stored in milk crates, a mattress on the floor for a bed, a second bedroom piled high with hoarded junk.

She went back to the living room.

No TV. There's always a TV.

She looked at the outlets in the kitchen. The one beside the refrigerator had a mini power strip. Plugged in were the refrigerator, a smartphone charger brick, a can opener, a coffeepot ... and an extra cord that went into a hole in the wall beside the refrigerator.

She yanked the refrigerator back from the wall with surprising strength and found a door carved in the drywall.

She motioned for Jamie. *But where the hell was he?*

Eliza looked over her shoulder and instead found Joe Costa standing behind her.

"Where's Jamie?" she hissed.

"Looking for signs of forced entry? I dunno," Joe said with faint disgust.

She shoved the door open, took cover to one side, and shouted, "*Police! Freeze!*"

The cord powered a ceiling fan with a light.

She heard something undefinable, then she heard the movement of clothing on clothing. Someone was down there.

"Fuck this shit." A SWAT team operator appeared beside her, all geared up, night vision goggles at the ready, ballistics shield on one arm. "You're in over your fucking head. Get out of the way and let us—"

But there was a disturbance on the other side of the house. Jamie was screaming at someone to freeze.

The SWAT team officer threw a flash-bang down the stairs and ran for the commotion. Eliza wondered where the rest of them were *after missing the goddamned hidden door!*

She heard several people laughing in Jamie's direction.

In front of Eliza, a man ran up the stairs.

Eliza drew her service weapon and backed up while the man walked the few steps from the door and stood with his back to the sink.

Pointing her weapon at his midsection, she said, "Down on your knees! Hands on your head!"

The man took a step toward her, and she hissed, "Give me a reason!" Then she yelled in a guttural, growling voice, "*Give me a reason!*"

As he complied, he said, "Do you have a dog?"

Joe Costa put him in cuffs. As Joe ushered Dyson out of the kitchen, Dr. Trivedi, who now stood in the entry to the kitchen, backed up to let them pass.

Eliza held her service weapon at low ready and went down the stairs.

There's the TV, she thought. Then she heard the screams, the begging, the dog. Lonnie Dyson had videoed his crimes, and there he was—a star in his own snuff film, starring Olivia D'Antonio, Ross D'Antonio, and Max. And Lonnie Dyson.

The room was so small, it took seconds to clear it. A couch with a table and a bottle of hand lotion. Walls painted black. Green shag carpet. TV on a console with fifteen DVDs.

All the while, she could see what he was doing to Olivia D'Antonio and ...

"*Clear!*" she called, and then she realized her mistake. She heard footsteps at the top of the stairs, and she turned around, but Officer Randall Jenkins and Joe Costa were already in the room.

"Who's got him?" Eliza asked.

"SWAT."

Jenkins was transfixed by the recording, breaking into a cold sweat and turning pale. He yelled, "*Jesus Christ! Oh, Jesus Christ!*"

Behind him, Joe Costa took one look at what was on the screen and gently said to Randall, "Hey, buddy. Turn around. Don't look."

Then Eliza heard more footsteps. *Badri!* She went up the stairs two at a time, blocking Dr. Trivedi halfway down.

"Turn around, Badri! *Turn around!*"

He looked startled. This was the first time she had ever addressed him by his first name. "What is—"

"*Everyone! Everyone! Turn around!*" she called. "*No one is coming down here but CSI until this scene is processed!*"

"If there are bodies," Dr. Trivedi said, "then—"

"Badri," Eliza said, shaking, gripping his forearm. He had a hold of hers from underneath. "Please, by all that's holy in this universe, I cannot let you see what's down there. You'll never sleep again."

"Remember who you are talking to, Eliza," he said in perplexity, "and my duties."

"There are no bodies down there, Badri! Just a video playing." At "video," her voice broke. "He videoed everything."

From the TV downstairs, there was the guttural wailing of a woman whose child has died, and Eliza felt Badri's hand go ice cold.

"Go back upstairs," Eliza nearly whispered. She took a deep

breath, looked over her shoulder, and shouted, "*Joe, turn it OFF! TURN IT OFF!*"

The screaming stopped, and Eliza realized that Badri still had a hold of her arm, and she hadn't let go of his. He looked haunted.

Eliza wondered who was giving comfort to whom.

She let go of his arm, and he hesitated before he let go of hers.

She suddenly felt bereft, and she turned around and went downstairs.

Eliza was filling out paperwork when Sergeant Roth took Jamie's chair and sat across from her. "Happy news," he said. He looked anything but happy.

"Oh?"

"Lonnie Dyson was murdered an hour ago in the jail."

Seeing his expression, she said, "No, no, no, Sarge! Please tell me you aren't putting me in charge of—"

"Fuck no. I asked the higher-ups to let the State Police take it. Too many of us would want to find out who offed him and pin a medal on their chest. They agreed."

"What happened?"

"Found dead in his cell stabbed, oh, about seventy or eighty times. Badri will have a blast counting the stab wounds."

"You don't look happy. Why don't you look happy?"

"Adrenaline crash. It's over. I was waiting for all of the motions before the thing had to go to trial. Then the trial. Maybe there's a conspiracy nut on the jury who lets him walk. Cases like that live with you, you know?"

Eliza knew. "Connecting the dots between the bodies we

found and the videos he took of the murders. You made the right decision, limiting access to those videos to just me and Jamie." She rubbed her eyes. "I may never get those images out of my head. Or the screams. Or the squeals of the dogs. But at least we won't have days of testimony. I won't have to look at those videos *again*."

"I'll feel relieved in a while, but not so much happy."

"How does this happen in a jail? In prison, yeah. Easy-peasy. But how does this happen in the jail?"

"I guess the State Police will find that out. Thank God I don't have to really care very much." After a few beats, he said, "Take some time off. That's an order. You have the annual leave for it. Give yourself two weeks."

"And do what?" She wanted to ask him how she was supposed to get the screams and images out of her head, but she was afraid of his response, which would likely be official and possibly put a dent in her badge.

"Try to remember who you are when you don't have a badge on."

Eliza laughed.

"I wasn't entirely joking."

"I know."

Jamie walked in looking numb, and he leaned on the desk next to Eliza. "Sarge, I'd track down Dyson's killer all right. Only to offer him a blow job though."

Sergeant Roth and Eliza laughed.

"I'll set him up with a lifetime supply of cupcakes," Eliza said. "You can handle the blow job, Jamie. Who will bring the wine?"

The three of them laughed, but there was an edge of hysteria.

Sergeant Roth turned to Jamie. "I ordered Eliza to take two weeks of paid leave. You too."

"Will do, Sarge," Jamie said. "I'm outta here." He started to walk away, his stooped posture making him look even more like a question mark than ever. He turned around and said, "I'll text you later, Eliza."

After Sergeant Roth walked away, Eliza got an email.

It was from Dr. Trivedi: See me. Now.

Intrigued, she got up.

When she settled into Dr. Trivedi's office, he said, "You have heard by now that Lonnie Dyson was murdered in the jail."

"Yes, I did. The State Police has the case, thank God. Jamie offered to track the killer down and give him a blow job."

"This case has taken a toll on you, has it not?"

"It has." She opened her mouth to be specific, but instead, she said, "You didn't see the videos Dyson took. I wouldn't have let you. I can't stop hearing the screams of the women and children and the squeals of the dogs in my head. You?"

"I saw the videos."

"*Why*, Badri? Tell me why you would do that to yourself!"

"It was necessary to compare the injuries as they were being inflicted to the findings documented in my reports, to verify that there was a correspondence. And ... it is possible that I may have been cross-examined on these."

"Sergeant Roth didn't tell me. Neither did you. I would have checked in with you. Wasn't just one video enough? I put a trigger warning on the case server, and Denny put one on the discovery so that Rafaella could decide to just say fuck it."

"One expects to encounter shocking deaths in this profession. These deaths strained me nearly to the breaking point. I hope I am not intruding on your time."

"Never. And ... I'm sorry. Denny saw the videos too. I couldn't tell her how much they wrecked me. Jamie sat there mangling paper clips. He does that. At the end of one video, he put his fist through a wall. No one even wrote him up. Sergeant Roth threatened to show the videos to HR. You didn't have anyone involved in the case to process it with. Hell, Badri, I did, and it's only helped a little. It was bad enough that for a second, I thought about inviting Rafaella out for a beer after he was arrested. She actually had to talk to him."

"Rafaella?"

"DeMeo. One of his lawyers."

"Yes, I know who she is. This surprises me."

"Well, it was a dumb idea. Badri, if I'd known you'd seen the videos, I'd have sought you out. God knows, we can't go to our families for support with this case. That's partly it, isn't it?"

"Indeed."

"I've been ordered to take two weeks' leave. Sergeant Roth also said, 'Try to remember who you are when you don't have a badge on.'"

"This is wise advice. And your husband certainly agrees with this, no?"

Eliza laughed silently. "No husband." She saw Badri relax, a nuance, but there was a sadness there that she couldn't interpret. "I think that was part of what informed Sergeant Roth's point. I really don't have much of a life outside of the job. You?"

"Sergeant Roth's advice is generalizable. I too do not have much of a life outside of the job."

"How by God's frisbee are you single? What are you, late thirties?"

"Forty, and one could ask the same of you."

"Oh, I'm uncomfortable around most people. The joke is,

the one person who always puts me at ease can't possibly love me back. Nor should he. And it's been a problem for years, and it's going to stay a problem. And here you are, with everything going for you, and you're alone. Seriously, someone needs to have a life around here."

He sighed. "A person who cannot love you back is a fool. I mix with others with difficulty. And I too love a person who cannot love me back. Nor should she. It is possible that I will continue to love her for years."

"Well, she's an idiot too. Maybe we should introduce the two idiots, and they'd get along."

Dr. Trivedi laughed again. Then he said, "And why could he not love you?"

"It would be stupid."

"Do I know this man?" he asked softly.

"Something tore loose in you," Eliza said. "This case, it's ripped us all to hell. But you're flooded, aren't you?"

"This is an interesting metaphor," he said. "I believe that you are correct. I would have had thirty-two autopsy reports to review. There would have been weeks of trial preparation with Denny. I would be testifying for weeks. Indeed, so would you. And now there is nothing to be done."

"There would have been so many motions, I'd have done better to put a bedroll in the courthouse. As the lead investigator, I'd be sitting there even if I weren't testifying. Reliving it over and over and over. *Seeing* him. Now he's dead. I'll get around to feeling relieved about that, but now we're left alone with our thoughts, aren't we? What we saw and heard. And what am I supposed to do? Because my sergeant is right. I *have* forgotten who I am when I don't have a badge on." She softened. "I'm glad you called on me. I think you and I lived with this case the most."

He sighed, then he looked at her with an expression she had not seen before—was that grief? "If I invited you to my home, would you misunderstand this?"

Touched, Eliza said, "No. And we can't just go grab a beer at The Lion, can we?"

On her way to Badri's house, she got another phone call.

ELIZA FOUND the snug brick house in an old, leafy neighborhood in Tauxenent County. It bordered on Difficult Branch, which allowed for some discretion.

When she got out, she saw thunderheads piled up and, in the distance, lightning, signaling one of the last afternoon thunderstorms of the season.

Badri wore a plain black T-shirt and faded jeans.

Eliza was wearing a white V-necked T-shirt and faded jeans, hoping to signal informality and I Know This Is Not A Date. Eliza wondered whether that was behind Badri's dress choices as well.

In a very slight nod to the fact that she was not at work, she wore her hair down. Although she had hesitated at first, she'd put on her Star of David necklace.

She took off her shoes inside the front door and lined them up with his and followed him to the living room.

To Eliza's delight, Badri's living room was lined with full bookcases. His home was as clean and orderly as she expected it to be.

She inspected his books and saw that he was a voracious reader of just about everything—except, she saw with relief, self-help books. On a side table beside a recliner in front of the fireplace was a book called *Suns of Glass*. Keeping the bookmark in place, she looked at the back, but it had nothing but testimonials. She put it down.

"Literary fiction," she said.

"You have read this?"

"No. It doesn't have a synopsis on the back. This is publisher-ese for 'If you haven't heard of this book, you are a benighted fool.'"

He laughed. Then he said, "Sit. Please."

She sat on the couch and tried to figure out what to do with her hands.

He came back with two bottles of beer and handed her one. Then he sat in the chair and took a deep drink of it.

"This is better," she said softly, then drank.

"It is that. I am presuming that your superiors would not agree."

"My superiors would be screaming their heads off. As would Denny. Joe Costa and Jamie would drag me out of here by my hair. I don't care very much about that right now. Jake Levy with those necropsies—he must wake up screaming. That case practically moved into my head, and it's been spraying blood on its metaphorical walls ever since. Yours too, no?"

"That is an apt metaphor," he said. His gaze shifted to the fireplace. "The book is speculative fiction about artificial intelligence in androids, but the android protagonist cannot tell who is Human and who is not. And ... he is curious about death, since he will not die."

"Hell of a book for you to read, no?"

"It is in part an exploration of the phenomenon of the near-death experience."

"Tell me you don't believe in that shit. Please."

He looked at her in some surprise. "This concerns you, what I believe?"

"The idea that you believe that NDEs are a window to some sort of beyond fills me with dread."

"Why?"

"Because one of the many things I like and admire about you is that you are a rational man."

He laughed quietly. "And yet I have invited a female homicide detective to my home alone. This does not strike you as irrational?"

"Oh," she said, laughing, "my coming here is one of the dumbest, most career-ending moves I could make. I should have gently said no and pretended you never, ever asked the question at all. And I am nevertheless sitting here in your living room. On the other hand, it beats a trip to Cameron Psych. Or, worse, *not* going to Cameron."

He looked at her sharply. "Are you having thoughts of—"

"You know who did. He came down the stairs right behind me. Randall."

"I know," he said quietly, studying her.

"Working with you was a bright spot in all that darkness. I wasn't in that basement, watching that video again. I was not in my office, making a spreadsheet of the lives of murder victims. The day before he was murdered, one of the preschoolers had been on a field trip to the zoo. And now I learn that you believe in NDEs?"

"I do not believe in them. There is no evidence for these. The protagonist in this book attempts to mimic the Human death experience, to his detriment. It is interesting to analyze the thinking of an immortal, sentient being." He suddenly gripped the bottle of beer so tightly that Eliza wondered if it would shatter. "I find my emotional responses in the aftermath of this case to be overwhelming, a thing I am not accustomed to." Before she could respond, he said, "But when you considered that I might believe in such nonsense, you were alarmed."

"This case overwhelmed everyone. I'm glad you sought me out. And ... we're going to have a thunderstorm pretty soon. If I were at home alone, it would not be pretty."

"You are afraid of thunder?"

"Not until this case. But, you know, the McMann house. The power went out. Sitting here with you though ... thunder can go back to being the sound of static electricity. Not when I'm alone. It's almost embarrassing to be a grown-up who is newly afraid of thunder."

At "with you," Badri became very still. Then he said, "I remember the house." He took another deep drink. "And I wish I did not."

Eliza buried her face in her hands and said through tears, "Bear was still alive! Badri ... how was Bear still alive?"

"I envy Detective Cloud," he said quietly, "that he felt free enough to put his fist through a wall. I transported Dr. Levy to Cameron Psychiatric Health Center after he euthanized Bear." He slid a box of tissues across the coffee table.

"I don't blame him," she said, wiping her eyes. "I'm glad he went, then." She looked at him for a moment. "Are you okay?" she said softly.

"I did not have suicidal ideation then. Nor do I now."

She relaxed.

He got up and came back with another bottle of beer for himself. "To return to our original topic ... and it would be best if we did this ... you were concerned that I believed in the existence of NDEs. Why?"

"Because a belief in garbage like that could inform your professional approach."

"And it has not."

"*Yet*. What happens when we get a case that could be interpreted in terms of the supernatural instead of as one big question mark? I couldn't come to you for help in a case like that, if you believe that someone's ancestors are at the end of a tunnel beckoning a dying person to cross to the other side, when it's just a soup of neurotransmitters in an anoxic brain—one of them being endorphins. Or why isn't it, at the end of that tunnel, ever your creepy uncle who got drunk on Thanksgiving and said racist shit and espoused conspiracy theories, your aunt who wondered why you weren't married yet while criticizing your body size, and that guy you slept with in college only once because he was terrible in bed and who died in a frat house of an overdose of grain alcohol?"

Badri laughed hard. "Alas, wishing for something does not make it true, no matter how desperately it is hoped for."

She tried to imagine Denny or Sergeant Roth in the room and what they would say, but that did not work. "If only. And I am filled with abject relief that in the event of a case involving a series of events that could either involve empirical evidence or spooky woo bullshit, I can count on you that you won't cough up fantasies about the supernatural or some such shit." She took another deep drink of beer. "I'm sorry that I lost it a little. You worried me."

He studied her. "Your curiosity was one of the reasons that I have agreed to consult with you so often. You are not curious about the unexplainable?"

"I'm confident that we're all bags of electrified meat and

that eventually we all die. We're either cremated or we rot. And you?"

"I have similar beliefs, although not in such graphic terms. I discount talk about tunnels and séances, and I do not believe in magic. It would similarly have alarmed me to discover that you believed in such things." Then he stopped. His expression grew haunted. "Eliza, the suffering of the victims, I could not bear this. And yet we both did."

"You weren't supposed to watch the videos. You see them when they're already dead—"

"And in this case, this was sufficient." His expression was bleak.

"But I could have watched them *with* you, so you didn't have to watch them alone!"

"In retrospect, that would have been wise."

"Odds are, we'll never have anything like this in Tauxenent County again. There are, what, thirty-five serial killers operating in the United States? This isn't Castle Rock, Maine."

"And I would tear up my diplomas before I would ever work there."

Eliza laughed. "The meetings we had ... I promise I never met with you for no reason."

"You did not."

"There was all that horror, and there you were, explaining it, breaking it down to a series of facts, making things make sense." She drank down half the bottle of beer at once. "My God. I desperately wish I could believe in heaven and hell."

"I am glad you do not."

"Because?"

He looked away.

Eliza thought about pushing the issue, but she let it pass.

He said, "You are Jewish, yes?"

"I am. We believe we were all at the foot of Mount Sinai when Moses came down with the Ten Commandments, and we made a covenant with God. I believe that. If that's a cognitive inconsistency, it's one I'm comfortable with. You don't need to tell me you're not Jewish, because I'd know. It has nothing to do with where you came from, because the exile sent us all over the world."

"You would know?" He looked amused.

"I would." She took another drink. "So, you?"

"I am an atheist."

"Interesting."

"This does not disturb you?"

"No."

"And yet you are not. What is the difference?"

"I still don't have to believe in heaven or hell. I wish the Messiah would hurry up, and yeah, I open the door for Elijah. And?"

"And I do not accept these things to be true."

"And Jews don't seek converts."

He smiled slightly. "This is fortunate. Similarly, I do not try to convince anyone of the absence of any deity."

"Huh. So is this woman you love an atheist?"

"She is not."

"And what happens if she loves you back? Is there a fist-fight about religion and kids?"

He laughed. Then he said sadly, "The issue is moot."

"You've decided this for her?"

"Exploring this issue is in no one's best interests."

She studied him. "Why won't you tell her?"

"Who is he? The man you alluded to in my office?"

"My God, here are two unavailable mystery people."

"How is it that you could not discuss your emotional responses to these cases with your partner?"

Eliza leaned her elbows on her thighs. Then she ran her hands through her hair.

He tensed.

"Jamie?" she said. "Have you *met* him? Talk about it? He got drunk at my house twice."

Badri went perfectly still.

"No, not that. He got drunk and watched football reruns. It was just better than wondering if he'd wrap his car around a tree or plow into a family of four while driving home from The Lion. He decided bravado was the best coping mechanism. Occasionally, it was drinking alone. Or more than occasionally. If he talked about it at all, it was to joke. Dark humor is thera-peutic, but it only takes you so far. And Joe Costa didn't want to discuss any of it." She finished her first beer and realized that it had gone to her head. "You refer to Sergeant Roth as 'Oren,' Krista Denbow as 'Denny,' and you call me by my first name. You have only ever referred to Jamie as 'your partner' or 'Detective Cloud.' What's that about?"

"This is nothing to concern yourself with."

"Oh? If this were a date, I would wonder if you were jealous of him. And if you were, I would tell you truthfully that he has an alarming taste in twentysomething badge groupies and exactly zero interest in me. In fact, I doubt the thought has ever occurred to him."

"You are more confident in his intentions than I am. And the matter is still nothing to concern yourself with. I will not discuss this matter further." He punctuated this by bringing her another bottle of beer.

She accepted it, then said, "I wonder what mix of qualities

some of our colleagues have that this case is rolling off their back as it is."

"This is the third time that you have mentioned this idea. How concerned should I be?"

"Not at all. I'm just curious how some of us can deal with it while some of us struggle. Randall was Dyson's thirty-third victim. Who knows if Jamie will back off his drinking? And me? I'm sitting in your living room. Yet the pressure to stay out of a professional's office is real. Could you imagine dealing with that on cross in a use-of-force case?"

"I can. You chose a moral, legal, and ethical response to a common pitfall of working in the criminal justice system."

Eliza thought for a moment. "Well, when you put it like that ..."

"I do. And ... concededly, my ability to compartmentalize has been strained by this case. Perhaps this is why I have invited you here."

"I'm glad you did."

But when they began to discuss the McMann case, they quickly changed the subject. Suddenly, Eliza said, "Did you hear what Jamie did when we went into Dyson's house?"

"Tell me."

"So I'm waiting for Dyson to get to the top of the stairs, and I hear Jamie screaming at someone to freeze. *Screaming* it. No authority in that voice at all. The room he was in was dim, I guess? And Jamie thought he had Dyson at gunpoint in a closet, but it was actually just a pile of hoarded clothes with a baseball cap on top of it. It turns out that's why I heard people laughing in the other part of the house. Did the SWAT operator go down the stairs when I found the hidden door? He did not."

Badri looked disgusted. "And you say this man is your friend."

"He does have, as they say, issues. Right now though, I'm basking in my abject relief that you aren't going to talk about hiring a psychic in the next case."

"Absolutely not. And I am similarly relieved that I will not have to discourage you from doing so."

"So who is she?"

"I am surprised that you ask this."

"Why?"

"My ability to predict the qualities and behaviors of others, it is a skill that I value. I am surprised that you do not have similar skills."

"We all have our blind spots, no?"

He locked eyes with her for a moment, then looked away.

"If you think that I already know, why won't you tell me? And if you think you already know, why do you keep asking?"

"Because the fact that I ask is important in itself, no?"

"No. It isn't. As far as whether I can read you? I can't. You're very controlled most of the time. My sense is that there is a lot going on under the surface, but nothing I can interpret."

"And yet you are here."

"I'm confused. Can you elaborate?"

"You are here alone, and we are drinking together. Yet you say you cannot ascertain my motives."

"And I never gamble what I can't afford to lose."

"What are you gambling on?"

She took a deep drink of beer. "Your motives."

He flushed. He started to say something but went with, "You must stop saying that I helped solve the case. I did not."

"Oh? Some of the injuries, you had a hypothesis of what made them. You repeated that observation regularly, all—"

"That observation merely stood out for you. I made many."

"Well, you kept making that one. It wasn't the only weapon used," and she ripped part of the label off the bottle and took another deep drink of beer. "There were banker's boxes worth of evidence. With all of that, it was your observation about a particular kind of injury and calling my attention to it repeatedly during the autopsies and in the photographs— it was only one of the many, many kinds of injuries that that animal inflicted on his victims—that caused me to change my approach. You laid out all the autopsy reports and crime scene photographs on your conference table as they came in, and you had to look at them over and over and over again instead of doing an autopsy and moving on to the kid who fell out of the boat and the old lady who died alone in her bed. And you saw those videos. Badri ... you didn't have to see them!"

"Perhaps my motives were selfish."

"Selfish how?"

"The faster you apprehended the suspect, the fewer such bodies I would receive. And ... the fewer such crime scenes you would have to process."

"I wouldn't call that selfish."

"Oh?"

"You wanted the killing to stop. How is that selfish?"

"I ..."

"You what?"

"It is of no moment."

Sensing his discomfort, she said, "Well, now that I know that you aren't deluded, I can now add that book to my to-be-read pile. It's already ridiculously huge, but I'll move this one to the top."

"Then you will tell me what you think of it. You are educated?"

"NYU. Cognitive anthropology. Wanted a PhD. Looked at academe. Stopped wanting the PhD. Picked this equally attractive alternative. Are you going to tell me I should have gone to law school too? Because I hope you don't. Lawyers give me hives, with the exception of Denny."

"I would not." Then he asked, "Do you find it necessary to agree philosophically with a person in order to befriend them?"

"Not at all. Not even a little bit."

"But my views matter to you. Why?"

"My older brother believes in past lives, and Jamie believes in space aliens, time travel, and, God help us all, telepathy. I don't care. I don't count on them the same way I count on you."

"And your ability to reason, it is one of the traits that I value in you."

"And yet here I am, alone in a male forensic pathologist's house, drinking alcohol. Periodically, we skirt the issue of love. So maybe I'm not the brightest bulb in the drawer."

"Eliza ... who is he?"

She looked at the yard, which had a large oak tree at the opposite end. The wind had picked up and the sky had darkened in anticipation of the storm, and she watched the branches sway. The leaves had flipped to show sage green.

Badri tensed.

"If you're counting on me to be the wiser one here," she said, "you misjudged me. I got a call from Jake Levy on the way here. Look at these guys here." She leaned over and handed him her phone.

The image was of two puppies, one a German shepherd mix and one a tricolor Danish-Swedish Farmdog. They were sitting beside each other, nearly touching. The shepherd mix was sitting sideways and had one ear up and one ear down, looking impossibly soft. The Danish-Swedish Farmdog, tiny in comparison, had a white blaze and soft brown eyes. There was also a video of them playing, the shepherd on his back and the small, solid-looking puppy pouncing on him. Another photo showed them sleeping in a little heap together.

"Jake says these two were dropped off at his office. Just ... dropped off. A couple was moving to a place that didn't allow dogs, didn't want the pound to put them under, and Jake was on TV."

"You wish to adopt these?" he said, putting her phone on the coffee table.

"I can't adopt dogs. Some days, I don't even go home. But you, on the other hand, have a yard and a normal workweek. That case ... seeing those images ... reading about the dogs. Well, here is an opportunity to take care of two dogs."

He looked at the photo of the dogs again, and his face softened. "Who could part with these two? One would have to adopt them together, as they are clearly bonded. But if I express an interest, Jake will know that we have spoken."

"And? He doesn't have to know we're having a sordid tryst involving us drinking beer and discussing impossible things."

At the word "tryst," Badri flushed. Then he sent a text, which Eliza surmised was to Dr. Levy.

"When you bring them home, I want to meet them. Assuming I'm not being a terrible guest right now. You've asked me a question three times, and I've refused to answer it three times. And instead of being candid with me, you're playing a guessing game, asking a question that, because of the way I'm constructed, I can't answer."

He got up and sat facing her, his arm behind her on the back of the couch. "Then I will speak plainly. If we referred to those not present, we would have said so. I also would not have invited you here despite the innocence of my motives, and you likewise would not have accepted my invitation despite the innocence of yours. I hope never again to see you as distraught as you were the day that you arrested that *thing*, and I find your presence comforting. Would you prefer that I return to my seat?"

Eliza's heart stuttered. "No."

He kissed her.

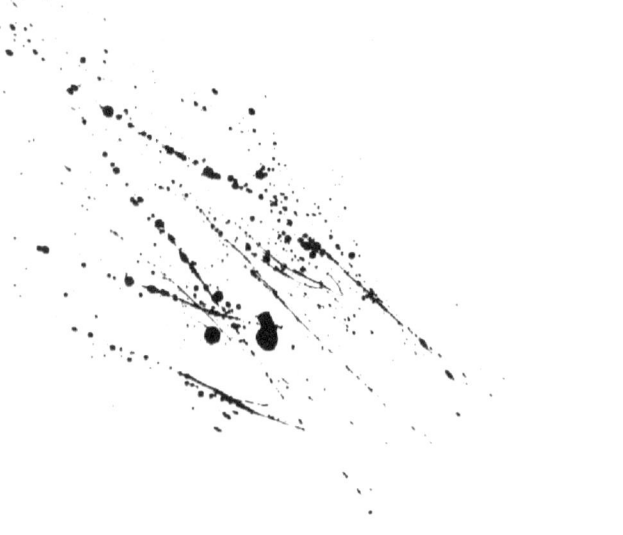

CHAPTER
NINE

BADRI HELD her in his arms afterward, which to Eliza felt glorious.

After several minutes, he began to seem as if he was about to speak, then brought himself short. Finally, he rolled on his side to face her. "I think you should remain here while you are on leave."

"I could do that ... but why?"

"If we are as compatible as I predict, we must determine how to address our situation professionally. If we are not, the issue is moot."

"You didn't sleep with me because you needed someone, did you?"

He pulled her to him and held her tight. "No. My feelings for you were a source of difficulty shortly after I met you. And while your looks caught my attention, these would not be sufficient in themselves."

"Same ... and same. Pathetically, I haven't been able to look at anyone else since then."

"Neither have I. And as soon as I was notified of Dyson's

death, I informed Richmond that I would be taking two weeks' leave."

"It will give us a taste of having to keep a secret like this one. We can't even go out with friends or meet our families. People just can't help but talk, even if they intend to keep a secret. Even a slip of the tongue in a hallway or someone talking about us where they could be overheard. A cell phone conversation in a grocery store could wreck us. We'll need burner phones in case we ever have to turn our personal phones over for discovery. It happened in Tidewater."

"I concur. Are you out often?"

Eliza laughed silently. "I'm at The Lion often enough to be polite. I practice a form of Krav Maga. Jamie and Joe drag me out every now and then."

In alarm, Badri told her where he practiced the same self-defense system.

"You would have seen me already," she said.

"It would have been unnerving to have to spar with you on the ground."

"We have two docs from Cameron Medical and one from StarSight Trauma. You could start a drive-though."

Badri belly laughed. Then he said quietly, "Our situation is perilous, is it not?"

"I could so see myself working as a convenience store security guard. You, on the other hand, would do your penance with the Board of Medicine and then go off to work for an insurance company withholding lifesaving healthcare from babies."

He held her tight. "We will do nothing of the kind. Perhaps it is premature to discuss this—"

"But it's probably not going to stop you."

"It may be possible for me to find a position in the UAE."

"*What?* If you're rushing me into a commitment, that's a big red flag, and—"

"I merely suggest this as a future alternative. The longer we stay involved, the likelier our exposure."

WHEN THEY HAD GOTTEN the call, Jamie had walked into the bathroom and thrown up. They couldn't leave until he had brushed his teeth, swallowed mouthwash, thrown up again, and repeated the process. He looked pale, and he wouldn't tell Eliza what was wrong.

When they got to the curb of Chloe Jackman's town house, Jamie put the car in park and turned to Eliza. "You're gonna have to read ahead."

"I read that part. We need to get a list of names and—"

"Warn everyone? *Everyone?* There are sixteen colonists on that ship!"

"And we've already met four of them. The surviving three can consider themselves duly warned. And Chloe is dead now too. So that leaves eleven. I still think the PIO needs to give a press conference—"

"And say *what*, exactly?" Jamie said. "Say *what*? 'Five people involved in two murder cases have the same names as the people in a best-selling science fiction book. Lock your doors.'?"

"When you put it like that—"

"Eliza, we still have work to do on that case. Maybe Glenn poked the brother with a stick. Or knew about something else and threatened to dime him out again. Or threatened to dime out someone at work, and they're not talking. Maybe Cody—"

"Has no motive. They were all going to live with the grandparents. He's a bright guy with everything to lose. No arrests, no bar fights, no DUIs, no sign of his being an impulsive, violent man. So why now? The killer is *out there*, and there's the book in common!"

"Badri told us not to get tunnel vision. So let's not get tunnel vision."

The detectives got out and noticed a group of people, some of whom were crying.

"Where's the caller?" Jamie asked the patrol officer.

"Over there," she said. "Victim's door was ajar. She pushed it open and called out her name and—"

"Any chance—"

"Any chance ninety-nine-year-old Doris Mendel disemboweled Chloe Jackman? I'm thinking nah. Doris is in great shape, understand, but she still walks with a cane."

"Any next of kin?" Eliza asked.

"Girlfriend's on the way. Roscoe already assisted in the death notification."

Eliza nodded. Lt. Roscoe was one of the department's chaplains and a trained crisis counselor.

"The neighbors"—the officer pointed to the group gathered in a knot across the narrow lane—"call each other by name. I haven't talked to them, but it seems like she's well liked. Doris is over there."

Eliza saw a woman wearing her hair in a fashionable bun,

gray curls spilling out of it and framing her face. She was standing next to a middle-aged woman in a pink tank top. The woman had her arm around Doris. Eliza approached them. She could see that Doris was crying.

"I'm Detective Eliza Benveniste. Are you Doris?"

"Doris Mendel." She began sobbing. Through her tears, she said, "Chloe was my dear friend! She was like a grand-daughter to me! Please, please catch the *thing* who did that to Chloe, my dear Chloe!"

"I'm so, so sorry for your loss, Ms. Mendel. I know you've been through a terrible shock, but I won't catch the beast who did that to Chloe any faster if you collapse. Can I walk you back to your house?"

"It's right there." Doris pointed to the house across the street from Chloe's. "My house."

The woman in the tank top said, "I'm Haleigh. I've been trying to get Doris to go inside for half an hour."

"I wanted to talk to a detective in person," Doris said in a steady voice.

"I promise, I plan to talk to you later," Eliza said. "But you can't talk to me if you have heatstroke." Eliza studied Doris. She looked pale. "I'd like some paramedics to come take a look at you."

"I'm old, not dead."

"You've seen something horrific, and you knew her—"

"She and her girlfriend were my friends."

"At least have a medic take a look at you. Humor me."

"My granddaughter's on the way too. She thinks I can't grieve without dropping dead."

"An eighteen-year-old would need to be looked at after seeing what you did. Do you live alone?"

A smile flashed across her face. "No, but my husband is in Chicago moving his sister into a nursing home, and it's about time too."

"How old is your husband?"

"Leo is a hundred and one. Don't look at me like that; he doesn't look like the Crypt Keeper. He'll be back tomorrow."

Doris was slender and dressed fashionably in a long-sleeved, flowy lavender shirt of linen that hung below her waist; loose yellow linen trousers; and black ballet flats. Her cane was polished dark wood, and the handle fit in her hand as if it had been made just for her. "Chloe's door was ajar. It's never ajar! So I stood in the doorway and called for her. No one answered, but something smelled ... off. I went in and—" Doris buried her face in a handkerchief and started to cry.

Eliza put her arm around her shoulder. Haleigh had hers around Doris's other shoulder. Doris was surprisingly muscular, but suddenly, she was swaying, and the two women helped Doris to an open police car and sat her in the back seat, facing the open door.

"I think I might need that ambulance after all," Doris said.

Haleigh came back with a bottle of water and some tissues. Doris wiped her eyes and accepted the water.

"Do you know of anyone who would want to hurt her?" Eliza said, nodding to a patrol officer, who looked at Doris and said something into her radio.

"No!" Doris said, crying again. "Everyone loved her! When her girlfriend Rafaella gets home—"

"Rafaella DeMeo?"

"How do you—oh, of course you would know her. She's a public defender."

"Yes."

But Doris was staring into space. "At first, I thought she

had fallen. Then I saw—oh, God! It's—I thought I was in a horror movie! I thought maybe the killer was—" Doris was gripping her cane so hard that Eliza could see the bones in her hand. She started sobbing again. Through her tears, she said, "Poor Chloe! I pray she was already dead when—when he did those things to her! I feared the killer was in the house. I could have hit him with this, I could have helped Chloe! But Chloe was already—I didn't go farther than the living room."

Eliza reached into her pocket and handed Doris a card.

"What is this?"

"It's the number for Victim-Witness. They can provide counseling services. What you saw was shocking. I promise I'll speak to you as soon as I can."

Eliza saw with satisfaction that an ambulance had pulled up. She met Jamie at the entrance to the crime scene. The iron smell of blood assaulted her.

On the floor in front of them was a heavy, cobalt blue glass statue, some sort of abstract, indefinable thing. It had made a dent in the drywall to their left, just in front of the door.

"Where's the blood?" Eliza asked. "Woman's throat is slit. She's disemboweled. Someone should have been tracking blood all over the place. Where is it?"

Jamie shrugged.

Nothing. There was nothing. They entered the fenced-in backyard and found nothing. No blood. No bloody fingerprints. No discarded gloves. No footprints. No knife. No nothing. The bar was set across the sliding glass door. The security camera didn't shine blue when they walked past it.

"Battery's dead," Eliza said. "How did this animal get in here and get out without being covered in blood?"

"Who knows?" Jamie had broken out into a cold sweat.

"One of these days," she said, "you're going to tell me what the hell is going on."

When they walked back to the front door, a CSI shook her head. "Nothing. Not a single thing. You want us to spray a little luminol in the kitchen, right?"

Eliza laughed. "Spoken like a pro, Rhonda."

"Fifteen years. And I've seen everything. After Dyson, this one is almost a cakewalk."

"You made that case a little easier."

Rhonda squeezed her shoulder.

Eliza looked at the floor and said, "Even if the killer cleaned up, you'd think there'd be blood in the grooves between the flooring. Nothing on the walls in the hallway. That cream-colored carpeting should have showed splotches of bleach if not footprints of blood. Anything. Good God, even if he had a transporter beam, there'd be footprints where he stood. So what the hell?"

The living room was tidy except for two empty wineglasses on the coffee table. Eliza looked again. Beside the empty glasses was an open, empty jewelry box small enough to contain a ring.

"Trophy?" Jamie asked.

"Or they got engaged."

Opposite the couch were two large aquariums, one containing the usual complement of ocean fish. The other one most prominently contained a lobster.

Eliza decided that the lobster was so ugly that it was cute.

"That's a two-hundred-gallon aquarium, and the lobster et al. have a one-hundred-gallon aquarium," Jamie said. "The two of those things together weigh over a ton. Literally. The table it's resting on has to be concrete."

It was made of concrete, painted white like the walls.

In desperation, Eliza asked the CSIs to dust it for prints, to dust the whole house.

On the wall above the aquariums was the TV. Chloe could sit on the couch and either watch TV or the marine life if she weren't currently decaying in the kitchen.

The two detectives couldn't inspect the other rooms of the house without interfering with CSI combing for hairs and other trace evidence.

A dining room chair was tipped over.

The blood started just outside the kitchen. There was blood spattering the legs of the kitchen table. There was blood on the kitchen ceiling, the cabinets, the countertops, and even the refrigerator. And a pool of blood had flowed to the opposite wall.

Chloe Jackman lay on her back on her kitchen floor between the kitchen island and the gas stove. On the bottom of the kitchen island, nearly on the floor, was a bloody handprint. Chloe's hair tumbled about her face and lay in the blood that surrounded her. There was a dishrag stuffed in her mouth. Her throat had been slit nearly to the spine.

She had been stabbed and disemboweled. Her internal organs lay obscenely between her knees. Her arms lay at her side palms up, and each hand held one of her eyeballs.

"Oh, God ... Doris saw that ..." Eliza said. She stood beside Jamie and studied Chloe's left hand. It was almost entirely obscured by blood, but she saw it. "There's the engagement ring," she said to Jamie and pointed.

He didn't look. "In the book ... the humanoids they met in the reeds got her," he said. He was looking at the handprint. "They ate other humanoids. And each other. So Cody named them Donners, and it stuck."

"In the book," Eliza said, still looking at the engagement

ring, "Glenn Sommars is shot by his son. Here, Glenn Sommars is shot—and, for the cherry on top—*in exactly the same parts of his body* as the Glenn in the book. In the book, Chloe was disemboweled by Donners. Here, Chloe here has been disemboweled. *Where is the author?*"

"All that blood on the walls," Jamie said. "Was it from the aorta or from the carotid?"

"Are you listening?"

"I'm listening. He's somewhere not being a murderer!"

"Where's the blood being tracked out of this kitchen and out the door or down the hall?" Eliza demanded, but Jamie was still staring at the handprint. "Look at me, Jamie!" He looked at a point over her shoulder. "The killer should have been covered in blood! All over his face. In his hair, in his clothes, on his shoes, dripping off his shoelaces. He was leaning over her. Someone should have walked out of here looking like a red popsicle. But there's nothing!"

They would be there for nearly ten hours. Luminol would show that there was no blood on the floors, the rug, or the bathroom.

And Doris had nothing to add.

At Eliza's insistence, Jamie joined her while she debriefed everyone north of them on the police department food chain, as well as the public information officer, Commonwealth's Attorney Michael Schiff, and Deputy Commonwealth's Attorney Krista Denbow. Denny would oversee any search warrants and, from that point on, go to any crime scenes that appeared to be connected to the book.

Jamie, Eliza, and Denny were assigned the task of reading *Rebellion at Broken Oar*.

The media started speculating about the Broken Oar Killer.

No one could find David Dove.

On the way out of the conference room, Eliza had to quietly explain to Jamie that a prosecutor accompanies detectives to a crime scene to be better prepared for trial. Jamie dropped a mangled paper clip into the trash can.

DENNY AND ELIZA sat at Eliza's kitchen table, drinking and taking notes from the book.

"Goddamn homework assignment," Denny said. "I hate this science fiction shit."

"What do you read?"

"I'm reading *The Sizzling Scar*, and before that I read *Painted Walls*."

"What's *Painted Walls* about?"

"Kid was created as an IVF embryo and gestated in an artificial uterus. Lots of screaming about the implications."

"Oh," Eliza said. "Speculative fiction. So how is science fiction different?"

"I have a no-aliens policy," Denny said. "Too much complicated bullshit involved in that whole concept."

Eliza laughed. Then she said, "Denny, what do we do if victims one by one turn up in this book?"

"We already need you to crawl up David Dove's asshole and find his social and business contacts and his bank accounts and his mother's favorite ice cream flavor and find out how he knows all these people. We'll just need that even more."

"The author doesn't have a website or a social media presence," Eliza said. "I checked."

"Which leads me to extra think he's our scumbag. I'm not even sure how this book even took off."

"What do you mean?"

"No marketing. No book signings. No website. No blog. No nothing."

"You got me. Without that, he should've sold fifty copies, max, based on what I've seen online. Denny, we're trying to figure out how these people might know someone named David Dove. So far, there's nothing."

"The killer's always in the file," Denny said. "Isn't that what Sergeant Roth always says?"

"It's true. The killer's always in the file."

Eliza asked Denny about the subpoenas to various online booksellers.

"The court signed off on the interstate subpoenas. But the companies are stonewalling us. They're yelling that they promised their authors intellectual whatever-the-fuck on their platforms and that the specter of police oversight—I could quote you their motions to quash, but I figure there's enough in your day to make you throw up."

Eliza said, "We need that information. We have nothing other than his name and a brief biography saying he lives in New York. We have no DOB and no photo. Maybe we can attach crime scene photos of Glenn and Chloe with their photos in life as exhibits in response to their motions to quash."

"I was planning to," Denny said. "With a nice, pretty chart to show the one-to-one correspondences between the victims and the book characters. We've never had to litigate these issues with e-book platforms before, but an office in Kentucky did, and they said it's gonna take some time. It pegs my shit detector to red that there are two bodies, and the author doesn't even have his headshot in the back of the book. And that with all of these copies sold, a traditional publisher hasn't already bought it from him."

"Two bodies *now*," Eliza said.

Denny hesitated a moment. "How are you handling the Dyson case?"

"He was murdered last year."

"I didn't ask you when the case ended," Denny said gently. "I asked you how you're handling it. I've never seen anything like it."

Eliza hesitated. "After the second baby and the third dog, I started having nightmares. I don't have any reason to avoid the houses or the streets or the turnoffs, because they're off my beaten path. But," and she took a deep drink of wine, "it's bad. I could never have a dog because my schedule really doesn't permit it, but I'd really love to. I'd spoil the hell out of them."

"Them? You'd get more than one?"

"No, I'd get one. I meant *them* though, because I don't refer to animals as *it*."

"No?" Denny sounded intrigued.

"Why refer to an animal with the same pronoun as a thing?"

"Funny, you're the third person this week who's said that. And it's in *Painted Walls*."

"It's in *Sizzling Scar* when you get further into it. When they start talking about the pigs."

"We're off topic. Did you know that Judge Dempsey and Badri both took two weeks' leave? At different times, of course.

Audra Dempsey stepped off the bench after the bond hearing and called in sick the next day. Then she took two weeks off."

"I'm not surprised."

Denny shook her head. "When Dyson was murdered, she was free. It was her case. After he died, do you know that she transferred to the civil division?"

"I didn't know that. My sergeant ordered me and Jamie both to take leave. You didn't take time off though."

"You have a big family," Denny said. A flash of sadness passed across her face. "Why didn't you just grab one or more of them and take off for parts unknown for a while?"

"And who am I going to talk to in my family about what we saw and heard?"

Rebellion at Broken Oar
Chapter 5
Ursinus b: Spring Equinox 50–noon

"What do we do with him?" Gino asked, pointing to Glenn's body.

No one answered.

Cody was crying in Maura's arms, and Kelly walked over, and then the three of them huddled together, crying.

Baines studied Cody's cool blue eyes, with their indigo specks. She saw no triumph there.

Banner walked up to the small family and put his hand on Maura's back.

Suddenly, numerous creatures crawled up onto Glenn's body as if the other Humans were not there. The creatures were the size of a cat's head, shaped like roly-polies, transparent, and eight-legged. They arrayed themselves across Glenn's body, their guts pulsing as they ate.

"Hey! What's that?" Banner yelled, looking up and covering his head.

Baines and the others looked up.

Above them, flying shapes with six-foot wingspans. When they landed, everyone stepped back. They were bats, from what Baines could tell—about the size of a house cat, orange pink like the soil, with a strange double coat. Their eyes also dilated open and closed.

Baines saw that some of the Banner's geckos' indigo prey settled on Glenn's eyeballs and dug their proboscises in.

"And here come the Banner's geckos," Cody said.

The geckos started tugging at Glenn's body and darting away from the bats. One of the bats grabbed a gecko by what turned out to be tail, which dropped off. The gecko scurried away. The bats ignored the isopods and the indigo arachnids.

"It probably gets cold suddenly," Cody said, very pale. "The bats' fur is raised right now, and you can see the lower coat. But I'll bet it closes tightly when it gets cold. They aren't molting, I think." He looked again. "That's weird. The bats have eight legs too, if you count the wings." Then he walked away from the group and vomited.

The rest of the group watched the scavengers in horror, including Maura.

The dead humanoid's body was covered in the same scavengers Glenn's was.

"Let's go," Gino said, "before I lose my shit.

Captain, with respect, Sommars over here just murdered his father. Then he gave us a documentary presentation. I'm hoping we're all going to talk about this later."

Baines turned to Gino. "Any of us have a clear line of fire on those things? Glenn made sure we didn't."

"But we can't take the law into our own hands!" Gino said.

"Oh?" Baines said. "We have no cops and no courts. This was a one-way trip. The *Peregrine* and the *Archer* might never show up. Glenn tried to murder his wife right in front of all of us and then killed Chloe—by on purpose—when he stood in the way. Then he said he never did, even though we all saw it with our own eyes. You want that time bomb sitting in the colony? Because I don't."

"And how can you trust him then?" He gestured at Cody. "You can't murder people for being assholes."

"I shot him," Cody said quietly, "because he murdered Chloe after trying to murder my mother. And we all know he'd try to kill my mother again and maybe one or two of the rest of us in the process. This after beating the shit out of Maura for six months while none of you noticed."

Maura put her backpack on the ground. Then she turned around and unzipped her jumpsuit. A bruise the size of a man's fist covered her shoulder blade. She replaced it and turned back around. She slipped her backpack on and stared at Gino. "Any questions?"

"Is that why you refused your physical?" Banner asked gently. "Why didn't you tell anyone?"

"How do you think that would have worked out? My grandmother looked at my bruises and explained to me they were an accident. Then called Glenn. I was out of school for a week."

"Let's go find Chloe," Baines said, putting her hand on Maura's shoulder. The discussion was over.

This time, the group had their lasepistols drawn, but the humanoids had gone.

They walked for about five minutes and approached a small clearing.

Gino stepped into it and yelled, *"Jesus Christ! Oh, Jesus Christ!"*

They had found what was obviously Chloe's body. Her abdominal cavity had been ripped open, and her internal organs were gone, as were her eyes. Blood coated the reeds and had soaked into the ground.

The group counted thirty sets of footprints.

✸

"Oh, my God," Denny said.

"You don't know the half of it," Eliza said, absently running her hand along the scar on her arm. "Our Cody has dark blue eyes with indigo specks. Our Kelly's eyes are so pale blue they're almost white. Our Maura has steel-blue eyes and shiny yellow hair! And she had a bruise in exactly the same spot! You could take photocopies of the book and add them as exhibits!"

"We will," Denny said. "Eliza, this is—"

"I feel sick."

"So do I," Denny said. "I just hope neither of us turn out to be in this fucking book."

"How would we?"

"Oh, after he learns what we're trying to do, he might just write a sequel."

CHAPTER
TWELVE

"DO WE HAVE ANYTHING?" Jamie asked the officers in the briefing. "Anything at all?"

"Everyone liked her. No one saw a thing."

"The neighbors blamed themselves for not seeing or hearing anything. Doris Mendel had a heart attack. She's going to be okay, but only because she went to the ER for a 'checkup.'"

Everyone heard the air quotes.

"Roscoe and I gave the death notification to Rafaella DeMeo. Rafaella suggested I go to Chloe's office personally. I did, with Roscoe. People were wailing."

"They said she didn't have any problems with anyone. They were wrecked. *Wrecked.*"

"Why are you keeping this case, with a PD as a victim?" an officer asked. "Or are you okay with a conflict of interest?"

"I told Roth we should hand the whole case over to the State Police," Jamie said, "but Rafaella's about to take the bench. Civil division. No more conflict."

"Or they could give the case to court-appointed counsel," another officer said without looking at Jamie.

He looked at a photo of Chloe. She had a long, slender neck and a cap of wild brown curls. Her head was tilted to one side, and she had a wide grin. She was leaning against a smiling Rafaella DeMeo.

CHAPTER
THIRTEEN

ELIZA SAT with Jamie at his computer, looking at the geolocation and phone results for the Sommars-Chatworth family.

"Nothing. No-goddamn-thing," Jamie said. "Corroborates everything the family said."

"Unless the kids left their phones at Grandma's," Eliza said. "Did Cody make any calls from the grandparents' house?"

"Called a pizza place, then hung up in fifteen seconds," Jamie said. "But that could have been anyone at the grandparents' house."

"And they had shitty overcooked steak, remember?"

"Maybe he decided not to insult Grandpa right away."

The two detectives scrolled through the text traffic.

Then Eliza stopped. "Can I say what a piece of work that grandmother is?"

"Explains how Kelly ended up with Glenn. Then it all went to hell when Cody came. Grandma gets a crush on her daughter's husband and beats her up by proxy for the next twenty years."

The two detectives saw that Maura's text traffic was limited to perfunctory texts to her mother and that all Kelly used hers for was to notify Glenn on an ongoing basis of her whereabouts.

"All their relationships off-grid," Eliza said softly.

"Glenn's search history has nothing but recipes for protein shakes and weight routines."

"Of course it does," Eliza said. "Denny's arguing a motion to quash the subpoena of his work emails. Old emails to Grandma about Kelly's 'episodes' and nothing else."

"Guy was a cipher, an absolute cipher."

"Annnd ... none of them have social media."

"Dammit. And we need to investigate the brother. What if he called Maura on a burner phone?"

"From federal prison?"

"A lot of things get smuggled into federal prison. Or it could be someone who knew the brother. What about the dissertation supervisor?"

"Nada. Kelly's well-liked by her students. Brilliant work. Sense of humor. That kinda thing." Eliza turned back to her desk and started looking at the list of Glenn's neighbors and colleagues and everyone in Chloe's life to see if there was a connection—to each other or to David Dove.

Rafaella sat in Eliza's interview room. She had insisted. "I want to see what my clients see."

Eliza sat across the table from her and handed her a mug of black coffee.

Rafaella stared at it for a moment.

"Doris told me that you liked your coffee black," Eliza said. "Like a sociopath."

Rafaella laughed, but it was nearly a sob. "Does that explain you?"

Eliza laughed too.

Rafaella's hair was fastened into a bun with two sticks. She was dressed in black, and there were dark circles under her black eyes. She was still wearing her engagement ring, a delicate, narrow band of gold, nearly a filament.

She picked up the mug in a delicate hand, saying, "To Doris," and drank. Then she said, "I need to see the crime scene photos. I know that Badri won't let me see the autopsy."

"Badri finished the autopsy. Why would you want to see either of those things?"

"Because I need to know. What I'm imagining right now is a lot worse than—"

"No," Eliza said. "It's not. Not at all."

"I need to. Maybe I'll stop driving toward her house on autopilot."

"You won't though," she said softly. "You always will. Or you'll reach for your phone. Or you'll see her in a crowd."

"You lost someone?"

"My baby brother David. He was fifteen. On his way to summer camp. I dropped him off. I watched him start to cross the street to wait with the youth group in front of the synagogue for the bus." Eliza stared at nothing, speaking softly. "Little side street. He was carrying a large duffel bag. In the middle of the crosswalk, he suddenly ... crumpled. But he fell face-first. He didn't even try to break his fall. Then he didn't get up. I got out of the car and ran to him. I thought, 'Okay, he's had a concussion.' But when I rolled him over, he had no pulse, he wasn't breathing. I started chest compressions while screaming to call 911. A couple of his friends came to block traffic. He ... it was an AVM. A knot of arteries and veins. In his brain stem. It burst. He probably died on his feet. We never knew it was there. Where it was, it couldn't even have been removed." She took a breath. "I was home from NYU. I was a freshman. David and I were close. I tell you this to help you understand that looking at those photos will not help you. I *still* reach for the phone to call him, and it's been fifteen years."

"You were there, though," Rafaella said, looking crazed with grief. "I took a 1:30 suppression hearing for Bell, allegedly because a temporary crown popped off. I was on my way out the door, and Bell was standing in the hallway, blocking it, holding the file. I didn't get out until after 5:00. Otherwise, I would have been done with court before lunch, and I was going home to do some paperwork, then over to see—" Sobbing, Rafaella covered her face with her hands and started rocking back and forth. "Bell didn't have a temporary crown."

Eliza waited. Then she said, "Of course he didn't. Bell's a lazy piece of shit. Everyone knows that. And I'm so sorry. I'm so, so sorry. But I've been doing this long enough that I can tell you with certainty—Rafaella, if you had been there, you'd have been victim number two. You couldn't have saved her."

Rafaella froze. Then she whispered, "I guess I hadn't thought of that."

"How could you have? But rest assured, none of this was your fault, and Chloe wouldn't have wanted you to be hurt."

Rafaella grabbed Eliza's hand so tightly it hurt. She quickly let go. "Thanks," she said. "I should have known that too."

"It's different when you're the victim. You've had a terrible shock."

"It just slays me that Chloe wanted soundproof construction in that town house. Maybe someone would have heard—someone would have heard her!"

"The killer would have just taken her somewhere else. The

what-ifs will keep you up at night, but in my judgment, nothing could have prevented this other than ESP."

"Keep reminding me of that."

"Where are Chloe's parents?"

"She won't talk about her family. I get the feeling her parents died young."

"Why do you think that?"

"They were like ... a blank spot in her life. She always changed the subject or looked at me like she didn't understand the concept."

Eliza felt a brief chill, like she was missing something. But the feeling passed. She made a mental note of her response, then asked, "How long had you been seeing each other?"

"Six months."

"You got engaged in six months?"

"And? Some people just know. We just knew."

"Some people just know. Where was she born?"

"I don't know. Chloe was a very private person. I know nothing about her past or her family." At Eliza's look, she said defensively, "I didn't need to. I guess that sounds weird given what I do, but my instincts are good."

"Did she act like she was hiding from someone? Or something?"

"No. As a matter of fact, I had to talk her into locking the door. And she was always walking that trail back there with her headphones on no matter how much I yelled at her."

"Was there anyone giving Chloe any trouble?"

"No," Rafaella said immediately. "And she would have told me. There wasn't even a pervert neighbor."

"No. There wasn't. You've got a close neighborhood."

"*Had*. I'm not moving in. I can't stand it!"

"I can understand that. Did she argue with anyone at all?"

"You mean did she argue with me. No. We had the normal spats occasionally. You know, please don't commit to our going out without asking. Why do you wait to get the oil changed on the car until I tell you? *When* were you going to take time off?'"

Eliza smiled slightly. "You had to remind her to change the oil."

"How do you know?"

"Because you never forget to do *anything*."

Rafaella laughed. "True that. But neither do you, dammit. That partner of yours, on the other hand ... why isn't he in the Auto Squad? Sorry, you guys present a united front on the outside, but all he ever did in Dyson was check for forced entry and debrief the officers who did the canvassing. Am I wrong about that?"

Eliza was silent. Then she said, "How did you handle that case? Did you watch the videos?"

"Started to watch one. Closed up the file. Thanks for the trigger warning. At first, I thought I could handle it. Then I knew why you put it there. I figured that I had plenty of time for that. But you did, and so did Badri."

Eliza took a deep breath, then let it out slowly. "Yeah."

"I read your reports—and Badri's. I get it. You two connected the dots. With that deadweight of a partner, what else could you do? Why didn't you ask to pair up with Cutter?"

"Anyone ever ask you to switch co-counsel?"

"We don't put anyone in Major Crimes who's deadweight. Bell's suppression motion was on a burglary, the lazy fuck. But *you* didn't want to rat out your partner, so you found an alternate one, in a manner of speaking. It was actually good for *us*. Word is, Badri made a finding of suicide in a dude who shot himself three times in the head a few years back. That was unexpected, but word also is, Jamie had a tantrum, and you came back with some studies and handed them to Roth."

"How do you know?"

"A little bird told me about the tantrum. Roth was decent enough to hand me the studies. Badri told me you asked for them."

"Yes. I'm relieved he figured it out." *Sergeant Roth?*

Rafaella smiled briefly. Then she said, "May I ask you a question? I don't mean to overstep."

Keeping a poker face, Eliza said, "Sure."

"Are you and Cloud together?"

"What on Earth gave you that idea? Is that why you think I didn't ask to switch?"

"He implied that you were."

"What. The. Hell. Did he *say*?"

"He said that you hogged the bed—not with that look you didn't."

Eliza was shaking with fury. "That piece of—"

"I'll be glad to confront him with you."

"I'll be confronting him on my own. He'll tell me he was joking, but he'll also get the point." She quickly changed the subject. "Was there anything missing in the house?"

"No ... nothing. You'd think the killer would have taken a trophy or something ... but no." Rafaella put her hands over her face and started crying again. "Oh God, oh God, oh God ..."

Eliza slid the box of tissues across the table.

After Rafaella calmed down, Eliza said, "Everyone at her job loved her. By report, people were wailing. Are you sure there was no one acting strangely? No one followed her home? No one intrusive at a coffee shop? Anything?"

"No. She'd have said something."

After a moment, Eliza said, "Is there anyone who'd want to hurt *you*?"

Rafaella barked out a laugh. "I'm the deputy public defender. Let me count the ways!" She sat back in her chair and thought a moment. "There was a time that I could tell you who in particular was a threat, but the only one I really worried about was murdered in prison last year. But ask me that question again after I start ruling on civil cases. You knew I was taking the bench, right?"

"Yes," Eliza said. "It's why Denny's not filing a motion to give it to court-appointed counsel."

After another hour with Rafaella, Eliza learned nothing new.

Jamie walked up to Eliza's desk and sat on the edge. "David Dove's in Costa Rica. He was in Costa Rica at the time of the murders."

Eliza looked up at him. He was staring off into space.

Finally, she said, "Maybe he and Glenn ended up in the same gate at the same airport. Maybe he overheard Glenn and thought, 'There are four names.' But what novelist writes characters that are clearly actual people? It's a phenomenal way to get sued! And do we honestly think Glenn gave complete physical descriptions of them all? And how does that explain Chloe?"

"David Dove didn't murder anybody!"

Everyone in the room looked at Jamie. "Hey, buddy, take it easy!" someone said.

Jamie moved to his chair and said to Eliza, "Why is everyone focused on the author? Either Cody or Gary murdered Glenn—or had him murdered—and we'll find another disemboweled woman, or maybe some killer has a perverse sense of humor! The *Broken Oar* book isn't David Dove's first book. His first one is called *The Shadows*. It isn't bad, and it's getting some traction, but"—Jamie gripped his pen so hard it snapped—"*The Shadows* has a scene in a small town."

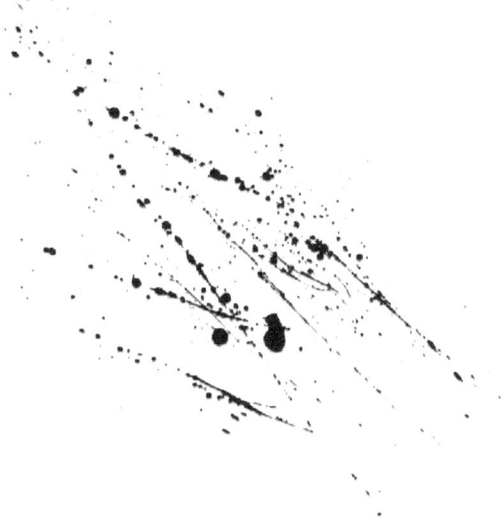

CHAPTER
FOURTEEN

ELIZA HAD INSISTED that Jamie come to her house for wings and beer. She hoped that he might tell her more after he'd had a few. While she waited for him, she read.

Rebellion at Broken Oar
Chapter 6
Ursinus b: Spring Equinox 50–1:00 p.m.

Polichek and Kinkead were still in Engineering. Dr. Bynum was trying to convince Maura to have a medical exam. Instead, Maura walked out of the ship with Cody.

Baines and Gino were on the bridge. Polichek walked in, looking grim. "Captain, Gino, you need to come with me."

He led them down the long, sterile, white-painted corridor into Engineering. He palmed the bio-key and they stepped down into a large, round, metal-floored room.

Gino saw that everything was clearly labeled in big letters and remembered that this was to prevent crew errors under stress.

Polichek led them to the workstation opposite the entrance, their boots clanging on the metal floor.

A casing door was open to the guts of the navigation system. Polichek knelt.

"See these circuits?" Polichek said. "They're fried. Completely fried."

"How did that happen?" Gino said, squatting beside him. "There's no way for that to happen!"

"Captain," Polichek said, "this could not have happened spontaneously. There's no mechanism here for that. It would be like flying a kite and having the string burst into flames. Someone had to go out of their way to destroy these components."

"With what?" Baines demanded.

Polichek pointed to a lasepistol on the floor beneath the casing. "He didn't even try to hide it."

"How did no one see this?" Baines asked.

"I checked the video, Captain. Glenn was alone in the room. He sabotaged the ship with this lasepistol right before descent."

"Let's find out why," Baines said.

They found Cody standing by one of the ponds at the base of a wash a few meters from the ship. Maura was squatting beside him. She stood and turned to face them.

"Do you know," Baines asked, "why your father would want to disable the ship?"

Maura said, "Why did he try to kill our mother? Why did he stand in the way when you wanted to save

Chloe? How did you not see this in the psych evals? Mom tried to tell you about him when the mission started. She tried to warn Space Force. They didn't listen, and neither did you. In fact, they almost left *her* behind. What kind of background check did they do? Did they do one at all? We tried to tell you!"

"But why would he do this?" Polichek asked.

"You want us to speculate?" Cody said. "Do you think he consulted *us*? Do you think he raised it with Mom? That could be an idea. Do you want to ask her? She's in her quarters, grieving. Chloe was her friend. Or you can stop speculating about why that twisted fuck broke the ship and be glad he's out there feeding the wildlife. Can it be fixed?"

Momentarily startled by Cody's description, Polichek quickly recovered. "No. We have some extra components, but we didn't bring a whole second ship with us." Polichek was almost as tall as Baines, and he at this point had a five o'clock shadow that was rapidly turning into a six o'clock shadow. "The ship can do everything but take off and fly. We're working on beefing up our sensors so that we can try to detect life forms on the planet. We're also running a diagnostic scan on the whole ship."

"Captain, why don't we wake up the dogs?" Cody said. "They'll probably hear the Donners before they get here. And we really need them after what happened."

"Donners?" Baines asked.

"The cannibals," Cody said. "The ones who ate Chloe."

"You are fucking *dark*," Gino said.

"But he has a point," Baines said. "Polichek, let's wake them up, and pray Glenn didn't hurt them."

Polichek ran to the ship and practically leaped up the ramp. He loved dogs.

"More bad news."

Shannon Rodgers walked up.

"I took some samples of those reeds you mentioned," she said. "They require a significant amount of water. I'm betting that if there are any lakes, they're through that forest."

"What about the reeds?" Cody asked.

"Them too."

"What about this way?" Gino asked. "Away from the, you know, monsters who can jump out at us from anywhere?"

"What do you see in that direction?" Shannon asked. "Nothing but what we're standing on right now. I'd like to send out some drones, Captain. Maybe even some minibots. This stuff"—she pointed to the foliage coiled on the ground—"grows into an impenetrable thicket over there. Ever hear of the gympie-gympie? They're in Australia and are also known as the suicide plant. *Dendrocnide moroides.* The stings from the plant hurt so bad that at least one soldier shot himself in the 1920s. We need to be wearing more than these jumpsuits if we're making close contact with plant life, sir."

"Glenn's sister lives there," Cody said, rolling his eyes. "I wonder if that's why we never heard from her."

"Right now, we need to start building the ecofarms," Baines said. "But we need to find a water source."

"Remind me why we can't just start planting?" Maura asked.

"Because," Shannon said, "we don't want the pollen from our crops to contaminate the ecosystem. Do you want to find a millet plant here and wonder if it came from us?"

"Is there any reason," Maura asked without looking at Shannon, "we can't just dig a well? If the dickweeds need a lot of water like you say, wouldn't there be groundwater? We're not going to build an aqueduct, are we? We'd have to go right through those reeds! I thought the whole point of this mission was to observe, not to do to a new planet what we did to ours."

"We're still going to have to find a source of water," Shannon said.

"Through the reed forest?" Maura asked. "We're going to make a *road* through the reed forest? We're not supposed to do that, remember?"

"Our ship sensors can't detect groundwater?" Baines demanded. "Let's check the sensors for groundwater."

"And these ponds," Cody said. "Can we get Yossi's take on whether they're permanent? It would help us to know how often it rains. There seems to be a complete ecosystem in this one. I guess it could spring up and then dry up, but it's hard to see how."

An eight-legged crustacean, approximately two centimeters long, swam up from the bottom, took a breath, and then swam back down.

As the group walked back to the ship, the siblings hung back. Behind her, Baines heard Maura ask, "How did Shannon not think to dig a well?"

CHAPTER
FIFTEEN

ELIZA WAS FILLING out paperwork and looked up to find Rafaella standing in front of her, shaking. "We need to talk," she said.

Eliza started to lead her into the conference room, but Rafaella said, "No. My clients would go to the interview room." She had the intense look of the accomplished trial lawyer, but Eliza refused to be intimidated. "You're not a suspect, Rafaella. You're a victim. Let me help."

In the conference room, Rafaella sat down, somehow looking small in the chair. She was still dressed in black, and her bun was held in place with two ballpoint pens. She looked, if possible, even more distraught than she had when Eliza first saw her.

"You didn't look in the car?" Rafaella demanded.

"Forensics did. Lots of photos."

"Well, when you guys unfroze the ... the crime scene, I finally went out to Chloe's car. I had to move it. And on the back seat, I found these." She opened up her briefcase and handed Eliza a stack of photos. "I printed them out for you."

"What am I looking at?"

"Chloe's car. The back seat. I went in the garage to move the car and found that shit in her car."

"Move the car?"

"The movers need to come in. I can't do this. I'm in her will. I'm the *only* one in her will. I thought about keeping the town house, but I can't bear to be there another second. I have to find a place in my home for Lancelot the Lobster and the other fish tank. I think I know enough to take care of them. But moving them's also going to take some logistics. And her car was in the way. The car had to be moved. And that's when I found *this* garbage."

Eliza gave a small nod. *I rambled like this when David died. I even saw myself doing it.*

And then Eliza saw it. A black jumpsuit and tactical boots. "Are ... are those *hers*?"

"No. They aren't. There's a CamelBak too, but it's empty. None of that belongs to her. What's it doing in her car?"

"Rafaella, the garage was closed and locked. We looked at the security footage, and between the time she got out of the car in the garage on Monday at 3:53 p.m. and the time we got there, no one went near the car. And after we left, we froze the scene. Did you look at the footage from after that?"

"Yes. The only other person who went near the car after you all left was me. The other cameras were down. The ones on the outside ran on rechargeable batteries, and Chloe must've never recharged them. I was too stupid to ask her. She forgot things. Now this means her killer might go on to kill again. The one in the garage was plugged in. That's great, right? Or else there'd be all kinds of speculation. The jumpsuit was rolled up on the seat. The CamelBak was on the floor next to the boots, just like in the pictures here."

"I don't know what to say. We'll collect the security

footage. We're also examining the footage from the neighbors' security cameras." *But so far there's nothing.*

Rafaella started sobbing, and Eliza put her arm around her. Then she held her, rocking.

Finally, Rafaella gathered herself. "Eliza, there would be no reason for her to have this. This getup is too close to the book, and I want to know who thought this was funny. I didn't touch anything. I saw it, and I left it."

Eliza nodded. "Not tainting the crime scene." She smiled sadly.

Rafaella handed her the key and the garage door opener. "I'll come back for them later."

After Rafaella left, Eliza took the photographs and went to find Jamie.

Eliza went to Jamie's desk and sat across from him. "This is well and truly fucked up," she said. She handed the photographs to Jamie, who sat back, shaken. "Do you know what this is?"

"It ... it looks like a jumpsuit from the *Broken Oar* book, based on the descriptions," he said. "And the boots too. Where did they come from?"

"Rafaella said that the jumpsuit was rolled up on the back seat of Chloe's car, and she found the boots and CamelBak on the floor between the front and back seats."

"We didn't miss anything! Is she claiming we missed something?"

"No."

"Then who put them there?" Jamie turned and logged on to the case server, where he found the photographs of the car.

"Here are all the pictures. There's nothing there. See? Right there. The floorboards and seats are clear. We need to get the footage from the garage cam from the past few days. And there'd better not be a break in the time stamps."

"Fair."

"And they didn't *really* come from a fictitious ship around a fictitious planet around a fictitious star in a fictitious universe! That's an insane idea! What did she do with them?"

"She left them in the car."

On the way to Chloe's house, Eliza said, "Rafaella told me that you said I hogged the bed."

Jamie's only response was to grip the steering wheel more tightly.

"Why would you tell her that? Why would you tell anyone that?"

"She was talking about how you and Badri spent so much time together. I was saving your ass."

"No, she wasn't."

"She—"

"She mentioned the reports, right?"

He went silent again.

"Right? She asked you where yours were? And you had to tell her she had all of them?"

He flipped the turn signal a little too hard.

"I'm right, aren't I?"

"You don't understand how it looks."

"What, that you generate a fraction of the reports in any given case? I agree. That looks like shit. The fact that Badri and I finally put together who the killer was while you did the bare minimum? I didn't bring that up to anyone. If you spent more time on things like, oh, I dunno, trying to find David Dove, that would be a hell of a lot better than accusing me of sleeping with Badri. Point taken?"

"Point taken."

When the duo entered the garage and inspected the car, they found the jumpsuit, the CamelBak, and boots right where Rafaella told them they were.

"Call CSI," she said. "They need to look for trace evidence before we package it."

"They're ... they're new," Jamie said, looking relieved.

As Jamie opened the trunk of their unmarked police car, she said, "Yes, but the person who put them there might have left trace evidence. And I don't know why you're happy they're new. It would be better if they weren't. We'd have a better chance of finding out whether any trace evidence on the clothes matches the trace evidence on the bedclothes in the Sommars house. We'll still try, but the odds aren't great. At least these were unwrapped."

Jamie said, "It's better that they're new." He leaned against the driver's side door and stared at the ground.

Eliza slammed the trunk closed, and it gave a satisfying *thunk*. She faced Jamie so that he was backed up against the driver's side door. "What on God's flying motorcycle is wrong with you? Did you think the boots would have Ursinus b dirt on them? Maybe a Banner's gecko in a jumpsuit pocket? Because that's crazy! At this point, we need to have David Dove in our interview room ASAP. I don't care whether he says he was in Costa Rica, he's—"

"*David Dove didn't kill anyone!*" A vein stood out on Jamie's forehead.

"How do you know him, Jamie? Is he a friend? I think I know everyone you know. Why are you protecting him?"

"I'm not protecting anyone!"

"Then why hasn't he been interviewed by *us*? Why won't you give me his phone number? Why have you lost your shit time and time again throughout this whole case?"

"I ... I wish I could tell you."

"What do you mean? Is he blackmailing you? You, Jamie? What'd you do? Take a label off a mattress?"

Eliza's phone vibrated. When she saw who it was, she answered. "Go ahead, Sarge. I'm here at the Jackman scene with Jamie, and you're on speakerphone."

"Another one," Sergeant Roth said.

"Another what?" Jamie asked.

"Are you awake?" Sergeant Roth demanded. "Another *body*!"

Jamie sat down on the ground next to the wheel well of the car and asked, "Who?"

"Jennifer Simms," Sergeant Roth said. "Name ring a bell? The chief called me screaming about some science fiction book. The *chief* called!"

From the ground, Jamie asked, "Is there a corrosive involved?"

"Someone took a large volume of concentrated acid and dumped it on her head, yes. It's not ours. It's in a garage in Seattle."

Jamie stood up. "She a farmer?"

"Runs a stable. How did you know?"

"The book, Sarge."

"The book? The book is a murder list? Cloud, figure this the fuck out."

"She's a stocky redhead, right?" Jamie said, leaning on the car. "Covered with freckles? Close-cropped hair? Blue eyes?"

"Where've you been for the past twelve hours?"

"This is Eliza. He had dinner at my place last night. It's obviously a character in the book. I haven't gotten that far into it. Do we have photos and the reports?"

"Yeah. Seattle transmitted them. Obviously, we have to treat it as a serial killer. God knows the public already is. Where's the author? Anyone track him down?"

Eliza looked hard at Jamie for a few beats and then said, "We're working on that."

"Well, work on it harder!"

They rode back to the department in silence.

CHAPTER
SIXTEEN

BACK AT THE OFFICE, the two detectives looked at the crime scene photos they'd received from Seattle.

Jennifer Simms lay on her back in her garage. She had been nearly skeletonized from the waist up. One hand clutched a crowbar.

"In the book," Jamie said, "one of the animals that Maura called a 'dickweed.' Jennifer Simms approached one to study it. Cody warned her, but she wouldn't stop. The thing sprayed something, and it went every-the-fuck-where. It basically melted her from the waist up. Weirdly, it didn't do anything to the dogs later, even though one peed on one. Probably a defense mechanism against the Donners. Cody called them *Macrodactylus fatalis*, but *dickweed* stuck."

"Tell me again," Eliza asked, "why we don't think David Dove came up with a really creative publicity stunt."

"He didn't."

"How do you know?"

"It wasn't David Dove!"

"Do you know him?"

Jamie got up and walked out.

Eliza sat at her desk, feeling sick. She toyed with going to Sergeant Roth and discussing David Dove and decided that throwing Jamie under the bus would backfire. She started to run David Dove through the national driver license database, grateful that it had been centralized ten years prior, praying he'd gotten a speeding ticket and there would be a name and address, or at least a date of birth. As she looked at the list in despair, she said, "So many David Doves, so little time."

NCIC—the National Crime Information Center—had proven fruitless. She was scheduled to speak with Badri about what she had found, and she got up and left.

Jamie was mangling a paper clip and staring at the photographs of the floor of Chloe's car when a shadow fell across his desk.

Denny pulled up Eliza's chair and sat down across from Jamie. "Your report has three lines where you spoke to the author. Give the author's phone number to Eliza, or I'll go to Roth."

"You're the boss." Jamie grabbed another paper clip.

Denny sat back. "You look like shit, Jamie. I have never seen you with dark circles under your eyes like this and playing with a paper clip while looking at the same screen. I was standing there for five minutes while you haven't done anything but look at photos of the floor of Chloe Jackman's car."

"Tell me," Jamie said, "how six months ago, an author had a premonition about a bruise."

CHAPTER
SEVENTEEN

AT ELIZA'S SUGGESTION, Badri had agreed that they would only discuss the details of ongoing cases at work just as they would have if they hadn't been having an affair.

"But why?" Badri had asked.

"Because what could happen is that you could inadvertently repeat a detail that you could only know about because you talked about it with me, but you would have had to see me when one or both of us wasn't working."

Badri had said, "You often encounter individuals who deceive others. It is unnerving to become one of them."

By this point, Eliza was going home primarily to get her mail. And Badri had adopted the dogs, whom he had named Skye and Luna.

Eliza needed to talk to Badri about the *Broken Oar* case, because she was at a loss.

As soon as Eliza settled into her seat, Badri said, "Your partner's accusations in the hallway, has he repeated these?"

"He told Rafaella that I hogged the bed."

Badri had a murderous expression that was gone as soon as

it had formed. "How did she respond when you corrected her?"

"About like what you'd think. She also said that it was a good thing that you and I conferred so much and brought up the Smallwood case. Our reports always have new substantive information because we only meet when we need to, so we're obviously working. She noticed this, clearly, because she did not suggest that we were doing anything improper. In fact, she brought you up in the context of her asking why I wasn't partnered up with Joe Cutter and saying that Jamie doesn't do shit on cases."

"And your partner?"

"He said he was saving my ass, and I lit into him."

"And?"

"He got the point. And if he decided that I was sleeping with you, he wouldn't say anything to anyone up the chain. But he might come here and confront you about it. If he does, go on the offensive. He's fundamentally a wimp."

"That is helpful." Then he said, "Has he ever made a declaration to you?"

"No. He has not. Why?"

"This could be another motive for his confrontation of you in the hallway, could it not?"

"Or he is protecting the author."

"As you walked toward the exit, he determined that voices carry in that corridor. If the circumstances were as they appeared to him, this would have been an effective means to keep you from me other than in a courthouse hallway."

"Yes. That would have worked. Because you would have noticed that I didn't deny anything explicitly, and you would have caught the lie if I had. I might as well have confessed to you directly. I wouldn't have set foot in your office ever again, and I may have even avoided you completely."

Badri's expression again flashed to murderous so briefly Eliza nearly missed it. "So what in this case has changed?"

"This book is full of these insane, dead-on coincidences. Jamie keeps denying they exist while acting like they do."

"Which coincidences?"

She took a sip of coffee and listed them all, which by this time went on and on, as she covered her scar with the other hand.

"So these statements in the media, these are not exaggerations. To the contrary, since you have followed the wise protocol of not sharing all the case details with the media, the facts are even worse. This is very odd. I do not even begin to have an explanation for this. Did anyone not inquire of Glenn Sommars's family whether they found these coincidences alarming?"

"I didn't know for certain about the connection to the book when I interviewed Kelly or Maura, but I reviewed the entire video of Jamie's interview of Cody. And after Jamie asked him about the one-to-one correspondences between his family and the characters in the book, Cody said, 'What's the saying? A million monkeys with a million laptops for a million years, one of them's gonna write Shakespeare? It's a coincidence. Weird, definitely, but a coincidence.' Also, Cody said he thought Jamie recognized him from somewhere, which makes me extra think Jamie is protecting the author."

Badri sat back for a moment, took a sip of tea, and thought. Then he said, "The son's suggestion is as reasonable an explanation for these correspondences as any. But only if the author is not involved. As we discussed last year, I do not believe in magic. And I am more firmly convinced that Detective Cloud is protecting the author in some way."

THREE YEARS AGO

Badri sat awkwardly at a bar called The Lion in a booth across from Eric Hill, who was the public defender. Next to Hill was Krista Denbow. Next to Badri was Sergeant Oren Roth. The commonwealth's attorney, Dennis Collins, was ascending to the bench, and this party was for him. Dennis sat at a table on the far end of the room and looked like he'd rather be anywhere else. Everyone in the criminal justice system was there.

The three at the table with Badri were on their second beers, and Badri was nursing his first Scotch. He was still wearing his customary white button-down shirt and trousers, but as a nod to the occasion, he had rolled up his sleeves.

Everyone in the bar was a cop, a defense attorney, or a prosecutor. And then there was Badri.

"So Gilmartin had the victim on the stand, and the victim was a great witness," Hill was saying. He turned to Badri and said, "Gilmartin's an ACA. This was a carjacking case. Someone hauled the victim out of her car in the parking lot outside Alley Steak House and beat the shit out of her, then took her car. My client had an alibi defense. He had a couple of witnesses in the hallway all ready to talk about their card game or some such shit. Who knows? Because Gilmartin finished direct by asking the victim, 'And do you see the man who robbed and beat you in the courtroom?' What happened next? Gilmartin didn't bat an eye. All she said was, 'Let the record reflect that the defendant is raising his hand.' Fuck me if he wasn't!"

Denny and Sergeant Roth burst out laughing.

"This is odd. Does this happen often?" Badri asked.

"Not often enough," Sergeant Roth said.

Hill laughed.

Badri's phone vibrated. It was a cousin in Sharjah. He excused himself and walked toward the front of the bar. He had meant to step out on the curb to take the call, then return and take his leave as soon as possible.

Then Badri saw Eliza on his way out. She was sitting at a table three meters from one of the exits, with Jamie Cloud and two women whom Badri could not place but who he guessed were detectives. Badri shifted his stance, debating whether to greet her.

A tall, stocky man with a salt-and-pepper crew cut and a five o'clock shadow walked over to Eliza's table. He was slightly unsteady on his feet. His gut pressed against his beige polo shirt. He looked at Jamie, looked at the three women, and took a chair from the next table. He turned it around and sat in it.

Badri noted that the man had bags under his eyes. He also had broken blood vessels on his face, and Badri hypothesized that he had alcoholism.

The man stroked the arm of one of the women, a fortysomething blond, and said, "Hey, baby!"

She jerked her arm away from him and said, "Fuck you, Boone."

In response, Boone laughed, got up, bent down between Eliza and the third woman, put his arms around them, and hugged them. He said, "Hey, ladies! Having fun?" Then, with his thumbs, he touched each woman on the side of her breast.

Badri started over to the table, but Eliza had already

grabbed Boone and got him into an arm bar, tipping over her chair in the process. Then she turned him around and shoved him away from the table.

Boone regained his balance and said, "Hey! Can't you take a joke?" He took a step toward Eliza.

From behind him, Jamie took Boone by the scruff of his neck and put him into another arm bar.

"Let go of me, pal!"

Jamie forced Boone past Badri toward the door, and as he passed him, Jamie looked at Badri out of the corner of his eye. The door led to a small service alley. Either direction led to the parking lot.

Eliza, shaking, followed Jamie. Badri followed Eliza, but she stopped in the doorway, turned around, put her hand gently on Badri's shoulder, and said, "Dr. Trivedi, you should probably turn around and go out a different exit." When the two made eye contact, Eliza flushed.

"I could kill him," Badri said quietly.

Eliza looked momentarily startled, then whispered, "I didn't hear that." Then she quickly squeezed his arm, went out, and stood in front of the door.

Over her shoulder, Badri saw Jamie shove Boone away from him, and when Boone rushed him, he punched Boone in the stomach and shoved him against a dumpster. Then he punched him in the face. Boone fell to his hands and knees, and Jamie said, "Now get the fuck out of here, you piece of shit!"

Badri stepped back, and two meters from the exit, he just stood there, at a loss for what to do. Speak to Eliza? Check on her welfare? Leave?

Eliza walked in and locked eyes with Badri once more, and his pulse spiked.

Jamie walked in behind Eliza. All of a sudden, Jamie put his hand on the back of Badri's neck and pulled him close. Then he said quietly, "Doc, she ditched a boyfriend to start this job. She's not going to fuck you and end it."

Then Jamie let him go roughly and followed Eliza back to the table.

Badri left the bar, shaken.

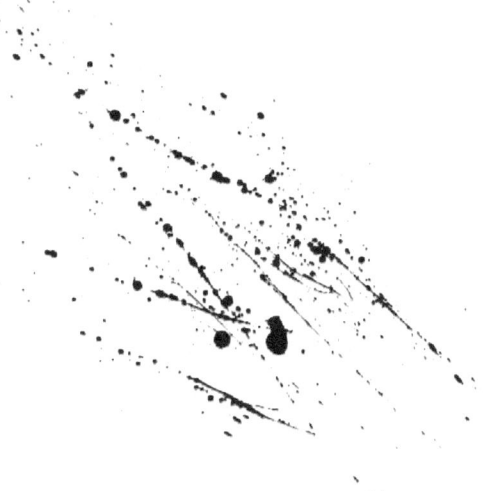

"JAMIE'S VERSION OF THINGS," Eliza said to Badri, "is that David Dove is in Costa Rica, as if that's the end of it. The addendum to his report says just about only that. 'Author in Costa Rica, location confirmed.' But confirmed how? Did he demand copies of airline tickets? Hotel receipts or leases? Did he try to get his credit card statements? He did not. Instead, he's almost perversely defensive about the idea that the author could be involved. And I can't find any more information about David Dove. In fact, Jamie didn't even list a phone number so that I could try to call him too. When I asked, Jamie yelled at me, even though we should be on a plane to Costa Rica right now.

"There are a number of subpoenas outstanding to various online publishers. Denny's going to have to litigate them. There's more: If Jamie knows David Dove, then knowing Jamie, I'd expect him to have told me how to find him so he could get out of the case. In fact, under any other circumstance, I could predict with certainty that he would, if nothing else because he's so lazy. Instead, he's passively written a three-line report with no phone number and is resisting the idea that the author was involved!"

"How did he respond to the notification of the second murder?"

"He looked so sick that when he ran into the bathroom, I followed him. He threw up, cleaned himself up, and then threw up again. He was shattered."

"And the third?"

"He slid down the car and sat next the wheel well."

Badri was silent. He poured himself more tea from a warmer behind him and said, "How long have you known him?"

"Five years."

"How well do you know him?"

"I thought I knew everything about him, but I guess not."

"Do you know the names of his friends?"

"I've met almost all of them. He's kind of, well, introverted in his private life, so none of them are particularly close. In fact, other than Joe Costa, who's a street cop, I'm it in terms of close friends. None of them named David Dove."

"This author, David Dove—how much do you know about him?"

"Just what Jamie tells me. Jamie says he has a phone number, but he won't give it to me. I'm this close to going to Sergeant Roth about it. It's a given that the killer is always in the file, and the evidence is pointing to David Dove."

"What of Detective Cloud's family?"

"I met them. His parents held a Christmas party, and I went." Then she sat back, pale. "Oh, no ... oh, no ... oh, no. Oh, my God."

"You know who this man is."

"David is my dead brother's name. Jamie's mother's last name is Tauber." Eliza's blood ran cold. "German for *dove*."

          ✳

Jamie flipped to the video of Kelly's interview and, with headphones on, watched it, taking notes on a legal pad that would soon be illegible even to him. Then he looked at Chloe's crime scene photographs. Then he looked at Jennifer Simms's photographs, the whole time mangling paper clips or taking notes.

With dread, he realized that Eliza had not been at her desk. "Trivedi," he said. He got up and walked out.

          ✳

Badri went completely still. Then he said, "You have not discussed this brother. Why not?"

"Because I didn't want you to see me as Tragic Woman with Dead Brother? I'd've brought it up eventually. Can we talk about the case now?"

"For *now*." He sighed. "Your hypothesis that your partner is David Dove is consistent with the evidence available. Yet this is not to say that he is a murderer. For example, Jennifer Simms was murdered in Seattle either while your partner was in Tauxenent County with you or within hours afterward. And you say that he appeared on time for his duty shift."

"Yes. He'd've needed a transporter beam."

Badri took a sip of tea, and Eliza waited.

"I speculate that his behavior is more consistent with someone who is witnessing murders committed by another and blames himself. When I told him that he was not responsible for the death of Glenn Sommars, his response was extreme." He poured tea into a cup and set it on his desk in front of Eliza.

She smiled briefly and took a sip, wishing it were coffee. Then she toyed with her pen. "Jamie would've had to form a relationship with someone in Glenn Sommars's family, enough to learn details about them that they were reluctant to share with outsiders but under the radar enough that none of the family recognized him. And Glenn Sommars isn't merely an abusive control freak; he also sabotages people. Those traits don't necessarily overlap. And even if Gary spilled the beans—"

"Who is Gary?"

"Gary is Glenn's brother. Glenn caused Gary to describe certain crimes over a speakerphone in the presence of law enforcement in an airport. Whether this was premeditated or not, only the IG's office or the State Police know right now. We were going to follow up with that. And Gary is in federal prison in Florida."

"Even if your partner somehow came into contact with this Gary individual in some way, this does not explain his knowledge of the other two. And if he had hired an individual, or individuals, to acquire enough data about persons so that he could render them as book characters, then murder them in the same way, only you can tell me whether his presentation would be consistent with one who is capable of doing these things. His response to these murders suggests that he is not."

Eliza took a sip of tea and sighed.

"You see?" Badri said. "Coffee does not have this effect."

Eliza smiled. Then she said, "I didn't know Jamie wrote books at all, and I thought I knew him well. He is irritatingly honest to the point of oversharing. And he still lives in a studio apartment and drives a three-year-old car. He doesn't have any new toys in his apartment, and he isn't flashing any jewelry. His spending, as far as I can tell, has not changed. He isn't motivated by money."

"I am not a psychiatrist, Eliza. I cannot determine whether your partner would take the time to construct an elaborate scheme to write a book and then carry out a series of murders. But the murders themselves appear to cause him great distress. Does he travel?"

"In five years, I cannot think of a single time that he's left the county, other than with me to interview witnesses. None of those places were even west of the Mississippi."

"It might have been possible for him to have employed a person, or persons, to carry out the murders," Badri said. "It is another matter entirely to have sought out information about various persons of different social circumstances and even locations. Does he take unnecessary risks in his personal life, such as with high-risk sports or like that?"

"He does not. He does the opposite of that."

"The undertaking we discuss here would be quite risky, even for one with a predisposition to kill. He would have had to cultivate certain relationships to the point of earning trust and to do so without your knowledge. These activities would be time-consuming. He would then need to find a skilled accomplice. Like almost all homicide detectives, he works a chaotic schedule. And you say he does not travel. It does not appear possible for him to do this."

"So are we saying that Jamie wrote fictional characters, and they turn out to correspond directly with six real people, three of them who died the same way as in the book?"

Badri poured himself more tea. "This would be consistent with his presentation and with the evidence. His unwillingness to discuss this is understandable under these circumstances."

"But how by God's flying tricycle does this even happen?"

Badri laughed. "I do not have an answer. As I said, I do not believe in magic. The explanation about the million monkeys is as good as any. But this does not appear to be a sufficient number of years—or monkeys."

"So that leaves us with the fact that a jumpsuit, a CamelBak, and a pair of tactical boots turn up in the car of a victim."

"What is the significance of this?"

Eliza told him.

"Well, this is odd. You did not fail to notice these items in the car when you first inspected it?"

"No. And Jamie and I even reviewed the photographs. Those items weren't in the car. Of course, we have to take a look at the security footage to ensure that Rafaella—or someone else—didn't return to the car to place them there, but Rafaella is emphatic that she did not."

"I think I am going to need more tea."

"I think I want something stronger than tea."

"Would he make an admission to you if you confront him?"

"I—I don't know."

He sat back. "I would like Detective Cloud to join us right now."

Eliza texted Jamie.

It took a long time for Jamie to reply.

Eliza's phone buzzed, and she picked it up. "Jamie! You're on speakerphone. Where are you?"

"Take it off speaker. Leave Trivedi out of this."

Eliza took it off speaker, looking at Badri. "You're off speaker."

"Meet me out front. I have something to tell you."

"You sound terrible. Come meet me in Badri's office."

"Eliza, I can't until we talk."

"If I come meet you, will you come back to talk about the case with us?"

"This an intervention?"

"No."

"Then sure, he can cross-examine us some more. Meet me out front."

She sighed. "Be right there, Jamie." After she ended the call, she said, "Badri, he wants me to meet him out front to talk. Then he's agreed to come back and speak with you. Do you have time?"

He checked the time on his phone. "Yes."

Eliza stepped out of Badri's office. Immediately, he heard her shout, "Hey! What the fuck?"

He stood up and ran to the door.

Eliza was gone.

She had not been buzzed out. She would not even have had time to get to the other end of the corridor.

DR. TRIVEDI WAS BEING INTERVIEWED ALONE in his office by Detective Joseph Cutter.

Sergeant Roth walked into Dr. Trivedi's conference room, where Jamie leaned back against the table, gripping the edges with both hands.

"We examined the video," Sergeant Roth said. "She walked out of Badri's office and just—the camera flickers, and then she's gone." He looked Jamie dead in the eye.

"Gone? How the fuck is she gone?" Jamie demanded. "Is this an interrogation? *Did she vanish the fuck into thin air?*"

"We're getting Forensics to look at the video more closely, but—"

Detective Cutter knocked on the door and said, "Sarge? I need a moment with you."

Sergeant Roth stepped out, closing the door behind him. After a few minutes, he shouted something and then strode into the room, slamming the door behind him. Jamie flinched.

Sergeant Roth crowded Jamie and said, "*You lied to me!* I asked you to find the author, and you *lied* to me! When were you going to tell me? *What are you hiding?*"

"*Nothing!*" Jamie said, his voice unnaturally high. "Except that my totally fictional *book characters* are turning up dead in Tauxenent County! They were from the twenty-third century and died on the other side of the galaxy, but the *very same people* were also murdered in Tauxenent County or Seattle less than a week ago! *I have no idea how any of this happened!* Do you think I teleported to Washington state to murder Jennifer Simms yesterday?" Then he collected himself and said, almost aggressively, "Do you want to pat me down now?"

Sergeant Roth backed up and looked at him in disgust.

With Cutter right behind him, Dr. Trivedi walked into the room looking sick. He was Jamie's age, and even though he was only five foot ten, he somehow looked taller.

"What have you done?" Dr. Trivedi said to Jamie. "Where is she?"

"What do you mean what have I done?"

"Do you need a dissertation?"

"I ... I wrote a story when I was in second grade about a dog with yellow eyes, slitted pupils, one lower fang, and an M on the forehead like a tabby cat. In my story, the dog could purr. Six months later, someone down the street rescued a puppy exactly like that in a sewer but couldn't keep her. People said, 'Give the freak dog to the loser kid,' and she ended up being mine. The story was written before she was even born. Kitty—the dog—lived to be twenty years old, like a cat. I wrote a bunch of stories after that. Never happened again. Coincidence, right? Did I write anything where Eliza disappears? I didn't write anything about Eliza! Are you out of your mind? I did not!"

"And do not," Dr. Trivedi said.

"But—"

Dr. Trivedi grabbed Jamie by the collar and jerked him to him. "Do not."

Dr. Trivedi let go of Jamie, who fell into the nearest chair like a sack of groceries. "You two," Dr. Trivedi said, "leave the room so that I might talk freely to Detective Cloud."

"No," Sergeant Roth said. "He's coming with me, and then he's headed to our interview room."

"Before you do these things, first I will speak with Detective Cloud. *Out!*"

No one there had ever heard Dr. Trivedi raise his voice before.

"This is an investigation, not a conference, Dr. Trivedi," Sergeant Roth said. "Stay out of this."

"And Eliza and I were able to deduce that Detective Cloud wrote the book when you could not. You knew the name of Eliza's deceased brother. You knew Detective Cloud's mother's name, Sergeant Roth. She is a circuit court judge."

"She transferred to the civil division when Detective Cloud joined the police department," Detective Cutter said. "That was before your time. How did you know?"

"I testified before Anita Tauber in a civil matter two years ago. She spoke to me of Detective Cloud while the jury was deliberating. It remained in my mind as an explanation for why an individual with such limited abilities as Detective Cloud managed to be promoted to Homicide."

Jamie turned red. "That's a hell of an accusation—"

"I wondered the same thing," Sergeant Roth said without looking at Jamie. "Eliza was a newbie, but she was good, so she worked around him. But—"

"I will reduce my findings to a report. I will summon a patrol officer to collect him when I have finished. And"— Dr. Trivedi looked Sergeant Roth in the eye—"this will permit you to confer with your superiors before arresting a fellow homicide detective. I said *out!*"

Sergeant Roth barked out a laugh. "You've got a point, Badri." Then he looked at Jamie as if he were a hair in his sandwich. "Don't move. That's an order."

Jamie stayed silent.

Sergeant Roth and Detective Cutter left.

Dr. Trivedi stood up and slammed the door shut. Jamie jumped.

He sat across from Jamie, who opened his mouth to speak.

"I am not a violent man," Dr. Trivedi said. "I have taken an oath to do no harm. You will answer me truthfully so that I may adhere to that oath. Did you write any other books where Eliza was a character?"

Jamie took a breath and hung his head. "Not a character, but—"

"Do not bother with technicalities. Tell me."

"I wrote a book about the Tauxenent Strangler. I can't publish it until I retire, but I wrote it." Jamie's green eyes were bright. "It's nonfiction. And in *Broken Oar*, Kelly reads that book."

Dr. Trivedi reached automatically for a cup of tea and was annoyed that he was not in his office. "It became immediately manifest when Glenn Sommars was murdered that your writing had this strange capacity to make real that which is not. Yet you concealed this. Now Eliza has disappeared. The evidence points to the fact that just as persons from this book world of yours can become part of this one, persons from this world can become part of that one. The facts are difficult to digest, but they are inescapable."

Jamie wiped his eyes with his handkerchief. "Tell me, Badri, if I went to anyone when Glenn ended up dead, handed them a copy of *Rebellion at Broken Oar*, and said, 'I wrote this, but I didn't murder them, it's just that omigod I have super-powers,' what do you think they would have then decided? I'd be on my way to a hospital on a seventy-two-hour hold! Then I'd be investigated for murder! And if they decided I was telling the truth, what can anyone do about it? Do you think I wanted any of this to happen? There was a dog in second grade! When Kitty came along, do you think that I then decided that I'd found some conduit between universes? You bet! So then I tried to write myself a velociraptor, but I couldn't even subsequently write myself a dinosaur set for Christmas. Do you think I'd have written so much violence if I knew that Kitty wasn't some coincidence?"

Dr. Trivedi said, "Come with me."

"Now what?!"

"I said *come with me!*" He led Jamie to his office. "I need a cup of tea. Perhaps you do too. We must talk."

With them both settled in, Dr. Trivedi took a sip of tea and said, "You have concealed key facts in a case involving a serial killer. Though you did not kill, you did file a false report, and you lied repeatedly by omission. Your career is finished, such as it was. You have written books, and some sort of strange problems have resulted from two of those. The book where Eliza is a character will be studied carefully and discussed widely. Many will whisper that you are a murderer. What do you think your mother will say? What will it cost her professionally under these circumstances, since she vouched for you? For you, all is lost, Detective Cloud. All is lost. These matters do not concern me. So I find myself making a strange request."

PART TWO

ELIZA FOUND herself standing on pink dirt at the edge of a cliff. At the bottom was a beach with white sand. The beach continued to her left and then, some distance away, there was a narrow, rocky cliff, with boulders and stones beneath, and a rocky coast. Then more sand. To her right, the same. In front of her, the water went all the way to the horizon. The sound of the waves was soothing. There was a breeze coming in from the water, and it smelled of ocean. She waited for the sound of seagulls, but there was only the sound of the waves. Flying animals soared above the water and occasionally dove in and flew out with prey. Eliza estimated that it was eighty degrees, and the air was humid.

She was standing on a trail. She looked to her right and saw that the ground sloped upward. In the distance, far from the cliff, was a dark gray structure that looked like a coliseum or—was that a walled village?

She looked up. The sky was dusky blue. The sun was close to the horizon, and it was too large. The light had a hint of orange, and low on the horizon at forty-five-degree angles from each other, there were two moons.

"*Ursinus b?* I'm on fucking *Ursinus b?* Is this a joke?" She turned around as if the doorway to Badri's office would be there, but there was just a trail. She paused in silence, heart pounding, wondering if Badri would step through next.

He didn't.

Eliza knew that she would never see him again, and she sobbed.

Then she said, "It's like I'm dead! To everyone I know, I'm dead! And I can't tell anyone where I am!" She took a breath to calm herself. "Badri will figure it out. But so what? I'm stuck here!" Eliza felt herself panicking again. "Badri will come and get me." She realized how ridiculous that sounded as soon as she said it.

With the ocean at her back, she saw a field of purple—fungus? ferns?—interspersed with coiled tree roots covered with what looked like lichen. And beyond it, the edge of the reed forest. In dread, she looked at the reed forest for signs of Donners. There weren't any.

She started to dig an *EB* into the dirt, deep enough that perhaps the wind wouldn't fill it in. But she could not dig anything in that hard-packed ground with her bare hands.

In tears, she looked about her for something hard enough to dig into the soil. Finally, she walked up to the lichenwood and took hold of some, hoping that it didn't have some sort of toxin on it or something horrifying beneath it.

It didn't, and there wasn't. She heard scurrying within the thicket but saw nothing.

She tugged, hard. Finally, some of it came up, a clump of it the size of a large head of broccoli. To her relief, she saw that the end of it was sharp.

She went back to the scratches in the dirt, and she started digging. She saw that as she dug, small rocks became visible, some the size of marbles, some of golf balls, all irregularly shaped. Periodically, she wiped sweat from her face with the bottom of her shirt. She was hot and thirsty.

At first, she was hypervigilant, even startling every time the waves broke. *What am I doing? I'm going to smell them before I see them.*

When she was done, she sat back on her haunches and examined her work. In the ground, at the edge of the trail, she had carved an *EB* the size of a large pizza, and above that, an arrow as long as a roll of paper towels. It pointed to what she hoped was a village and not a ruin. Beside her, she had a small pile of rocks, and out of them she built a cairn beside her markings. Beside the cairn, she left the bunch of lichenwood.

Then, thinking of Badri, she started softly to cry.

Miserably, she brushed off her hands on her trousers and started up the trail, wishing that she had worn something cooler than tactical boots and more resistant to climate than a polo shirt.

The trail curved around the hill, away from the cliffs, and she lost sight of where she had first appeared on Ursinus b. Next to her was a slight rise that obscured her view of the reed forest. She drew her service weapon and held it at low ready, walking quietly and keeping her eyes on the hill.

Suddenly, she gagged: spoiled meat and unflushed toilet.

Eliza looked wildly around but couldn't see where the Donners were.

Then two of them appeared on the trail ahead of her and immediately charged her. She fired three shots at each of them, but they didn't stop. She holstered her sidearm. As the nearest one got close, she kicked it in the chest as hard as she could, her foot slick against the creature's indigo blood. It stopped. But the other one grabbed her from behind. She dropped her weight and pounded it on the groin, coming in contact with slime, screaming *"Fuck you! Fuck you! Fuck you!"* as it dragged her. She elbowed it in the gut and stomped on its instep. It didn't work. She entangled her legs behind the Donner's knees, and it fell backward with her on top of it. She rolled over and pounded it in the chest and face repeatedly. She stood, heart pounding, getting ready to run.

She heard a noise. The remaining Donner dropped.

At her feet, her Donner was twitching, its lips split.

A man walked past her and shot them both. Then he holstered what she assumed was a lasepistol. He was about six feet tall and solidly built. His black hair was in a topknot. His large, intelligent eyes were the color of cinnamon, and his pupils were slitted. His eyelashes were thick. He had prominent brow ridges, upswept eyebrows, and a high forehead. His skin was dark but with a blue undertone. He was wearing a cream-colored tunic, black pants, and soft black boots. From his left hip hung a large knife or short sword in an ornate gray scabbard. The handle was black with metal studs.

"Thank you."

He replied in his language, a staccato, deep burst.

She realized she had already tapped and racked her sidearm and then reholstered it.

He took something out of his ear and held it out to her, motioning for her to put it in hers. She wiped Donner blood, slime, dirt, and stray bits of lichen off her palms and fists and onto her work trousers. Wondering if the slime was ejaculate, she made a sound of disgust.

Her hands still shaking from the fight with the Donners, she took what he gave her. It was an earpiece of some kind. She put it in her ear, grateful that it fit. She felt it expand.

"Could you understand me?" Eliza asked.

"I could." His voice was very deep. "I said, 'You're welcome.' Let's get out of here. My name's Kolokh."

She saw that he had canine teeth and only then knew for sure that he was not Human. And with only one translator, she could half hear what his untranslated speech sounded like. It was like talking to someone next to someone else who was having a loud conversation on a cell phone. Eliza saw that he was studying her.

"My name's—"

"No one from the *Broken Oar* mentioned you—" He grabbed her forearm roughly and inspected her. He was looking at her scars.

Eliza decided not to be afraid or offended. Yet.

His hand felt ice cold, and he was turning her arm this way and that.

"Please let go now," Eliza said.

He let go. Then he saw the cloth police department badge stitched to her shirt. "You're a detective, right? What are you doing here?"

"Jamie!" she said in despair. "What the fuck has he done? Yes, my name is Eliza Benveniste—"

"Of the Tauxenent County Police Department." He peered at her. "You look as I thought you would. But what are you doing *here*? Who is Jamie?"

"I really don't want to know how much you already know about me."

"Just what I know from the book. But what is a person from a book doing here, standing right here? Detective Benveniste—"

"Please, just call me Eliza!"

"Eliza, who is Jamie, what is *fuck*, and what has he done?"

"How do you know me?" Eliza had to restrain the urge to just run screaming down the trail. "And what book?"

"It's called *The Tauxenent Strangler*, about a serial killer. Kelly brought it. I'd never heard of a serial killer before, and I was curious to read it, so she somehow converted it into an audiobook so that I could. Kelly told me that not all of your books suck that bad."

"Who wrote it?"

"The author was David Dove."

Eliza put her hands on her thighs and started laughing helplessly.

"What is the matter with you?"

"David Dove is a—Jamie Cloud wrote a different book under the pseudonym David Dove. I guess he wrote more than one." Then she looked at the reed forest, and the pair resumed walking quickly. "The Humans. Cody, Maura, and Kelly Chatworth? Dr. Banner Colson? Captain Baines? Gino Accardi? There should be thirteen of them now."

"Yes. And there are other Humans too." He stopped and looked down at her. "But you didn't know about me, so am I in that book as well?"

"I didn't read that far. And then I ended up here. God knows how."

"I don't understand this. I do not. Let us not juggle stars. Explain this word *fuck*."

Eliza was wildly grateful that she could say words that were ordinary. "The word *fuck* is a complicated word. On paper, it's a crude word for sexual intercourse. I meant it as a means of emphasis for something mystifying and wrong. It's best that when you hear a Human say any form of that word, you ask for clarification. And don't use it first until you know how. And never in front of children. Even if they, uh, use it themselves."

"Your explanation of the word *fuck* is water by the firepit."

"So who are you? And did you get here the same way that I did?"

"Our planet, Kharq, is fifty thousand light-years from here. We don't know how our ship crashed here. It should have taken five thousand years to get here, and it was *not* our destination. We didn't even know it existed. We only live three hundred years. My nephew Malit is four years old and blind. On our continent, they take kids with birth defects to the middle of the Q'un Desert and dump them there to die. On other continents, they're dumped into the ocean, or worse. My sister, Lita, and her husband, Zhan, hid Malit instead. Someone dimed us out. Lita and Zhan would have been beheaded, the rest of the adults stripped of our names and dropped separately into the desert to die alone. Malit too. The young children would be placed with foster families and raised to curse us. We had planned for this eventuality. We had a ship ready, and our entire clan fled Kharq. Our destination was a neighboring system, but when we left orbit, we immediately saw this planet in our viewscreens. The way our ship malfunctioned melted it into slag. We almost didn't make it out of the ship in time. The name-stripping means the government takes your estate, by the way, so your children don't inherit your property."

Eliza realized that at least some of what Kolokh said was at such low frequencies that she could nearly feel his speech in her chest cavity.

Abruptly, Kolokh said, "Wreck."

Eliza did not know what he meant until she smelled the Donners and nearly vomited.

Kolokh's sense of smell.

A herd of them were running toward them from the reed forest.

Kolokh said, "You can't outrun them, though I can. Get behind me." He shoved her behind him before she had a chance to get there on her own. "This is gonna suck."

Suddenly, Eliza heard the sound of two enraged dogs running toward the Donners. The Donners crouched, looked at the dogs, and fled.

WALKING PURPOSEFULLY UP the trail behind the dogs was Badri Trivedi.

"Be right back," Eliza said to Kolokh.

Eliza ran to Badri, and he took Eliza into his arms, hugging her so tightly she thought her ribs might break.

She said tearfully, "I thought I'd never see you again."

"I thought the same."

Finally, they let go of each other, mindful of the fact that Kolokh was there.

Badri was wearing a black T-shirt with a colorful anatomy of the central nervous system on the front, along with a backpack. He was also wearing faded jeans instead of trousers.

"Your clothes are stained with a substance that I hypothesize is blood," Badri said. "I have brought additional clothing for you. We will turn our backs so that you may change your clothes. You cannot go around looking like that."

In fact, the blood on her clothes stank. *Stank.*

"Why do we need to turn our backs?" Kolokh asked.

"Just do it," Badri said.

Standing with their backs turned to Eliza and facing the

sea, Badri said, "In our culture, an adult does not uncover in front of another person unless certain exceptions apply. They do not apply here."

After Eliza changed, she wiped her hands off as best she could with her old polo shirt. She said, "I'm done. But I can't just drop these on the ground." He had packed her fresh clothing except, instead of polo shirt, a matching black T-shirt. She transferred her holster and sidearm and, with hesitation, she put her badge in her pocket.

He stuffed the stained and stinking clothing into the backpack.

Eliza considered her surroundings and wondered for a moment if she had taken drugs without noticing it or just lost her mind in general.

Badri's dogs studied Kolokh, crouching and moving their heads up, down, and side to side, creeping forward, then retreating, as dogs will when they see something they cannot recognize and have not decided whether they fear it.

To Eliza's surprise, Kolokh knew to ignore the dogs and let them approach him. Very shortly, they were greeting him.

"No one knew that dogs scare off Donners," Kolokh said, then studied Badri for a moment. "Dr. Badri Trivedi. You also look like I pictured you."

Badri said, "It is interesting to discover that Detective Cloud is capable of accuracy, regardless of whatever else might be said of him." He bent and leashed Skye and Luna, and the trio started walking. "Please call me Badri."

"Are the service dogs okay?" Eliza asked. "The crew would already know the Donners scare the dogs, yes?"

"The *Broken Oar* crew said they didn't see any Donners when they arrived with their dogs," Kolokh said. "Perhaps that's why."

"I'm so glad the dogs are okay," Eliza said. "Hey, how come you understand each other?"

"Jamie supplied me with translators."

"How did you get here?"

Badri told her.

Kolokh was fascinated. "Eliza told me before. I needed time to fill the cup. Is he the only Human who can do this?"

"We know of no other who can do this thing than Jamie Cloud," Badri said. "We are proceeding at a pace that is too taxing for me. Traveling to this place has exhausted me. You may have to—"

"We can slow down. Donners are afraid of dogs," Kolokh said. "David Dove didn't mention that you had dogs."

"Jamie Cloud didn't know that Badri had dogs," Eliza said.

When they saw the dead Donners, Badri said, "Who killed these?"

"We both did," Kolokh said.

"Shooting one of them didn't stop it immediately," Eliza said. "It was a good thing you showed up, Kolokh."

The trio resumed walking. Eliza was glad her clothing didn't stink to high heaven, but she was still thirsty.

"These translators don't footnote manners, customs, other relevant things," Badri said to Kolokh.

"There have been issues."

The Humans laughed.

At Kolokh's look, Eliza said, "When Humans laugh, it is best to seek clarification. We weren't laughing at you. We were imagining things that could go wrong."

Kolokh laughed too.

"This is interesting," Badri said. "You are not Human, but your facial expressions correspond to ours, and here you just laughed. One would expect more differences. And yet there are not."

"The sun is the sun," Kolokh said.

"Are there other species in that structure?"

"There are."

"Do they also laugh and smile?"

"No. Among outsiders, Kanninoin only raise their eyebrow. What it signifies, who knows? Otherwise, they have a half-smile. It is said they can be violent. I do not know how they laugh or if they laugh. I have not talked to many other species. They tend to keep to themselves."

"Pity," Badri said.

Suddenly, Eliza turned to Badri. "Jamie. Is he coming?"

"Sergeant Roth had neglected to confiscate Jamie's service weapon. He shot himself. He simultaneously sent a bullet into his brain and propelled me here. I found myself here immediately with the dogs."

"He what?" Eliza said through her tears. "You—"

"Was Detective Cloud your husband?" Kolokh said. "He wrote that you were going to marry. Or that you had. He was not clear."

"Oh, my God!"

"Absolutely not!" Badri said, resting his hand on Eliza's shoulder.

"Never!" Eliza said. "He was my partner and my friend. Then he ... he lost his way. Why didn't my sergeant confiscate his service weapon—oh, I know Roth. He'd have wanted to clear it with the whiteshirts first. But then someone should have stayed with Jamie."

"Someone did," Badri said. "Had he not ended his life, it is likely that he would have written about you despite his promises, and if not, he would have written other things, and more people would have disappeared or died."

CHAPTER
TWENTY-TWO

THE STRUCTURE WAS four stories tall. It was distant enough from the shore that the sound of the waves was very faint. By this time, it was nearly dark.

The walls were made of stone, and there were equally spaced turrets on top. In front of them was a door approximately one story tall and two meters wide.

Kolokh walked to the entrance and stood there.

Badri and Eliza traded looks.

The door dilated.

"How did you accomplish this?" Badri asked after they walked in.

Eliza looked back. The door had already shut behind them.

"I didn't. The gate reads DNA."

Badri opened his mouth to speak, but they found themselves in a dark stone hallway. Eliza realized that the walls must be at least fifty feet thick. With the door closed, the hallway was dimly lit with path lights.

As Kolokh approached the second door, it dilated open.

It was an entire village on a red brick plaza. Most of it was open to the sky. The roof overhung what looked like four-story apartment buildings, and Eliza guessed they were all around the village. The upper levels appeared to be reached by stone staircases with metal railings. Eliza could not see the opposite wall, because other buildings blocked her view.

Streetlights encircled the village all the way around—upright poles with globes on top that reminded Eliza of the streetlights in Washington, DC. The light was good, but not overwhelming.

There were what resembled picnic tables in front of each dwelling, and people of various species were sitting at them. Not all of them were humanoid. Some that looked like gigantic furry spiders had gathered on top of a table speaking with a group of giant land octopuses.

The eyes of these octopuses were slightly higher up the body, their pupils horizontal slits, their tentacles functioning more like legs. Several sets of tentacles ended in opposable digits. They were gesticulating animatedly and occasionally changing colors.

"Those are Kovians," Kolokh said, "and Spiders."

"Thank you. I hope I get to meet them."

There were detached white one-story buildings in the center of the village. They had sage green iron roofs. Around each detached building was a riot of flowering bushes.

"How many people live here?" Eliza asked.

"Maybe two hundred. These around the edges are homes. There is a hospital. There is also a village square and two social halls, one small, one large. There are fenced areas for animals to run. There are some areas for games. The Spiders play some sort of a ball game."

"Amazing! How many species live here?" Eliza asked.

Kolokh ticked off names on his fingers. "Along with us, there are Kanninoin, Spiders, Kovians, Tenurians, an Ursan, a

Marsh Ursan, and Humans. We also have Q'ua'to, which are pets. Humans have dogs. Kovians have—" and the translator winked out.

"Where are the crew of the *Broken Oar*?" Badri asked.

"They live on the other side."

"Are the residents segregated by species?" Badri asked. "I hope this is not the case."

"Most aren't. Some are, by choice. With those, it is best for everyone."

Eliza was about to ask about that, but a woman walked up. She was Eliza's height, with white hair in a long, sparse braid. Her skin was a waxy white. Her yellow eyes were three times bigger than Human eyes, and her pupils were slitted. She had a nose like a cat's. *She's nocturnal? Why is she up?* She had a thick black unibrow, and her ears began at her jaw all the way to her forehead and extended upward like a cat's. Her ears were thin enough that Eliza could see the light and blood vessels through them.

The woman wore a simple cream tunic and leggings, but she was barefoot. She had objects in her hand, which turned out to be two of the same translators that Kolokh had given her.

Eliza took the one she was wearing out of her ear and handed it to Kolokh. For a moment, she did not understand a word this woman or Kolokh was saying. She even had trouble picking out words at all. Kolokh's language was staccato and guttural. The language sounded harsh, but then he gestured at Eliza and gave a kind of silky growl. Sometimes he spoke at low frequencies that she felt as well as heard. The woman's language sounded nearly musical, sometimes almost like a call. Sometimes, there was a shriek. Some of the sounds she made were at nearly too high a frequency for her to hear. Eliza wondered how much of their speech was at frequencies that Humans could not hear at all.

Eliza put the devices in her ears.

When the woman saw that Eliza's translators were in place, she said, "I'm Inani." She raised her unibrow. "I have turned into a welcoming committee of sorts. The other Humans who arrived were fascinated, but they were also disoriented until the issue of language could be sorted out."

"Find them an apartment," Kolokh said. "Tell everyone that these dogs chased off fifteen—" and here the translator winked out, but Eliza inferred that he was referring to Donners. "The woman is Detective Eliza Benveniste. She neutralized two of them. The man is Dr. Badri Trivedi."

Inani's unibrow almost went into orbit. "This is fascinating news about these dogs! I will send this out on blast. In these homes, you'll find communication equipment and computers so you will be able to send and receive news. You will be given comm-watches that can send and receive information. I sense that Dr. Trivedi and Detective Benveniste are exhausted."

"Please, call me Eliza."

"That is not our custom."

Eliza looked at Badri pointedly. Then she said, "I'm so thirsty. And I'd be really grateful to be able to rest for a time. It has been a—an exhausting day."

Inani's unibrow went up again. "There are vacant homes. I'll put you in one across from our medical center, given your profession, Dr. Trivedi. Or we can find you separate apartments."

Badri took Eliza by the upper arm with a strong grip. "We will share a home. We already parted under unexpected circumstances once."

Thinking of how she had stepped out of his office and ended up here, she said, "Yes." Eliza moved closer to him.

"What's the matter with you?" Kolokh said.

"The other Humans that arrived did not look as you did," Inani said. "Are you ill?"

"We are merely fatigued," Badri said. "Our method of arrival was ..."

"Different universe," Eliza said.

Inani was studying the two Humans. "Well, this is unexpected," she said. "Some of the scientists among us will wish to discuss this with you and—"

"It won't help. We don't know how we got here."

"You will have a chance to get some education now that you are here."

"Badri is a medical doctor. I have a bachelor's degree in cognitive anthropology. Do your universities confer doctorates in book-portal-ology?"

Kolokh snickered.

Inani's unibrow went up again. "Something has clearly been lost in translation."

"Something hasn't," Kolokh said.

"This does not make sense," Inani said.

"Eliza already made this observation," Badri said.

As they walked, various people looked up from tables and some greeted Inani and Kolokh. Some greeted Eliza and Badri too, and they greeted them back.

Two of the Spiders raised their two front legs at them, and Eliza waved.

Next to her, Inani tensed.

In a saccadic movement, one of the Spiders quickly blocked their path. They were ten feet away, but to Eliza, they might as well have been in her lap. The Spider was black and furry, with two fangs. Their eight eyes were even with Eliza's face.

Skye went purely crazy, and Luna hid behind Badri's legs, barking.

"Enough!" Badri said, and the dogs silenced. "Down!"

The dogs went down, but their hackles were raised, and they were quietly growling.

"Why did you threaten me?" the Spider said, raising both front legs.

"I didn't," Eliza said calmly. "I meant to politely greet you. I'm sorry if I made the wrong gesture. I didn't know it was wrong. What should I do next time?"

The Spider lowered their legs. "I'm—" and the translator winked out. "None of you monkeys can even say that. So call me ... oh, hell ... Wolf. Does that work for you, prairie ape?"

"Yes. How did I offend you?"

"You're a monkey. Your kind jokes about killing us with fire. How does the little mammal taste?"

"I didn't threaten you, I was saying hi. *Empty-handed.* Was that hostile of me?"

"Luna is a companion, not food," Badri said.

"You monkeys are idiots." Wolf began to advance on Luna.

"Hey!" Eliza said, drawing her service weapon and pointing it at Wolf. "Stop!"

Wolf stopped, but his front arms raised again.

"Go suck a fly's dick, you asshole! Fuck you!"

Eliza had never heard a spider laugh before. "Next time, don't stare. And keep your hands down, monkey."

"Deal."

Eliza holstered her weapon, and they walked on.

After they had walked a few moments, Eliza started crying softly.

"You're brave!" Kolokh said. "I would've been shitting in my pants!"

Inani looked completely calm.

"I am once again grateful for your bravery and quick thinking," Badri said. "I'm sorry that I—"

"You were unarmed," Eliza said. "The dogs needed your protection. Inani, how often does this kind of thing happen?"

"The Spiders are irritable, suspicious of bipeds."

"When were you gonna cough up that factoid?"

"I didn't have time. Most Humans pretend not to see them, fearing Spiders. You're the first Human who actually greeted one."

"Anyone else here who'd just as soon kill us as look at us, or have we met the only murder contingent in town?"

Kolokh laughed so hard he had to hold his ribs.

Inani stood in her path. "The only murder contingent we're aware of here is you. The crew of the *Broken Oar* has one killer among its number."

"I'll be glad to talk to you about justifiable homicide another time."

"I would find that fascinating."

"It would cause an attitude adjustment."

The group walked on in silence.

"We are here. That building is the hospital." Inani pointed to a structure not a hundred feet away. "Please study the markings on your door. This will prevent you from walking into the wrong one. Each of you palm the door three times. This will enable the locking mechanism to work."

Eliza looked at the incomprehensible markings, which were nearly symbols, and realized that they still couldn't read even if they could communicate in words. "Why can't anyone do that and get in?"

"Because when you get inside, you will do the same thing. Only in this way will the door lock. Some people have different ideas about knocking before entering."

Her tone caused Eliza to believe that this had happened before.

"What is that expression you are making?" Inani asked.

Eliza realized that Human facial expressions might be less subtle to some species here. "I was thinking that you sounded like this had happened before."

Kolokh belly laughed. Eliza wondered what his laughter would sound like without the translators. "Kano ran into her house while she and her spouses were—"

"Kano is impulsive. Let us speak no more about this."

"How ... how long is the day here?" Eliza asked.

"Twenty-four hours."

Jamie. "Months in a year?"

"The year is three hundred days long. We divide them by equinoxes and solstices. To answer your next question, hurricane season is approaching. Our summer solstice started eleven days ago. This is Summer Solstice 11."

"You don't name the days of the—the solstice?"

"It is not necessary."

"How long have the people from the *Broken Oar* been here?" Eliza asked.

"They arrived here on Spring Equinox 55," Inani said, with the same edge to her voice as someone at 4:45 p.m. on Friday would have while answering an unnecessary yet longwinded question at a staff meeting. "Let's go in."

"Good," she said. "I'm thirsty." Eliza struggled to do the math on how long the *Kestrel* crew had been at Broken Oar and decided that it was about a month ago.

Eliza walked in. The air was cool, and she relaxed. Badri unleashed the dogs, and they started sniffing about.

The home was very large, about 1,500 square feet, with walls and floors of orange-brown wood. The light was warm and not too bright.

On the same wall as the door was a large window, seven feet tall, ten feet wide. The bottom edge was three feet from the floor, the top edge was three feet from the ceiling, and it was in the center of the wall.

"Is that one-way glass?" Eliza asked, wishing that there were a cat sitting on the windowsill.

"Yes," Inani said, and Eliza relaxed.

To their left, perpendicular to the door, was a wooden breakfast bar with four chairs on either side. It was more solidly built than the Sommars's sideboard, but for a moment, Eliza looked for the tiny vase full of plastic daisies. On the other side of the breakfast bar was what looked to be a kitchen, but with devices she did not recognize.

To her right was a waist-high, thick wooden divider between the hallway and what appeared to be a sunken living room. In the living room were a couch, a love seat, a chair, a coffee table and, beside what was obviously a fireplace, a small stack of wood and a device that Eliza guessed to be some kind of lighter. The living room was accessible on either end of the divider by three low steps.

To Eliza, the dark brown furniture looked like it belonged in a private law office's waiting room.

Across from her, on the other side of the living room, was a sliding glass door. On either side of the sliding glass door was a short hallway.

"To the left is a bedroom. To the right is a den—and another bathroom," Inani said. "It is not modest to have guests walk through someone else's bedroom in order to relieve themselves, no matter what the Kharkuns say."

"I'm really thirsty," Eliza said. "And I really need to wash my hands." She saw a small sink in the center of the countertop, and she immediately washed her hands.

Inani handed her a towel and soap, and Eliza wondered where it came from.

"I'm so thirsty I could cry at this point," Eliza said.

Eliza realized that Kolokh had left without saying goodbye and decided that this was customary.

"*He* does not enter a home without a specific invitation," Inani said, "unlike Kano. And Kharkuns do not say goodbye. They just leave."

"You're good with facial expressions in context," Eliza said, wondering how many Humans had decided Inani was telepathic.

"Yes."

Inani walked to a device beside the granite countertop where an oven would be in an Earth kitchen. It had several buttons on the side. "You can either push a button or speak to the computer. Its voice recognition is quite good. This will dispense food and beverages."

She pushed a button, and the door slid up. There was a glass pitcher full of water and two glasses. She handed Eliza the pitcher, which was ice cold. Condensation was already forming on it. She put it on the countertop and poured water for herself and Badri.

Eliza drank her first glass so fast she barely had time to breathe. Then she drank a second and then a third glass. Feeling better, she said, "Where do these go?"

Inani said, "Here. You've never seen a dishwasher before? These don't use water. Once they start, they'll lock." She took the glasses and the pitcher and put them in the dishwasher. "The waste disposal is here." She pointed to a large round area on the countertop to the left of the sink and said, "The waste is converted to compost below-ground. Then it is recycled. You open the disposal by palming this console." This was a small console against the green backsplash on the other side of the circle.

"I'm sure we won't recognize any of the technology here," Eliza asked. "Can you show us?"

Imani palmed a console inside the front door. "This button adjusts the lights. This one lowers the curtains." A copper-colored screen fell and obscured the window completely. "This is a communications console. There is one in every room in the house, with the exception of the bathroom. Some species lack sufficient modesty. This is a thermostat. If you want to set it higher—"

"*No!*" Eliza said. "No. Thank you. This is perfect."

Badri went and put his arm around her shoulders and said quietly, "That house is a universe away."

Inani said, "Sometimes, Eliza, you seem to dissociate. Is this customary?"

Eliza took a breath. "It's … it's nothing."

Inani studied her. "No, it's something. And it's obviously distressing. You should stop."

Inani took them down the short hall on the left and slid open the bedroom door. In the back of the bedroom, there was an entrance to what had to be a bathroom. The wooden door locked from the inside, she saw with relief.

"The bathroom is soundproof too," Inani said. "It seems like whoever constructed these dwellings had the Kharkuns in mind."

Badri started to speak but appeared to think better of it.

Inside, there was a toilet with a bidet, a countertop, a sink, and a large mirror. The shower and whirlpool tub looked like they did at home. Eliza looked in the bottom of the tub and Badri whispered, "There is nothing there."

"Why would there be?" Inani said.

"It's a long story," Eliza said.

"You are inappropriately alarmed by nonevents. Badri, is she ill?"

"I'm right here. No. And you're violating my privacy by asking about it. Please stop."

Inani's unibrow went up, and Eliza had to remind herself that the gesture could signify anything.

Eliza realized that she had been staring at the toilet and started laughing. Through her giggles, she said, "This bathroom is the most familiar thing I've seen since I got here!"

Badri looked around, and then he laughed too.

Inani stared at the two of them for a moment, and she said, "Is this humor?"

"You should try it sometime," Eliza said, wondering why she was starting to dislike the Kanninoin.

Indeed, everything about the bathroom looked as it would have at home, including the bidet.

To the inside right of the bathroom door, there was a recessed wall and three more devices. "This dispenses textiles." Inani pointed to an object set into the wall that opened outward like a dresser drawer. "It is voice activated. When textiles need to be cleaned, put them in the—" and here the translator failed. Inani said two incomprehensible syllables while pointing to a device that looked like a top-loading washing machine. "And the device will clean your clothes without the excess use of water and return them dried. This"—

she pointed to a smaller device—"will dispense toiletries and soaps."

Inani peered at the two Humans and pushed some buttons on the clothes dispenser. Towels, washcloths, and what looked like pajamas popped out of it. "This is what the other Humans wear and use. I estimated for the two of you."

Inani had Eliza and Badri use each machine until they knew what to do.

Eliza tried to get the food dispenser to issue a muffin, and she got one the size of a basketball. Appalled, she started laughing. Badri tried to get a cup of tea out of it, which came in a cup the size of an eggshell.

"Omigod," Eliza said around her laughter.

"This is impossible!" Badri said. "Must we specify volume and mass?"

"This is a Tenurian muffin," Inani said. "Do not eat it, and do not give it to your animals."

Eliza saw that it was flatter than a normal muffin, light blue, with coarse crystals on top that looked to be sugar. It smelled wonderful, and she was grateful for the warning. She quickly put it in the trash device so that the dogs would not get it.

"Thank you," Badri said. "Their names are Skye and Luna."

"Their causing Donners to retreat gives them some use, but you use these for ... companionship?"

"We do not *use* them. We are interdependent," Badri said. "For thirty thousand years."

"You're thirty thousand years old?"

"No. The dog species, *Canis lupus familiaris*, and our species, *Homo sapiens sapiens*, have been interdependent for thirty thousand years. I am forty-one Earth years old. Eliza is thirty-three."

"But ... this one is now lying on your feet. This does not disturb you?"

"It does not."

"The formal name for your species suggests that there is another subspecies of *Homo sapiens*. Is that correct?"

"*Homo sapiens neanderthalensis* is one subspecies," Badri answered, "but they are extinct. There were others, who are also extinct."

"And your subspecies drove them extinct," Inani said, her ears reddened.

"Actually, no," Eliza said. "Neanderthals had no appetite for innovation, they lived in small family groups, and the climate was going through rapid shifts. They couldn't adapt. They also would have been more susceptible to diseases given that they lived in such small family groups. We actually interbred with them, but no, we didn't wipe them out. Why, were there other sapient species on your planet?"

"No."

"Figures."

Inani pushed some buttons so rapidly that neither Human could see what she was doing. "I have calibrated the device to your species. I have also included information about these two dogs. Human and canine dietary requirements and biochemistry are in our database. A Tenurian muffin contains high levels of organophosphates, which are an essential part of the Tenurian diet. One of the Humans from the *Broken Oar* ate one and reached our hospital in agony. She would have died if someone had not carried her there, drooling, seizing, and vomiting. Now that the dispenser has been programmed, it will not provide any foods toxic to Humans unless you enter the request manually. Now, try again."

Eliza tried a glass of zinfandel and got one. Badri got a glass of Scotch. Badri then requested water in a large dog dish and got one and set it on the floor at the end of the breakfast bar.

When the dogs started drinking, Inani said, "This sound is ... pleasant. And they chase off the Donners. Perhaps they are not so objectionable after all."

Badri tried the dispenser again and it produced two bowls of kibble. Badri set it beside the water.

Inani listened to the dogs eat and said, "This too is a very pleasant sound. I have rethought these animals. Perhaps they are not as disturbing as I had supposed."

"Why didn't you like them at first?" Eliza blurted.

"They appear tumultuous."

Eliza and Badri traded looks.

She led Eliza and Badri back to the living room and pointed to the sliding glass door. "This window can be closed with this console here."

Eliza expected to see an orb weaver in its web and was relieved that she did not. She saw that the yard was big enough for the dogs, although not as big as Badri's. "The walls out there," Eliza said. "Are they the wall of the village or is it a separate wall?"

"This is the border of the—" and the translator winked out again. "The stone walls that divide the yards obviously are not."

The yard had an indigo lawn and ordinary deck furniture. Eliza estimated that the walls dividing the yards were more than fifteen feet high.

Inani looked at the dogs, then at Badri. "Since you keep

these emotional creatures, please understand that you must clean up after them. There are waste stations throughout what you Humans call Broken Oar because some species are less modest than others." She took Eliza and Badri and showed them how to get the dispenser to make dog waste bags.

"What if they urinate?" Badri asked.

"Bring a bottle of—" and the translator winked out. "Spray it on. It will cause this to evaporate."

"I could not understand the word you used," Badri said.

She typed some characters into the dispenser. "Call it urine cleaner," she said. "You are not the only species to keep pets, and we had to get the Kharkuns to stop pissing against the walls. Put the dog food in this tub here."

Eliza noticed some kind of flat-screen TV facing the couch. She saw that everyone in the room could watch it without sitting sideways. Below it was the fireplace.

Inani said, "This viewing screen can show entertaining programs. You can also ask the computer for instructional and educational materials. The database is quite large by now. You will find two additional computers in the den. You will have to control them by voice, since you cannot read."

"Please instruct me on the use of this device," Badri said.

"Certainly."

"I'm going to go take a shower," Eliza said. "Thank you so much, Inani."

"Of course."

After she'd finished, Eliza walked to the doorway of the bedroom dressed in a soft, cream-colored cotton tank top and loose cotton trousers.

Inani looked at them both and quickly said, "I'll leave you to yourselves. If you need to call for help, there is this button on the console. Yelling won't help, since the soundproofing is very good. Kharkuns can be loud." Then Inani left.

As soon as the door closed, Badri palmed the door three times to lock it, then took Eliza in his arms.

Once in bed, they made love as a couple would who had thought they'd lost each other.

ELIZA SET down a cup of coffee, and Badri said, "I will cure you of that habit one day."

Eliza laughed. "You've been saying that for almost a year." She sat beside him on the same side of the breakfast bar.

Badri looked at her arm. "Did this happen last night?"

"What do you mean?"

But her forearm was bruised.

"Wow, that's really something," she said, looking at the bruises. "Kolokh must have done it by mistake. He saw the scars there and realized that he knew me and grabbed my arm to inspect them. I was at that point still adrenalized and wouldn't have noticed if he'd set me on fire."

Badri laughed again. Then he turned serious. "I never asked you how that happened."

"I always wondered why you hadn't."

"It seemed an invasion of privacy."

"You know what I look like naked."

He blushed. "Yet you did not tell me of your brother's death. I opined that you are a private person."

Eliza sighed. Then she told him about how David had died, white-knuckling her composure, but she was shaking.

Badri took her in his arms and said softly, "It is impressive that you began chest compressions. Many individuals would have panicked."

Eliza laughed silently. "I never panic. But please, I'll tell you about the aftermath of David's death some point, just not now."

"I would like to know what happened. But you—"

"And the scars? I'd been on the street for a year. I'd pulled over a drugged driver. Asshole weaving all over the road, crossing the double-yellow lines, braking at random, almost running off the road at the fog line. In his favor, he hadn't actually collided with anyone yet. I stopped him right at the intersection. I'd just stepped out of my marked police cruiser when he got out of his car and charged me, butcher knife in his right hand. Even if there weren't bystanders in the line of fire, he was just too close. I could've emptied my Glock into him, and he still could have finished me. I mean, our vests don't stop knives. So I used empty-hand tactics. He's on the ground decorticate posturing. I radioed for backup. I'm bleeding like crazy. I could kneel and handcuff him and bleed out, or I could count on the fact that he's down for now and deal with the mess on my arm. All of the smartphones out, no one called 911. I ran to the car for a first aid kit. I put a tourniquet on myself and ran back to the knifer. He was breathing, and he had a pulse, so I just sat there. Turns out he had a warrant out for failure to appear on some minor felony, which would have gotten his probation yanked on a burglary charge. Just a stellar specimen."

Badri thought for a moment. "I believe I performed his autopsy. I remember this because it was a police-involved death.

He had died in a skilled nursing facility. I do not recall his name."

"Shane Turner. He'd been high on halo. He died?" Eliza felt sick.

"I do not recall the mechanism of death. And your parents did not urge you to find another line of work?"

"Wait, Shane Turner died?"

"This has upset you? You were forced to defend yourself!"

"It doesn't make me feel any less awful." She wiped her eyes roughly. "He was supposed to discharge from the hospital and get his scumbag ass sent to jail, not end up ... Holy shit."

"Your martial arts training, this is funded by the police department?"

"Wait, give me a moment. Okay, it's going to take me some time to process that death. I don't know why either. Anyway, no, that training is not funded by the police department. The Risk Management department wouldn't touch that with a ten-foot pole. But I think all able-bodied Jews should learn Krav Maga."

"It does not concern you that I am not Jewish."

"How have we not had this discussion already?"

"Perhaps it was one we were avoiding."

"I wasn't avoiding a thing. You haven't celebrated a single religious holiday since I've known you. You are from a family of atheists? Because my mother would never let me get away with skipping Passover."

"I was in high school when I declared that there was no evidence of any deity."

"We discussed this, yes. I never asked you how your parents took that."

"They reacted in the same fashion as yours did when you announced your intention to become a police officer. Whatever faith a child of mine is raised in does not concern me, but the child must be permitted to make up their own mind when they are older."

"They do anyway. This is a discussion we could have had a year ago, Badri. If religion had been an issue, I wouldn't have slept with you in the first place."

"That seems reasonable in hindsight." Then he said, "You left an inscription in the ground. Did you make this for me?"

Eliza took a sip of coffee. "Yes."

"You knew that I would find it?"

"I didn't know. I ... It was the only thing I could do." Then she sat up. "Oh, no—"

"The thing was not a pentagram, Eliza. It did not conjure me here. It was a road sign. Do not concern yourself with this."

"I wouldn't have—"

"*Enough*, Eliza! It was my choice. The thing is done!"

"I appreciate the emphasis, Badri. But I'm sitting close enough to hear you."

Badri flushed. "Please forgive me."

She stared pointedly at him for a moment. "How ... how did it feel going from your office to here? I felt like someone had grabbed me by the hair. Then I was looking at the ocean."

"The last thing that I recall was ... was a gunshot and the—the aftermath. And then I appeared exactly where you did. Detective Cloud was capable of some accuracy at least. It is a shame that he never devoted that amount of effort to his sparse reports."

"To everyone back home, we're everywhere and nowhere. They'll think they see us in a crowd, and then the person will turn around and ..." She started crying softly. "If I keep thinking about this now, I'll fall apart."

Badri's expression was bleak. Eliza sat very close to him and put her hand on his back.

Then he said softly, "After you disappeared, I was without you. This was intolerable. My parents were elderly. After they died, I would have been without them and still you. I would not have known whether you were safe, injured, or deceased. Your opportunity to say farewell to your family was stolen from you. I could at least send a text, a wretched, insufficient thing, but I sent one timed for twelve hours hence. If Detective Cloud's efforts had failed, I would simply have deleted it. This text, it informed my parents, Denny, and Oren that we were well but that we had been forced to flee for the safety of all and that we could not return. To assure them that this text was genuine, I included certain details that only Oren and I would know. I asked Denny to communicate with your parents. I instructed her to tell your parents and your siblings that you would dearly miss them." Then he held her so tightly that Eliza could hardly breathe, and then he kissed her, hard. His arms still around her, hands in her hair, he said, "The decision to follow you, it was not one that I made lightly."

And he gripped her arm tightly and led her into the bedroom.

Afterward, they held each other tightly, as if one of them might disappear again.

Eliza rolled on her back and stared at the ceiling. She felt Badri's gaze on her, and she said, "I'm hungry. And now we can just walk into the other room and push some buttons and get whatever we want to eat. I don't know what I think of that."

"I am hungry too. And the dispenser is the least disorienting feature of our new surroundings."

At the food dispenser, Eliza said, "I wish there were a menu, like … 'Give me something a Kanninoin would eat.'"

"There will be time for this."

But a shallow bowl of a white substance appeared. "Hello!" Eliza said. She took it to her seat and sat down. "It's ..." She poked it with a spoon, and the mass in the bowl dimpled inward. "Here goes nothing." As soon as she put the spoonful in her mouth, she gagged. Forcing it down, she said, "It tastes like, just ... congealed flour ... in Crisco and unflavored gelatin. I give up."

She soon sat back down with a slice of cheese pizza. "I need some comfort food after *that*." Badri studied her, and she said, "No, don't even try it. Just imagine Play-Doh in white school glue."

"I am convinced." Badri took a sip of tea and said, "Who do you think will solve those cases now that we are gone?"

"Hey, we're in the future. Why couldn't we find news articles about it?"

But when they tried to look it up, they saw that American history was confined to events at the national level or those with a global concern. "Well, our disappearances and a bizarre series of murders didn't make the cut," Eliza said. "I don't want to think about what that means. Wait, the Lonnie Dyson murders aren't listed either. So—"

"It appears that the local historical database is limited to that supplied by the *Kestrel* crew. It is clear that we can learn nothing of the fates of our loved ones, about which I am filled in equal measures with relief and despair."

"And then ... a man who wrote a science fiction book and had the opportunity to enter it chose to stay behind. Why?"

"I read the beginning of this book when the connection between the murders and the book became manifest. When you disappeared, I recalled these Donners. I almost threw him into the wall. Repeatedly."

Oh no, oh no, oh no. "Badri," she said quietly, "you said Jamie knew certain things that caused him to shoot himself, but I know him. He was processing nothing. He might not even have grasped just how fucked he was. Isn't his mom a judge? Maybe he even thought she'd get him out of it. He would have woken up in the morning with his service weapon gone, maybe even in lockup. What did you say to him?"

"I told him the truth."

Eliza whispered, "You told him the truth? What do you mean? Help me understand the sequence of events. I disappeared. You called 911 surely—"

"When Detective Cloud entered my office, he said something crude about what he expected to find us doing there. When I informed him of the sequence of events, he sat in my office in hysterics. I called Oren."

"Who came?"

"Oren Roth and Joseph Cutter."

"And they separated you and Jamie, right? They wouldn't talk to two witnesses in the same place at the same time no matter who they were. Who else was there?"

"Only Oren and Joseph—and Joseph spoke to me while Oren took Jamie into my conference room. One of them had attempted to summon Denny, but she was in a hearing."

"And you told Joseph that Jamie wrote the book and then he told Oren and ... But they didn't take Jamie's badge and gun and cart him off for an interview?"

"Oren wanted to do this thing."

"And you told him not to."

"I sent them away so that your partner could write what had to be written. Worse, if possible, he would have continued to write. This conclusion is inescapable."

"So you got Jamie alone, got him to write you and your dogs here, and triggered him to die by suicide?"

"It was not my intention to do this. I gave him the opportunity to join me. Had he done this, he would be here too."

"He didn't want to walk away from his family! How could he be expected to do that?"

"Eliza," Badri said, raising his voice, "he did not cast you into exile in a foreign country! *He consigned you to a different universe!* There was no one and nothing familiar! It was impossible for you to tell anyone where you had gone or to ask for help! He was willing to leave you here to *rot* for all he knew! He said he could not face you. It was his responsibility to face you! Instead, during the pendency of the investigation, he challenged your observations at every turn, stormed out of rooms like a coward, and then he orchestrated a confrontation within my hearing! If you had materialized in front of a horde of those creatures, what then? Or you could have appeared in a wasteland! Consider the likelihood that he would have continued to write and that more people would lose their lives for his self-indulgence."

Eliza, shaking, said, "I need to take a walk." Crying silently, she stopped first and said, "I'll be back." Then she walked out.

Eliza nearly collided with two women after she got their front door open. She recognized them immediately—Kelly Chatworth and ... and that had to be Dina Baines.

"You're Eliza Benveniste," Kelly said to her. "Why are you crying?" She pushed her way in, and the other woman followed.

Eliza turned and saw that Badri was clearly upset. He picked up his mug of tea with a shaking hand.

Then Eliza looked at the women. "Kelly Chatworth … and you have to be Captain Baines," she said wonderingly. "These are Kelly Chatworth and Captain Baines. Holy hell."

Looking at the two women, Badri said, "The correspondences are shocking. And, Kelly, I have done nothing. This dispute is between us."

As soon as he finished speaking, Kelly said, "You both look like you've had a bad argument. Between your appearance and your voice, you're Dr. Badri Trivedi, right? Your accent is barely perceptible. David Dove described you as being from India, and his depiction of your accent was … unique." Kelly rolled her eyes.

"I am not from India," he said in disgust. "I was born and brought up in United Arab Emirates. I grew up speaking English, Arabic, Hindi, and Marwari. I am not surprised that his depiction of me would be … a ghastly caricature."

"Why are you so upset that he was wrong about where you're from?" Baines asked.

"Asking for the national origins of individuals with accents is a breach of etiquette, to say the least. In his case, his speculations were as clueless as he was. Ironically, I have never been to the Indian subcontinent." Then Badri studied Kelly. "You *are* Kelly Chatworth."

"That's right. According to the book I read, you're a know-it-all. Now you show up here, and Eliza's crying. What did you do?"

Badri immediately belly laughed.

Eliza said, "Jamie Cloud was intimidated by Badri's expertise."

"David Dove knew about that?" Kelly asked. "And how do you know who I am?"

"David Dove *is* Detective Jamie Cloud, and—"

"Figures," Kelly said. "Detective Cloud in the book is a complete tool."

"You don't know the half of it," Eliza said. "That's how we all know each other. David Dove is a pseudonym used by Jamie Cloud. We're all real people, and we're also depicted in books. You exist as book characters in a novel called *Rebellion at Broken Oar*. Badri and I exist as characters in a true crime book called *The Tauxenent Strangler*. Jamie wrote both books. *The Tauxenent Strangler* book pulled me here, and then Jamie wrote a piece of flash fiction to send Badri after me. The way Badri got here resulted in David Dove's—Jamie Cloud's—suicide, and I'm crying because I'm still processing why he died."

"What the fuck?" Kelly said. "Hold on a minute." She took her translators out. "Say something to me."

"Right before I got here, Badri and I were in his office discussing the murders of Glenn Sommars, Chloe Jackman, and Jennifer Simms. We'd just figured out that Detective Jamie Cloud was David Dove, author of *Rebellion at Broken Oar*, which was about Ursinus b and all of *you*, so I was on my way to meet Jamie in front of the Office of the Medical Examiner so that I could bring him back to Badri's office. Badri and I planned to confront him together there."

Kelly had just been standing there, but as Eliza spoke, she walked to the breakfast bar and sat across from Badri, staring intently at Eliza.

"But," Eliza went on, "I was yanked from the hallway by my hair and ended up staring at the ocean down the trail from here."

When Eliza spoke, Kelly's eyes grew wider and wider. She ran a hand through her hair, and it fell back into place. "Give me something with slang in it."

Eliza thought for a moment. "What kind of slang? How many different ways do you want me to use the words *fuck*, *shit*, and *ass*—"

"Timeless words don't count."

Eliza snickered. "We might informally tell someone who is agitated to *chill out*. If you cease all forms of social contact with someone without warning, you've *ghosted* them. You might refer to a beloved pet as a *furbaby*. An *incel* is an involuntarily celibate misogynist who believes that women owe him sex. For menstruation, there's *that time of the month*, *Aunt Flo*, or *got my period*. And more. If you agree with someone so strongly you could have said it yourself, you say *I know, right?* The minimum wage is only twenty-five dollars an hour even though that means that minimum-wage workers have to live in private dormitories instead of apartments. We call those dormitories *sardine cans* or *cans*. My mother used to say *yeet* to mean discard by throwing far away or *yoink* to grab something quickly. How's that?"

Kelly rubbed the bridge of her nose. Then she replaced her translators and asked, "How many pronouns do you use?"

"For people? Three. Male, female, and singular *they*."

"And you always use several pronouns?"

"Yes, why?" Eliza said, glancing at Baines and then back to Kelly. "I mean, the captain's subordinates call her 'sir' in the book."

Kelly shook her head. "No, we don't. No, we fucking don't. That's some real *Star Trek* shit, is what that is. We use a pronoun-referent prefix. It's a grammatical placeholder. If I hadn't read *The Tauxenent Strangler* and listened to your archaic English, I'd say you were delusional or lying. But this is something out of *The Twilight Zone* or *The Invisible Sky*. Walk with us, Eliza."

"Wait, tell me what year it is."

"*It is,*" Kelly said, mocking Eliza, "the year of our Lord 2203."

Eliza and Badri traded looks.

"So you're a widow, and you jumped in the sack with him right away?" Baines said, gesturing at Badri.

"No!" Eliza said. "I was never involved with Jamie Cloud! Not *ever*. Have you asked me why he's not here? He could have been!" Then she followed Kelly and Baines to the doorway, turned to Badri, and said, "We're not done with this."

"Oh? These are the second and third persons who believe that Detective Cloud was your husband. But he still betrayed you and left you to your fate."

"And I'm a homicide detective! Or I was when—"

"James Roland Cloud could have followed you to the place where he sent you," Badri said. "Then he would be sitting at his breakfast table writing more chaos, playing Russian roulette with the fate of others. Instead, he stayed and destroyed himself."

"Eliza," Baines said, "you and Kelly and I are going to have ourselves a little talk. Badri, can you be trusted to keep calm while we're talking some sense into your girlfriend?"

Eliza sat in Kelly's apartment, which was identical in almost every respect to the one she shared with Badri. Kelly had somehow found a way to get the dispensers to make a black cotton area rug and two sage green throw blankets.

The three of them sat at the breakfast bar, and Kelly said, "What are you drinking?"

"Just some coffee."

Kelly set a pitcher of beer and some mugs on the breakfast bar, then she put a pizza before them and sat down. Baines and Kelly sat together, and Eliza sat across from Kelly.

Kelly suddenly saw Eliza's bruise. "And you say you were just arguing. I guess that's technically true but—"

"That was Kolokh." Eliza saw something in Kelly's manner that she couldn't describe.

"Kolokh?" Kelly asked.

"He's the one who found me. He saw the scars and grabbed my arm to inspect them. I didn't even notice that it had happened. I guess he didn't know his own strength." She looked again at Kelly. "You and he are a couple?"

"And?"

"Look, I really don't give a shit one way or another. With all of these species living close together, it wouldn't surprise me if it happened a lot. But take it down a few notches, okay? Speaking of which, Kolokh hits you?"

"Kharkuns can be rough with each other. He knows better now."

"Going from Glenn to someone who can be—"

"Save it," Kelly said. "Never in a million years."

"What's going on?" Baines asked. "Jamie Cloud suggested the two of you are married and we walked in on you and Dr. Trivedi. You two were fucking each other's brains out during a criminal investigation?"

Eliza told the two women about finding Glenn's body and the subsequent events, adding that she and Badri became a couple *after* coming to Ursinus b. They had time to devour the entire pizza during her account.

"That," Kelly said, "is creepy."

"How did the crew take what happened to Glenn here?" Eliza asked.

Kelly looked down.

"Oh," Baines said, "Gino lost it, but he got over it."

THE CREW SAT in the mess hall, some still in tears. The mess hall consisted of round tables with plastic cafeteria chairs, the white walls plastered with murals of the artist's most optimistic conceptions of Ursinus b. One of them had an image of a blond White male in a Space Force coverall, feet planted shoulder-width apart, one hand on a shovel, other hand on his hip, while he looked up at a small orange sun. The crew had taken to calling that one the *Fatherland Mural*.

Another mural featured various colonists standing behind a little green man while a female colonist held out a basket of fruit, the green man looking up adoringly. The other murals were somehow even worse.

The group agreed that these murals would be painted over as soon as the ship landed. The lone dissenter was Dr. John Bynum, who was sure that the colonists would be received in just that way and that the "aliens" on Ursinus b would need what he called "Human guidance and husbandry."

Now the group sat, the mood bleak.

"Kelly, you've gotta eat something," Baines said.

Cody returned to his seat beside his mother with tomato soup, a grilled cheese sandwich, and a mug of hot tea. He set the plate in front of his mother and said, "You used to make this for me and Maura when things were awful, remember?"

Gino was drunk and sitting at the next table. "You mean things like murdering your dad?"

John Bynum strode across the room. He took an empty chair from the next table and sat down next to Gino. "Sommars didn't murder enough of the crew for you? What's the lucky number before you decided he was a liability?"

"This isn't how it's supposed to be handled."

"Oh? How should it have been?" Bynum replied. "We could summon the police. They would arrive in two years. How many of us would be left to inform the police of the day's events?"

"It was murder."

Bynum said, "The series of events as described to me—"

"Had nothing to do with murder," Banner said. "Were we gonna work as Kelly's bodyguards in shifts? Since he sabotaged the ship, would you have trusted him with the crops or the dogs?"

"Gino," Cody said, "what if we had landed in an ocean or across a nasty fault line? He was willing to risk that just to make someone feel incompetent. You'd say, 'There's a Donner over there,' and he'd say, 'No, there isn't, go on ahead. There never was a Donner, you just can't handle the pressure,' or 'I don't know what happened to Gino, you know how he always gets lost. No, he didn't go east, he went west.' You'd try to shoot a herd of Donners and he'd stand in your way again. He'd have found a different way to murder my mother. We're out here on our own now. This isn't Earth. This is here."

"Oh," Bynum said, "Chloe was careless. In this outpost,

only the strong survive. Glenn was constantly insubordinate to Captain Baines, and if we're colonizing a planet, we need order."

Cody started to brush his forelock from his face and kept his hand where it was.

"WOW," Eliza said. "Those murals ... And how did you take what Bynum said?"

"Those walls were going to be covered over with a nice coat of paint," Baines said.

"But Space Force decided those murals were a good idea," Eliza replied. "Covering them up, does it erase Space Force's philosophy?"

"What do you mean?"

"Are the people on the other ships going to be like Glenn and Bynum or like you all?"

Eliza couldn't interpret the look on Baines's face.

Kelly turned the handle of her mug the other way.

Remembering Kelly turning her travel mug around during the interrogation on Earth, Eliza's guts filled with cold water.

Baines broke the awkward silence. "Bynum thinks we should kill all the Donners and that the aliens in this village are in the way. He's an asshole, but he's a doctor, and he doesn't call those particular shots."

"Kelly?" Eliza said.

"Detective Benveniste, you're not on Earth. There are no police, no lawyers, and no courts. You can die if people fuck with your head, interfere with a rescue, or push people in the way of monsters."

"So you and Badri were what, the dynamic duo?" Baines asked. "Which one of you is the sidekick?"

"Neither of us is Sherlock or Watson. Dr. Watson wasn't as smart as Sherlock and so the comparison doesn't even make sense. Together, we solve cases that otherwise wouldn't have been."

"Who?" Baines asked.

"You've never heard of Sherlock Holmes and Dr. Watson?"

Kelly shook her head. "No idea. Were his stories written with a quill pen or in cuneiform? Who calls the shots and who follows?"

"Neither of us. Do you talk to your shipmates like this?"

"You walked out of that house in tears," Kelly said.

"We had an argument about Jamie's death. I was going to take a walk and think."

Baines set another beer in front of Eliza, then asked, "And how did he murder Jamie Cloud?"

Eliza told the two of them what happened.

"How's that murder?" Kelly demanded. "He could have joined Badri. He'd have had to look you in the eye, but that's a lot better than what he was looking at there—a total shitshow. If Badri had let him be hauled off for questioning, he wouldn't have been able to get to him to write that piece of flash fiction, and you'd have been here alone, the only person in our universe who came from where you're from. The political and social events that happened to you are history to us, and some of the folks here haven't even heard of them, but the ones that we went through, you don't know about. Our experiences growing up, the entertainment we watched ... all of it. Badri's right."

"Not to mention that Jamie had his finger on the button for at least two universes," Baines said.

Eliza wondered whether Baines had actually said "finger on the button" or knew where the expression came from.

Kelly shifted her weight onto one elbow and took a deep drink of beer. "Jamie wrote that you and Badri went off to a conference together one year. His description of Badri's motives wasn't pretty. What happened in Baltimore?"

The beer had gone to Eliza's head. "Nothing. I was a female detective in the same place at the same time as a male forensic pathologist, and people talk. We never said or did anything that couldn't have appeared on the front page of the *Washington Post*. We always sat with, talked to, and ate with a group of people. We traveled in two cars to the conference, and when he drove us anywhere, there were always two others in the back seat. I did get to know that he too drives a stick shift and also was not a left-lane camper who drove below the speed limit and that he doesn't make infuriating eating noises, but our feelings did not come up."

They laughed again.

"But he wasn't even staying in the same building as me. I was there to learn, and I learned a lot. There's no way in hell I would have risked my career and reputation by saying or doing anything inappropriate, even if I thought that Badri saw me that way at the time, and I didn't. Was it painful? It surely was. And?"

"No lingering looks? No standing too close? No come-hither in the elevator?"

Eliza shook her head. "No. Not at all. If you haven't noticed, Badri's on the formal and reserved side, and he's not an idiot either. What's bothering me? Badri thinks Jamie wants me. Jamie thinks Badri wants me. Very faint and wavy love triangle, no? Then Badri gives Jamie an ice-cold reality check so that Jamie doesn't follow, bumping Jamie out of the picture. That's what's bothering me."

"If Jamie hadn't been so gutless, none of this would have happened," Kelly said. "He could have dropped a copy of the book on your desk and told you he was the author. He could have told you how he felt about you. He could have followed you anyway."

Eliza sighed. "He knew I wasn't interested. The book? Ironically, if he had gone to the sergeant and handed him a copy, everyone would have thought the bad guy was out there." She gestured. "By hiding it, he made himself the suspect—wait a minute. You read paperbacks?"

"It's old-timey, I know. But people are nostalgic, and you can't read an e-book when your device needs charging."

Then Eliza looked around and then back at the two women and said, "This doesn't seem real. I half expect to suddenly find myself sitting at my desk watching Jamie playing with a paper clip."

"A what?" Baines said.

"You don't use paper?"

"Almost never. Except for books."

Eliza ran her hands through her hair. "So what do people do with themselves all day? There's free food, clothing, shelter, and medical care, so no work."

"People work. This is a very small town with a lot of interesting people and a lot to learn," Baines said. "Eventually, when we find our feet, we'll go exploring."

Kelly looked at Baines sharply.

"That's why we're *here*, Lieutenant Commander," Baines said.

"We could at least prepare ourselves by sending up d—"

"No drones," Baines said.

Eliza watched this tableau, perplexed. "I'm a cop. You need street cops here? Or homicide detectives? Or forensic pathologists? I'm pretty sure Badri hasn't treated a live patient since medical school. What do we do?"

"You'll adapt," Baines said, shrugging.

"Okay, but what is this place?"

"No one knows," Kelly said. "Not even the Ursans."

"That's ... almost like it's a zoo exhibit."

"A what?" Baines said. "Oh, right. You guys held animals captive for entertainment."

"To be fair, in the best zoos, they kept the animals from going extinct."

"Something you had to worry about," Baines said. "We didn't. Instead—"

"It was here when everyone got here," Kelly said. "We don't know for how long, and Belek's people—the Ursans—have a weird problem with the concept of time. You know about the Holocaust refugees on the other side of us?"

"There are? Omigod."

"You'll meet them."

"That's fantastic! And I've always wanted to meet people from other planets."

"Exactly," Baines said with shining eyes.

"Could I borrow *The Tauxenent Strangler*?" Eliza asked.

"Sure. Look," Kelly said, "Badri did the right thing. Sorry Jamie was your partner, but you might want to go count the sex scenes in that book before you weep too much over him."

"Sex scenes?"

"Between you and Detective Throbbing Manhood. Yeah."

"That's ... that's disgusting. We never—that never happened. That almost feels like—"

"Being violated," Kelly said.

"How you figure?" Baines asked. "I'm sure that Eliza over here had some pretty racy thoughts about Badri before they got together—"

"Oh, yeah," Eliza said.

"But she didn't turn around and put them in a book that everyone was supposed to think was true or write porn about the two of them and post it in a blog," Kelly said.

"That's exactly what it's like," Eliza said.

"*Did* Jamie figure out who the Tauxenent Strangler was?" Kelly asked.

"That piece of shit," Eliza said, wonderingly. "That slime-ball! He took credit for that? He looked for signs of forced entry and spoke to the occasional witness. In fact, he failed to notice that Dyson showed up to at least two crime scenes. Jamie never would have solved that case."

"Was he convicted?" Baines asked.

"Dyson was murdered in the jail." Eliza took a deep drink of beer. "Captain, the title of Jamie's other book is *Rebellion at Broken Oar*. Has ... has there *been* a rebellion?"

"Against what?" Kelly said. "There isn't really even a government here to speak of."

"There's no one who could land here and try to take over?"

Baines said, "We're it. The *Peregrine* and the *Archer* are on their way, but they're Space Force. If you're asking us if we have weapons, we do, but I can't see us needing them."

"But you're not from here either," Eliza said. "We should ask Inani."

"Will do," Baines said.

"So go home," Kelly said. "Go thank your boyfriend. Then meet us at the dog park. We'll point it out on the way back." Then she got up and came back with the book.

Eliza looked at the cover, then at the two women. "This ... this doesn't look like either of us! And *he* was screaming at a pile of clothes in a closet. *I* had Dyson at gunpoint." The breasts of the Eliza in the photo were cartoonishly large, almost bursting out of a thin button-down shirt open to the cleavage. "Well, maybe he got the *rebellion* part wrong too."

When Eliza walked in, Badri was sitting on the love seat talking animatedly with a Kharkun and a man who Eliza guessed was Dr. Banner Colson. Badri was drinking Scotch. Banner had a beer. The Kharkun was drinking something white. They had put a medical tutorial on the TV, but they had it on pause. The dogs were curled up next to Badri, Skye's head in Badri's lap.

Badri looked up. At Eliza's expression, he said, "I see that they have gotten you to see reason."

"They did. That was before I learned that, in his book, Jamie took credit for solving the Dyson case. He also had a lot of sex scenes between me and him."

"He what?"

"Oh," she laughed darkly. "I corrected them. About all of it." She turned to Banner and the Kharkun. "I might be able to tell you what really happened in this case once I—"

"Badri told us," Banner said quietly. "I'm Banner Colson, but you probably already know that." He smiled a little at that.

"My name is Ror. Like them, I'm a doctor. I have a last name too, but we only use those in formal government documents, generally when we're being sentenced to death. Just call me Ror."

Eliza laughed. "Done. Pleased to meet you both—and you're right, Banner."

Ror's eyes were so black that Eliza could barely see his slitted pupils. His head was shaved. He had a scar running from his left temple to the corner of his mouth. His skin was olive, like Eliza's. He was dressed entirely in cream, with a symbol on the breast of his long-sleeved tunic. He was barrel-chested, and she estimated that he was Banner's height. On his feet were what Eliza swore looked like sage green Crocs.

She walked over and handed the book to Badri, who looked at the cover and tossed the book onto the coffee table like it was a piece of garbage. "This is contemptible."

"Wow, really?" Banner said. "That's ... that's disgusting. That doesn't even look like you! Did he look like that?"

"No, the figure in the illustration went to the gym every now and then. Anyway, I'm headed to the dog park. Do you want me to take Skye and Luna?"

She left the three men, smiling to herself.

Eliza walked farther into the interior of the village that Baines's people called Broken Oar.

She passed various aliens but made eye contact with no one in case she offended someone else. The dogs seemed to have the same idea, because they looked forward unless they looked up at her.

She noted that at the dog park, entry and exit was through two side-by-side chain-link sally ports with chain-link gates on either end, just like the dog parks back home.

As soon as the inside gate closed behind her, she let the dogs off leash, and they tore into the park.

The park itself wasn't fenced in with chain links. Instead, enclosing the park were trees with thick, pale gray trunks, fencelike masses of intertwining branches, and round leaves the size of saucers that were black with streaks of orange and dark green. The effect was of a thick, leafy, ornate wicker basket surrounding the park.

On the far end, there were various play structures set up for dogs.

Sitting at a picnic table were people Eliza recognized and people she did not. As she approached the table, a man stood up. He had to be Gino Accardi. He looked at Eliza with expressive eyes, extended his hand, and said, "Gino Accardi."

"Eliza Benveniste. Please just call me Eliza."

They shook hands.

"I thought Polichek was the one who loved dogs," she said.

"Tony's over there." Gino pointed at a tall man at the far end of the park playing tug of war with an animal that looked like a large otter. "It's a dog park. A dog park on another planet!" He shook his head. "This continues to bewilder me."

"And the bathrooms," Eliza said. "There's a machine that can give you food when you ask it to, and then you go into the bathroom, and there's a whirlpool tub and a very artsy vanity and a shower."

"I can't believe this shit. You know us, Kelly knows you. I have a headache."

Eliza laughed. "At least you're in your own universe!"

"On a planet we're marooned on. It was supposed to be a one-way trip, you understand, but our ship is completely grounded. It's a good thing we didn't land on an iceberg, or we'd've been fucked—uh, sorry. By report, you curse like a sailor."

Eliza laughed. "Oh, yeah."

Kolokh was sitting beside Kelly, along with a boy who looked to be about eight years old. Kolokh stood and introduced him as Malit, who had some kind of a bone in his hand that was about as big around as a thick cucumber. His short hair had loose, light brown curls, and his face still had the roundness of a child.

The boy said, "You're the lady who knocked out two—" and the translator winked out again.

"Beginner's luck," she said. "How old are you?"

"I'm four. Are you going to ask me if I'm big for my age too? Because I wish you wouldn't."

"Never." She saw that Malit was looking in her direction but that his eyes did not focus on her. His eyes were white, with barely visible slitted pupils. She remembered that he was blind. "Do you have dogs where you come from?"

"We have pets too. That's mine. Her name is Suk." He pointed at a sand-colored animal that looked like an otter, if otters had longer claws and tufted ears.

Eliza wondered how Malit knew what direction to point in.

Eliza said, "Suk has one end of a rope toy, and a yellow dog has the other end, and they're each pulling backward, playing. There are other animals like Suk, and two creatures in the corner digging holes." They looked like sand-colored, feathered armadillos, until one looked up and its mouth was a round tube with sharp teeth.

"Thank you. I can hear it, including the rope toy."

"That's amazing. Our hearing isn't anywhere as good as yours."

"You're weaker than we are too!" he said with enthusiasm. "But I like you anyway."

Eliza laughed.

Malit bit into the bone as if it were a very large cookie. Then he offered her a bite. His forearm was the chubby forearm of a very young Human child.

Touched, Eliza said, "That's very kind of you. But that would break my teeth."

"You can't eat Q'a'ta bones? They're yummy."

"I wish. But my teeth aren't built to eat bones."

"That's sad."

"It is. But I can eat lots of other things."

Suddenly Inani was at her elbow. "Detective Benveniste, you'll probably like this." She handed her a goblet of something pink and foamy.

"Thank you," she said, and drank. It was warm and thick, with a flavor reminiscent of cotton candy, and she suddenly felt more awake. "Ohh, this is lovely," she said. "What is it?"

"Naiya," she said. "A stimulant. It comes from a fruit on our home world."

Eliza pronounced the word in her head. *Nigh-yah.* "It's delicious. Just sweet enough and not too sweet."

"Sweet?" Inani cocked her head. "We find it savory, with a peppery bite."

"You can't taste sweet?"

"I've—I've never heard of it."

"Well, hang on." She walked up to a mini-dispenser and said, "How do I get this thing to make a peach smoothie? Can you drink milk from mammals?"

Inani's ears pulled back like an angry cat's.

"Oat milk it is!"

And Eliza handed her one in a glass mug, thinking of the

Kanninoin resemblance to cats and the feline inability to taste sweetness.

Inani drank. She raised her unibrow. Her ears went back to normal. "Properly creamy, spicy. This is fascinating. You taste something else entirely?"

"You're vegetarian?"

"We don't speak of our dietary preferences," she said with her ears pulled back.

Another Kanninoin quickly introduced himself as Kano. "Johalo and I are going to be trying to breed some of those dogs of yours," he said. "My family finds them engaging." Kano was shorter than Inani, but his skin was no less waxy and corpselike. His black hair was worn loose, and he wore a black vest with no shirt and, to Eliza's surprise, a pair of faded denim jeans. Like Inani, he too was barefoot.

"You know how to do that?" Eliza asked.

"Yes. We can make gametes out of stem cells. And though there is not enough genetic diversity to breed the resulting puppies, we can clone them."

Eliza suddenly thought of Denny's book, *Painted Walls*, and wished desperately that Denny was here. "That's ..."

"Interesting," Kano said. "Other Humans have had similar reactions. Do you find the idea ... immoral?"

Eliza shifted her stance and thought for a moment. "I guess what bothers me is the idea that an individual—a dog—could be considered replaceable. They aren't. You could clone Luna and Skye, but they wouldn't *be* Luna and Skye; they would be two different dogs entirely. A Human can grieve for a dog forever. Handing that Human a clone of that dog? I don't know."

"Do Humans bear identical twins?"

"We do."

"If one twin dies, do the parents respond to this by saying that they have one left, or do they grieve the death of that twin? Our spouses often bear triplets, and we view them as different children, not clones."

"We don't see them as clones. They're individuals. In fact, they don't even always have the same personalities. There is nothing worse to a Human than losing their child. They would grieve for that twin as a separate child."

"You see a clone as a different organism than a twin, then?" Kano asked. "You would not have a new Luna and Skye; you would have their twins. You would think of them as entirely different dogs, not copies of the two who live now."

Eliza considered. "If it's viewed in that way, then I think it would be a good idea to have more dogs in this village."

Then Eliza gasped. Cody and Maura walked in and sat with Kelly. Cody gave Kolokh a high-five. When he saw Eliza, Cody walked up to her.

"My God," Eliza said. "You look just like—"

"Yeah, well, so do you. I heard whoever killed Glenn in your world's gonna walk. Good for him, whoever it was."

"Well, I'm not a cop anymore." At this, she felt a wave of grief. "From what I know about what happened to Glenn here, it sounds like justifiable homicide."

Cody relaxed. "It was."

"Oh, hey!" Maura walked up. "Here's the porn star!"

Eliza blushed. "Your mom told you that—"

"That David Dove had a lurid imagination, with shitty sex writing to go along with it? Yeah. Mom didn't read the shitty sex porn to me though, because she doesn't hate me. You gonna try to lock up my brother here?"

"For justifiable homicide? Just so you know, the Glenn where we came from was ... even if we'd figured out who offed him, the jury would have probably pinned a medal on their chest, because our Glenn was a fucking monster."

Maura and Cody laughed.

"I'm really sorry about the hell he put you all through."

Kano studied Eliza. "You just changed personalities."

"How you figure? Oh, you mean register. I spoke informally. I didn't change personalities."

Maura had turned on her heel and walked away.

At Eliza's expression, Cody said, "She really doesn't want to deal with any of it. And I don't blame her. And if Eliza used speech that was too informal in court, anything could happen, from alienating jurors to being walked out in handcuffs."

Eliza laughed. "Oh, yeah."

"So Humans can change vocabulary and tone based on the listener?"

"And the circumstances, yes. We have to," Eliza said, "or we can break some intense social rules."

"There are social rules involving tone and vocabulary? How can that be? Language is language. It does not change."

"Your language is static? Cody and Maura speak one of the same languages I do, English. But English has changed so much between our time and theirs that we need translators to talk to each other. I don't even know how Kelly understood Jamie's book. There are also over seven thousand languages and even more dialects where we come from. And some languages go extinct."

"We have different languages too. Geography is geography. But our languages are the same today as they were ten thousand years ago, upon the development of writing. Extra vocabulary words are added as new objects and phenomena appear, but the language is otherwise the same."

"We didn't even *have* writing ten thousand years ago." Eliza thought about asking Kano about pronunciation, but she didn't feel like discussing the Great Vowel Shift, the Mid-Atlantic accent, or the exclamatory syllable quite yet.

"So give me the story from the top," Gino said. "I'm tired of this weird game of telephone."

Eliza gave him a brief synopsis, looking forward to the time when she did not have to repeat it.

"So Sommars was a piece of shit in your world too."

"God, yes. I figured I'd end up as much a defense witness as I would a prosecution witness. But," she said, looking at Cody, "we had no suspects. And none of the Chatworths would talk about what he did to them."

Cody shifted his stance and put his hands in his front pockets, looking suddenly vulnerable.

Eliza hesitated. Then she said, "Cody, the aliens here. Spiders, octopuses, and humanoids. Also bats. How is that? Why do they all look like Earth counterparts? Why do they all communicate by sound? Shouldn't they look completely different?"

"I thought about that. The best I could come up with is that this is convergent evolution on steroids."

"Convergent evolution?"

"Different animals of different genetic lineages evolving similar traits in response to similar environmental pressures. The biggest example is eyes. Or thylacines and red foxes. Birds, pterosaurs, and bats. Caffeine in coffee, tea, cacao, and guarana."

"What's ... what's a thylacine? Are they here?"

"No, they lived in Australia. Basically, big marsupial foxes even though they were called Tasmanian tigers. They're extinct, because Humans suck."

"Humans do. But what does caffeine have to do with evolution?"

"Natural pesticide, but the pollen gives the pollinators a buzz to make them want to come back. And it kills off plant competition. To be fair, the Kovians and the Spiders are telepathic. I wish I could find the mechanism for that, but none of them will agree to get into a Hansen scanner, so that's out. And the Kovians do communicate with each other by color also, often in shades that Humans can't see, and the Ursans use pheromones to create a tonal and emotional subtext. When we got here, Bynum was sure that the Kharkuns were a primitive warrior culture, kind of like *Star Trek*'s Klingons. He's wrong. They're starting to reject infanticide and collective punishment, which is why they're here, but they haven't fought wars in centuries. Inani comes off like the ultimate pacifist, but she's a raving hypocrite, and almost none of her people agree with her. They're just shockingly naïve, but she's in charge, so."

"Why aren't the Ursans mad that there are other species squatting in their village?"

"Because it isn't their village. Their own cities are underground by way of the water. By report, they're a lot nicer than here, and they think we're short-lived barbarians. Belek is the only one who shows up, and I'm half-convinced he's here to show the primitives how to behave. I asked to see one of his cities, but he put me off."

She laughed. "I'll have to meet him!"

"He's right over there!"

Cody pointed at what looked like a giant lobster with two thick pairs of jointed arms instead of claws, and each hand with two thumbs, each digit with fingernails. Belek's six feet tapped the ground as he moved, and his eyes were higher than Eliza's head. He had a sheaf of antennae encircling his eyes, and his shell was maroon. He had eight appendages to an Earth lobster's ten, she noted.

Belek attempted to play ball with an alien animal that looked like an armadillo the size of a Galápagos tortoise, but instead, the armadillo tortoise climbed on it, rolled over, and started tossing it into the air with its jointed legs.

Belek's carapace immediately changed from maroon to dull green, and he clacked his antennae.

"Is that animal his pet?" Eliza asked.

"No, Belek just … hangs out here sometimes. Like an anthropologist or something. Anyway, nice to meet you. I'm glad you're not an idiot. Based on the book, my mother thought you were." Then he followed his sister and sat next to his mother and Kolokh.

"What does it mean when Belek clacks his antennae?" Eliza asked Gino.

"I dunno. Frustration? Applause? Indigestion?"

She realized that she and Gino had walked into the depths of the park, which was huge. They were now alone.

"Lieutenant, did Captain Baines tell you about the fact that David Dove's book was called *Rebellion at Broken Oar*?"

"She did. Inani didn't know what Dove was talking about. Also, Baines isn't here pulling rank that doesn't exist anymore. Please call me Gino."

Eliza was tempted to ask Gino about Baines's relationship with the rest of the crew, but she let it pass. "Will do! Well, *The Tauxenent Strangler* sounds like it had a negligible connection to the truth. Maybe he's wrong about a rebellion too. Maybe."

"Well, there isn't anything like that going on now, and this place has been here for who knows how long."

"And nobody knows who built it?"

"Not even the Ursans. Word is, it just … appeared one day.

They don't know when, because Ursans can't tell time, apparently."

Eliza shuddered. "That's just spooky."

"You don't write, do you?" Gino asked. He looked as if he was asking her if she were a covert sex offender.

"No, other than for work."

"I can't tell you how happy I am about that. And yes, that was also me changing the subject."

"I understand why—hey, I wonder what that's about." Kolokh had pinned Kelly's hand to the table by the wrist. "There's a male Kanninoin speaking with her. Is Kolokh that possessive?"

"That's Johalo, Inani's husband. I asked Lita about that, Kolokh's sister. Yeah, they do that. Lita's husband, Zhan, does it too. Kelly swore to me that Kolokh does not abuse her, but Lita tells me that as a species, they're pretty rough in bed."

Lita had silky, tortoiseshell hair that fell below her shoulders. Her eyes were rust-brown and had slitted pupils. Her upswept eyebrows were the color of turmeric. Eliza thought that she was beautiful. Zhan was a bulky redhead with coarse hair, and his pupils were round. His ruddy skin was covered with freckles. She pegged him at six-eight and 275.

Eliza looked at Kelly thoughtfully. "There can be some pretty intense, persistent relationship patterns, but then, Cody and Maura don't seem to be worried about it." Eliza looked at Kelly again. "Kolokh doesn't even notice he's doing it! And Kelly doesn't seem to notice either. That's ... really ... unnerving." She looked into the center of the park. "Are those three dogs yours?"

"Yeah. The otter-looking guys belong to the Kharkuns, except one that belongs to Inani's mother. I can never remember what the hell they're called. The Kanninoin all of a sudden want pets."

A black Lab suddenly bounded up to Gino with the total exuberance exhibited only by dogs. "Hey there, Ralph!"

Ralph was carrying a ball and what looked like an unknotted rawhide, but he dropped them at Gino's feet and took two steps back, looking up at him expectantly and wagging his tail.

He turned to Eliza and said, "I love how he does that." Gino threw the ball and Ralph picked it up, trotting back and looking proud of himself.

Bear. He looks like Bear. She dropped to her knees and greeted the dog, who was licking her studiously on the chin, and she began scratching him behind the ears. "You look just like—"

It had been a town house. Bear's owner, Nikki, had been found in the same room on a couch, and Bear had been—

Eliza found that Ralph was pushing on her shoulder and nosing her under the chin repeatedly, and she wrapped her arms around his neck and realized that she was shaking.

Badri was suddenly standing next to her, and she quickly stood up. She said, "Dyson." Before Badri could react, she wiped her eyes roughly. "Nikki McMann. I didn't see you come into the park!"

"Banner and Ror needed to return to the hospital."

Kelly was suddenly beside Eliza and put her arm around her shoulder. "What happened?"

"The Tauxenent Strangler was an exceptionally brutal serial killer," Badri said. "Those involved in the investigation and prosecution of these cases saw things in the course of their duties that ..." Badri went very still. Then he briefly explained Dyson's pattern but without specifics.

Gino said, "Jesus, really?"

Fighting for control, Eliza said, "And Bear was still alive."

At the crime scene, she had approached the dog and found herself screaming for the veterinarian, Dr. Jake Levy, who had started accompanying them on these calls. Dr. Levy had examined the dog and quickly euthanized him. Then he had stepped out to the front of the house and thrown up.

"Wait," Kelly said. "In the book, you threw yourself into Jamie's arms, and he called for the vet."

Badri said, deadly calm, "I wish I had killed him with my bare hands. In these cases, I insisted on going to the scene. When Eliza was kneeling by Bear, Detective Cloud had indicated that he was going to search the house for signs of forced entry and went upstairs. Dr. Levy, the veterinarian who ultimately euthanized Bear, was standing a few feet behind Eliza when she started calling for him in a state of great distress. Detective Cloud came down the stairs, but he did nothing but look at Detective Cutter and Dr. Levy and say, 'You guys got this?' He briefly looked at me and pointed to the body on the couch behind me and said, 'You got *that*, right?' Then he went to look for other signs of forced entry. No one present made physical contact with Eliza during that incident."

Eliza said, "As Jamie walked past Nikki and Bear, he said, 'That's gotta hurt!' He was absolutely rattled."

Kelly hugged her. "Why wasn't Bear already receiving care when you arrived? Or why hadn't he already been euthanized?"

"Dyson was booby-trapping houses. Citizens started calling us once they saw the—what Dyson was leaving in the windows. In the first case, a patrol officer who made entry into the home was nearly killed by a crossbow bolt. The State Police Bomb Squad started sending bots into the crime scenes first."

"Here's a drink," Kolokh said. "This is what Humans do." He handed her a strawberry margarita.

It took Eliza all she had not to laugh, but Kelly and Tony were laughing so hard their eyes were watering.

"What the fuck is the matter with you?" Kolokh said. "This is the proper usage, Eliza, correct?"

"Yes, it is. Perfect. And I'm so grateful," Eliza said. "I had a lot to drink this morning with Kelly, and you could not have known that."

Lita was standing next to Kolokh, bristling.

Uh-oh.

Eliza said, "In our culture, refusing a gift of food or drink is not an insult as it is with yours. It is extremely common, and it is only considered rude or contemptuous when not greeted with thanks."

"Eliza did drink with us this morning," Kelly said. "Furthermore, when experiencing ongoing trauma, it isn't healthy for a Human to drink when reliving it, or the Human could develop a dependence on alcohol. And a margarita is consumed on happy occasions. Later, Eliza will drink a beer with all of us, which is the custom."

Lita settled down. "In our culture, refusing food is a serious insult. I see that in yours, it is not."

Cody walked up. "Was David Dove telling the truth about how you got your scars?"

"That depends on what he said."

"Something about a drunk driver and a butcher knife."

"Eliza concurs," Inani said.

"Don't speak for me, Inani," Eliza said. "And thank you for calling me by my preferred name."

"You Kanninoin are telepathic?" Cody asked.

"No. Her expressions and body language are obvious."

"Inani," Kelly said, "don't speak for Humans who are able to answer for themselves."

"She was taking too long."

Cody traded looks with Eliza and said, "I came over to ask if you all wanted to spar. Hey, Badri, you know how to fight?"

"Somewhat."

"How is it that you Humans all fight?" Kano asked.

"Mass shootings," Eliza said. "Etcetera. Where do we go?"

ELIZA AND BADRI FOLLOWED CODY, Kelly, and Kolokh into a low building on the far end of the village. After a moment, Kyr and Enkhid—Kolokh and Lita's uncles— joined them.

There were rows of a garment that she didn't recognize.

Cody handed her one. It was yet another Ursan cream-colored piece of clothing, but with an attached helmet. She ran her hands along the cloth, expecting to feel light cotton, but it was like touching a giant bead of mercury.

"What the hell is this?" she asked.

"It's a pressure-damper suit. It allows us to fight as hard as we want to without, you know, killing and maiming each other. It lights up to show injuries. It also shows your heart rate." Cody pointed to an indicator cuff on the right wrist. "It warns you when you're overdoing it. This thing goes over your head. If you would have died, the whole thing turns red. You can feel some of it, but you won't get hurt."

Eliza looked at it again. The whole helmet looked like it was made of some kind of thick glass. "This is a pressure-damper?

It looks like a good kick could shatter this and put out your eyes."

"Not with a pressure-damper. It's not that kind of glass."

"Tell me why you wouldn't just wear that thing in combat the whole time."

"Because it doesn't stop lasepistol fire."

"Intriguing," she said. "Why isn't Maura here?"

"Why do you think?" Kelly asked. "Combat gives her flashbacks."

"Why is there no treatment available for posttraumatic stress disorder?" Badri demanded. "Surely, it is endemic here."

"No therapists," Kelly said.

"This place has no contact with others in space?" Badri asked.

"No. It's a total backwater."

"It was visible from Earth," Badri said. "Surely it is visible to others!"

"It's visible, Badri," Kelly said, "but that doesn't mean it's accessible. That wormhole can only be reached from our end of the galaxy. It would take forever to get here without it."

"But what about from this side of the galaxy?" Eliza asked.

"There are no space-faring peoples within 25,000 light-years of Ursinus b," Kolokh said. "At least, that's what Zhan tells me."

"That's a good thing," Kyr said. "Trust me."

"Why?" Cody asked.

"You don't want to know," Kolokh said.

Badri opened his mouth to speak, and Kolokh said, "Wreck," and Enkhid said, "It's ugly. Don't ask. At all. Ever."

"I didn't mean to interrupt you," Kolokh told Enkhid.

"But you also interrupted them"—Enkhid gestured at the Humans—"so it's fine."

So Eliza asked "We keep our street clothes on underneath?" instead of "What the hell happened?" and "If I described the Dyson videos, maybe you'll believe it can't be worse."

"Yes," Cody said.

After everyone had suited up, they did some basic warm-ups, punching pillar bags at one end of the large room. To Eliza's surprise, Badri gave one a punch and it tipped over. That usually took a hard kick, and only from the strongest fighters.

Kyr and Enkhid could do this too, but no one else.

Cody said, "One-on-one, who's first?"

Kolokh said, "Me against Eliza."

Kyr and Enkhid traded looks.

"If you're thirsty, why do you swallow a raindrop?" Kyr exclaimed, gesturing at Eliza.

"These two," Enkhid said, gesturing at Kolokh and Kyr, "and their folksy, old-timey sayings. Kolokh is starting small."

"Apparently," Eliza said. "Don't blink or you'll miss it."

"You're the who's survived a Donner attack," Kolokh said.

"Only sort of," she said, "out of pure luck." And she walked out onto the mat.

Kolokh picked her up and slammed her on the ground. She did a perfect breakfall. She kicked out at him. He grabbed her by the foot. She axe-kicked his hand. He loosened his grip. She kicked out at his groin. He straddled her. He tried to put his hands around her throat. She shrugged. Turned her head before he could get a grip. Pulled his forearms down and against her chest. Explosively bridged her hips. Rolled on top of him, using one leg as a kickstand. Tried to stand. He stood up. He took an angle. He kicked her in the head. Her suit turned red.

"Your hands are freezing, Kolokh," she said, standing up.

"One can perceive temperature through these suits?" Badri asked.

Cody pushed a button on the wrist of her suit to reset it. "Yes."

"Rematch," Kolokh said.

This time, when Kolokh tried to pick her up, she was ready. She dove, her left arm around his gut, her right one behind and between his legs, where she grabbed his belt and yanked. He landed face-first on the mat with a cry of surprise, and she jumped on his back, quickly put him in an arm bar, and started pounding on the back of his head with her free hand. He shook this off as if it were a light breeze and stood up. She fell backward, and he was on top of her in a split second. Her suit turned red.

"Rematch."

This time, she tried to determine whether he was more easily winded than she was.

He was not.

"Re—"

"You're boring everyone," Eliza said.

"May I?" Badri said.

Cody laughed.

"This is funny?" Badri said.

"Have you ever had to defend yourself on the street?"

"I have not." But Badri impassively walked out onto the mat with Kolokh.

Kolokh took a swing, and Badri crouched, immediately throwing an uppercut to Kolokh's armpit. Kolokh gasped and went to his knees. Badri took an angle, grabbed him by the top of his suit, and kneed him under the chin. Kolokh fell back, and Badri punched him in the throat. Kolokh's suit turned red.

The room went completely silent.

"Do it again," Kolokh said.

This time, Badri took an angle and kicked Kolokh behind the knee. Kolokh toppled and landed on his back. Badri kicked Kolokh under the chin and axe-kicked him the throat, and Kolokh's suit turned red.

"What did you do?" Eliza asked. "Because that was incredible."

"I have merely been studying Kharkun anatomy. Speaking informally, in Kharkuns, there is a bundle of nerves under the arm and behind the knee that have an effect similar in quality, although not in mechanism, to kicking a Human male in the testicles. An uppercut exploits another anatomical weakness. Kharkun skulls are more durable than those of Humans, and the cerebrospinal fluid of the Kharkun is viscous. Thus, it is much more difficult to inflict a concussion on such an individual. But Kharkun skeletal and neurological anatomy causes this vulnerability in the chin. Further, Kharkuns have no more anatomical defenses in the throat than a Human does. This is true, is it not, Kolokh?"

"How the hell would I know?" Kolokh said. "I taught high school history!"

Eliza wondered what the literal translation of "high school" was.

Kyr said, "Pilot. I didn't know either. Do all you Humans learn anatomy and physiology?"

"Sadly, no," Cody said.

Enkhid said, "I'm a veterinarian. We don't even learn comparative anatomy."

"You have not exploited this anatomic vulnerability in combat?" Badri asked.

"We don't fight hand to hand. We used—" and Kolokh walked over to a row of weapons in the back of the room and picked out what looked like a machete. "We used these. And now we use lasepistols!"

"Those look brutal," Eliza asked. "Does Lita know how to use one?"

"To run a coffee shop?" Kolokh asked, nonplussed. "We learn how to use these in high school. It's an elective. But we don't use them anymore after that."

"But if you have that ... that knee testicle problem—"

The Kharkuns howled with laughter.

"That knee testicle problem, how come you aren't always accidentally hurting yourselves when you bump into chairs?"

"I used a considerable amount of force, Eliza," Badri said. "These nerve bundles are far beneath the skin."

"What's the Q'a't for?" Cody asked. "The short sword you carry."

Kolokh paused. "Thousands of years ago, when a Kharkun soldier was too hurt or sick to fight anymore, he used it for suicide. We also used them in duels to protect the honor of self or clan. But you can't waste time and money training someone who goes and dies in a bar fight. We also don't particularly need to go to war anymore. We don't use them for executions either, because our executioners are too chickenshit to look the condemned in the eye. Now, they just identify a Kharkun's clan, which is stupid, since you still have to show your ID. Why do you need a Q'a't? Almost no one under the age of twenty wants one, and Malit says he doesn't."

"See?" Enkhid said to the room. "Old-timey."

Suddenly, Kolokh ran at Eliza with the machete in his right hand. Eliza deflected the blade by striking Kolokh's inner arm lengthwise with her left forearm. The machete went flying. She hit him with an elbow strike to the chin, then to the throat. Kolokh's suit turned red.

"That sent a jolt up my arm," Kolokh said, laughing.

"Mine too."

"How'd you do that?" Cody asked. "You're smaller and weaker than he is!"

"Physics."

"Please show me how to do this," Kyr said.

"Next time."

The Humans sparred each other in turn.

When Eliza was sparring with Badri, she realized that neither of them was doing a very good job. Neither of them could go full bore against the other.

Out of the corner of her eye, she could see Kelly watching this intently.

At one point, Badri got Eliza on her back in guard position, Badri between her legs, holding her wrists down. She stopped fighting. She locked eyes with him and whispered, "Hey, I like this position."

Kelly shouted, "You two, get a room!"

The room broke up, even Badri, who was blushing furiously.

Eliza took advantage of his hesitation to twist to one side, push her lower leg against his hip, and push him backward with her other leg. Then she got up. Badri was already standing.

"You could have rolled on top of me," he whispered to Eliza. "I saw you do this with Kelly." He threw a punch.

She ducked. "I never get on top," she whispered to him, and he blushed again.

"Behave," he whispered.

"Later," she whispered.

He froze in embarrassment, and she got him with a body shot. Then she walked over to Kelly before he could respond, leaving Badri blushing, but he locked eyes with her.

Kolokh was fighting Kyr. Eliza noted that all three of the Kharkuns had incorporated Badri's techniques, but the fights still lasted for several minutes. At the end, none of the Kharkuns were even breathing hard.

"Okay," Cody said. "I'm hungry."

"You don't want to go two on one?" Eliza said.

"Tomorrow!"

"Cody," Badri said, "your heart rate remained consistent whether you were punching a pillar bag or fighting an opponent. Did you know this?"

"I do now. And?"

"Are there simulated lasepistols here?" Badri asked.

ON THEIR WAY out of the sparring center, Kelly said, "Some of us are going back to the ship for supplies. Why don't you come along?"

"I'll go," Eliza said.

"Thank you for the invitation," Badri said, "but I intend to meet with Ror and Banner."

Everyone had wolfed down a quick meal and showered. Ruefully, Eliza put her service weapon and magazine in a drawer. Her badge was already in this drawer, and she picked it up for a moment and stared at it before replacing it sadly. She took a lasepistol and holstered it.

Then it had taken time to get properly equipped.

Soon after, she, Baines, Gino, Kelly, an alien Eliza guessed was a Tenurian, and a Kovian met at the gate and headed out. Joining them were Duncan and Scout, the two other service dogs from the *Kestrel*. When Eliza introduced herself to the Kovian, he turned bright purple for a moment and told her to call him Kovian 2.

She turned to the Tenurian and said, "I'm Eliza Benveniste."

He didn't respond.

The Kovian, whose skin seemed to have a baseline color that matched the soil, suddenly adopted the texture of the gravel and trail and said something like, "Uh-oh."

Eliza remembered that octopuses on Earth could match the texture of their surroundings too.

"Address him by name first," Kelly stage-whispered. "And Kovian 2 thinks you're offended. As far as we can tell, that color is when there are misunderstandings."

"Tenurians don't respond unless you call them by name," Baines said. "That's Senn."

Senn was lanky, tall, orange, and reptilian, with spikes above his small yellow eyes. He had slitted pupils and recessed ears. He wore a sleeveless tunic of the perennial Ursan cream and brown leggings stuffed inside leather boots. He wore leather bracelets that extended from wrist to elbow. His belt buckle was dark orange and inlaid with five ivory ovals almost like flower petals. His muzzle ended in something that looked like a pink vestigial beak. She considered his long fingers and decided Tenurians must have evolved from birds.

"Hi, Senn, my name is Eliza Benveniste."

In a saccadic movement, Senn tilted his head and then looked down at her. "Eliza."

Senn's eyes closed, first with a film over them—a nictitating membrane—and then they opened, and the nictitating membrane slid back last. Eliza pictured his pre-humanoid ancestors as a flock in a thick forest, not able to see who was calling to whom, and this linguistic quirk developing to avoid the I-wasn't-talking-to-you-Kevin problem.

"That means *hello*," Kelly said. "When they close their eyes, it's a form of trust, right, Senn?"

"Kelly, Eliza is actually very friendly, kind, and amusing,

which is mostly because she is not trying to kill me." His voice was not sibilant, as she'd expected, but deep.

Eliza looked at Kelly, who nodded. "Senn, pleased to meet you. How long have you been here?"

"Eliza, egg's length."

"So, about a year," Kelly said. "They lay eggs, the mothers guard them, the fathers feed the mothers, and then, well, the young hatch and eat their mothers."

Senn blinked again.

"Oh," Eliza said. "Wow. Okay. Well ... Senn, how did you end up here? At Broken Oar," she added.

"Eliza, Keel didn't die. Then we were here."

He was breathing so rapidly that she wondered how he managed to talk, then realized that he was practically holding his breath when he did, as a Human would when they blew up a balloon. "Senn, do you mean the mother?"

"Eliza, Keel fed the hatchlings a k'k'kah. This is a large mammal." He blinked at her again. "A primate."

"Senn, do you mean that she left the eggs?"

"Eliza, I brought the primate to her." His voice sounded breathless, and there was a quick panting before he inhaled again.

"So she is here?" Then she said, "Senn, does this mean she is here?"

"Eliza, she is at home in the village."

"Senn, how do the hatchlings take this?"

"Eliza, they know no different."

"Senn, is it just the—"

"One of them was eaten by Donners," Baines said quietly. "There were six young."

"Six is a death number," Senn said.

"Senn, you didn't get to the village in time?"

"Keel chucked one of them at the Donners, Eliza," Kelly said, poorly concealing her disgust.

Kovian 2 turned red again, then indigo and red.

Eliza didn't know what to say to this either, so instead, she turned and asked, "Senn, does the weather ever change here?"

He didn't acknowledge that she had spoken. Then he said, "Eliza, define change."

"Senn, temperature, cloud cover, wind speed, humidity, precipitation, or a combination of these."

"Soon," he said, tilting his head again.

"Senn, what time span do you mean by 'soon'?"

He looked at the group as a whole. "'Soon' means soon. Hot and more hot, more water and more water in the air, wind and more wind. Lightning and noise. Many rain."

"Now he's addressing all of us," Kelly said. "So no name signifier needed."

"I'm assuming there's a drainage system for Broken Oar," Eliza said.

"You missed it?" Kelly asked. "All around the edge, right at the thresholds. Water flows into the drainage slits and out the far side through a massive drainpipe. Kolokh says it's dramatic. The winds can get faster than 160 kilometers an hour."

"How fast is that? We don't use the metric system where I come from."

"So ... what," Gino said playfully, "egg squirts per cow? Inches per avalanche? That's a hundred miles an hour, and we get Category 2 hurricanes all summer."

Eliza burst out laughing. Then she said, "My God, I'd hate to get caught out in that." She saw that the Kovian 2 had turned pink.

"Well, the village is fortified against these storms," Kelly said.

"Oh, good," Eliza said. "And you said no one knows who built this place?"

"Like I said, not even the Ursans know, and no one's found any remains," Gino answered.

"I wonder if Jamie wrote it." Then Eliza realized her mistake.

"You mean like a habitat for a pet hamster?" Gino asked. "I hope you really don't think that, because that's crazy."

"No, I guess I don't. But you can understand my—"

"I can understand the idea of a book as a doorway. Sort of. But plopping a whole village in the middle of a planet and sticking us all here like toys? Nope, not at all."

"I'm with Gino," Baines said. "That's really completely creepy. I remember my whole childhood. No way that shithead wrote all that."

"No," Gino said, "she thinks he *invented* us."

Kovian 2 immediately matched the texture of the ground as well as the color.

"We're not arguing," Eliza said to Kovian 2.

"No," Gino said. "We're not arguing. We're pointing out that Eliza's idea is insane. Eliza, tell me you see now that that idea is insane."

"Yes. Yes, I guess it is. But you didn't walk out of an office to find yourself on a trail in a universe depicted in your partner's novel and end up in a village that magically appeared one day either. You arrived here on purpose on a ship using technology that breaks the laws of physics in my universe, and now we can ask a machine to make something for us and then it magically appears. Then there are these translator thingies. If, God forbid, I somehow ended up back where I came from and told my superiors what had happened to me here and who I'd met, they'd send me for a psych consult. And I'd never work again."

The Kovian turned back to his baseline Ursinus soil color and normal texture. "She's making a kind of sense. She read about you, and now she's talking to you. She's not saying you're not real. Right?"

Eliza nearly felt like crying. Then she imagined Badri back at Broken Oar and relaxed. "Right. I never said you weren't real. I never even said you were book characters."

"Then what are you saying?" Gino said. "Clarify this for me."

"Nothing about that village weirds you out? None of it? Tell me the mechanism by which those dispensers work. Tell me how these translators work. I'm not saying Jamie created *you*, but you can understand—"

"Jamie created a portal with his words," Kovian 2 said. "He didn't put anything here. He saw and heard, but imperfectly. For example, the book is about a rebellion, and there's nothing here to rebel *against*. I agree with you, Eliza, that the rest of it is ... I have no words. Gino, you'd admit the village and the technology in it are surreal."

"It's mystifying."

"He's not a god, Eliza," Kelly said. "He's a shitty historian. About the rest of this? Who the fuck knows. I guess we'll figure it out eventually."

"Or not," Gino said.

Kovian 2 managed to keep up, each tentacle moving faster than the average snake on Earth.

The dogs avoided Senn.

The weather was hot and humid, and to Eliza, this was thunderstorm weather. Thinking of Tauxenent County, she said, "Captain, has anyone checked the weather forecast?"

"Oh," Baines said, "we're only gonna be gone three hours. The wet season isn't for a few weeks yet."

"How often have you made this trip, Captain?"

"We go several times a week. We're gradually trying to bring our seed stores over, and ship rations, in case those dispensers break."

"Cody comes back out to study the—the *Macrodactylus fatalis,*" Kelly said. "He's still not sure what they eat or how they mate, just that they grow alongside freshwater ponds, streams, and so on. After—after what happened to Jennifer, he thought they might have some intelligence, given that they've never attacked the dogs."

"Will I be able to *meet* a dickweed?" Eliza said.

"Whoa!" Gino said.

"It's okay, Gino," Kelly said. "I'll read her the sex scenes between her and Jamie in *The Tauxenent Strangler.*"

"You will *not*!" Eliza said.

"Don't worry, they're so awful they're funny."

"We keep trying to think of something more formal to call the *Macrodactylus,* but we never can," Kelly said. "There are smaller ones in ponds and streams."

"Do they ever monitor weather at Broken Oar?" Eliza asked.

"Yes. But this is a short trip."

"What about these jumpsuits? How resistant are they?"

"We wear these when it's hot."

"And if the temperature drops?"

"You know you can just go back, right?" Kelly said.

"That's not why I'm asking." It *was* why she was asking. But she couldn't bring herself to turn around. She feared it would do permanent damage to her relationship with the group.

After twenty more minutes of walking, they passed the inscription she'd made in the ground. Something had toppled the cairn, and the lichenwood bunch was gone.

Kelly pointed and asked, "What's that about?"

"It's ... it's where I appeared. I'd stepped out of Badri's office to go talk to Jamie and ended up here. I didn't know what else to do. I thought it was ... maybe a connection to someone I would never see again." She bent and put the cairn back together. "And then it was a road sign." Thinking of Badri back at the village with Ror and Banner, her relief was almost visceral.

"It's a nice view of the ocean at least," Kelly said. "You could have appeared a mile offshore."

"Or in the middle of the reed forest," Baines said. "This Jamie of yours was a piece of work."

"I keep trying to reach around my back for the knife." Still, Eliza got a flash of him sitting across a table from her at The Lion and had to control her tears.

"Well, you're here now," Baines said. "We're all trying to get used to it all, but there's so much to see and learn!"

About twenty minutes later, Eliza saw, about seventy-five feet away, a herd of eight-legged animals eating the lichenwood surrounding the purple ferns. They reminded her of Highland cattle, but their shaggy fur was black and green in a calico pattern, camouflage against the lichenwood, and they had reed-colored armor in a saddle pattern. Their large, soft, dark brown eyes dilated open and shut. Their tails were shaggy, with a blunted end. The largest ones had horns. The calves were lichenwood gray. The animals ripped the lichenwood out of the ground, constantly eating. Even as far away as she was, she could smell a faint musk coming from them. They all looked so sweet that Eliza wanted to kiss one on the muzzle.

She expected the Highland cattle to lumber when they moved, but they were graceful. Their hooves were cloven. "How are they not too hot?" she said softly. Then she remembered that thick fur can shield the skin too.

In the background, there were eight-legged wolves. They had a double coat of green-and-black calico fur and shaggy tails. She wondered if the tails dropped off and grew back and wondered what could eat a Banner's wolf.

The Highland cattle were bigger, but they were also slower and less agile than the Banner's wolves.

The Banner's wolves were converging on a calf, but the herd surrounded the calf. The Banner's wolves harried the calf's mother—biting at her face and throat. She turned around and slammed one of them with her tail. The wolf squealed and limped to the back of the pack.

Over time, the pack gradually cut off a different calf from the herd. Eliza saw that the wolf who had taken a hit had shaken it off.

The calf they'd isolated was lame. The wolf pack brought it down easily, biting its other hind leg and, to Eliza's relief, ripping open the calf's neck and not starting in the middle. Or worse.

Its mother issued a loud call, but the pack was too large for her to attack them on her own, and the rest of the herd seemed more invested in protecting the calves in the middle than in protecting the lame one.

Bats started dive-bombing the kill almost immediately. One bat miscalculated, and a Highland reared up, took it by the wing, shook it like a dog would, and ate it.

"Ungulates on Ursinus b are facultative herbivores too," Eliza said. "Who knew?"

"Whats are what?" Gino asked.

"Ungulates are hoofed mammals," Eliza said. "Facultative herbivores are—what you just saw. There are videos of cows on Earth eating snakes, and deer eat birds. Like that—that Highland cow just did."

"No way!" Kelly said. "How do you know?"

"A forensic anthropologist told me."

Gino laughed in horror.

"This is what we came for," Baines said, staring at the animals, eyes glittering.

Gino and Kelly traded looks.

After a time, they walked down a low ridge to the ocean. This was spiral beach. Cliffs, rocks, and boulders, then sand, then more cliffs, rocks, and boulders as far as Eliza could see. The waves weren't more than four feet high. The beach was strewn with seaweed—some indigo, some black—and it had a sharp, kelp-like smell. Small crustaceans crawled in the seaweed. Flying creatures who looked like bats dove into the water and flew up again with what looked like fish. She wished they'd made seagull sounds. Their absence made the beach seem incomplete.

"Which way to the ship?" Eliza asked.

"If you don't take this turnoff and you stay on the trail, you walk through the reed forest and you get to the ship," Gino said. "It was half an hour from the village to the inscription and the cairn where you—where you came through. From Broken Oar, it's an hour to the ship."

Duncan and Scout were having none of the ocean, sniffing at the sand as the water receded and retreating as the water flowed back in.

Eliza stooped to let the water flow between her fingers, and the water was warm.

※

Before the group reached the second cliff, they turned left, walking up a trail. They followed the trail back inland until they reached the reed forest.

"Why didn't we just take a straight path?" Eliza asked.

"We wanted to give you a walk on the beach," Baines said.

"Thanks." Looking at Gino, she said, "I hope you're still not mad at me."

"Your situation is definitely fucked up. No."

Someone had, indeed, built a trail through the reed forest. Eliza looked up at Baines and said, "Maura must have been furious."

Baines said, "How do you—oh, right. Yes, she was. But we're still going back and forth from ship to town, and we have to avoid being ambushed."

"Speaking of which, why haven't any Donners shown up?"

"Maybe because of the dogs," Gino said.

"What do the Ursans know about them?"

"Well, a practically immortal species," Gino said, "turns out to be stunningly time-blind. They don't know when the Donners showed up."

"Time-blind?"

"Don't keep track of when things happened. In Humans, it makes them chronically late. Or a doctor says, 'When did that start hurting?' and the time-blind patient says, 'Fuck, I dunno, Doc.' Ursans live forever, or at least they practically do. What does time matter to them?"

Eliza considered. "I guess that makes sense. I'll analyze that in more detail after I get used to those dispensers. What do you know about the Donners?"

"Not much," Baines said. "They don't use tools. We've never heard them make a sound, except a weird, monotonous high squeal when they die. Cody says they sound like desert rain frogs."

Eliza laughed. "Those aren't much bigger than a golf ball! And that sound! I've seen videos."

"Yep," Gino said. "Pretty weird for something so big and miserably dangerous."

The soil made a gravel sound under their feet and the wind made shushing sounds in the tops of the reeds. When the stalks collided, they made wind chime sounds. The forest smelled a bit like fallen leaves. Above them, they saw what looked like bees landing on the tufts and flying away. In the background were what sounded like cicadas.

The group fell silent to take it all in.

At one point, the reeds collided, and the cicadas' calls abruptly stopped. Eliza stopped for a moment, but Gino said, "We always smell 'em first."

"But it's something."

"It's something not headed our way," he replied.

Crawling up and down the reeds were Banner's geckos.

Eliza took a breath. "Did you ever get to pet one? They look like feathery little dogs!"

"No one's tried," Baines said. "They get pretty tense if you get too near them. Cody thinks they're pretty easily stressed. The bats eat them, and sometimes the—what did you call them?—the Highland cows will grab one if they get too far out of the forest."

On another reed, she saw some of the indigo animals. One had its proboscis deep into a reed. Several were walking up the reeds. Suddenly, one flew at Eliza, and she ducked.

"Oh, God! Let's get *out* of here!"

But it collided with a thicker reed and landed in the dirt.

Throughout their walk, Eliza heard the reeds collide on one side or the other off the trail, and she could hear, faintly, animal footsteps.

"Whatever it is," Kelly said, rolling her eyes, "they never bother us. So stop being so jumpy. You're making me nervous."

"Sorry. New here. Have you ever seen what makes that sound? It sounds pretty big."

"We haven't identified all the animals here," Baines said. "We haven't been here that long. First time we heard that sound was our second day here. They probably are big. They've never bothered us. Maybe they eat Donners. I don't know. I don't care."

Eliza cared, but nothing had crossed their path, and she fervently hoped they ate Donners.

Eventually, they went through a clearing, and Eliza saw footprints and a flat marker in the ground at the edge of it, and she realized this was Chloe's headstone.

The group stood next to it for a moment with their heads bowed. The wind made soft sounds through the reeds, and the musical notes seemed more muted. Kelly was whispering. Then she quickly walked down the trail.

"She gives her updates," Gino said to Eliza quietly.

Eliza remembered Chloe's photograph in the case file and the crime scene in her town house, and she thought about asking if Chloe's fiancée was named Rafaella. Suddenly, it seemed very important that she do that. "Did—did she have a fiancée named Rafaella DeMeo?"

Kelly looked at Eliza sharply. "Used to. She's still on Earth —oh."

"Yeah," Eliza said. "She was appointed on the Dyson case too. She wasn't in the book?"

"No."

"You have no idea how desperately I'm trying to avoid running screaming into the wilderness right now," Gino said in a conversational tone.

"I understand more and more why you're so troubled, Eliza," Kovian 2 said.

"Thank you."

They walked a few minutes in silence.

Suddenly, she smelled Donners. The group heard a sharper sound of reed on reed. To her horror, Eliza heard the sound of flesh being torn from bone. Remembering Dyson's videos, she froze.

The dogs began growling.

Through the reeds, they saw two Donners squatting over another one, their faces covered with indigo gore, but they looked up and stared straight at the group with their inanimate, expressionless eyes.

They had been feasting on the body of a Donner on the ground.

Duncan and Scout started murder-barking, hackles up.

The Donners stood up, the movement oddly graceful, and Eliza drew her lasepistol, but they fairly melted into the reed forest.

Duncan and Scout quieted themselves. Gino rewarded both of them with a treat and a "Good doggies for saving us from those horrors."

After a moment, Eliza said, "They smell like someone had turned off the climate control in Badri's morgue."

The humanoids laughed, with the exception of Senn, who tilted his head with that saccadic movement and closed his eyes.

Kovian 2 turned pink.

"They eat each other," Gino said. "Figures."

After they had walked a few meters out of the reed forest, Eliza could see the ship in the distance, and she longed to see it up close, to walk around inside it—a real starship!

But in the air in front of the group, there were black, shadowy animals built like tailless manta rays floating sideways, moving with the undulating motion of fish and forming a school. She counted six of them. They had no eyes or mouth as far as Eliza could tell. They were the size of a car door.

Eliza noted that Duncan and Scout hadn't uttered a sound.

"Hold up," Baines said. "What are those?"

"How ... how are they staying up there?" Gino whispered.

"They're beautiful," Eliza said.

Kovian 2 turned black.

When he did, the Shadows "swam" in his direction. Kovian 2 immediately turned red and then camouflaged himself, looking almost like he was at one with the ground. Eliza stifled a laugh. It so resembled "Never mind!"

Senn pulled his lasepistol out and Eliza took it from him. "Senn, what the hell do you think you're doing?"

"Six is a death number," he said, rubbing his long trigger finger. "Eliza, return that please."

"Senn, nope," Eliza said. "With you just gratuitously going to shoot them?"

Gino said, "Senn, the fuck? I thought we got past this shit."

"Six is a death number."

Eliza wondered if the Kharkuns could hear the heartbeat of a Tenurian and thought of how exhausting that sound would eventually become.

"Senn, it sure as hell will be if I send your ass back to Broken Oar alone!" Gino said.

Gino got within two inches of Senn, who was taller, and

Eliza wondered if there would be a fight. Kovian 2 turned bright red.

"And Donners, they don't like Tenurians," Kelly said. "Right, Senn?"

Senn looked at the six beings in the sky, turned on his heel, and walked in the other direction.

"Hey, Senn!" Gino said. "Come back! You trying to kill yourself?"

But Senn kept walking.

"Tenurians are insane," Baines said.

"Ironically," Eliza said, "it turns out that there are a whole lot more than six of them!"

In fact, there were more and more gradually converging above them, so many that Eliza lost count.

Mating? Migration? she wondered.

As soon as Senn was out of sight, a Shadow quickly dove, wrapped itself around Eliza like a blanket, did a figure eight, and wrapped around Gino, then "swam" back into the air.

Eliza hit the ground in agony, hearing the crackle of lichen-wood. She curled in a fetal position, shouting, "Don't hurt them! Don't hurt them!"

Next to her, she heard Gino on the ground, moaning.

Someone touched her shoulder. She realized she'd been squeezing her eyes shut and opened them. Then she realized that she was completely blind.

Next to her, Gino was screaming, "I can't see! I can't see! Fuck my life, I can't see!"

The pain subsiding, Eliza stood, and she said, "They made contact with the two people who were protecting them." *When they touched me, they were so deliciously soft.*

"That's a hell of a thank-you!" Baines said.

"It was," Eliza said. "They're sentient." She realized that she could see what they saw. "Gino?"

"Fuck me," Gino replied, "but this is weird. I can see what they see. Eliza's right, Captain. They're harmless, and they're sentient."

Eliza said, "At ninety degrees, there's a herd of Donners headed our way. Thirty of them. They're about a quarter of a mile that way," and she pointed.

"We're downwind of them," Gino said. "That'll suck and be great at the same time."

"Thanks, guys!" Eliza called to the Shadows.

"Do we have time to turn around and go back?" Baines asked.

"Yes, Captain," Gino said. "In fact, we should."

"Let's go," Baines ordered, "before we *have* to shoot one."

Eliza realized that she could now communicate with Kovian 2 telepathically. She got an image of Kovian 2 ripping Senn apart and eating his entrails, and she shuddered, desperately grateful that the image wasn't strong enough to taste as well as see.

"*I can dream*," Kovian 2 thought to her, turning dark red.

Eliza laughed. Then she said, "*I forgot you're telepathic.*"

"*Only with each other and the Spiders. Only when we're close. Now with the Shadows and you.*"

"*Are you talking to Gino too?*"

"*Too many number thoughts.*"

Eliza laughed again.

"Why are you laughing?" Baines demanded.

"*Can I tell her?*" Eliza asked Kovian 2.

Eliza got a barrage of imagery and emotion that in part consisted of Kovian 2 eating a mollusk and decided that it was fine.

"Kovian 2's telepathic," Eliza said. "And the Shadows are telling us to hurry. There's a storm coming off the coast. We have about two hours. I thought we had a few weeks!" She didn't mention that the mollusk had tasted good, even if it was raw.

"We'll barely make it!" Gino said.

"I thought we had a few weeks!" Eliza said again.

"Weather doesn't send us a damn memo!" Baines said.

The thunderheads were so thick that it was almost dark. Suddenly, there was a thunderclap and Eliza jumped. Kovian 2 went multicolor. "*Too close,*" he said to her. His gills were rippling.

When the group got to where Eliza knew her inscription was, the Shadow had gotten too high, and she couldn't see it. But she saw the top of her own head.

"Gino, I see myself from above! This is fucked up. One more fucked-up thing."

Gino barked out a laugh.

She started at another thunderclap. The lightning was so close it looked like broad daylight for a microsecond.

The group started running.

None of us are in good enough shape to run the whole way, Eliza thought, panicking. *We won't get there fast enough!*

"Where's Senn?" Eliza asked.

"Who knows?" Kelly said over the wind.

Eliza stared at the Ursan lightning show above her and, for a moment, she was sitting on her porch back home and watching the sky. Then she realized that she would have taken a look at a storm like this one and gone inside and unplugged all her electronics.

All at once, the temperature plummeted. She gasped at the cold. She saw from above that they were still fifteen minutes from Broken Oar, but a freezing gust of wind knocked them nearly off their feet. She wondered about the dogs.

"*Too cold for me. Too fucking cold for me,*" Kovian 2 said.

Then the downpour came, and the world went black for Eliza.

"Blind again!" Gino called from ahead of her.

"Me too, Gino!"

From the sounds of the thunder, Eliza guessed that the lightning was yards from them, not miles from them.

She felt a hand on her forearm, then heard a voice right up near her ear. "It's me. Kelly. I'll guide you. Captain's got Gino up ahead."

Eliza nodded and said, "Thanks!"

The wind was manageable, but the gusts were getting faster. She was nearly knocked off her feet, and she heard Scout yelp.

Thinking of Bear, Eliza said, "Can you and Captain Baines carry the dogs?"

"We could!" Kelly yelled over the wind. "But we can't guide you and Gino at the same time!"

"Get the dogs inside the village! I'll wait here!"

"Are you insane?" Kelly replied. "You could get hypothermia out here!"

"And the dogs could get blown into the reed forest! Kovian 2 can guide Gino! We're not *that* far! Someone can come back in a few minutes! I'll sit on the ground and stay put, I promise! Please save the dogs! I'll be here!" And then Eliza sat.

CHAPTER
TWENTY-EIGHT

AS SOON AS the group's footsteps receded, Eliza started crying quietly from the cold. She was shivering violently. Then the hair on Eliza's arms stood up. Anticipating a lightning strike, she balanced on the balls of her feet, hugged her shins, and buried her face against her thighs. The thunderclap was so loud that her ears started ringing.

The gusts of wind grew stronger. Miserable, Eliza was at least grateful there were no branches or trash can lids flying in the air.

Then something that felt like hail started pelting her, and she covered her head. By now, she was full-on sobbing.

She remembered that Baines told her there was a pup tent in her backpack, which Baines had shown her before they left the village. The captain had described it as "a thick square." Eliza took off the backpack and did a methodical search with her hands.

There wasn't one. There was nothing square-shaped in the backpack at all. Eliza zipped the pack back up and put it on her back again, wondering what the hell good the backpack would do her.

She was soaked through, and the cold was agonizing.

The thunderclaps were closer and closer together and louder and louder.

Eliza thought about trying to crawl back to Broken Oar, or at least meeting someone halfway. The wind was practically blowing through her.

Even with the wind and thunder, she could hear the ocean, and every time the surf broke, she jumped.

Heart pounding in terror, she started crawling, feeling the water running down the trail and the gravel against her palms, figuring that she could stay on the part of the trail abutting the lichenwood and follow the runoff upstream. That would keep her away from the cliff and also help guide her to the village. As she crawled, she fell over, seized with vertigo. She vomited, then got back up on her hands and knees. Even moving her mouth was too much, and eventually, she started vomiting bile.

From the nausea and the vertigo, she was nearly glued to the ground. As miserable as the cold was, the nausea and vertigo were worse.

She tried to move anyway. She realized that if she didn't, she could freeze to death out here. The gusting wind actually nudged her in the ribs even though she was stationary on her hands and knees.

I can't leave Badri alone here. That would be the worst dirty trick I could ever play.

She started crawling. Every time she fell, she got back up. Occasionally, a bout of vomiting seized her, but her stomach was empty. Each time, she got back up and resumed crawling.

She was having difficulty judging textures with her numb fingertips. She couldn't feel the rainwater anymore. She decided to inch her way forward, hoping that if she somehow came to the edge of the cliff, she'd feel it and pull back in time.

Only a moment later, Eliza felt the ground give, and she clawed and groped at the ground for purchase, but it wasn't enough.

✳

The group arrived at the gate of the village. After the door opened, they stepped inside out of the weather. Baines turned to make sure that everyone was accounted for. Both of the dogs shook themselves off.

"Eliza stayed out there," Kovian 2 said. He was the color of skim milk.

"*Are you out of your mind?*" Gino yelled. "It's freezing out there, and the wind is gusting to fuck-me kilometers per hour! Why didn't you warn her?"

Through chattering teeth, Kelly said, "I told you that she wouldn't budge! She sat down and wouldn't come with us. She was too worried about the dogs getting thrown into the reed forest."

"She was right," Gino said. "She also asked about the weather."

After a moment of uncomfortable silence, Kelly said, "You don't look good, Kovian 2."

"We have to go back for her," Baines said. "But first, we have to get Gino to the hospital."

Kovian 2 said, "It's too cold for me. I've got to get warm or else I'll end up hibernating. I'm sorry. Please go find her!" And he left.

As the trio entered the hospital, Badri met them at the door. "Where is Eliza?"

Ignoring him, Baines said, "Could someone please give us some help here? Gino's blind! And someone get us some dry clothes!"

Belek came forward. He and a Kanninoin lifted Gino onto a gurney, and the Kanninoin ferried him into one of the bays in the back.

Belek looked at Baines and Kelly and said, "You two, out of those wet clothes!"

"You don't have to tell us twice," Kelly said, teeth chattering.

Belek's feet tapped the floor as he moved, and the stalks of his eyes were even with Baines's. "Johalo will do his best with Gino until a Human doctor gets here—one who treats *live* patients."

"Where is Eliza?" Badri asked again.

But the two women moved behind a curtain to change clothes.

"Where is Eliza? Tell me!"

From behind the curtain, Kelly said, "She's still out there wait—"

"In that weather? Why did you leave her?"

Baines came out, dressed in dry clothes. "I didn't leave anyone. She sat down and wouldn't budge."

Badri was deadly calm. He walked up and crowded her. "Why would she do this?"

"Back off!" Baines said. "I'm captain here!"

Badri looked at her like she was talking backward. "We have to bring her back. And I am not in your chain of command! I am in *no one's chain of command!*"

"The dogs," Kelly said, brushing the curtain back and walking out. "We couldn't carry the dogs and lead Eliza too. She's blind. The dogs could have been blown into the reed forest, and she was afraid."

Belek checked a computer, his feet tapping the floor,

antenna pointing at Badri. "It's too dangerous for any of us. Our instruments show that winds are gusting to 110 kilometers per hour right now. The temperature out there is three degrees Celsius. There is hail. And the lightning strikes are too frequent and too close. It's too dangerous."

"She can't survive out there under those conditions!" Badri said, eyes welling up. "Why did you not drag her here by force?"

"Because," Kelly said, "she wouldn't go! I told you that!"

There was a chair in front of a computer console a few feet away, and Badri sat down in it. "How long do these storms last?"

"Hours or days," Belek said. "Or maybe solstices. There's no way to know."

"And you have food dispensers but no motor vehicles?" Badri asked.

"No one has ever needed them, Dr. Trivedi," the Ursan said.

"Well, you do now." He looked at the floor and said, nearly too low for Baines to hear, "This will be a recovery and not a rescue."

Baines now wore a long, cream-colored tunic and leggings, but she'd brought her backpack in with her, which was still cold, wet, and uncomfortable to carry.

Having only been in the hospital before briefly, Baines looked around. The door to the hospital was in the corner. To its left was a wall. Perpendicular to the wall, there were four gurneys separated by curtains. On her right, along the same wall of the room as the door, there was a long, narrow table, on which she saw two computer consoles and beneath which were transparent cabinets containing shelves of supplies and several machines. Above the table were more cabinets. At the far end, Baines thought she recognized a large Hansen scanner. There were two crash carts and a large device that she did not recognize. Otherwise, there was all the equipment and supplies she remembered from her own trips to the ER. Across from the four gurneys, on the opposite wall, there were four more.

If she walked down the wide space between the gurneys toward the back of the room, she'd get to a set of double doors. Above them, there was writing in black that no one could read, sharp-edged, with dots, curves, parallel lines, and half circles. This writing was identical to the markings beside the apartment doors, she realized.

The walls and floors were white.

She wondered why she couldn't smell any disinfectant, as she would have back on Earth.

Kelly walked over to her, dressed in the same clothing as Baines.

Badri was still sitting on a chair and staring at the door.

"You're not going out there," Baines said to him. Then she opened the backpack and pulled out a rectangle that looked like foil and was the size of a sheet of printer paper and as thick as the average-sized paperback. She put this rectangle on the floor and pulled a tab on the side.

It inflated into a pup tent.

Badri said, "What is this?"

"If you opened this up on the ground instead of a tile floor, it would spike itself into the soil. It can withstand winds up to 150 kilometers per hour, and it preserves body heat. If it gets too cold, it heats up. It's climate-controlled for twenty-four hours. Eliza knew this was in her backpack because I told her about it before we left. She's probably sitting in hers right now."

"Yet you did not do this for her, nor did you use this on your own."

"She's barely a kilometer from the door, Badri," Kelly said. "She was worried about the dogs."

Badri gestured at Baines. "And that one did not provide for her safety."

"Badri, you can't do anything right now," Kelly said. "Go home. Take care of your own dogs. Then get some sleep if you can. Trust that Eliza has some survival skills. We'll go find her tomorrow. It will take all of ten minutes."

Badri stared at the tent for a moment, then he got up and walked out.

Kelly and Baines traded looks.

"No, he's not that stupid," Baines said. "In his line of work, he knows how often untrained rescuers end up in his morgue."

ELIZA LANDED HARD. The pain on impact was excruciating. When she cried out, she heard an echo.

She lay there stunned and suddenly, inexplicably warm. The warmth was delicious, but she was afraid of how badly she might have been hurt.

Eliza realized that she'd landed on some kind of rock ledge. Where her head was facing, she felt warmth. Then she reached out and felt around, realizing that it was a tunnel. She crawled into it, aiming for the warmth, stopping often because of the abject misery of the vertigo, until she no longer felt the wind and the rain, just warmth and discomfort from lying on the cold, rocky floor in damp clothes.

She had feeling and motion in all her extremities. It hurt to breathe.

She rolled over on her side, hyperventilating from the vertigo.

Then she fell asleep.

✳

When Eliza woke up, still in her damp clothes, she was warm. She remembered where she was. But as soon as she moved, the vertigo returned. It was so severe, she could not tell which way was up.

Given how the thunder caused her ears to ring, Eliza knew that there was a massive electrical storm outside. She could hear the waves below. She wondered idly what *thing* she might have awakened in the tunnel.

Her body hurt all over, and she was hungry and thirsty. She reached around for the tube leading to the CamelBak and was immediately overcome with vertigo. She curled into a fetal position, holding her head.

When it passed, she tried closing her eyes again and felt a little bit better. But every time she moved, the vertigo returned. She lay on the floor of the tunnel, miserable.

After a time, Eliza realized that she had somehow dozed off again. She tried gingerly to move. The vertigo had morphed into a raging headache. She wondered how long she had been asleep. She could hear that it was still raining outside.

She opened her eyes. Her breath caught. *I can see again!* She blinked a few times. It was still dark aside from the almost constant lightning.

The tunnel, though, was like an amplifier to the thunder, and she prayed that the lightning couldn't strike her where she sat. She also wondered why her ears had stopped ringing.

Eliza reached for the tube connected to the CamelBak and drank deeply. Then she reached into the knapsack to take a quick inventory in the light of the electrical storm. She searched for a change of clothes and found none.

Of course not, she thought in disgust.

She found a packet labeled CAL-POD. The other bit of

writing on the label made it clear it was an emergency food source, so she opened it. It fit in her palm, was football-shaped, and had the color and texture of a stale brownie. She stuffed the empty packet into the backpack. Then she bit into the Cal-Pod. It was delicious, but the aftertaste nearly made her gag. She wolfed it down anyway, trying to clear the taste out of her mouth with more water. She decided not to contemplate what might be living in the tunnels or whether they were drainage tunnels.

Her headache was getting worse.

After her meal, she was feeling a little better. She reached to her hip for her smartphone and realized that her smartphone and lasepistol were gone. Her comm-watch was cracked and nonfunctional.

She opened another compartment in her knapsack and found a first aid kit. There was writing on some of the items, and she prayed that she could read it and that if she could read it, she could understand it. She took out a pill bottle and inspected it.

PAIN RELIEF, SEDATING. CAUTION: RESPIRATORY DEPRESSANT.

She did not want to be sedated.

Eliza pulled out another pill container: PAIN RELIEF, MILD.

Who knew what this was? She didn't care. TAKE ONE OR TWO CAPSULES EVERY 4–6 HOURS.

She opened up the bottle and took two pills, smiling grimly at the familiar bitter aftertaste.

She dug around some more and found another Cal-Pod and then a device the size of a smartphone. She looked at it: GEOLOCATION.

Geolocation?

Geolocation! "They can find me with this!"

There was a button marked ON. She pushed it.

BAINES WOKE up and walked out her front door. Though the sky was overcast, the rain had stopped. She went back inside and called Kelly.

After Baines dressed and ate, she went to Badri's door and knocked.

After a moment, he opened it. He looked like he'd been up all night.

"Let's go get your girlfriend, Badri."

"If she is unharmed, why has she not returned on her own?"

"Let's go—"

Badri came out, dressed in blue jeans and a black T-shirt with a colorful diagram of a Human heart.

When they got to the entrance of the village, they found Kelly and Belek. Belek was carrying objects on his flanks from a harness on his back. Also on his back was a gurney. "You primates really are limited in what you can carry, aren't you?" he remarked.

"Yep," Baines said, "we Humans seem to suck at everything."

Kolokh and Scout walked up.

"Belek, what have you brought with you?" Badri asked in horror.

"A gurney. MediKit. And—"

"And rope," Badri said, "for ..."

"To recover her body, Badri. In case she is dead."

The group walked out the gate, Baines wondering how Belek's carapace changed color. When they got to where Kelly had left Eliza, Baines stopped, staring pointlessly at the ground.

"Where is she?" Badri demanded. "You say you left her here. *Where is she?*"

"There are no Donners out, Badri," Baines said. "Not in this. Let's just keep walking."

It was overcast and muggy, and the surf was still high. The trail was wet, and the group occasionally stepped in puddles with a slapping sound. Scout stopped to drink from one and then trotted along behind them.

After about twenty minutes, Badri stopped. The *EB* and the arrow were full of water, and the cairn had blown over.

Scout walked to the cliff and started barking furiously.

Kolokh saw it before Badri did. He stood in Badri's path and said, "Go back."

"What have you found?"

"Human, turn around and go back and wait."

"I will go through you, if I must, Kharkun or not."

With a look of sympathy, Kolokh moved aside.

There were marks on the edge of the cliff, and new dirt caved in. Below, the beach was spotted with kelp, and from the debris, it was clear that at the height of the storm, the tide had covered the beach.

*

Eliza woke up. She was sore all over, and worse, she desperately had to urinate.

What now?

She opened up the backpack again. After rifling through it for a few minutes, she found a flat object the size of a sheet of paper. TOILET.

Eliza smiled. "Space Force thought of everything!"

She pushed the button, and the object opened into what looked like a child's potty. Eliza laughed, with an edge of hysteria. The thing also included a packet of wipes, which were helpfully labeled WIPES.

When she finished, it folded up like a clamshell—a sealed clamshell, she noted with relief.

Eliza went to the mouth of the tunnel, and she saw that the ledge overlooked the ocean. She looked at the clamshell, looked in the tunnel, looked at the sea, and thought, *I'm a piece of shit.* And she hurled it over the side. It fell in and disappeared.

As it fell, she decided that she was about ninety feet above the shore. She looked up and realized that she had not fallen far at all.

Eliza used the rest of the wipes to clean her face. She braced herself and ate another Cal-Pod and drank some more water. Then she wondered what to do with herself.

She touched the walls, and they were smooth. So was the floor of the tunnel.

Next, she sifted through the backpack's contents again and this time found a pack of STIMULANT GUM.

She popped a piece in her mouth and quickly started feeling better.

Eliza thought for a moment and found the geolocator. She saw that it was still working. She wondered whether the thick rock overhead would interfere with transmission and decided to move it closer to the mouth of the tunnel.

"They have to be looking for me. Badri will make them." Then she covered her face in shame. *I almost left him alone here.*

Scout was still barking like mad.

Baines's comm-watch lit up. "Hey," she said, "there's a geolocation beacon going off!" Then she looked around quizzically. "Down there?"

Belek unloaded his equipment.

AFTER KOLOKH UNHOOKED Eliza and she stood up, Badri held her so hard she could hardly breathe. Her ribs were so sore that she cried out in pain.

He took a step back and said, "That was selfish and cruel, this risk that you took."

"Badri, I thought I'd be okay, but the dogs would've been blown into the reeds where the Donners are! I didn't know how bad it would get!"

"You had only *two hours* in those conditions!" Badri said, despair in his voice.

"And I knew that how? Baines said there was a pup tent in my pack, and there wasn't one! Where is it, Baines?" Eliza handed Baines the backpack.

Baines dumped it out. The bladder of water fell to the ground with the slap of a dying fish, but there was no pup tent.

"Well, shit," Baines said. "I must have forgotten! I'm sorry, we were only gonna be gone a little bit! The storms weren't supposed to start for another few weeks!"

"Badri, I couldn't have known!" Eliza said, ignoring Baines. "I've never seen conditions like this before. My hiking experience is walking to my office from my car! I didn't think I was risking my life!"

"But you thought the dogs were risking their lives?"

"How would they have done in the reed forest, do you think? Why would Baines have led a group into conditions that could have killed us? Why wasn't the pup tent in my pack?"

"She has done this before, has she not?" Badri looked at Baines in fury. "Your recklessness has caused two deaths and almost a third. Perhaps," he said cryptically, "there could have been a fourth."

"You're wrong, Badri," Baines replied. "I have the psychological profile of an adventurer!"

"Reckless. Shamefully reckless. Have you learned nothing?"

"What do you mean a fourth?" Belek asked.

"Be angry at me for being ignorant," Eliza said tearfully. "Everyone thought this season was weeks away! I didn't think I could have died when I decided to wait!"

"The sun is the sun!" Kolokh said angrily.

Eliza felt his speech in her chest.

"Did you know about these tunnels, Baines?" Badri asked.

"That's *Captain* Baines. And no, I didn't."

Eliza's steps were tentative. She had hurt her hip and her ribs in the fall. Finally, Belek placed the gurney on the ground and said, "Get on. You're slowing us down."

Humiliated, Eliza tried to climb on, but her body ached too much. Badri gently picked her up and laid her on the gurney.

She took his hand. "I would never leave you on purpose," she said quietly, locking eyes with him.

"I understand now that you have only seen my reports concerning the bodies of those who putatively died at the hand of another and not concerning those who had died of exposure to the elements."

Suddenly, Scout jumped up onto the gurney with Eliza and rested her head in the crook of her arm. Eliza stroked her head and scratched her ears, and Scout wagged her tail, thumping it against the mattress.

Belek put yet another Ursinus b cream-colored textile over her. The blanket was soft, and she covered herself completely, even her head. She lay on the gurney in mortified silence. She listened to Kolokh's deep voice, Belek's near-whisper, and Kelly and Baines's quiet conversation. Badri was silent.

She was surprised at how smoothly the gurney moved and relieved that the ride was not bumpy.

As the group was just approaching Broken Oar, it started raining again. When the group got into the village, Eliza immediately tried to get down.

"No," Belek said.

"I just have a headache! Can I get something for the headache?"

"Well, I'm glad that's over," Baines said to Eliza, watching Kelly and Kolokh walk away, Scout in tow. "Your boyfriend over here was a mess. I'm going to go—"

"You are leaving? What is this outrage?" Badri asked. "You were the one who led her into that storm and failed to—"

Baines turned on Badri. "Now you listen to me. This is an

alien planet, not a beach resort. She knew the risks when she—"

"*She* did not," Eliza said. "I asked you about the weather multiple times. And there was no pup tent even though—"

"Why don't you try taking responsibility for yourself for a change? If you choose to come to another world, you—"

"I didn't choose to come to another world! And I relied on you, a leader, someone who knew the planet already, to know what you were doing. I asked you over and over about the weather, and you blew me off over and over. The next time, the third time, you have to lead anyone anywhere, maybe think on the conditions and plan ahead."

Baines stormed off.

"I wouldn't trust her to lead me to dinner," Belek said to the two Humans. "And neither should you."

"Never," Badri said.

"The Shadows," Eliza said. "Belek, have you ever seen them before?"

"Yes. This is their season."

"What do you know about them?"

"They appear, gather in flocks, and disappear again." But his carapace turned momentarily black.

After Belek wheeled Eliza into the hospital, Badri gently helped her move to a gurney in the hospital bay. He brushed her hair off her forehead.

A man walked up who Eliza surmised was John Bynum. He had short blond hair in a crew cut, blue eyes, and a round face. He had a paunch, and his hands were small and plump. His expression telegraphed intelligence.

Dr. Bynum sat on a stool. "You need to remove your clothing before I can examine you."

"Could you and Belek step out then?"

"I've seen a naked woman before."

"In our world," Badri said, "It is not customary for a patient to—"

"I don't care, Dr. Trivedi."

"I will cover you with this blanket," Badri told Eliza, "so that you may disrobe with sufficient modesty."

Eliza undressed under the blanket, leaving her undergarment on.

Dr. Bynum pulled the blanket off and dumped it on the floor. "The blanket is in the way."

In a rage, Badri closed the curtain, saying, "This is improper—"

"You're very thin," Dr. Bynum said. "Do you have an eating disorder?"

Eliza reached for her coverall and covered her body with it as best she could. "Can we finish my exam, please, so I can go home? That includes, you know, asking me what happened, performing an exam about it, and telling me what to do."

"Then we will discuss your weight at follow-up."

"I'm here after falling ten feet onto a rock, and I had severe vertigo. I'm here to find out if I broke something or if I can just go home. Can you help with that?"

He turned to Belek. "Now you're getting hysterical. Belek, please get me two milligrams of Ativan."

"Shouldn't I be getting an X-ray or something right now?"

Belek wasn't moving.

"Are you always this hysterical? Or are you drug-seeking?" Bynum said.

"If I were *drug-seeking*, I would've asked for the Ativan. I'm getting out of here."

"You're getting your Hansen scan." Dr. Bynum turned abruptly and motioned to Belek impatiently, who brought what looked to Eliza like a mini-MRI machine—and another blanket, which Badri put over Eliza's body.

"Thank you, Belek," Eliza whispered.

Belek's carapace flushed blue for a moment. He said, "This a Hansen scanner. The device will go over your head and body to—"

"Just do it, Belek." He looked at Badri when he said this. Then Dr. Bynum leaned over Eliza. "Was your stunt an attention-seeking tool? You don't need an audience to get a Hansen scan."

Belek finished his explanation.

"Dr. Trivedi, please step out," Dr. Bynum said.

"No," Eliza said. "I don't want him to step out."

"This is my exam room. I can't work with him breathing down my neck."

"You're working right now?" Eliza said. "I can't tell."

"I will not move," Badri said.

Belek hurriedly activated the machine. It made a slight humming sound.

Dr. Bynum studied the results on the console beside him. "I already examined Lieutenant Accardi, and I see that missy here bore the brunt of the attack, Dr. Trivedi. There is damage to the hippocampus, the amygdala, and the medial frontal cortex. There is also inflammation of the optic nerve and alteration of visual cortex activity. She has some bruising to the ribs, pelvis, and greater trochanter on her left side."

"I'm right here. Can I please have something for the pain?"

"Here we go," Dr. Bynum said, rolling his eyes.

Eliza said through her teeth. "And I only know what a greater trochanter is because I'm a homicide cop. It's at the top of the femur, right? All of those other things are in the brain. I don't know what they do. Badri, what is he talking about?"

"No need for histrionics, missy," Bynum said. "There is a procedure, although experimental, to repair your brain damage. We'll need to get your head shaved and—"

"No, you won't. I don't consent. I also don't consider that the Shadows *attacked* me."

"Well, they're a menace. It's a shame something can't be done about them."

"That's reprehensible." Eliza started to get up off the gurney. "You're reprehensible. I'm leaving."

"Dr. Bynum, have you have not seen posttraumatic stress disorder before? The damage to the hippocampus, the amygdala, and the medial frontal cortex are consistent with posttraumatic stress disorder. If you take scans of Kelly's brain, you will note the same findings. Your treatment plan is butchery. Eliza, we will follow up with Dr. Colson to see if any further treatment is required."

"She doesn't know what she's saying, Dr. Trivedi."

Eliza was sitting up and about to get off the gurney, but Dr. Bynum started to put his hand on Eliza's shoulder.

Eliza quickly deflected his hand. "Dr. Bynum, if you touch me again, I will break your hand."

"She is agitated now. Belek, sedate her."

"Move," Badri said, crowding Dr. Bynum, "or I will pick you up and throw you across the room."

"Or I will," Belek said.

"Lobster," Dr. Bynum said, "you are a medic, not a physician. Do as you're told."

Eliza gasped.

"And I'm a lot bigger than you are," Belek said. "Wanna find out why that matters?"

"Badri, can you get me out of here?"

ELIZA HAD SLEPT on and off for the rest of the day.

When Badri came to bed, she woke up. He took her into his arms, and she lay with her head on his chest. Eliza had had countless nightmares about what she had almost done to Badri. "If I didn't have PTSD before I saw Dr. Bynum, I would now."

"Banner was appalled. He said that he understood now why Maura would not see Dr. Bynum. This dynamic, you have seen this before?"

"Very occasionally. My mother had horror stories." Thinking of her mother, Eliza started softly to cry. Then she sobbed.

Badri held her close, rocking her. "I miss my parents too."

"Tell me about them?" He had spoken of them for a year, but Eliza did not care.

He rolled over, into her arms, and quietly sobbed, about his parents, about what he saw in the videos, about Bear—who had still been alive. And about months of looking over his shoulder, afraid they would be found out. And she held him and stroked his hair.

Eventually, he fell asleep.

After a time, she got up and walked painfully into the bathroom. She saw that her whole left side was black and blue, with her hip taking the brunt of the fall. She also had some bruising from what she guessed was hailstones. Thinking back to her experience with Dr. Bynum, she thought about taking another shower, but she washed up and went back to bed, calmer now.

When she got into bed, Badri was awake again.

"What is it?" Eliza said quietly.

"My cousin was getting married today. We are in a strange place, and we will never see our families again."

"I wish they at least knew where we were. I keep looking for a phone to call them."

"As do I. If you mean to apologize once again for my following you here, do not. I would do it again."

"Do you fit in with Banner and Ror?"

"I do. Very much so."

Eliza wondered what she was feeling for a moment and realized that it was contentment.

"What is it?" Badri asked.

"What was what?"

"Your affect changed."

"I'm glad that your life has changed at least a little for the better for having come here. And I like those two."

"And you?"

"I ... I don't know. I'm sure that I'll make a friend or two here. I mean, it's inevitable in a place like this. Not Baines, though. Not Kelly." Then she sat up. "How by God's flying tricycle did Space Force pick these people? Baines is a loose cannon. Glenn was a sadist and so is Bynum. What the everloving airborne fuck?"

"They selected for bravery and found foolhardiness. They selected for adaptability. Glenn Sommars was manifestly adaptive—to a superior degree—but Space Force failed to rule out exploitative and predatory character traits. Dr. Bynum was likely selected for his knowledge of theory, but they failed to select for sound judgment. Or compassion. Indeed, he has none."

"What the hell happened to NASA in 158 years? They'd never have allowed this!"

"Would a government agency like NASA have had the funding to build these ships? It is quite possible that they did not. Perhaps Space Force is a private concern. It is clear that their selection protocols are ... dangerous."

"My God. Maybe it's the *Archer* or the *Peregrine* that tries to take over Broken Oar!"

"It is possible. We will insist that this issue be explored."

"I should have predicted how reckless Baines was from the book, but Kelly—"

"—was obeying orders," Badri said.

"Why did you make that point about Cody and his heart rate?"

"Even when one's life is not at risk, engaging in real combat is stressful. One would expect the appropriate physical response. Cody did not have this."

"And?"

"Such a person would be very likely to fire a semiautomatic handgun fifteen times and hit their target fifteen times."

Eliza nodded. "You think our Cody killed our Glenn?"

"This is my hypothesis, but we will never learn the truth."

"I'm not sold, though. I mean, why would our Cody do that?"

"We do not have enough data to be certain. Perhaps our Glenn caught our Maura packing to leave and rearranging her room in defiance, and Cody had accompanied her."

"Or Maura was rearranging her room because she knew her father would be dead soon." Then she sat up and gasped. "Malit."

"You consider that these ... Shadows ... could temporarily correct his vision? Only Ror could say if he has the neurological structures to support vision at all."

"Malit wouldn't know either way. I worry about him trying to get to them on his own."

"No one is leaving this place under these conditions. The wind would blow him off his feet. And I have learned that Kharkuns have little tolerance for the cold."

"This storm won't last forever."

Badri pushed a button on the communication console, which lit up, but neither Badri nor Eliza could read the display. They looked at each other, and Eliza shrugged.

So Badri pressed another button and said, "Contact Lita."

The display turned red and then shut off.

"The storm has affected communications," Badri said. "Perhaps those who know the boy will be able to predict whether he would try to find the Shadows or whether he has the ability to negotiate the trail without falling to his death."

ELIZA AWOKE to the sound of Badri in the next room, and she heard a tutorial about trauma surgery. She smiled to herself.

She was in more pain this morning than she'd been the day before. If anything, her headache was worse.

After limping into the bathroom, Eliza looked at the soaking tub, thinking it would help, but she could not bring herself to get into it, so she showered. Considering the pain in her hip, she put on loose trousers that closed with a drawstring and a light T-shirt of sage green and walked painfully out to the living room.

"Were you able to get in touch with Lita?" Eliza went to the dispenser and got herself a mug of naiya, hoping it would make her feel better.

It didn't.

"Neither Lita nor Zhan would answer."

No sooner did they sit down to breakfast, Badri with tea and Eliza with coffee, than there was a knock on the door.

It was Banner. He sat down at the breakfast bar and said, "Malit took off this morning."

"Alone?" Eliza asked. "Oh, God."

"Cody and Zhan went after him. They took Duncan and Scout. They'll catch up to him."

"But that cliff!" Eliza said.

"Kharkun hearing is not to be believed. He'll be able to avoid the cliffs, but not the Donners. Eliza, Belek told me what happened last night. We told Dr. Bynum to stay out of the hospital. His treatment of you was appalling."

"He went quietly?" Eliza asked in disbelief.

"He was ... *helped* out of the hospital by Belek."

Eliza snorted. "I wish I'd been there to see that." Then she said, "He called Belek a 'lobster.'"

"What he said to Belek after you left was even more disgusting. I won't repeat it. And I did review your scans. I don't think there's anything that needs to be done at this point. I do wish we had some way of getting you some talk therapy, but we don't have anyone here to do that. How's your pain?"

"The PTSD is manageable. I'm in a lot of pain from the fall."

Banner got up and went to the dispenser. He hesitated. "Is there any chance that you could be pregnant?"

"No, I'm using a contraceptive implant."

He nodded. "That widens the field in terms of what I can give you, then."

He rapidly typed and then, equally rapidly, pushed some buttons. Out of the dispenser came a pill bottle. Eliza smiled at the familiarity.

"This is tramadol extended release," Banner said. "Instructions on the side. Don't take it with booze." Then he swiftly entered another series of numbers. "This is the aptly named curamide. It has anti-inflammatory properties, and it will heal bone injuries very rapidly, including joints. You take this once a day—with food unless you want a hole in your stomach."

"Thank you—oh! Do you want anything to eat or drink? I can push this button over here and—"

Banner laughed. "No, thank you. And those things weird me out as much as they do you."

"Well, I'm hungry." Eliza got herself another mug of black coffee and a plate of shakshouka. Then she took her medication.

"What's that?" Banner asked, pointing to her plate.

"Eggs poached in a tomato sauce and—"

"How did Dr. Bynum respond to your decision?" Badri asked.

"He said that Belek would taste good with garlic butter and that I was allowing bad elements to control me."

"*Oh my God!* That's a threat!" Eliza said.

"Bynum doesn't want to be thrown out of the village," Banner said. He sighed. "This isn't the first time I've been concerned about Space Force's decision-making. That started when they gave us a sixteen-year-old. After Glenn, I gave up being surprised about it. Now I'm waiting for the other shoe to drop."

"We were discussing this," Badri said. "We are concerned that this rebellion that Detective Cloud refers to in his book involves one or both of the remaining ships. Neither of us read the thing to the end."

Banner rubbed the bridge of his nose with his fingers and thumb and said, "If true, I ... I hope there's something we can do about that."

"Do they even have big enough weapons here?" Eliza asked. "They can't fight off a starship with lasepistols."

"We'll all put our heads together," Banner said. "This is

crazy. I'm also here to speak with you, Badri. We need to get you trained. Right now, I'm the only one who can treat Humans—well, and Dr. Meyer Brodt—and Leon Glass, who's an ob-gyn—but they're from, you know, 1941, so not exactly current. We have no anesthesiologists, just a bot that barely does the job, and no nurses, so we're already winging it."

"I must repeat an internship and residency," Badri said. "I am not competent to treat patients at this time. It has been many years."

"We'll take you up on that."

Eliza said, "How did the Shadows float like that? They were sideways!"

"Cody has no idea," Banner said. "Neither does Kinkead. Eliza, it must have been very frightening."

"It wasn't. It was wonderful. And they were so, so soft."

"Interesting. Gino said pretty close to the same thing. After he stopped throwing up."

Eliza walked over to the coffee table and picked up *The Tauxenent Strangler*. At Badri's look, she said, "Don't worry, I'll be skipping the sex scenes."

"I do not know why you bother."

"What are you reading?"

"I am studying a medical text. The formal English of scientific texts is more understandable than I feared, and this has a dictionary."

"Well, that's a relief." She sat down and opened the novel.

I was looking at the man who had murdered sixteen helpless women, one of whom was a baby of three months. He had made the women watch as their dogs and their children were tortured horribly to death, and then he tortured the women and strangled them to death. He made evil videos of every moment of his dastardly crimes.

I had finally hunted down this man.

"Oh, Jamie! I'm so glad you finally found him!" Eliza said to me. Her luscious lips parted, and I knew that tonight, we would be making love again.

"Oh, good God!" Eliza said. "It's disgusting right away."

"You do not need to read this, Eliza. I do not know why you are."

"Morbid curiosity."

Badri looked back down at his tablet.

Eliza watched him. He was staring at it without reading. She went back to her book.

Deputy Commonwealth's Attorney Krista "Denny" Denbow stood on my other side. She stood five foot eight and she was statuesque, with the same curls as Eliza's. Like Eliza, she tethered hers in a topknot. Her neck was long, her nose pert, and she had a cleft chin. I know that Eliza envied Denny's classical beauty. Denny, in her turn, longed for Eliza's sultry, exotic look and sultry voice.

"You have done it again, Jamie," she said with an

indefinable twang to her voice. Like Eliza, she cursed like a sailor, but whenever she spoke to me, the look in her golden-brown eyes softened.

"I can't with this thing!" Eliza said. "He wrote, 'the man who had murdered sixteen helpless women, one of whom was a baby of three months.' *Really?* And he even used 'sultry' twice in the same sentence. It isn't a true crime book, it's terrible erotic fiction!"

She read these excerpts aloud to Badri, who said, "*Enough, Eliza!*"

The dogs jumped off the couch and ran to their beds by the sliding glass door.

"Oh my God. This is the second time you've talked to me like that, and it's not okay. Are you going to yell all the time? Because I won't—oh, shit!"

Denny. Kolokh and Kelly had read about Eliza and pulled her here. Did she just do that to Denny? Eliza quickly got up, grateful for the tramadol, and hurled the book into the disposal, with force, since she was angry. Then she went and sat on the coffee table across from Badri.

"Don't yell at me again."

"Reading this to me was disrespectful!"

"I don't deserve to get yelled at! I won't live like that. And I was reading the words of a pathetic dead man, not a passionate love letter. The book was disgusting. Next time, just ask me to stop, and I will."

Badri took her hand between his. "I am sorry. You are correct in this. I will not lose my temper with you again in this way."

She withdrew her hand, and he tensed. "I really hope this book didn't call Denny here just because I read it."

"This is why you disposed of this book?"

"Yes. I'm hoping that because Jamie is dead ..." and Eliza wiped her eyes roughly, "... because Jamie is dead, that book is just a book. Do *not* be confused! I didn't throw it out because you yelled at me. I threw it out because I'm concerned that reading about someone will bring them here. And it was excruciating. I expected to read at least some of his thoughts on the case, not to be violated on page 1."

"I am relieved that you did not throw the book away on my account, Eliza," Badri said, kissing her forehead.

Eliza relaxed. "It's forgiven. And I'm sorry I inflicted that garbage on you. I shouldn't have. And if you're learning medical stuff, would it help if I quizzed you?"

"This would be helpful, yes."

"Badri? I didn't apologize for staying behind in the storm. I could have left you alone here, and I see that now. In fact, I thought about that when I was stuck in the tunnel."

"I do not understand why Baines's crew still regards her as their commanding officer."

"They don't. Did you notice? They don't do what she says, and she really doesn't give orders anymore."

"They nevertheless have not sent drones."

"Maybe they don't have any here."

Badri and Eliza sat across from each other at the breakfast bar, and Eliza quizzed Badri on the material.

At one point, she mispronounced a word, and he laughed silently. He corrected her and she smiled. "I'm glad I can finally help you for a change."

"How have you not helped me?"

"I would come to you to discuss my cases, and together we

would come to a conclusion. Or you would help me to come to a conclusion. That was you helping me, not me helping you."

"Eliza, most of the bodies I received were those who were not victims of homicides. For example, they were unattended deaths—elderly persons who had died alone, or individuals in one-car collisions, or like that. When the bodies were those of homicide victims, my role was limited to what I could discern from their bodies. It was well that I could help you determine who killed them. It permitted me to perform an additional service on their behalf."

After nearly an hour and a half of work, Badri said he'd had enough. Eliza found it exciting, but not surprising, how rapidly he mastered the lessons.

A bit later, Eliza returned from taking Skye and Luna for a walk and went into their bedroom to lie down.

She awakened to the sound of Badri speaking with someone in the other room.

Then he came into the bedroom, saying, "Malit left the village in the night. Zhan is dead. The Kanninoin have accused Cody of murder."

"Wait, what? What about Malit?"

Badri sat beside her. "Cody and Malit returned with Duncan and Scout but without Zhan. Cody's clothing was stained with what was determined to be Kharkun blood. Cody was not injured, but he was vomiting and feverish. Cody said that he entered the reed forest with Zhan, Scout, and Duncan and regained consciousness beside Zhan. Zhan's ceremonial knife was protruding from his body. The dogs were missing.

Cody reports that he tried to perform lifesaving measures, but Zhan was already deceased, cold even for a Kharkun.

"He located Malit standing at the edge of the reed forest and the dogs beside him. Cody and Malit returned with the dogs. Since Cody has killed before, Inani accuses him of murder."

"What do the Kharkuns say?"

"They do not accept this."

Eliza relaxed. "If Cody was unconscious that long, how brain-injured—"

"When Cody returned, he had a high fever and was nearly delirious. A Hansen scan yielded no evidence of a closed head injury."

"That's a relief. Any idea why?"

"No."

Eliza groaned. "We're ... we're back on the job now, aren't we?"

"It seems so. Let us go and address this current crisis together."

"Have they left Zhan's body where it was?"

"Fortunately, I was able to convince them to do this. Da'in, Kyr, Enkhid, and Kano have remained at the crime scene to preserve it. They have taken two of the service dogs."

"Where's Kolokh?"

"With Lita."

"I'm assuming they've verified that the blood on Cody is Kharkun blood."

"Ror did. It is Kharkun blood, and further, after taking a cheek swab from Malit, Ror was able to ascertain that the blood belonged to Zhan."

"Did they photograph Cody as he was when he returned?"

"Yes. The Kanninoin are quite thorough. They fortunately recorded all the data as it came in."

"They saved the clothes too?"

"They did, in the appropriate packaging."

As Badri and Eliza started to walk out of the house, Kelly and Maura were in the process of knocking.

We have to stop meeting this way, Eliza thought.

Kelly looked distraught. "Are you planning on railroading my son?"

"For what?" Eliza asked.

"I told you, Mom!" Maura said.

"Well," Kelly said through gritted teeth, "they've locked Cody in his home."

"*Who* has?" Eliza asked.

"The Kanninoin."

"Not the Kharkuns?"

"No. And I'm doing my level best to control myself so as not to provoke a war between us and the Kanninoin, but fix it, Eliza."

"What?" Eliza said. "Who elected me—"

"You're the one with the badge!" Kelly snapped. "Fix it."

INANI STOOD in front of Eliza with Lita, Kolokh, Kano, and Johalo. The group had gathered in front of the hospital.

"I'm so sorry for your loss," Eliza said softly to Lita. "I plan to find out who murdered your—"

"We know who murdered Zhan, Eliza," Inani said. "There is no need to waste time with a so-called 'investigation.'"

Eliza heard the air quotes and was momentarily fascinated that Kanninoin used them too. "Let Cody out, Inani."

"Cody murdered a man."

"He *didn't* murder my husband," Lita said, teeth bared and fangs showing.

Inani looked at her with a half-smile and said, "You don't know these Humans."

"You haven't even begun to know us Humans," Eliza said. "For instance, do these lasepistols have a stun function? No? Too bad."

Inani tried to look at Kano, but he was looking at Eliza.

"That sounds like a threat," Inani said to the group.

"Not yet," Eliza said. "Kelly has very kindly agreed to take the diplomatic approach for now, but I suspect that her patience will wear thin sooner rather than later. As will mine. If this were happening where I come from, you'd already be in handcuffs and on the way to the county jail."

"And you should not be interfering with our culture."

"This is not your planet, nor is it subject to Kanninoin jurisdiction, nor would I even give a flying goat's syphilitic fuck."

"You do not have a directive against interference with other cultures? Because—"

"That *directive* exists in fiction, Inani," Eliza said. "Nor am I subject to it."

"Nor are we," Lita said to Inani through gritted teeth. "You test our tolerance."

Johalo was standing beside Inani and shifting his weight from foot to foot. Kano looked at Inani with an expression that Eliza could not interpret.

"This is awful, Inani," Kano said. "Let the kid out. Stop this before—"

"He's not a kid. He's a grown man. Old enough to know the punishment for murder."

"You can't lock him in there forever," Kano said.

"I can," Inani said.

Lita growled something that Eliza's translator could not grab.

"Inani?" Johalo was looking at her with his pale yellow eyes. He traded looks with Kano, who nodded briefly. "Where is Rasan'in?"

Inani flushed. She looked to Eliza as if she had a horrific sunburn, but then her control returned. "The danata is the danata. This was in cold blood! Premeditated barbarity!"

Kano said, "I'm letting him out."

Inani's ears tilted back. "You are not. Are you challenging me? This is a violation of our traditions! It isn't done—"

"Of course it's never done," Kano said, ears reddening. "We never discuss murder outside the family."

"You have completely lost control of yourself, Kano. Are you entering the danata? You should go home to R'ani and Sha'in before tragedy strikes."

"It struck *your* house," Kano said.

"This is a private matter!" she said to Kano, pupils fully dilated.

Johalo and Kano fairly stared Inani down, and she looked at the ground, lips tight. Then she locked eyes with Eliza. "Humans kill because they can."

"Cody had no choice," Eliza said, loathing Inani. "He was defending his mother and his crewmates in a place with no courts and no jails. We live in Broken Oar, but others might have chosen not to. Or hadn't you thought of that?" At Inani's look, she said, "Of course not."

"He's a Human," Inani said. "This will color your investigation."

"Kano," Eliza began.

From behind Eliza, someone said, "This is a lot of to-do about nothing."

She turned around. John Bynum was leaning against the edge of a picnic table with his arms crossed.

"In what way, Dr. Bynum, is it a to-do?" Eliza demanded.

"If Cody hadn't murdered Zhan, someone else would have. They're brutes. Look at those brow ridges. Their language consists of grunts and growls, they insist on carrying knives, and they stink. And before you got here, they were urinating against the walls. What is your life expectancy, miss?" He was looking at Lita. "Forty years?"

"Three hundred."

Bynum shook his head and laughed, "Kharkuness, perhaps I should teach you to count."

Lita looked at Eliza, and Eliza said, "He's a piece of shit."

"You're from a primitive time," Bynum said to Eliza, "with a primitive vocabulary and understanding to match. This is a violent, backward species. That's why Inani is concerned, and they're not. Look at her," he said, pointing to Lita. "She doesn't even express grief. Like animals, they only think about the present. Cody didn't commit murder, he rid this colony of vermin." He looked at Lita. "What are you, dear, twenty? With an eight-year-old? Stop hyperventilating, Miss Eliza, about what you don't understand."

"Trepanation went out of fashion in the Paleolithic," Eliza said without looking at him. "And that's *Detective Benveniste* to you." She turned to Inani, loathing her half-smile, and said, "I—"

Maura walked up. "When are you letting my brother out of there, you pompous bitch?"

"We're getting him out of there," Eliza said. "Your mother is urging diplomacy, and I reluctantly agree. For now."

Maura backed Inani into the door. "The next time I come back, I'll bring more Humans. You might want to let him out before I do."

"Your grief is clouding your judgment, little lady," Bynum said.

Maura turned her back to him and walked away, holding her hands in the air and simultaneously flipping him off with both of them.

We're going to have a problem when the Peregrine *and the* Archer *get here*, Eliza thought.

Eliza and Badri arrived at the crime scene with Skye. Luna was too excitable. Ror and Kano had accompanied the Humans.

Kyr was staring at Zhan, looking shell-shocked. Ror said something to Kyr that the translator couldn't grab.

Enkhid said something that the translator also couldn't grab, but Eliza felt it in her chest.

Eliza did not recognize the other Kanninoin present.

"Where is Cody?" Kyr asked.

"Inani won't let him out," Kano said. "We are grateful that the Humans have chosen restraint."

"For now," Eliza said. She could smell decomposition, and the odor was comparable to the unique, unmistakable smell of Human decay. "Let's get this case solved in the meantime."

Da'in approached her. They were wearing a vest of the same fashion as Kolokh, but no shirt. They had thick black fur on their torso, which had a pouch and three breasts. They were bald. Their ginger-colored unibrow was thick, reaching to the middle of their forehead. Their face had Inani's softness, and their eyes were even larger than Inani's. "We took some photographs and video."

Eliza imagined blurry photographs of irrelevant things, but after she reviewed the photographs and the video on Da'in's tablet, she looked at Da'in with respect. "Thank you! You even videoed the trail ahead of you before you stepped on it!"

She looked again. "How did you get these closeups of Zhan's injuries? You didn't turn him—"

"No," Da'in said. "It's possible to take detailed photographs from a distance. We also collected what appears to be vomit from a spot distant from Zhan. It's likely Cody's, but we don't want to make assumptions."

"Wow, you're as good as the CSIs I used to work with!"

Da'in was expressionless. Like all Kanninoin, they stood closer to people than arm's length. She took a step back.

Zhan was lying on the ground in an odd position. Eliza pictured him having lain in a loose fetal position and then being flipped on his back. The clan knife protruded from his right side. A few feet from Zhan was what looked like vomit. The back of Zhan's skull was caved in, and she could see brain matter and, from the cracks in the skull, a clear, viscous fluid leaking onto the ground. Eliza noted that Zhan had the same expression in death that Humans had and was glad for a moment that Malit was blind.

She noted that there were eight-legged winged insects in and around Zhan's eyes and mouth and clustered on his skull and stab wounds, as were small, nearly translucent crabs. There were also maggots the color of the soil clustered around the viscous fluid.

Someone had crushed one of the roly-polies that were about to go to Zhan's body.

She could see that Badri was fascinated.

Zhan's abdomen was swollen, and he had the familiar green marbling of decomposition there.

"This is odd," Badri said to Ror. He knelt and pointed to Zhan's face. "I have minimal acquaintance with your species, and I will speak informally. The presence of livor is inconsistent with his having died in this position. Did Cody indicate to anyone that he had moved him?"

"Cody said that he found Zhan lying on the ground there and tried to do chest compressions. He indicated that he left

Zhan as he found him." He sighed. "The Kharkun heart is not located there."

"Would it have helped if the compressions had been done properly?" Eliza asked.

"No," Ror replied. "Zhan had been dead for some time based on the decomposition I see here."

"Where did the blood on Cody come from?" Badri asked. "I see none here."

Ror studied the ground. "There isn't any."

"And would Zhan's blood have clotted fast enough for him not to have bled?" Badri asked.

"No. In you Humans, a stab wound to the abdomen would cause internal bleeding, with relatively little blood elsewhere. Not in Kharkuns. Each of our four livers make erythropoietin very rapidly, and as a result of other anatomical structures, he could replace his blood volume within minutes. Since he would not have applied pressure to this wound to stop the bleeding, there should be a notable presence of blood."

"Ror, have you ever testified in court before?" Eliza asked.

"I'm a trauma surgeon," he said, smiling a little, "not a medical examiner. Why?"

"You act like someone who would have been completely at home on a witness stand."

"On my planet, that would not be a virtue," he said. "But you are paying me a compliment, and I shall receive it as such."

"I'm suggesting that if there is a trial, you might—"

"What? A trial?" Kyr said, nonplussed.

"Yes, a trial. Why not? If we find a suspect, they have to have a—"

"This could be caused by a blunt instrument," Ror said. "There's a scalp laceration here."

At that location, the scalp looked like someone had pulled a sheet back on a bed.

"In Humans, there are arteries in the skin of the head," Badri said. "Is this likewise true of Kharkuns?"

"Yes. It is not possible for Zhan to have died here."

"Did ... how were you related to Zhan, Ror?" Eliza asked tentatively.

"I'm not related to any Kharkun here. When he was two, Malit ran through a sliding glass door. My name is not unknown to those with children like Malit. I treated him in secret, as I did all patients like him. We were able to bribe the bookkeeper in our hospital so that she wouldn't report the discrepancy between on-the-books requisitions and our actual use of medications and supplies. Then she retired. The new hospital bookkeeper found the discrepancies and reported them. When the new bookkeeper sent his findings to his superiors, he triggered an audit. The authorities thought they were looking for a thief. They would have traced those missing supplies and medications back to me and my few trusted colleagues. I learned of the audit in time."

"And your family?" Eliza asked softly.

"My clan escaped to the neighboring system. My wife and daughters were on that ship. I remained behind to warn all of my patients, who also fled. I was to leave with Malit's clan and meet my family on Uruk." Ror became very still. "Was your question for any specific purpose?"

"Yes. It was. I knew a paramedic who responded to a mass shooting in a grocery store, and one of the victims was his brother. It affected how I inter—asked him about the events."

Ror's smile was so brief that Eliza almost missed it.

Eliza studied Zhan's body for a moment. "Can you estimate Zhan's weight, Ror?"

"I estimate that he was around a hundred and twenty-five kilograms. Our bones are thicker and denser than yours, and he was over two hundred centimeters tall."

At Eliza's look of confusion, Badri said, "That is two hundred and seventy-five pounds and approximately six foot five inches."

"Thanks." Eliza walked across the trail from the crime scene into the edge of reed forest on the other side, Da'in documenting this with video.

Eliza returned to the group. "How did Zhan's body get here? Did Cody carry Kolokh firefighter-style, you know, using a shoulder pull? Then where are the marks in the soil? Could Cody have gotten a Kharkun of Zhan's size off the ground, lifted him across his shoulders, and carried him? Cody's pretty strong, but he's also not that big. I'm guessing five-eleven, one sixty. And he's no powerlifter. Did Cody have any Kharkun blood on his shoulders?"

Da'in searched through his tablet. Eliza, Ror, and Badri gathered around.

"No," Eliza said. "So he didn't carry Zhan on his shoulders to get him here. Where are the drag marks?"

Eliza walked carefully in an ever-widening arc from Zhan's body into the reed forest, Da'in filming the whole time. A few feet from the scene, *three sets of footprints!* She followed these carefully until she found what looked like a streak of Kharkun blood on the reeds along one side. She briefly considered following the footsteps into the reed forest, then imagined what she might find there. *Nope.* Da'in photographed these footprints close up, then photographed the blood on the reeds. From his knapsack, he pulled out a vial and carefully took a blood sample from each reed. He sealed the envelope and signed across it.

They walked back to the group, careful not to disturb the footprints. "Hey, y'all," Eliza said, "I found three sets of footprints going off into the reed forest. Cody was set up."

Da'in showed the photographs to everyone.

"What's that way?" and she pointed. "We need to follow these footprints. Three Human men working together could have heaved Zhan's body into this clearing without stepping into it." Then she stopped. *Oh, shit.* "Does anyone at Broken Oar monitor the skies?"

"Why would they?" Kano asked. "This planet is remote from all planets that support carbon-based life forms."

"Oh," Eliza said, "I dunno. Because there are two more ships where the *Broken Oar* came from?"

Back in the village, Badri and Ror escorted the body, covered with a sheet, into the hospital, which was now a makeshift morgue. The ground beneath Zhan's body, and postmortem abrasions, confirmed that he had been tossed there. There was no more crime scene to guard.

Eliza brought up the rear with everyone else.

To her surprise, they encountered Wolf.

"How's my pet monkey doing?"

"Good to see you too, Wolf," Eliza said. "We can catch up on old times another day."

He laughed. Then he said, "Come to the park and play—" and the translator winked out. "You know, ball? Net? Hitting it back and forth? You know how to play games, little monkey? I think your fellow prairie apes are afraid of us."

Touched, she said, "I'll take you up on that. I can't now."

"I can teach you the rules."

"I'd like that," she said again. "Zhan was murdered and—"

"And you're at work."

"I live here," and she pointed. "I'll be busy for the next day or so—but come find me then, and I'll join you."

"Much more fun than sucking a fly's dick," Wolf said, laughing.

"Who knew?" Eliza said, smiling, wondering if she'd ever get used to the sound of a spider laughing. She looked at him again. Although he walked on them, his front four limbs were actually six-fingered hands with two opposable thumbs. He also had fingernails. She realized that any animal with a thumb needed fingernails for proper grip, for sensing pressure, perhaps for self-defense, and for scratching.

After Wolf had been gone for a moment, Kano said, "You ... are friends?"

"Oh," she said, "he threatened to eat Badri's dog, and I threatened to kill him and then uttered a string of obscenities at him, as one does. Apparently, it was the beginning of a warm friendship."

"*Prairie ape?*" Kyr asked.

"It's almost accurate," Eliza said. "Kyr, I would like to talk to Malit for a few moments. Would that be okay?"

"I'll ask," Kyr said. "But he is probably at the q'a'hin'qe. The funeral meal."

Out of curiosity, Eliza took the translators out of her ears. "Can you repeat that?"

A *q* sound, but back in the throat. Then the translator winked out. *A* as in *apple*. Then the translator winked out. Then *hin* as in *hint*. Then the translator winked out. Then that *q* sound and *e* as in *egg*. Eliza realized that the translator wasn't picking up the low-frequency sounds that Humans couldn't hear and was essentially leaving those sounds "blank." Then she wondered about Da'in's name. She put the translators back in.

"What was that about?" Kyr asked.

"We Humans can't hear all the sounds in that word," Eliza said. "I won't try to say it, because I'll get it wrong."

"Thank you, Eliza."

"Thank you, Kyr. If this isn't a good time for Lita and Malit, it can wait."

Kyr left, and Eliza remembered that Kharkuns didn't say goodbye.

"Eliza," Kano said, "may I have a moment?"

"Sure."

Kano took her to a picnic table a short distance from the hospital. Then he sat across from her, keeping his arms to his sides. "Inani's treatment of Cody is barbaric," he said quietly. His untethered hair was long, black, and straight, making his pallor even more stark. His lack of facial expression was similarly unnerving, and Eliza had to remind herself that he was being kind. "Our family agrees with you that Cody is innocent. Inani's belief is irrational. It is not traditional to discuss these matters to outsiders. But these are not traditional times. Our people do not support her decision, but we are bound by it."

"No," she said. "These are not traditional times. Not for any of us. But it's time to release Cody."

He shook his head. "I feel at liberty to discuss these issues because of your rational approach with regard to the dogs. Many here do not see it as you do, and an exploration of the issue did not change their minds. It is this cognitive flexibility that permits me to speak freely."

"Cody was trying to save Malit even though a month ago, he didn't even know that Kharkuns existed." Eliza was surprised that yet another non-Human species here used the same gestures or facial expressions as Humans did and wondered if any others could be misinterpreted, as her waving at Wolf was misinterpreted. "What is ultimately going to happen is that someone is going to free Cody by force. Because at this point, if I did have to arrest anyone, it would be Inani."

"I will discuss your thoughts with others in the family. The next in line of succession is my wife, R'ani, but we are expecting triplets, and R'ani does not want—" he seemed to catch himself. "I hope you find who murdered Zhan."

"That will make the issue moot for you?" Eliza said. "So you don't have to stand up for what's right? You did hear me, right? Inani runs your family, but she doesn't run this village. If you all don't let him out, someone will get him out. Then there will be violence."

Kano turned red. He reminded Eliza of a burn victim. "This is not a traditional approach."

"Then what is your tradition even good for?"

"You have convinced me that it is necessary to countermand Inani. I will do so, though I might end up living next door to the Tenurians." He got up and left.

"You're Wolf's little pet," said a voice coming from behind Eliza.

Eliza turned around. A Spider crouched in front of her, looking very nearly like a cat in loaf pose.

She smiled. "I guess I am. I'm Eliza."

The Spider hesitated, first giving her a name that Eliza could not even make out, let alone pronounce.

At Eliza's apparent confusion, she said, "Oh, little monkey.

Wolf told me you can't understand our names. Call me Aphrodite." Then she started grooming herself.

"Pleased to meet you. I didn't realize that cursing at Wolf was such a popular idea. Do people often curse at Wolf?"

Aphrodite laughed. "No. You're the only primate who ever greeted one of us. When Wolf lost his temper, you apologized for upsetting him and asked for the polite way to greet him *next time*. Even your anger was a person-to-person affair, not superior-to-subordinate or person-to-vermin. Wolf lost his temper at you because one primate pointed a lasepistol at me as soon as he got here."

"Which primate pointed a weapon at you?" Eliza asked, looking around. She realized she had her hand on her lasepistol. Startled, she took her hand off it.

Aphrodite snorted. "A Kovian scared him off."

"One of the *Broken Oar* crew? I want to know who to—"

"A Kovian put him in his place. Then another member of that crew put him in his place. He won't bother any of us."

"I don't want to befriend someone who treats you all like that."

"He doesn't have any friends. You've met him."

"Oh. Him." Then Eliza looked around. "Where are the Ursans? I only ever see Belek."

"They come and go. They only talk to Belek when they show up. Otherwise, they watch us. Almost like we're an exhibit. They live in the marshes down the coast and inland a ways."

"An exhibit?" Eliza asked. "And they say they don't know how long this place has been here?"

"They don't do well with the concept of time. And it's easy to get bored if you're immortal, no? We're a novelty."

"That's ... I don't know what I think of that. If they're studying us, they should ask our permission first. I'm serious."

"Interesting," Aphrodite said. "I hadn't thought of that. I'm not sure I'd be too keen on saying anything though. Especially since Belek really is a very good paramedic."

"Fair point."

"I don't mind if they watch us. What else do they do with their time, watch the reeds grow?"

"What do you know about them?" Eliza asked. "I don't even know what they eat."

"Oh, carrion. Dead Donners. They'll eat a baby Donner if they can get one. The occasional fish. Plants. Algae. They make some kind of sweet out of algae and cicada honey. Sometimes they ferment it and get drunk. Ever see a drunk Ursan? They still have no sense of humor."

Eliza laughed. *A baby Donner?* "The Ursans live underwater?"

"They don't live all the way underwater. You only get to their cities through water."

Eliza imagined a beaver's lodge for a moment.

"And here's an odd thing. They just keep growing bigger. What do you do with yourself if you never die? They used to have wars. They say they've outgrown them. Some Ursans are a hundred thousand years old. When one of them gets sick, they don't know what to do!"

"They must think we're all—"

"Belek quoted one of your thinkers. They think our lives are solitary, poor, nasty, brutish, and short."

Eliza burst out laughing. "I guess to them ... and yet Belek is a paramedic."

"His people think he's a weirdo. Like I said, they come and go."

She thought of the spiders back home and blurted, "Your people are long-lived too, I hope?"

"That matters to you?"

"Well, yes, of course!"

"Why?" But Aphrodite sounded kind, not demanding.

"Because I have a strange affection for Wolf, and because I think you and I could be friends."

Aphrodite laughed. "A strange affection? He was aggressive toward you, yet you feel affection for him?"

"If I thought someone wanted to kill my people, I would be a little aggressive too."

"Fair point. Some of your old-fashioned jokes are not funny."

"They aren't my old-fashioned jokes. Thank God there's only one of that evil type of Human here. You know, it's not cute, so kill it?"

"We live to be around a hundred years old, like you. And eventually, how that Human's story will end ...?" She raised one leg and lowered it, and Eliza wondered if it was a Spider equivalent of a shrug. "We get stupid questions like do we eat our mates, but that's the orbs back home. *They* do that. Deviants."

Eliza laughed, relieved.

"And while Belek's people die of infection or something if they lose a limb somehow, we can grow ours back."

"Omigod. We can't."

"That's sad."

"Do you have family here?"

"At home, we raise them in dens—houses. Here, well ..." She lifted her leg in a shrug. "My younger kids are at home now, all twelve of them. We actually have three apartments, but we built doors to connect them."

"And you're not from Ursinus either?"

"No. We ... found ourselves right where you showed up. We had just been attacked by orb weavers. Something's wrong with them. They were always a coldhearted, joyless bunch, but we coexisted. Then over the last year, more and more of them started getting together in mobs and killing us, raping us, burning us out of our homes. Before that, they were never violent—unless you count the marital cannibalism. Awful people, really. If we called law enforcement, some of them were orbs, and they wouldn't get involved. Anyway, about four months ago, relatively speaking, we were celebrating a birthday at a restaurant. A gang of orbs streamed in. They'd blocked the exits. They poured accelerants, and then they started a fire. When they started running out, we tried to follow them, but there were too many orbs. We were trapped, and we would have all died. We were choking to death and vainly trying to put out the fire. In an instant, we were here. Except for my husband. He was burned to death."

"I'm sorry," Eliza said softly. "That's awful."

"Theoretically. He was having an affair with the birthday girl." She raised her foreleg and lowered it again. "It's okay, you can laugh."

"I feel better about my wanting to laugh. Is the birthday girl here?"

"She'd left with someone else before the orbs got there, for which I am glad. Who knows what stories he told her? And good for her for leaving with someone else."

"And no one had any idea what was going on with the orbs?"

"I don't know. I hope they find out."

"So many of us are refugees," Eliza said. "I mean, I'm not, except to the extent that my position back home was ... precarious at best. And then my work partner had powers I'm not sure I understand."

Aphrodite sighed. "This situation with the Kanninoin, I hope it doesn't get ugly."

"Me too."

"And you're expected to keep order by yourself."

"I don't like keeping order."

"Isn't that what you do?"

"I protect people. I thought that at least here, people didn't need protecting."

"And no other primate is telepathic. I understand it gave Gino a panic attack. Well, between what's going on now and your telepathy, it must be lonely for you. If you want to come over one day and drink whatever it is that you all drink, I'd like that."

"So would I," Eliza said.

MALIT LIVED on the second floor two doors down from Eliza and Badri.

When Eliza entered, the first thing she noticed besides Lita, Malit, and Suk was the lack of furniture in the living room, just a low round table and some manila-colored woven mats. The light was lower than in Kelly's or her own apartment, and the temperature was slightly higher.

There was a dark orange cushion by the fire that Eliza guessed was for Suk, but Suk was lying on the floor next to Malit with her head in Malit's lap. Eliza smiled at the familiarity of this.

Malit was cross-legged sitting at the table by himself, eating a slice of raw meat with a knife and fork. He also had another Q'a'ta bone. He put his fork down and took a drink of something red out of a bowl. He was dressed in a simple, loose, sleeveless black tunic, and Eliza was struck that he had the well-developed muscles of a Human in his late teens. Then she saw that his elbows had the dimples of a Human toddler.

Eliza sat across from him and said softly, "Hi, Malit, how are you?"

Suk opened her eyes and looked at Eliza intently. Her eyes were black, with white around them like eye shadow. She reminded Eliza of Luna.

Malit took a swallow of whatever it was he was drinking and said, "My father is dead."

Hearing this response, Suk put her head back in Malit's lap and closed her eyes again.

"This is the q'a'hin'qe. The funeral meal," Lita said, sitting cross-legged beside Malit. "It is our tradition after a death that the elderly, the sick, the expectant mothers, and the children must eat," Lita said. "For the first three nights, a—" and the translator winked out—"must watch over them, even as they sleep. Three days after the death, our clan will gather for the funeral. Zhan's body will be cremated."

Eliza's eyes welled up. "Watching those loved ones eat and watching them sleep ... that's a custom that we Humans should adopt." She wondered if this meant that Lita would be up for three nights or if someone would spell her. She also recalled with disgust Inani's saying that Kharkuns don't respect their dead. Then she asked Malit, "Can you tell me about what happened?"

Lita asked, "What do you want to eat?"

Eliza tried not to stare. This woman was in deep mourning, and her son had lost his father, but she was playing hostess. Eliza thought back to her brother and how wrecked she had been when he died and wondered at this contrast. *This is their custom. Shut up*, she told herself, realizing the last thing she had eaten was almost twelve hours prior. So, even though at home she would have been the one bringing food, she said, "Oh, thank you. I would be grateful for a rare burger and french fries with ketchup and unsweetened iced tea to drink. Also, a bowl of blueberries." Eliza was nearly squirming from the awkwardness of this request.

When her food was in front of her, Malit said, "What's that smell? Can I have some?"

In case she might be construed as refusing the plate in front of her and insulting Lita, Eliza took a bite of her burger first and looked at Lita for approval.

But Lita had already appeared with the same meal as Eliza's and set the plate and bowl in front of Malit, smiling indulgently at her son.

Then Lita came back with a mug of something red that smelled to Eliza faintly of blood, and she realized that it was the same substance that Malit was drinking. Lita sat so that the three of them formed a triangle. "I've eaten already." Then she smiled, watching Eliza nearly wolf down the food and drink the tea almost without breathing.

Malit took a bite of the burger and said, "Ew! That's cooked! Gross!" He plopped the burger back onto his plate.

Eliza tried hard not to laugh.

Then he dipped a french fry in ketchup and ate it. "These are pretty good! Mom, you should have some! What are they made of?"

"There's a leafy plant. The plants are pulled out of the ground and attached are potatoes, the roots. They're sliced and fried. We eat potatoes other ways too, but french fries are my favorite."

"Mine too!" he said. Then he happily ate the rest of them, Lita and Eliza looking on.

Eliza noted that Malit never tried to give table scraps to Suk and wondered what she ate. She was nonplussed at the behavior of Lita and Malit. It was as if they were all out to eat together on an ordinary day.

Malit popped a blueberry in his mouth. Then his expression changed. "*Mom!* Eat one!"

Smiling at her son, she took a blueberry, inspected it, and put it in her mouth. She looked like she'd just eaten something amazing, much as Eliza thought she looked when she had tasted the naiya that Inani had given her. "This is a blueberry?"

"They grow wild on bushes back home. All over the place."

But Lita had already returned with a bowl, and Eliza was struck by how fast Kharkuns moved.

"Do you eat dairy products?" Eliza asked. "Sugar?"

"We use all parts of the Q'a'ta," she said. "We eat sugar rarely."

"Does the milk make cream?"

"It does. This is a delicacy."

"So if you serve blueberries with cream and sugar, it's a dessert. I'm not having that now because that's an awful lot of food to eat at once, but for future reference."

Lita smiled. Then she said, "The Holocaust survivors are Jews too. Some of them don't mix meat and milk. You do?"

"I'm relatively assimilated, or I wouldn't either." Eliza was emboldened. "I notice that you and Malit have slitted pupils and Zhan didn't."

"We're from the South. We were separated from the Northerners for millennia by a desert that no one can cross. Where we come from, there are months where the sun does not rise and months where the sun doesn't set. We live by the ocean, so we can eat fish. Fish makes Northerners sick. If only one parent has slitted pupils, the child will too."

"Are your languages mutually intelligible?"

"No. There are many different Kharkun languages just as there are with you Humans. Zhan speaks mine. His accent is noticeable, but he is fluent. The Kanninoin have one language, and it has never changed. They are strange." Then she became quiet and looked haunted. "Zhan's accent was—" She took a sudden breath.

"I'm so sorry," Eliza said softly.

"There is a lifetime left to mourn him."

They sat in silence. Ordinarily, she would wait for an interviewee to speak first. But she said, "So let's talk about what happened, so we can get justice for you and Zhan."

"Malit will eat his heart out of his chest."

Eliza really wished she could interview these two apart. Remembering their custom, she did not ask. "Can you think of any reason why anyone would want to hurt Zhan?"

"No," Lita said. "But Kolokh says Cody has a sand dune heart."

"You mean that his heart rate doesn't change when he fights?"

"Yes. This is true of murderers on our home world."

"Well, that's true of many people where I come from too. Not all of them are murderers. This includes astronauts and some pilots. But in order to also kill people for terrible reasons, such Humans also have to lack empathy and enjoy the suffering of others. Or seek power and control. When Kolokh pinned Kelly's forearm to the table—"

"This is the kulit. It is traditional when another man approaches a man and his partner."

"Okay, but this is not traditional with us. In fact, with us— not with you, with us—it is, to us only, typically something an abusive and controlling man would do to a woman." Eliza tensed, hoping she had qualified this statement enough.

Lita looked as if she had suddenly understood something. "This is why Kelly looked frightened when Kolokh did the kulit with her. But he is her partner, and this is what is done."

"And did he do this in front of Cody and Maura?"

"He did. Cody asked Kolokh, 'What the hell do you think you're doing?'"

"And Maura?"

"Maura spoke to her mother. She said, 'Why are you letting him do that to you?' She started to cry. Cody went to her and put her arm around Maura's shoulder and asked his mother if she was afraid."

"What happened?"

"The custom was explained to both Cody and Maura."

"And did Cody say anything about this?"

"He asked if there was a tradition of domestic violence. There is not. This satisfied him."

"And he went out to find Malit at some risk to himself," Eliza said, "even though Malit is not his relative. When he informed you of Zhan's death, what was Cody's heart rate like?"

"Malit said it was fast."

Malit took another drink out of his bowl and nodded.

"Cody has empathy. If he was worried about Malit, he would be worried about Malit losing Zhan. Would he not?"

Lita relaxed. "This seems so."

"In fact, if he were going to attack anyone, it would have been Kolokh, no?"

"Yes."

"Does Cody behave in a disrespectful fashion toward Kolokh?"

"No."

"There are techniques that a Human could use against a Kharkun, but a Human could not crush the skull of a Kharkun, let alone take a knife from a Kharkun and use it. Is this true?"

"It is true."

"Cody was armed with a lasepistol. With the ... *massive* strength difference, why use a knife or a club?"

"You're quick to admit the weakness of your species."

"It's obvious."

"The sun is the sun. But the Kanninoin are weaker than Humans."

"How do you know?"

But Malit stood up and left the table, Suk following behind. Then he came back, and Eliza inferred that he had washed.

Suk said, "Night-night, Suk!" Suk's voice was the same as Malit's, after the fashion of gray parrots.

Malit smiled and said, "Night-night, Suk!" He handed something to Suk, and she ate it.

Suk then went and curled up on her cushion. Malit went over to her, knelt beside her, and rubbed the side of her cheek. Suk purred and pressed her head against his hand and Malit kissed the top of her head and came back to the table.

Suk went to sleep, tail over her nose. Eliza guessed that Suk was guarding Malit as he ate, not waiting for table scraps.

"Can you tell me what happened, Malit?" Eliza asked.

"Gino was blind. Kolokh said Human senses were not as good as ours, and Gino was afraid. He said that the Shadows helped him and you see but then you were blind after they left. You were missing and Baines called you a dumbass. Kelly said it was about the dogs."

Eliza laughed.

Lita said, "Malit, language!"

"Sorry, Mom. That's what she said." Then he said to Eliza, "Badri called you selfish."

"This conversation happened in front of you?"

"Yes, I was there when Kolokh told my mother. Kolokh told me that it was very, very cold outside and that we could die if we went out in that storm. Kolokh told Mani and me that you were dead. It was too cold even for Humans." Eliza inferred that "Mani" meant "mother."

"And he told you not to go out in that storm."

"Yes. He told me not to go out in the cold to find the Shadows. But you can see, and I can't. I wanted to be able to see."

"When did you decide to do this?"

"After everyone was asleep. After it stopped raining." As an afterthought, Malit said, "I'm glad you're not dead."

Eliza smiled a little. "Me too. Wasn't it still cold?"

"No, it got warmer. I wore a coat."

"Between the time that you left your house and the time that you walked out of Broken Oar, did you hear anyone?"

"Keel was there."

"Did she say anything to you?"

"No. She was ... she was walking and sleeping. She said, 'Don't let my children find me.' But she was across the way anyway. And then I left. Mani, is it true that Tenurian babies eat their mothers?"

Eliza shuddered. "I don't know, Malit."

But Malit scooted over and crawled into his mother's lap. Then he hugged her. "They're bad."

Lita gathered him up in her arms for a moment and rocked him, and Malit smiled. Eliza wondered if he was feeling drowsy.

Lita let go of Malit, but she tousled his hair.

Touched, Eliza said, "What happened next?"

"I was scared of the Donners," Malit said. "I knew I could outrun them. The bats were flying into the ocean, and they were loud."

"Are they always loud?"

"Uh-huh! In the reed forest, I was scared. I wondered how far the Donners were. I thought I heard three of them laughing. But they didn't smell like Donners."

"Do Donners laugh?" Eliza asked Lita.

"They make some sort of chatter with each other," Lita said. "But they have never laughed. I think their sounds are tree branches against tin. Wind and noise."

"Other than Humans and Kharkuns, does anyone else here laugh?"

"The Spiders," Lita said.

"They weren't Spiders," Malit said. "Spiders crackle when they move."

"What did the people who laughed smell like?"

"I don't know," Malit said, furrowing his brow.

"Do people who live here smell the same?"

"What do you mean?"

"Do you remember your home world?"

"Yes."

"Did your mother and father smell the same way there as they do here?"

Malit thought for a moment. "No."

Lita and Eliza traded looks.

We have to find those people!

"What happened next?"

"Duncan and Scout came."

"What happened then?"

"I asked them if they wanted to see the Shadows too. But they didn't answer. I knew they weren't mad at me, because they leaned against me. So I sat down, and they snuggled up against me. The ground was wet, but I didn't care."

"Dogs can't talk. What can Suk say?"

"She is a Q'ua'to. They can talk a little. She can tell me when she's hungry or thirsty. Or if she has to go number one or number two. She can tell me some other stuff. Dogs can't talk? Really?"

"It's very sad. They can't."

"That's not fair. I thought the dogs at the dog park weren't talking because they were playing."

"It's sad that dogs can't talk. Duncan and Scout weren't mad at you. They leaned against you. That's not what dogs do when they're mad. What happened when Cody came to you?"

"He ran and knelt on the ground and hugged me. He was crying. He said, 'Oh, thank God you're okay!'" Then Malit frowned again. "Cody was too hot. His body was very hot. And he kept throwing up."

"Was his heart like sand dunes?"

"No, it was beating very fast. You Humans have very thin chests. Like when Suk play-growls under a blanket."

"How did you learn that your father was dead?"

"Cody told me."

"What did he say?"

"He said, 'Malit, I'm so sorry. Something happened to your father. I tried to save him, but I couldn't! He's dead.'"

"And what—"

"He smelled a way. When Kelly, Dina, Gino, and Cody came back without Jennifer, they all smelled like that. They were crying then too."

"You can smell grief."

Malit considered. "Yes."

"Then what happened?"

"Cody said we had to hurry. I was waiting for the Shadows, but they never came."

"They were probably migrating away from the storm when we saw them."

"So they weren't hiding from me?" Malit furrowed his brow again.

"No, Malit. They weren't. What do you think could happen to a Shadow in those winds?"

"They would ... bad things. It would hurt them. So ... they weren't hiding because they didn't like me ... they had flown away from the storm!" He gave a slow, sweet smile.

"That's right. Why did Cody say you had to hurry?"

"He was worried about Donners and another storm."

She looked at Malit and saw that his eyes were welling up.

"What happened next?" she said softly.

"We went to where my father was." Malit suddenly wailed, hugging himself and rocking back and forth. He sobbed until his sobs gave way to wailing again, and Lita gathered him into her lap.

In tears, Eliza stood to leave. She locked eyes with Lita and said, "I'm so sorry."

When the door closed, the wailing stopped as if Malit and Lita had never existed.

STILL SHAKEN from her interview with Malit, Eliza knocked on Inani's door. "You're coming with me to unlock Cody's door."

Inani said, "He could kill again."

"Get over yourself. He's not going anywhere. Is he going to flee Broken Oar? He could run to the ship by himself if he could avoid getting eaten alive by Donners, right? And then what? You all could certainly find him there. So—"

"You can go in. He will stay where he is."

Inani had covered the palm pad on Cody's door with a device that looked like a metallic hand. "Take that thing off the door," Eliza said, "and escort him then, until the village figures out what to do about this."

"This is not the village's concern."

Eliza ignored this.

Eliza walked in to find Cody watching a movie that she didn't recognize. Cody was wearing a green-and-white raglan shirt and navy blue pajama pants, and he was barefoot. Next to him was a glass of hot tea and a mug of chicken soup.

When he looked up, she said, "I tried to get Inani to unlock that door, but she won't. Is she always that pompous?"

Cody said, "Sit. Yes. Do you want some tea?" His voice was hoarse, and he had a dry cough.

"No, thanks. You drink tea and not coffee?"

"In stories, does anyone calm a person who's upset by saying 'Here, take this big-ass cup of coffee and then you can tell us about the headless horseman'?"

She laughed, but she saw by his eyes that he was sick. He was also feverish.

"Can you take anything for that fever? Maybe go to the hospital?"

"I already took something. I feel less awful than I did when I got back to Broken Oar."

"You should be in the hospital."

"Tell that to the Wicked Witch of the West out there. She thinks I'm the monster out of the *Ghost in the Cabin in the Woods*—sorry, after your time." Then he said, "Ironically, every four months, Kanninoin go into heat. If there's no one to mate with, they get manic—the irritable kind, not the grandiose kind. No matter what, it passes. Then they're all *Happy Clam Kids* again. Sorry, after your time again. Ask Inani. She and Johalo weren't married to Da'in first. Their third spouse was Rasan'in. Rasan'in had been out of town at some sort of conference when they went into their breeding cycle, and they got home three days in, and Inani killed them."

"And they've locked *you* up?" Eliza sat on the floor across from him on the other side of the coffee table. "Who told you this?"

"Da'in. They talked about it like it was a divorce. Sort of. I get the feeling that their marriage is on the rocks. Not because of that, though. Da'in went into that marriage knowing what happened."

"Wow. That's ..." She sighed. "I'd like to record this conversation. Would that be okay?"

"Fine by me."

Eliza took a device out of her satchel and set it on the edge of the table. Then she stated the date, the time, and who was present.

"I'm just trying to get a sense of what happened. You don't have to talk to me if you don't want to."

"I want to. I know, I have the right to remain silent ..." And he recited his own Miranda warnings to himself. "Yes, I want to talk to you. I want to find out who killed Zhan even more than you do."

"I know. I know you do. So tell me what happened."

"Zhan and I took off after Malit with Duncan and Scout. We made it into the reed forest. Several feet in, I saw Banner's geckos ... their tails were going nuts. That means they're stressed. This time of year, at that time of day, there are crustaceans that sound like cicadas, but they were silent. The dogs were growling. Zhan said there was something there. He counted three sets of footprints. Next thing I know, I'm lying next to Zhan with his blood on my clothes." Cody had tears running down his cheeks. "His clan knife, his Q'a't, was sticking out of his side." Cody wiped his eyes. "His head was bashed in. The dogs were gone. I was puking my guts out."

"Because you were afraid?"

"No. I was sick. My stomach hurt. And I threw up so hard it came out my nose. But I had to find Malit, that little goofball. I was afraid something had happened to him." After a round of coughing, he said, "I heard about the Shadows. So I went to find him. You might find some more—I threw up all the way to the clearing where I found Malit, until it was dry heaves. I don't know how we made it back." Then he said, "Malit chattered all the way—"

Cody put his head in his hands, and Eliza saw that his shoulders were shaking. She waited.

He roughly wiped his face on his sleeve and said, "I need you to catch the fucker who did this."

"On it," Eliza said grimly.

"I don't remember what happened when I got back to the village. When I came to, I was in the hospital. I had a fever. Almost forty degrees."

"Do you know what that is in Fahrenheit?"

Cody smiled a little. "It was a hundred and three point four degrees Fahrenheit."

"That's awful."

"I felt like I was dying. They gave me IV fluids and something for the fever. I feel like I'm at about seventy percent now. I just woke up a few minutes before you got here."

"How close to Zhan were you when you woke up in the forest?"

"Close."

"Point to an object that is as close as you were to him."

Cody pointed to the far end of the table.

"So about six feet."

"So one point eight meters, yes."

"Tell me exactly what you saw."

"Zhan was lying on his back, but ... it was like he had been lying on his side in a loose fetal position and his head lying to one side, and then someone had flipped him over on his back." Cody wiped his eyes. "He wasn't bloody. There were holes that looked like stab wounds. He had ... he had a dent in his skull. Eliza, there was no blood except on me and him! If he was stabbed that many times, where was the blood? Humans might not bleed from a stab wound to the abdomen, but a Kharkun sure as hell would."

"Badri and Ror didn't know either."

"But I had Kharkun blood on my coverall. Not a lot. And Zhan had a pinprick on his neck. Wait—" Cody took off his shirt.

On his back was a pinprick with an ugly bruise telescoping from it. Eliza took multiple photographs of this, including some with a tape measure beside it.

She looked at the door for a moment. Then she said, "Cody, I'm going to go out there and try to make Inani let you out. If she won't, I'm going to shoot the gizmo off the door. I want you out of the line of fire. Stay on the couch, okay?"

"Thanks, Eliza."

Inani was sitting cross-legged on a picnic table across from Cody's door with her eyes closed, her hands clasped over her navel.

"Unlock that door," Eliza said.

Inani opened her eyes and took a moment to focus. "Someone must—"

"Unlock that door."

"He will escape and kill again."

"When were you going to tell everyone that you're a murderer?"

"I didn't know what I was doing. It was the danata."

"Oh? Where I come from you'd've been arrested for homicide. Cody killed Glenn Sommars in defense of his shipmates."

"Violence is always wrong."

"If you don't unlock the door, I'll blow it up."

Impassively, Inani palmed the device over the entry console. Eliza noticed that the device remained.

"Take it off," Eliza said through gritted teeth.

After Inani did so, Eliza said, "Put it on the ground."

"Why?"

"Do it."

Inani laid it gently on the ground instead of dropping it.

Eliza unholstered her lasepistol, aimed it, and fired. The device melted into slag. "If you put another one on any door without a village consensus, I'm going to arrest you. Do you understand?"

Without waiting for a reply, Eliza went in to inform Cody that he was free to come and go, but he was lying on the couch having chills, and his breathing was labored. Eliza put her hand on Cody's forehead and immediately went to the console and summoned Dr. Colson. Then she notified Kelly.

Cody lay on the gurney in the hospital being tended to by Banner, Belek, and a man Eliza did not recognize. Banner was giving that man instructions, and she realized that it must be Dr. Brodt. Eliza saw that Cody had an IV in his arm and that they monitored vital signs the same way they had back home. Cody had an oxygen mask on his face.

Banner closed the curtain.

Kelly walked in, and Eliza said, "Cody didn't do it. The three suspects are in the reeds."

Eliza looked around her. She saw that this resembled the Level 1 trauma center in Tauxenent County, without the chaos of multiple patients and multiple alarms. At home, if area patients weren't air-ambulanced to Shock Trauma, they went to Cameron.

Badri led Eliza through the double doors. At the far end of the hall was another set of double doors, and Eliza thought of the sally port outside Badri's office.

The light in the hallway was dim, but when they were halfway down, she followed Badri through a door on the right and into a brightly lit morgue. Ror was sitting at a computer terminal making notes, but he looked up when Eliza walked in.

"Can we access the gate scan data from this console?" Eliza asked.

Ror shrugged, which absolutely floored Eliza. *Kharkuns shrug too!* "I'll see." He then began working intently on the computer.

He studied the screen for a moment. Then he said, "No one in or out that we don't already know about. The footsteps belong to strangers."

Badri showed her a photograph of Zhan's back. There was an ugly, target-shaped bruise around a pinprick.

"The stab wounds and the open fractures of the occipital bone were postmortem," Ror said.

"Zhan died from an injection of COVID zeta," Badri said. "How is it that biological weapons were kept on that ship, Ror? Do you know?"

"Wait, Cody has COVID zeta?" Eliza asked. "Badri, we're immune! But what about everyone else?"

"Fortunately," Ror said, "Banner has access to effective antivirals, and Johalo has been manufacturing the vaccine. We can bring the villagers to the social hall to be vaccinated and to receive prophylactic antivirals."

Eliza showed the two men the photograph of Cody's back.

"They gave it to Cody too. They didn't just mean to kill Zhan."

"I ask again, how is it that there were biological weapons on that ship?"

"Well, there was Glenn on the *Kestrel*," Ror said. "We should adjust our expectations accordingly."

"How accordingly?" Eliza said. "Did the *Kestrel* crew bring bioweapons too? Bynum is more than capable of that."

"What of it?" Badri said. "The *Kestrel* is inaccessible to him."

"For now," Eliza said. "Worse, if all those ships are equipped with them, were they all equipped with the same ones?"

Badri and Ror exchanged looks of dread.

"We must confront him," Badri said.

"We will," Ror said, a look of brutality flashing across his face. "First things first, since he can't get to the *Kestrel* now."

"How did Zhan die that fast?" Eliza asked.

Ror said, "Kharkuns have no resistance to coronaviruses, including the one of many that causes your common cold. Zhan's lungs were full of fluid. Our superior immune system rendered COVID zeta almost immediately fatal." Then he said, "I'm sorry about the word 'superior.'"

"We're not proud," Eliza said with a small smile. "But wouldn't a strong immune system be helpful?"

"No. It can induce a cytokine storm, a fatal autoimmune response, just as it does with your species."

"Can Kharkuns take our vaccine, and will it work?"

"Our immune systems have similar elements to yours, and they operate similarly, although somewhat more efficiently. I've received one," Ror said. "I'm still well, at least."

"What about the others?"

"Kanninoin have never been exposed to coronaviruses," Ror said.

"But the Spiders? The Kovians?"

"They won't discuss it with us."

"Why not?"

"They don't like primates," Ror said.

Eliza laughed. "Wait—the Kovians don't like primates either?"

"They merely do not *trust* primates. After all, they've met Inani and Bynum."

"Fair. Well, I had a telepathic link to Kovian 2 during the incident with the Shadows. Maybe I can still talk to him telepathically. And I'm on strangely good terms with Wolf, and Aphrodite likes me. We need to know!" Then she thought about the order to go to the social hall, and she got a sick feeling. "Dr. Brodt, Yossi, Jonah, and I need to go talk to the Holocaust survivors. Being ordered to a central location ... that's what happened to them before they got here."

"And who," Badri asked, "will be able to determine if any other ships have landed?"

Banner walked in, shaken. "Cody is stable, but Kinkead tells me that the *Peregrine* landed two days ago."

PART THREE

PART THREE

CHAPTER
THIRTY-SEVEN

"CAN you ask Kovian 2 and Wolf to come to the hospital?" Eliza said to Banner. "I'd like the two of us to talk to them."

"Really? You want to talk to a Spider?" Banner asked. "They're pretty cranky, you know. One of them almost ate Ralph."

"The key word is *almost*. Wolf almost ate Luna too, but last night, she buried a dog biscuit under my pillow, so she's clearly among the living. And Aphrodite is my friend."

Banner went to the computer console and started typing.

"Hey, how do you and Ror know how to use those consoles?" Eliza asked. "We can't read them. The letters look like the ones over the door!"

Banner showed them.

"A drop-down menu?" Eliza said, laughing. "Cool!"

"Murdering Zhan makes sense for barbarians," Ror said. "But why try to frame Cody?"

"I hypothesize that they will announce that they will 'rescue' us from the epidemic," Badri said in disgust, "and further, that they expect to find us all at war, and they will take advantage of this."

"We have to be ready for them!" Eliza said.

"Well, they can't get into the village without their bioscans in the database," Ror said. "Do they have shuttles?"

"They don't," Banner said. "The *Enterprise* will, because they don't plan on landing it. There will be three hundred colonists on the *Enterprise*."

Eliza felt sick. "Someone needs to stop the *Enterprise*. We can't trust who Space Force has put there. We won't be able to fight them off. I can't imagine what will happen when it gets here. Does the *Kestrel* have probes? If Ursinus b turned out to be uninhabitable, you were going to warn everyone to turn around, right?"

"We would have," Banner said. "A probe can get to Earth much faster too."

"Fast enough to intercept the *Enterprise*?"

"The *Enterprise* was going to leave for Ursinus b in two years. A probe could get there in eighteen months."

"Can it get to space from the surface?"

"It could. Someone's going to have to get past those assholes to the ship though."

"When Bynum hears that COVID zeta kills Kharkuns ..." Eliza said.

She walked into the infirmary with Banner and saw a man who could have been her grandfather, if her grandfather had been in his forties.

"Dr. Brodt?" Eliza said.

"The one, but it seems that the tradition here is to use first names. Call me Meyer."

Eliza's eyes welled up. "Eliza Benveniste. I'm glad you're here. How many—"

"Thirty-one. Some are Germans from Berlin—lawyers and their families. Some of us are from Warsaw. You Sephardic?"

"Yes. My father's people went from exile to Spain to Transylvania to Israel to the United States. Yes. My mother's people are Ashkenazim, like you. They went from exile to Poland to Israel to the United States. How are you all adjusting?"

"As well as you are. The Kanninoin first thought we would be sitting naked around a fire and grunting."

Eliza laughed.

"We're also not getting murdered by Nazi bastards. My son is learning to be a veterinary technician from Enkhid. Kovian 10 is now attending Torah study, and so is Kyr. They're curious and that's nice. Will they try to convert? Who would want to join this club, do you think?"

"I think they'd need a psych consult," Eliza said.

Meyer laughed. "I don't know what that is, but I can guess."

"The requirement is probably in the Talmud," Eliza said. "Or it should be."

"The Talmud?" Banner asked.

"More Jewish law," Meyer said, smiling. "Yossi and Jonathan are also studying Torah."

"Your families?" Eliza took a breath. *Kyr?*

"There are eight families. Twenty children. It's a little hard, because the Berliners are more assimilated than we are, but we were all in the process of being deported. Then we all woke up here. We've got a small school going in our social hall—not the main social hall, of course. The rabbi is having a headache trying to figure out the Jewish calendar with this three-hundred-day year. We may need to throw in a couple of extra leap months. You're welcome to come to Shabbos services, if you don't mind the mechitza."

"A *mechitza* is a barrier to separate men and women in

Orthodox Jewish synagogues," Eliza said to Banner. "I'd love to join you, Meyer, and I don't care about the mechitza. Also, I'm fluent in Hebrew. I guess it doesn't matter with these translators, does it?"

"Oh, we sometimes take them out. How can you hear the Torah chanted otherwise?"

Eliza relaxed. "You can't. Meyer, the plan is to get everyone to the social hall to be vaccinated against COVID zeta. That's going to be a sensitive issue now, isn't it?"

"It will, but between me, you, Yossi, Jonathan, and our non-Human friends, I think we can reassure everyone that we're not being rounded up."

"Good. It was a delight meeting you," Eliza said. But Meyer pulled her into a hug.

Eliza smiled at him, and he left. She turned around and found Kovian 2, another Kovian, and Wolf. Behind Wolf was a Spider whom Eliza had not met. She saw that that Spider had white patches around the eyes. She wondered whether that was a sign of age.

The five of them stood in between the rows of gurneys, and Eliza was grateful that the room was big enough. Meyer, she noticed, had gone behind the curtain with Cody, but she didn't know if that was because he was afraid of the Spiders or not.

"Prairie ape!" Wolf said warmly out loud. Then he used his two front legs to pull her close.

Eliza realized that she had a telepathic link with Wolf by way of touch. She decided not to be afraid as he hugged her.

"Stop!" Banner shouted, furious.

"This is telepathy, not lunch," Wolf said to him. "What is wrong with you?"

"Sorry. You can see how I'd think that."

"No, actually, I can't. And I don't trust primates, Humans the least. I prefer to use telepathy because the rest of you primates can't hear us."

Eliza heard Badri running and shouting, "Stop!"

"Calm down, primate!" Wolf said. "I'm not going to eat my pet prairie ape."

Eliza smiled at Wolf, then telepathically said, *"Banner's got some questions for you. So that you all don't, you know, die. Can Kovian 2 join the call or is that too many?"*

Wolf laughed. *"A conference call—"*

"I don't need to touch you, Eliza," Kovian 2 said, sounding hurt.

"I guess I don't know how many people can talk telepathically at the same time."

"I've brought Kovian 35. She's a doctor. And you have a lot to learn about telepathy."

"Clearly. Just out of curiosity, what did you do before you got here, Kovian 2?"

"Machinist."

"Are you a good shot with a lasepistol?"

"Yes."

"What about you, Wolf? What did you do before you got here?"

Eliza got a rush of images of sculptures. They were beautiful.

"And I'm a good shot with a lasepistol too. I learned when I got here."

The other Spider refused to touch Eliza, saying aloud, "I don't touch monkeys. I don't even want to look at you. Someone needs to put down that monkey in the bed."

"Wolf, are all your friends going to hate me?"

"No. He's an asshole, but he's also a doctor."

Eliza laughed.

When Kovian 35 tried to speak to Eliza telepathically, she could not.

"Well, shit," Kovian 2 said.

The Spider doctor refused to identify himself by name to Eliza, so she decided that he was Dr. Spider. Eliza would never be able to pronounce their real names out loud in any case.

After nearly an hour of questions back and forth between Banner and the four eight-legged aliens, some via telepathy with Eliza, Wolf relayed that a Human coming into the village had had a cold. Jhuq, a Kharkun boy, had gotten violently ill and had to be quarantined in a hospital room on the other side of the double doors. Bynum had been furious. Some of the other Humans had caught the cold and had mild symptoms, but the Kovians and the Spiders were unaffected. Banner confirmed this.

Wolf let Eliza go and turned to Dr. Spider. Wolf first addressed him by name, and the translator winked out again. Then he said, "The monkey over here didn't have to say a thing to us, you know. She didn't know that we couldn't catch that plague—and when we met, I wasn't exactly cuddly with her. How many bipeds would have kept their mouths shut and watched us die if they could?"

"They're dirty."

Eliza froze. She remembered her grandmotherly neighbor calling her "dirty Jew" when she was eight. "You crackle when you walk."

Wolf belly laughed. To Eliza's shock, Dr. Spider laughed too.

"That was pretty funny, monkey," Dr. Spider said, laughing. "You're still disgusting. Can we go back to sleep now? I can't tolerate the noise of that thing in the bed."

As they all trooped out of the hospital, Eliza was hit with another wave of vertigo, and she grabbed Badri's arm for support. "Vertigo," she said.

Badri tried to pick her up, but she said, "No! No! Don't make me move!"

"You will fall," he said.

When Badri got her onto a gurney, she rolled over to the side opposite him and vomited until her stomach was empty, then she moved into a fetal position, feeling mortified.

"I have seen vomitus before, Eliza," Badri said.

"Not mine," she said, then started retching again.

The vertigo grew so intense that moving her mouth to speak was agony.

Meyer came to her bedside. He said, "I'm going to give you some medications for the vertigo. They're called meclizine and ondansetron. I'm going to give them to you by injection because you won't tolerate having anything put into your mouth. You're going to feel the disinfectant on your skin, and it will be cold, then the injection's gonna hurt a little for a second."

Once the medication took effect, she felt the vertigo recede, but then a headache came. She grabbed her head and went into a fetal position.

"You are in pain?"

Badri.

"Did this happen the last time you—you had this form of communication with them?" Dr. Brodt asked.

"I'd only ever talked to Kovian 2," Eliza said, holding her

head in agony. "Yes. I thought it was from the Shadows. I guess it wasn't."

"Meyer, let's get her some tramadol," Banner said. "We're gonna give her a lighter dose since she already has the other meds on board, but she's looking pretty bad."

A GROUP ELIZA thought of as the village leadership met in the room opposite the morgue to discuss strategy.

Also appearing was an alien the size of bathtub who turned varying shades of green and looked like a gigantic flatworm that moved by creating tendrils from the body and pulling itself forward with them. The tendrils reminded Eliza of lightning bolts.

The Tenurians refused to show up. Senn was nowhere to be found.

Everyone bristled at Inani's presence, Eliza noted, but Kano told her quietly that without Inani, the Kanninoin could not participate.

The flatworm alien crawled on top of the counter with surprising speed and communicated with the group by telepathy with Kovian 2. Kovian 2 let everyone know that the alien had picked a name that everyone present would understand based on a sweeping tumultuous saga published in 2070 called *George's Fire*. George went on to announce that they were intersex and native to the marshes around the Ursan mating ponds, where they ate the eggs of Belek's species.

"Call us Marsh Ursans," George said through Kovian 2.

"How are you gonna work alongside George, Belek?" Baines asked. "Their people eat your kids."

Belek clacked his antennae together. "The women of our species lay approximately a thousand eggs once every fifty Ursan years. Of these, most are eaten, but a large fraction of these hatch into larvae. Of those, approximately one survives to leave our breeding ponds. Most but not all of us survive our first molt. I read some Human history after you arrived. I was born a few Earth years before Genghis Khan centralized his power in 1206 by your reckoning, and the most recent of my ancestors to die did so shortly after your Permian extinction event, what your scientists call the *Great Dying*—"

Eliza had never heard of it before, but before she had time to decide it was just a really long time ago, Gino said, "That's two hundred and fifty-two *million* years ago. Really?"

"Two hundred and fifty-one point nine," Badri said.

"Oh, well, that changes everything," Gino said.

"Badri is correct," Belek said, his carapace turning a swirl of indigos, oranges, black, and red. Eliza wondered if that was how Ursans laughed. "Yes. If all of our eggs survived to adulthood, *we* would experience a mass extinction. Our larvae are expected to manage to survive to adulthood. If they cannot, what of it?"

The room was silent.

"They've never heard of birth control, obviously," Gino stage-whispered to Eliza.

"So," Eliza said, trying not to belly laugh, "Kinkead, can you get the probe in the air if someone goes to the *Kestrel* and gets it?"

"There's only one?" Belek asked.

"There are two of them," Kinkead said. "Yes, I can. They're

built for that, in fact. There might be conditions in the atmosphere that ..." and he gave a lecture that lasted fifteen minutes.

Belek clacked his antennae together as a sign of impatience, and Kovian had turned white, but Kinkead only stopped his disquisition when George poured themself down the computer monitor and came to rest as a puddle on the desk.

Only Badri was listening intently.

Eliza thought that Kinkead was about five-six, maybe one twenty-five. He had thinning, messy black hair and wore a cream-colored knee-length tunic, cream-colored trousers, and sandals.

"Where are they?" Wolf asked. "The probes, in case we all forgot what we were talking about."

"They're stored in a compartment beneath the bridge," Kinkead said, face bright red.

Eliza decided that he was used to this kind of reception.

"How far is the *Peregrine* from here?" Kolokh asked.

"About ten kilometers northeast," Kinkead said. "There's a cove there. In fact—"

"Well, some of them have come our way, but maybe not all of them," Banner said, deliberately interrupting.

Fanny Brodt sent Banner an adoring look.

"There are sixteen of them," Kolokh said. "There are two hundred of us. Why are we afraid?"

"Who in your family are you willing to sacrifice before we stop them?" Wolf demanded. "You can kill a lot of people with a lasepistol before someone rips your head off."

"I see this now," Kolokh said.

"Are there Donners there?" Gino asked.

"Yes," Kinkead said. "Drone data shows that there are a lot of them. They must like the fresh water. I noticed that—"

"Good," Gino said. "I hope the Donners open a restaurant right outside their ship."

Rabbi Einhorn laughed. "We'll need training to use those lasepistols. I'm not sure I know which end to hold on to." The rabbi was broad-shouldered, with a neatly combed black beard and earlocks. He wore a kippa, but he was wearing an Ursan cream shirt, a black vest, and black trousers. He looked like he could wrestle a Highland cow to the ground.

"We'll need to train all of the adults," Kolokh said.

"No Kanninoin will use a lasepistol," Inani said. "And your approach is disproportionate."

"You can't negotiate with murderers," Rabbi Einhorn said. "Even you must somehow know that."

"How if we could get their dogs away from them?" Enkhid asked.

Gino gave an evil grin.

"We'd have to send one group to the *Peregrine* and another to the *Kestrel*," Kovian 2 said. "Too many lives."

"There are three from the *Peregrine* nearby," Kyr said. "That would leave thirteen. They are already outnumbered."

"Is Kolokh correct about the population of the *Peregrine*, Kelly?" Badri asked.

Eliza noted that Badri did not address Baines.

So did Kelly.

So did Baines.

"Yes," Kelly said, "and the *Archer* as well, if the crew doesn't eat each other alive before they get here."

"But why go through all this headache over the *Peregrine*?" Fanny asked. "The probes, I can understand, but the crew of that other ship can't get in, can they? Could they really shoot through all of that rock?"

"They won't want to live in the ships," Banner said. "They're too small. And if they knock down the walls, the Donners will be on top of them forevermore. The problem is that they'll have us pinned in here. And Bynum will let them in."

"Even though they've murdered Zhan?" Rabbi Einhorn asked.

"Because they murdered Zhan," Eliza said.

"How did your Space Force let such a man aboard?" Rabbi Einhorn asked Baines.

"He doesn't make policy," Baines snapped. "That's not his job."

"So what?" Rabbi Einhorn said.

"Can you neutralize his gate bioscan?" Meyer asked.

"No," Belek said.

"Well, shit," Baines said.

"There's at least one tunnel," Eliza said. "Can you find out if there are more of them, Kinkead?"

"I'm an astrophysicist," he said, bemused.

"Yes, with equipment to be able to see stuff," Eliza said. "Can you?"

"Can do."

"Why do we need to know?" Inani asked.

"Because," Eliza said without looking at her, "if they get in here, we might want the more vulnerable among us to hide out while we take out the trash. That okay with you?"

"Why won't you try negotiating first?" Inani responded.

"You've never faced an existential threat, have you?" Rabbi Einhorn said, also without looking at her.

"There's no such thing," Inani said.

Rabbi Einhorn said, "I could give you a history lesson but—"

"Negotiate how?" Eliza demanded. "They use bioweapons."

"Split the village with them," Inani said, "or help them build one nearby."

Eliza laughed helplessly.

Rabbi Einhorn gave her a look of disgust. "You don't negotiate with butchers—"

"She'll agree to sacrifice us in the name of diplomacy," Ror said.

"We should show you the murals inside our own ship so you can get an idea of their mindset," Gino said. "This planet is huge. This village is tiny. They can go fuck themselves."

"Our doors lock," Inani said, her ears pulled back. "Why do we need tunnels?"

"So they do," Eliza said. "Can you open one with a lasepistol? Speaking of which, how are we with weapons?"

"We can manufacture weapons with the dispensers," said Kelly.

"We need to manufacture a lot of them," Banner said. "What are those turrets for?"

Belek remained silent.

"We'll investigate the turrets," Wolf said.

"Thank you, Wolf," Banner said. "What do we tell everyone else?"

"We each talk to our families," Rabbi Einhorn said, "or congregation. We don't give Bynum the floor."

"I just messaged Yossi," Kinkead said. "He says he thinks this storm will be sitting on top of us for the next three days."

"So let's use the time to figure out the tunnels and work out a plan in case this place is invaded," Banner said.

"When this place is invaded," Ror said.

＊

When the council regrouped, Banner immediately asked, "What did we find?"

Kinkead sent a map to their comm-watches and projected it on a large screen in the room.

It showed a network of tunnels with a central living area.

"How much space is there?" Rabbi Einhorn asked.

"Enough for the colony. Bigger than the big social hall," Kinkead said.

There was an access point to the tunnels from the first floor of every building. The upper floors could get to them via the fire escapes behind the units.

"What about the drainage pipes?" the rabbi asked.

"The drainage system is self-contained," Kinkead said. "We couldn't get into the pipes if we wanted to, and they don't intersect the tunnels we would use. I've already been to Eliza's tunnel. No one will get in through there again because I sealed it off. Now, the tunnels open up in these corners of the small social hall under the floorboards and the great social hall in the same location. Each first-floor house has an entrance in a den closet. The hospital has two. Follow me."

Kinkead led the group to the room on the left at the end of the hall. Eliza saw a hatch in the corner of the room, barely visible, and a small button the size of a thumbprint. Kinkead pushed the button, and the hatch dilated open into a tunnel with a ladder.

The entrance was big enough, Eliza saw, to accommodate even Belek. They went down the ladder and saw that the tunnel was dimly lit with path lights. The tunnel was about eight feet high, to Eliza's relief. They would not have to go through the tunnels on their bellies.

"How do the dogs get into the tunnel?" Badri said. There was a dull echo when he spoke.

"Someone's going to have to hand them down," Kinkead said.

"This sounds risky," Badri said.

"That it does," Banner said. "Kinkead, could you figure something out?"

"I'll ask Tony Polichek."

"Please," said Kelly. "And there will need to be five of whatever you come up with—for our dogs and Badri's too."

Kinkead nodded. Then he started to explain the mechanics of how this could be done.

"All right, already!" Meyer said. "Don't knock a teapot!"

Kinkead turned red again.

"Do these tunnels echo?" Kelly asked. "It could get awfully loud with everyone down here."

"It doesn't seem to," Kinkead said. "But the acoustics"—everyone tensed—"seem to suggest not." He flushed again.

"Thank you, Kinkead," Eliza said to him, but loudly enough for the whole group to hear, "for finding the tunnels, scouting out the tunnels—*and* thinking to seal off the entrance to my tunnel too. I don't know how many of us would have thought to seal up my tunnel."

"I'm sure it would've been forgotten in all the hubbub," Gino said. He clapped Kinkead on the shoulder. "Way to go, man."

"Thank *you*, Eliza," said Kinkead.

Eliza noticed that every few feet on the tunnel floor, there was a grate about three feet long. Eliza felt a draft coming through them. When she looked down, she saw only blackness.

"There are also compartments here," Kinkead said, pointing to a dark square the size of his hand. He walked across the tunnel, knelt, and pressed it.

The face of the tunnel wall slid aside to reveal a storage area that reminded Eliza of overhead airplane compartments.

"There is one of these every meter or so," Kinkead said. "We need to fill these with weapons and foodstuffs in case the dispensers break somehow. And I recommend adding additional translators too. I've programmed this to recognize every villager's bioprint, with the exception of Bynum's."

"Have you tried to reason with Bynum?" Inani asked.

"Rain is wet," Kolokh said.

"He understands," Rabbi Einhorn said. "To him, you're either inferior, dangerous, or both. And you're in the way."

"To him, you're just another alien," Eliza said, "just one who he knows will go quietly." She thought of the many, many science fiction books and TV shows where aliens were seen as wiser and more peaceful and imagined those Human characters responding to Inani.

"He's confused about why we can't hunt the local wildlife," Banner said. "He wants to domesticate those ungulates out there—the ones Eliza aptly named Highland cows. Including by slaughtering them. And he made a joke about eating Kovians. Those crewmembers are his allies."

"*Someone should set him on fire,*" Eliza said to Kovian 2 telepathically.

"*Someone might have to.*"

"*You're right.*" Eliza knew she was asking for another bout of vertigo, but she felt just fine about that.

"But not all of them are necessarily his allies," Inani said.

"Bioweapons," Eliza said.

"How do we get the news out about the tunnels?" Fanny

said. "We can't—how do you say it? Make it blast and not have Bynum find out."

"Put it on blast," Banner said, smiling a little.

Fanny smiled back. "You learn something new every day. How about that, Meyer? Put it on blast."

"We'll have to do it family group by group," Banner said.

"You cannot create a message and manually choose the addressees?" Badri demanded.

"What?" Banner asked.

"They've never needed an email chain before, Badri," Eliza said, laughing.

Ror punched some characters in his comm-watch. Wolf, Badri, and Kovian 2 each got a message. "I chose the three of you. Did you get it?"

A chorus of *yes*es.

"Any others receive my message?"

A chorus of *no*s.

"So much for the echo problem," Rabbi Einhorn said. "There isn't any."

Badri smiled and showed Eliza the message.

Eliza exploded into laughter. "A cat picture?" At Ror's look, she said, "Metaphorically."

It was a picture of a Q'ua'to, this one a tabby.

"This is Quna!" Ror said, confused. "I don't know what a cat is. You've seen a Q'ua'to before!"

"Our internet communications were heavily dominated by domestic cats," Badri said. "*Felis catus*. I will show you an image of one when we return to the surface."

"I'd like that," Ror said.

"We'll fill these compartments with supplies," Wolf said.

"Tell everyone that if they see an image of a Kovian turned red, it's time to evacuate," Kovian 2 said.

We need to run drills," Kelly said. "People should keep close to buildings and out of the open. After an alarm, villagers need to get into the tunnels within ten seconds. It's as fast as practical."

"Where is the oxygen coming from?" Fanny asked. "In the middle of that central shelter, will we be able to breathe? The tunnels will be sealed."

Kinkead pointed to a grate in the floor. "There's a draft coming through here. You notice these are every meter or so."

Fanny started weeping. Meyer put an arm around her, and Rabbi Einhorn said, "It's just oxygen. It's just oxygen."

Eliza went and put her arm around Fanny's waist. "We're safe here," she said. But she was crying too.

"What is this? Why are you crying?" Kovian 2 asked, distressed.

"Humans cry without reason," Inani said coldly to Kovian 2.

"Only the Jews are weeping," said Wolf, putting a hand on Eliza's shoulder.

"What are Jews? A different species?" Inani asked seriously.

Meyer laughed bitterly.

Eliza spoke telepathically to Wolf and Kovian 2 at length.

Then Wolf turned to Inani and said, "They understand Bynum all too well. So should you."

"What's going on?" Rabbi Einhorn. "The three of you—is that the telepathy that Meyer spoke of? I read a few novels about this. I never thought I'd see it. One was *Last and First Men*."

"They can talk silently?" Fanny said. "How about that!"

"What just happened?" Ror asked.

"It's a very long story," Eliza said, "with so many chapters repeating themselves, all ending the same way. Yes. Let's get back to work."

"These vents could be blocked, couldn't they?" Kano asked.

"That's an awful lot of blocking," Banner said, "for sixteen people to accomplish—and in terms of mechanical aptitude, Bynum couldn't find his ass with both hands. But where's the air coming from?"

"As best I can tell," Kinkead said, "there's a deep pocket of oxygen beneath the village. It extends into the reed forest and beyond. There are life signs under there. Perhaps the oxygen is their waste. But it seems to be self-contained. I don't detect any openings to the surface."

"How come we can't detect life signs anywhere else?" Gino demanded.

"Range," Kinkead said.

"Wolf," Eliza said with tears in her eyes, "I'm terrified to think about what those monsters would try to do to you and your people."

"I fear," said Badri, "that secrets do not keep."

In the social hall, Humans and Kharkuns stood in line, and Badri, Meyer, Leon, Ror, Johalo, and Banner were administering vaccines. At Meyer's insistence and to Ror's confusion, there were small treats for each child. Only Banner and Badri had ever seen a lollipop. Kharkun children were each given the tooth of an ungulate the name of which, for the non-Kharkuns, the translator couldn't grab. The Kanninoin objected to treats on principle until Badri suggested Rubik's cubes.

The social hall was about five thousand square feet. The walls were made of wood. In the front, there was a series of round tables and chairs, with food dispensers on each table. On each side of the hall stood a set of three doors, and toward the back was an open area.

Even though lots of people were talking, sound did not carry, and Eliza wondered what accounted for this. Then she decided that a culture that had left the dispensers behind could somehow make apparently wooden walls dampen ambient noise.

She saw Jonathan speaking with Fanny Brodt and a girl beside her who Eliza guessed was Fanny's daughter. Jonathan was stocky, with coarse black hair, black eyes, and a fashionable five o'clock shadow. Eliza estimated the girl's age at thirteen. She had a guitar hanging from a strap.

Fanny laughed at something Jonathan said and made a gesture that Eliza's mother's mother would have made. It meant "Nu? So?"

All three of them had their translators out, speaking Yiddish animatedly.

Not far away, Rabbi Einhorn was talking with Kyr and a Kanninoin whom Eliza hadn't met.

As Eliza scanned the room, to Eliza's surprise, she saw the remaining flock of Tenurians.

George's people, Eliza saw, were on the walls, all touching.

The girl with the guitar walked up to Eliza. She was plump and not much taller than Eliza, with her black hair in braids.

"I'm Channa Brodt."

"Eliza Benveniste."

"My parents told me what's going on. How can I help?" Channa had soft brown eyes, but she had the determined look of the born organizer. "We got the comm-watch messages. We found our tunnels already. You could miss that button if you weren't paying attention." Then she furrowed her brow, immediately reminding Eliza of Malit. "What about bathrooms?"

Eliza face-palmed. "Of course! Omigod! We'll have two hundred people in those tunnels. I'll talk to Kinkead."

"That would be a good idea." She hesitated. "You know, hiding from an enemy that's hunting for us ... bring treats for the kids. Plenty of water. Lots of food."

"There are dispensers in the central hall. We saw them."

"That's spooky, don't you think so?"

Eliza nodded. "It kind of is ... in a good way, except Humans might make a mess of it all again."

"Not if we can help it."

"I'm really glad you brought up the bathrooms. Otherwise—"

"*I'll* talk to Kinkead," Channa said, looking around the room. "There he is."

Kinkead was across the room talking to a Kovian, who actually appeared to be interested, to Eliza's relief.

Channa embarked on an earnest conversation with him, including the Kovian in the discussion. After it ended, she turned her attention to two juvenile Spiders playing with a Kharkun girl and a Human girl. The four were playing a kind of volleyball with a ball of web. Channa went over to join them, smiling.

Eliza watched Channa approach the young Spiders and her friends. She couldn't hear what they were saying, but suddenly, there were five children, three of them non-Human, laughing together.

"This is quite the gathering."

Eliza turned around to see Aphrodite. "I never thought I'd ever live to see this," Eliza said.

"See what?"

"Other species."

"You must have been disoriented when you got here."

Eliza laughed quietly. "Kind of. What do you make of this place?"

"I don't know. So many bipeds."

"You don't have bipeds at home?"

"We don't have mammals at home. You really must come over and drink whatever it is you drink."

"When?" Eliza said, meaning it.

"Come over for dinner the day after tomorrow. Six o'clock."

"Deal. I'd ask what I should bring, but those dispensers are—"

"I don't like them."

"I'm starting to see what you mean by that. They're ... I don't know, like we're—"

"Like we're caged animals being fed by a keeper."

Eliza tilted her head. "You're not the first person I've heard express that one way or another. Plus, we can't prepare our own food according to our own recipes. I had to tell the damned thing to put dill in the chicken soup, and it came out green. I had to negotiate it. Even then ..." Eliza shook her head.

"I'm not sure it matters what chicken soup is, because I absolutely understand. We don't want to eat the local wildlife. One of us is trying to build an enclosure with ratflies and—" here the translator winked out, and it seems like Aphrodite was rattling off a shopping list. "But as it stands, there isn't enough room to feed us all. The dispensers won't give us live food, so we're making do. But even if it did, we still hunted our prey, and now we can't."

"What's a ratfly?"

Aphrodite moved the hands of her front arms about three feet apart. "This long. About two feet around. Gray. Squishy. Burrows underground. If we catch it just as it metamorphoses into a fly, it's a delicacy. Really, they're delicious throughout their life cycle, but when they're still all ..." She hesitated. "I gather that your people don't eat insects, so I won't go into detail."

Eliza smiled a little. "Some Humans do back home, but not in my culture. It would be ... upsetting for us. I wish you could eat like you're accustomed to, though. When I first got here, I was happy that food scarcity wasn't a problem. So I'm kind of feeling a little bit spoiled. But there's no happy medium in this place. So yeah, almost like a zoo."

Eliza began to ask Aphrodite how she was related to Wolf, but Channa came back, distracting her. "Kinkead's on the bathroom situation. He said to tell you they won't be portable toilets. What are portable toilets?"

"Absolutely disgusting," Eliza said. "Thank you, Channa."

When Eliza turned back, Aphrodite had disappeared.

Channa sat on one of the tables and began to play the guitar. Eliza guessed that she was playing old youth group songs. Sitting next to her, munching on another Q'a'ta bone, was Malit, completely entranced.

The children, Eliza saw, were making friends. One Human boy was squatting, looking over the shoulder of a Kharkun at a portable video game console, and a group of three Human children were trying to teach a Kanninoin child and a juvenile Spider how to play what looked like chess. There were, she guessed, about fifty children in the room. Some hung back, some looked afraid, but most were trying to make friends. There was a toddler sitting on a woman's lap, staring intently at his mother's food and ignoring his own.

Another young Spider joined the volleyball game. At one point, Eliza heard the Human say to the Spider, "The sun is the sun."

Several Kovian children were sitting with Kanninoin children and a Human, also playing what appeared to be video games. Eliza smiled.

A few Ursans looked on, but a smaller Ursan tentatively joined the children playing chess, clacking their antennae in what Eliza had learned to recognize as intense emotion.

Belek looked riveted, his carapace changing from maroon to green to blue.

The Tenurians sat in a cluster, avoiding everyone. They occasionally made what Eliza thought might be warding signs at everyone. Then one Tenurian chick tentatively approached a group playing video games and squatted too. The chick's mouth was unnaturally large for the head, and Eliza shuddered.

Then she heard the chick introduce herself as Keela.

Eliza thought Channa's music lovely. A blond Kharkun boy walked up to Channa with a flute, and then a Human girl came with a clarinet.

Channa said, "Jhuq, sit here!" and patted the table beside her. Then she said to the girl with the clarinet, "And you sit next to him!"

As both of the children took a seat, Malit continued to watch Channa play, Suk curled on Malit's lap. Malit offered some of his Q'a'ta bone to Suk, who took a bite. At one point, Malit saw Eliza and gave a slow, sweet smile before turning his attention back to Channa.

Eliza watched Malit and Channa and realized that for the first time since she and Jamie had responded to Dyson's first victim, she was calm, even happy. Then she thought of the

Peregrine and of Bynum and was filled with rage. Looking at the two children, she knew what she had to do.

Badri was cleaning up the supplies, and he watched Eliza about six meters away to his left. She was sitting at a table watching the children, and he could see her expression clearly. She looked relaxed in a way that he had not seen her since before Lonnie Dyson had started his bloodbath. He could determine that she had formed a bond with the boy Malit and now with the girl with the guitar.

Eliza occasionally transferred her gaze to the children around the room.

Eliza looked again at Malit and Channa, and her vision clouded.

She stood up with an expression on her face that was familiar and that Badri wished that he could place.

Kovian 2 put a tentacle on her shoulder and turned red, and Wolf was standing at the side door to Badri's right, perhaps fifteen meters away.

She, Kovian 2, and Wolf stood by the door for a moment. As Eliza stood in the doorway, she locked eyes with Badri for a moment, and then Badri remembered with dread when he had last seen that look in Eliza's eyes.

CHAPTER
THIRTY-NINE

ELIZA STAGGERED into the house and saw Badri sitting on the couch with his dogs and watching a tutorial on medicine, 2200s-style. She leaned on the kitchen counter, quickly took a meclizine out of the bottle, and slipped it under her tongue, grateful that she didn't have to push it out of a blister pack. But the floor began to shift, and she lay down on the kitchen floor waiting for the vertigo to pass and the meclizine to dissolve.

Badri appeared almost immediately in the kitchen and sat beside her, stroking her hair, waiting for the medication to take effect. Both of them stayed silent.

As soon as Eliza said she was starting to feel better, Badri picked her up and carried her to their room, laying her on the bed, where she rolled onto her side, grabbing her head.

He left the room for a moment and came back with a tramadol tablet and a glass of water. "You must take this before your headache develops."

She did.

Badri got into bed fully clothed, lying behind her and

taking her into his arms. "You have changed your clothes," he said.

"I wasn't with anyone!"

Badri laughed silently. "I know this. You have been communicating telepathically with Wolf or Kovian 2. Perhaps both. And then something took place that required you to change your clothes. But why did you three need to talk telepathically? And what caused you to need to change your clothes?"

"Couldn't we just have wanted to talk for a while? Couldn't I have just changed my clothes because I felt like it?"

"You could have wanted this."

They lay in silence for many minutes, but Eliza was used to using silence to elicit the statements of others.

"Eliza." He stroked her face. "Eliza, what have you done?"

She did not answer. They lay in silence again,

"There are some things that are best left unsaid," she finally told him. "Do you agree?"

"I do not agree. There are some secrets that couples should not keep from each other. This is one."

"You followed me to a door once. Haven't you learned?"

"Roll over and look me in the eye."

Eliza did.

Badri pulled her close and went forehead to forehead with her and stroked her hair. "I followed you to a door once. And it cost us both nothing. Except that I learned what Detective Cloud was capable of if a man took from you what he himself wanted." He kissed her on the forehead.

"You didn't take anything. I gave it."

"Do not bother with technicalities, Eliza. I understand the subtext of what you are saying, and I also know that it has diverted us from my original question. Eliza, what have you done?"

"There are two others affected if I tell you what happened. What of them? Will you be silent on our account?"

"I will."

She took a breath, then looked him in the eye again.

EARLIER THAT EVENING

John Bynum opened his door and found Eliza standing there, crying hard. "Dr. Bynum," she said, congested from crying, "I can't take it anymore! I can't! I need to talk to you! I need you to do the surgery."

Bynum smiled. He said, "Calm down! No need for hysterics. Let's get you to the hospital. Ideally, you'd be on an empty stomach, but you don't have time—"

"No, not the hospital! Badri has to check on Cody! If he sees me, he'll stop me! He can't be allowed to do that! He'll go to bed in a couple of hours. Can I hide here? He doesn't know what you know! Please?"

Bynum sighed. "Come in," and he stepped back from the door.

Eliza held the door open.

"Well, come in!" Bynum said impatiently.

Wolf came in.

Eliza and Kovian 2 followed, the door closing behind them.

She saw with satisfaction that Bynum's floor was bare, and she palmed the window closed. She noted that the sliding glass window was already closed, and she smiled.

"What is this all about?" Bynum asked, looking at each of them in turn.

Wolf's front legs were up.

"Taking out the trash," Eliza said. "You'd have let them in. Even though they tried to kill us all."

"They wanted to get this colony under control, as they should," Bynum said. "Some of these species could be put to work. Others should be exterminated to make room for Human expansion. You're delusional if you think these"—he gestured at the other two—"are your equals. And look what's happened to Kelly—she's letting one pollute her!"

Wolf gave an ugly laugh.

Bynum jumped, then gestured to Wolf. "Why have you brought this thing with you?" As Bynum was talking, he was edging gradually to the fireplace lighter. "It's little more than a parrot, and it'll turn on you eventually. If you had half a brain, you'd take a lasepistol to it immediately. You can stuff it afterward and put it next to your fireplace."

"Oh, honey," Eliza said gently. "We can't take a lasepistol to *anything* in here. It will go through the walls and hurt someone!"

Bynum dove for the fireplace lighter, but he didn't get to it, because Kovian 2 was faster. He jerked Bynum back from the fireplace and toward the center of the room. With two tentacles, he lifted up the coffee table and tossed it over the couch, and it landed in the hallway with a crash that even made Eliza jump.

Kovian 2 yanked Bynum backward and held him against his body, and Bynum realized his mistake.

"You're a police officer!" he said to Eliza in a high voice. *"Stop them!"*

"*Stop* them? I brought them here!"

Kovian 2 held him still, and Bynum started screaming, *"Help me! Somebody help me!"*

"The apartments are soundproof, Bynum," Eliza said. "Scream all you want to. It still won't be as awful as the sound of a little boy wailing over the body of his dead father." Then she went to the dispenser.

Wolf put each of his front arms on Bynum's shoulders. By this time, Bynum was hysterical. After a few moments, Wolf sank his fangs into Bynum's chest. Bynum shrieked and tried to struggle, but Kovian 2 held him fast. Bynum twisted and gave Eliza a pleading look.

After a moment, Wolf disengaged, saying, "Yeah, I'm telepathic. I'm going to have to drink a lot of maggot blood tonight to wash away the filth of your thoughts. I'm not eating you, though. Why do you think that is? Because you're somehow sentient, you virulent bag of maggot pus. Once I got a brainful of you, I withheld the anesthetic. Your guts are going to turn to soup pretty soon. You'll be bleeding out of every orifice. Your bones will start to dissolve. And it's gonna hurt."

Bynum broke out in a cold sweat.

"You knew," Eliza said with loathing, "that a patient could aspirate vomit on a full stomach during surgery and suffocate or die of pneumonia, you coldhearted butcher, but you were willing to take that chance with me tonight, because any of those doctors would recognize a lobotomy if they saw one."

Bynum coughed, then said, "Not just a—"

"Ror's a night owl, right?" Eliza interrupted. "You needed to hurry up before he showed up and stopped you."

"You savages m-might have a low pain threshold, but n-not a Human man," Bynum said to Wolf. "I can take a little ... a little heartburn. Eliza's j-just trying to scare me, but she's coming to her senses, because she's a p-police officer and I'm a Human."

"No sedative or anesthetic," Wolf said. "Not for you. Payback for Malit, Lita, and Zhan."

Bynum vomited blood and started screaming again.

Eliza hurried to him, and Bynum had a fleeting expression of hope. But then he saw what she had in her hand. Eliza grabbed him by the shoulder and stabbed Bynum multiple times where she thought his aorta and liver would be. His abdominal cavity would slowly fill up with blood.

In less than a minute, he started bleeding from every orifice and from his gums. Kovian 2 dropped Bynum, and he fell like concrete, flailing as if trying to throw something off himself, screaming hoarsely. Then he lost the ability to control his legs.

He looked at Eliza with bleeding eyes, and she said, "Nothing would help. It's too late."

"Not even if you were in the hospital," Wolf said roughly.

Bynum closed his eyes. Occasionally, he would scream as if aroused from a nightmare, and every time he did, Eliza was reminded of Dyson. She walked over and, turning her face to one side so as not to get a mouthful of blood, she slit his throat. He still had decent blood pressure, somehow, because she heard the spray of blood, and her cheek and hair became drenched in it.

Eliza knew he was dead before she checked his pulse. His jugular gave when she touched it, and blood seeped out of the spot where she had put pressure.

"Why did you stab him?" Wolf asked.

"I couldn't just be the one who got you in the door, then stand around doing nothing." She took the knife, which had a broad hilt, to the disposal and dropped it in. Then she checked her hands. She saw no cuts and no red marks that would turn into bruises.

"*Then why did we need Wolf?*" Kovian 2 asked. "*Or me?*"

"Because if I came in here and just started stabbing," Eliza said aloud, "he'd've fought me, and I'd have signs of a fight, like bruises or worse. He might've even had time to flee. Blood makes people slippery. Then there would be the problem of how to dispose of his body. You held him still so Wolf and I could go to work. And we need you to help dispose of his remains."

"Why did you check your hands, little monkey?" Wolf asked.

"Because when people stab other people, sometimes their hand slides down the knife and they slice their own hands. I had a large hilt on mine, but I could still have bruises. If Badri or Banner saw the bruises, they might ask questions."

The group went to work according to plan. As the three of them knew it would, the venom had started to dissolve Bynum's skeleton.

They waited twenty minutes in silence. Then Wolf said, "I think he's done now."

Kovian 2 poked one of Bynum's cheeks with a tentacle—and the skull gave. "I think so." He wrapped a tentacle around Bynum's right arm and ripped it off like a chicken wing.

Eliza was brought back to Dyson's videos, and she broke out in a cold sweat.

Blood spilled all over the floor and splashed the three of them. They were now covered with blood.

Kovian 2 stuffed Bynum's body into the disposal in chunks.

After Kovian 2 had finished, the three of them had to shower in turn to clean the blood off so that it didn't drip off them when they cleaned up the house, including the ceiling, and then each showered again in turn. Eliza changed her clothes for the second time, wrapped her blood-soaked ones in a towel, and dumped the bundle into the disposal.

It didn't take them as long as she feared it would.

The three of them exited by tunnel, and Eliza emerged from the hospital and headed for home.

The vertigo hit her hard just as she passed the hospital, and she barely managed to stumble the short distance to and through the front door.

BY THE TIME Eliza finished her account, she was speaking through her tears.

Badri got up and left the house.

Eliza started sobbing uncontrollably. She touched her hair for a moment, but there was no blood in it.

She thought back to Bynum lying on the floor and how she'd said to him, "It's too late." She thought about Malit's wailing and knew that she had done the right thing, but it was hard to reason with herself about this and remember the sensation of the knife as it went into Bynum's body, the spray of blood. It had even been in her hair.

Eliza couldn't cope with the Dyson case on her own, and she thought about how she would cope with her guilt on her own.

There were sounds in the other room and she got up expectantly, but it was just Skye scratching his ear.

Crawling back into bed, she replayed the murder in her mind, scene by scene, then finally got up again and took another shower.

It felt like Badri had been gone for hours. She knew that he was gone forever, and she knew what she needed to do.

She went and got her service weapon and her badge. What would she do with the badge?

After a moment, she left the badge on her pillow, one more thing lost. She put her service weapon in her holster and put on a jacket to cover it.

When she walked out of the bedroom and into the hall, she saw Skye and Luna curled up in a heap on the couch. She went to them and gave them each a kiss on the muzzle while their wagging tails thumped the couch.

Eliza briefly wondered why Badri hadn't taken the dogs. She decided he was looking for a vacant apartment and would return for them in the morning.

Then she walked outside.

She stared at the gate, which glinted in the light of the two moons.

She thought of who was waiting outside the gate.

Then she walked to the other side of the village, then toward one of the vacant apartments.

Badri walked into the apartment, thinking he would find Eliza asleep. When he got to the bedroom, he saw that Eliza was not there. He searched the apartment and realized that she had left. He went back into the bedroom, which is when saw he that something was on her pillow.

Her badge.

He picked it up. The badge was cold. Badri considered the meaning of the badge, and he was filled with dread.

"I should have told her where I was going and what I intended to do there," he said. Then he thought about where she could have gone and realized that she would not have left the village.

A vacant apartment.

He put down what he had brought to the house and went out to search for her.

Eliza hesitated, hoping she was right and that the apartment she was walking into actually was vacant. Wolf barred Eliza's way. "What are you going to do, my little monkey? ... Eliza? What are you going to do?"

She opened her mouth to speak, but Wolf grabbed her upper arm with a forehand, palmed the door open, and pushed her in. The apartment was dark and cold.

Wolf palmed the window closed and turned on the lights. "Now we can talk without being overheard," he said. "Now, tell me."

"I murdered a man!" Eliza said. "And Badri despises me for it! How can I live with both of those things together?"

"And what of it?" Wolf said. "I made contact with what passed for Bynum's mind. We had to stop him. And, Eliza, you don't think I know what Badri did to your friend? That love triangle wasn't very thin and wavy, was it? Is Badri a hypocrite?"

"He thinks Jamie had a choice. He doesn't see it—"

"Well, he should. If he doesn't, that should be on *his* conscience. It means you misjudged him. Will he tell the village about what we did?"

"No. He wouldn't. Or I wouldn't have told him. When he

calms down, he'll even understand that it was the right thing to do. He was as worried about Bynum as we were."

"So he wanted someone else to do it, just not you. Or him either. Or maybe he wanted the murder done prettier. How could it have been? We couldn't open the village gate. We couldn't risk lasepistol fire through the walls. And what were we supposed to do with Bynum's corpse? Prop it up in his chair? Badri added to your friend's despair at his lowest moment. How was that a clean kill?"

"It wasn't."

"Well, you have me, little sister. And Kovian 2. Hold up a minute. I want to try something." ... *"Can you hear me?"*

"Wait, that was telepathic!" Then, *"But you aren't touching me!"*

"Welcome to the Spider family."

Eliza laughed, with no edge of hysteria to it.

"I'll walk you home," Wolf said. *"These thoughts of yours will pass in the morning. There is a vacant apartment on the far end of the village, on the fourth floor. We will move you there tomorrow. That's where you'll live."*

"How do you know?" she asked aloud.

"Because no one wants to live near the Tenurians. They shit on their doorsteps. But the place is vacant, closer to our group, and away from your hypocritical friend. These feelings of yours will pass. You will feel better and stronger in the morning. I need you to promise me that you won't hurt yourself. In my culture, a female and a male cannot cohabit unless they are mated. You are like a sister, little one, and that would be vile."

Eliza laughed.

"You can still laugh. Can I trust you that once you enter your house, you will stay there and not harm yourself?"

"I promise."

As Wolf and Eliza stepped off the sidewalk in front of the apartment, Badri walked up to Eliza and grabbed her arm. "What were you going to do?" he asked.

"Let go of me. Now."

"Well, look who's here!" Wolf said. "You left her. What do you care what she was going to do?"

Badri let go. "I did not leave her. Come back home, Eliza. Wolf, you will join us for a moment."

Inside the house, Eliza moved the coffee table out of the way, and Wolf crouched in the middle of the room.

The dogs were growling and barking, furious, but Badri silenced them.

Eliza sat on the couch, and the dogs jumped up beside her and went immediately to sleep, Skye's head on her leg.

Wolf said to Badri, "What in the blocked-up hidey-hole were you thinking?"

AN HOUR EARLIER

Badri went to the hospital and found no one but Belek.

"I urgently need to speak to Dr. Colson," Badri said to him.

Belek clacked his antennae together and typed into his communication console. Banner answered immediately. "What's going on, Belek?"

"Badri's here. He's looking ... he does not look good."

After a few moments, Banner walked into the hospital. "What's going on, Badri?"

"Eliza's episodes of vertigo and headache are increasing in severity, but now they co-occur. She left the social hall before dinner. When I returned from the social hall shortly afterward, I found her on the kitchen floor, unable to speak. I gave her meclizine, which has reduced the severity of the vertigo. Even after the meclizine, she could not sit up without holding my arm for support, and even then, she vomited on the floor, to her mortification. This medication is no longer effective enough. After the meclizine took effect, she apologized profusely for vomiting, as she put it, 'every-the-fuck-where' before she succeeded in crawling to the bedroom." Badri shook his head and sighed. "There is no accounting for the appetites of dogs."

Banner laughed. "I'm sorry. It's not funny, but it's funny."

"Eliza informed me that she, Kovian 2, and Wolf had spoken telepathically at length. She said that she finds this intriguing and that their communication is more thorough in this way. I fear that she will not cease this. She took the tramadol tonight, but the headache is quite severe, and she insists that this is the last time that she will take this. Are there treatments currently for pain that do not involve addictive substances? She said to me at one point, 'If I had to live with this pain for the rest of my life, my life would be short.'"

Banner looked alarmed. "Bring her in."

"She is somewhat disoriented and panicked. I do not wish to stress her any more than is necessary tonight. It is my hope that a sedative may be tried tonight and that she present here in the morning for further treatment as needed."

"Ordinarily, I would insist that she come in and be seen before I treat her."

"I cannot convince her to do so now. She has had a recent Hansen scan, when she appeared with this same complaint. It is my belief that the sequelae of telepathic communication increase in severity with repetition. I have attempted to get Eliza to see reason—"

"But no other humanoid in the village has been able to communicate telepathically with anyone. Gino said he'd rather slide down concertina wire into a vat of battery acid than ever go through that again."

Badri didn't laugh. So Banner said, "I'll give you something for Eliza, but she needs to be here in the morning."

Banner went to a dispenser and quickly typed. Then he pulled out a sealed packet. "This is a psychotropic medication, amatrazine, that is prescribed in part to those suffering acute severe trauma reactions. It has also been used off label for vertigo and nausea. She places it under her tongue, and it melts. It's a good medication, but some people have slept for twenty hours straight. Very rarely, about one time in a thousand, someone sleeps for three days. About one time in ten thousand, it works the other way, and they can't sleep at all, and they become manic. I'm just letting you know that this stuff isn't anything to mess around with."

Badri relaxed. "Thank you. I will insist that she present herself here in the morning."

When Badri stopped speaking, Wolf said, "You should have told her where you were going. She's dealing with guilt and horror. I am too. But I gave her the support that you didn't. I'm surprised that you didn't guess what she would do, when I did. I waited in the shadows for her to come out of here and she did."

"Thank you, Wolf," Eliza said.

"I left quickly because time was of the essence," Badri said.

"There almost was no one to save," Wolf said.

"You were punishing me," Eliza said. "You were off to give me an alibi, but you wanted it to sting."

"I was not. I assumed that you trusted me."

"I've known you *professionally* for five years. We've been a couple for less than one. And even if we had been *married* for five years, I violated my oath and murdered someone. You might have been able to predict how I would behave in my personal life—"

"I am sure of it."

"Oh? Did you predict that I was capable of murder?"

Badri sat back. Then he looked at Wolf and then at Eliza. "Three years ago, on Saturday, June 7, 2042, sometime after eight p.m., a man sexually assaulted you. Your partner forced him into an alley, and you blocked my path. There, your partner beat that man. I nevertheless took you into my bed, then into my home. Today, a man who would have murdered everyone in this village, you destroyed him. These two acts are of a piece, no?"

"Why didn't one of you arrest him?" Wolf asked Eliza, astonished.

"He claims it was an accident and he walks. Or maybe he spends some time in jail. Since he's a cop, he could have been maimed or murdered by inmates. What he did was disgusting, and it was a crime. It didn't warrant the death penalty. Jamie pushed him into the alley. If he had taken off, Jamie would have let him alone."

"You have not engaged in extrajudicial acts with civilians

and neither, as far as I know, had your partner," Badri said. "In fact, the man who put these scars on you, when I told you that he had died, you were distressed."

"Shane Turner. That's correct. And I still am."

"We have deviated from the point, Eliza," Badri said. "Who other in this small village might have arrived at same conclusion that you did? Now that Bynum has disappeared, who will concern themselves to make the inquiry, despite those entry and exit logs?"

"Where is Cody?" Wolf asked.

"He is still in the hospital, still quite ill. No one could accuse him of this. And Eliza was quite ill as well. And you found her, quite disoriented and looking for the hospital. You were able to ascertain that she was ill, and we brought her home together, where I administered amatrazine to her and then she slept. Eliza, I shall keep this medication in the event that you ever present as you did when you returned home this evening. Now I must know what your reasoning was when you decided to end your life."

"I can't stop thinking of how the knife felt going into him," Eliza said. "Not just that he was murdered, but how we —I—murdered him. Only a few hours ago, I shed someone's blood, and his blood was in my hair. I thought you would see me that way forever."

"*We* did it, Eliza. That murder plagues my conscience too."

"And if I had thought these things you feared," Badri said, "you would nevertheless have had a different perspective in the morning when your high emotions had passed. It is a tragedy beyond tragedy that Ira Smallwood and Jamie Cloud had not given themselves a chance to learn that for themselves. Although, in Jamie Cloud's case, perhaps not such a tragedy."

"Yes," Eliza said, "I see that now. All of those things. Except those two dealt with a situational problem, and so did I. What about people with depression? You think they can just sleep it off?"

"Nevertheless," Badri said.

"Not *nevertheless*. That's what hospitals and medications are for," Eliza replied.

"Concededly. But not in your case. Nor in the cases I spoke of. Your impulsivity has almost cost you your life twice in the past four days. After years of self-control."

"The first time, I didn't know I was risking my life—and that's the last time I'll put my life in the hands of someone I don't trust. The second time, I'd just committed murder. What I did, I'll have to spend the rest of my life learning to live with. I don't regret that I did it. It had to be done. That doesn't make the memory less hellish."

"Eliza, the responses you feared, I did not have them. Wolf, you must speak with Kovian 2."

"Kovians are incapable of ambivalence."

Eliza laughed. Then she said, "I'm glad for him, then. Wolf, thank you."

ELIZA SAT UP IN BED, reaching for her hair, heart pounding.

Badri came into the room and said quietly, "Banner is here to examine you. You are still drowsy. Your mouth is dry. Take this water."

She nodded and then he left the room. She really *was* drowsy.

Badri returned to the door with Banner.

"How are you, Eliza?" Banner asked.

Banner looked hollow-eyed.

Eliza drained the glass of water. Then she said, "Drowsy. My mouth is dry. I could sleep a hundred years." She studied him. "You okay?"

"You have dark circles under your eyes," Banner said, ignoring her question. "How did you sleep?"

"Like a rock." She smelled something delicious.

Badri had come in with a cup of black coffee, and she took it.

She drank some and sighed. "When will this drowsiness wear off? I just want to sleep!"

"It could take another day or so," Banner said. "Can you two come out to the living room? I have something to talk about."

Eliza nodded. "Give me a minute."

Shortly afterward, Eliza walked into the living room, damp hair twisted into a braid. She wore another sage green shirt and soft pants, wondering if she could ever figure out how to get anything to come out of the dispenser besides sage or cream.

Banner looked terrible. He sat in the love seat, his left foot awkwardly turned blade up.

Eliza sat cross-legged beside Badri on the couch. "Banner, what's wrong?"

"I have a confession to make," Banner said. He pulled out a syringe, which had a red cap on it. And eight vials. He put them on the coffee table, but when Skye and Luna walked up to inspect them all, Banner quickly pocketed them again. "I went looking for Bynum with this."

"What is it?" Eliza asked, but she noticed Badri was looking at Banner intently.

"Eight grams of pancuronium and a gram of potassium chloride." Banner's eyes welled up. "I took an oath!"

"And?" Eliza said roughly.

"That's cold," Banner said.

"Bynum would have—"

"You can be forgiven for this," Badri said. "I wonder how many others here have contemplated what you have. Perhaps someone else succeeded when you had not. It is well that you did not find him, for what if you had been unable to overpower him?"

Banner laughed a little and said, "I hadn't thought of that."

"My morgue was full of those who overestimated their own

strength." Badri extended his hand, and Banner gave him the vials and the syringe. Badri got up and put them down the disposal. Then he returned. "Eliza and I will not speak of this with anyone. Who else have you told?"

"Just you two."

"This is proper. Did anyone see you take these out of the hospital?"

"No. Funny thing. When I got there, Belek was gone. Ursans don't sleep, but he was gone. Meyer had just finished rounding on Cody and then we made small talk, and he left."

"I wonder how many people have been hunting for Bynum since our announcement," Eliza said. "My suggestion is that you don't ask aloud where he is or mention his name ever again. If he doesn't turn up, we can all heave a sigh of relief." Then she yawned. She was awash in drowsiness. "Please forgive me. I could chew on a pound of coffee beans, and I'd still be tired. Do you two mind if I take a nap?"

When Badri stood, Banner pulled him into a hug. To Eliza's surprise, the formal Badri hugged him back.

When Banner had gone, Eliza said, "Badri, did you give me any of that stuff?"

"No, Eliza. Never without your consent." And he showed her where the packet was, and it was sealed. "I suspect that your continued use of telepathy is exhausting to you, and I am concerned about your continuing to engage in it."

"I know," she said, and crawled into bed.

※

EARTH: WEDNESDAY, JULY 19, 2045

Denny walked out of her town house to retrieve a package and felt someone give her a shove from behind. "What the hell?"

DENNY FOUND herself standing on a cliff looking at an ocean. The sky was the wrong color. The sunlight was the wrong color. And there were the two moons.

Ursinus b? Well, shit. There were thunderheads in the distance, with their menacing dark blue undersides that seemed to join with the ocean, the puffy tops towering in the dusky sky. She turned around as if her front door would be behind her, but there was just that strange plant covering on the ground, and beyond it, the reed forest. Up the trail, though ... was that the Broken Oar village?

Now what?

At her feet were some marks in the soil. *EB* and an arrow. *Eliza and Badri? That's where those two went!* Desperately grateful she'd read the whole book, she started walking, looking over her shoulders for Donners. *I have to tell them.*

✳

Eliza was awakened by Badri.

"Denny is here," he said.

Eliza got up. "Are they letting her in?"

"They sought confirmation of her identity from me and I gave it. They are letting her in."

"Have they been watching from the turrets?"

"The Kanninoin had just returned from a meal break when Denny arrived."

"What."

"I am not certain who assigned the Kanninoin this task. Since the gate was unsupervised, then opened, Ror ordered the village into the tunnels. It remains to be seen who chose to stay above ground."

In fact, when Eliza and Badri went outside, they looked around, they saw no one.

"Who let her in?" Eliza asked.

"Inani."

Eliza laughed helplessly.

When they got to the gate, they saw Denny. She had broken into a cold sweat, but she looked calm. A man in a Space Force uniform was pointing a lasepistol at her head, his other arm holding her against him like a live shield. He looked like the epitome of Aryan manhood. Three others were looking speculatively at the doorways of the village.

"Oh, thank God!" Eliza said with an air of desperate gratitude. "There's an outbreak of COVID zeta here! Do you have a cure?"

"Don't move," the Aryan said, pointing the gun at her and tightening his grip on Denny.

A Kanninoin whom Eliza did not know trotted over from the direction of the turrets.

It seemed as if the Kanninoin would reach the four men, but the Aryan shot him in the gut, and the Kanninoin dropped, shuddering.

"Where are the rest of them?" the Aryan said. "You talk like you're out of a history book. I can barely understand you. Speak English."

"Them?" Eliza said, as if a gut-shot Kanninoin weren't lying on the ground in agony ten feet away from her.

"Where are the rest of the aliens? We detected nearly two hundred life signs here and now we detect only a handful. *Where did they go?*"

"Out the back gate!" Eliza said, looking as stupid as possible. She pointed in a random direction. The Kanninoin was still writhing on the ground. "That way! They're foraging for food!"

"What?"

"Something about a gate and food?" one of the other crewmembers said. He shifted from foot to foot.

"They're not Star Service," said the Aryan.

Eliza channeled the horror she was feeling into tears. "I don't understand! We don't understand! We want your help!"

"You don't need the gun," Denny said. "I'm with you!"

The four men looked slightly confused.

"Do you understand what the hell they're saying?" the Aryan asked one of the men with him.

"She doesn't understand something," the man replied. "Something about a gun. They don't have guns. We searched this one."

The Kanninoin was trying to drag himself to an apartment, and the Aryan rolled his eyes and shot him in the head.

Eliza jumped, despite herself.

Furious, the Aryan let go of Denny and walked toward Eliza, shouting, "*Where are they, you dumb bitch?*"

To Eliza's visceral relief, he stuck the lasepistol in her face.

Eliza grabbed the lasepistol by the barrel and redirected it in two tenths of a second. The muzzle was now pointed at his midsection. She cupped the grip with her other hand, still holding on to the barrel. She kicked the Aryan in the testicles until he doubled over. She rolled the lasepistol over his thumb and yanked it away, hearing the satisfying sound of his trigger finger breaking. He was still doubled over, vomiting and cursing. Badri took the lasepistol from her, and she grabbed the Aryan by the shoulder, forearm grinding into his jaw, the other hand on his bicep, and kneed him in the gut, then in the face. He went to his hands and knees, retching, and she kicked him in the head until he stopped moving.

When she stopped, she saw that the other three *Peregrine* crewmembers were on the ground, shot with a lasepistol.

Badri was standing above them, looking as if he had surprised himself. Then he said, "There are more coming through the gate."

To Eliza's shock, Badri shot the Aryan in the head with his own lasepistol.

Eliza looked at Denny and yelled, "Go!"

All three of them ran.

A few yards from the gate, Eliza saw Malit huddled behind the corner of a building. She ran toward him, hauled him over her shoulder, and sprinted for the hospital.

Twenty feet away, a crewmember shot a Tenurian. The Tenurian collapsed, guts spilling open. She tried to get up and caught her knee on her own intestines. She collapsed, then tried to stagger to her feet.

A blond Kharkun charged the crewmember, who shot him. The Kharkun kept running at him, blood everywhere, and the crewmember shot him again. Half of the Kharkun's face vaporized, but he fell on top of the crewman and literally ripped his throat out before he died.

The other *Peregrine* crew were going door to door.

Kelly and Kolokh ran for Kelly's apartment. "Kolokh, go ahead! I can't keep up with you!"

Kolokh picked her up.

Aphrodite was ahead of them.

A member of the *Peregrine* crew followed them into the house before they could get the door closed.

This was a short woman with a long lower jaw and short-cropped blond hair. She pointed a lasepistol at the three of them.

Kolokh set Kelly back on her feet.

"Why was that thing carrying you?" the woman demanded, jerking her chin at Kolokh.

"His name is Kolokh," Kelly said. "I'm Lieutenant Commander Kelly Chatworth of the SS *Kestrel*. What's your name and rank?"

"Lieutenant Valerie Fehr of the SS *Peregrine*, and we're here to clean this place up!"

"I outrank you. Lower your weapon! That's an order!"

"What kind of freak giant spider has two sets of hands? Is that some kind of weird salute or a threat?"

"Come find out, prairie ape!" Aphrodite said.

Valerie shot Aphrodite instead. Her abdomen exploded in a spray of red.

Kolokh growled something.

Valerie dropped her lasepistol and tried to take the

crossbow bolt out of her chest, but she took one in the forehead before she could. She dropped like a sack of garbage.

Kelly dropped to her knees beside Aphrodite's body, weeping. Enkhid stood beside Kelly, still holding his crossbow.

Kolokh gently helped Kelly up and led her into the tunnel, with Enkhid right behind them.

CHAPTER
FORTY-THREE

DENNY FOLLOWED Badri into the tunnel and nearly headlong into a gigantic spider. She started, despite herself. *A Spider*, she reminded herself.

"Wait, where did these dogs come from?" Denny asked.

The Spider looked at her and then at Badri and spoke.

"I need a translator," Denny said. Then she said to Badri, "I read the book."

"We need to go back for Eliza," Badri said. "This is the second time that she has done this!"

"What, the little kid? You wanted her to leave the little kid? What's wrong with you? She hauled him over her shoulder and ran into the building closest to your house. She's *fine*! There are tunnels in there!"

Badri opened his mouth and then closed it. He went to a nearby compartment and handed her a set of translators, and she put them in her ears.

"That's better," she said.

"Badri, do you know this monkey, or is she with that floating garbage can?"

Monkey?

"She is from our world. Her name is Krista Denbow, but she is called Denny."

"What in the high holy hell is going on around here?" Denny demanded. "I read *The Rebellion at Broken Oar*, *The Tauxenent Strangler*—it was on his laptop—and Jamie's last story, the short one he wrote before he blew his brains out. What the hell happened?"

"Detective Cloud found or created a portal between worlds," Badri said. "The wretched book he wrote about Lonnie Dyson, he somehow felt that this would be read even in 2203. Thus, he put it into the possession of Kelly Chatworth, who—"

"What do you mean by that?" Denny leaned against the tunnel wall. "Are you saying that everyone and everything is a creation of Jamie—"

"No. He merely had access to this portal. My hypothesis is that he sent the true crime book to this world just as he sent me here. Kelly read this book, and it caused Eliza to appear here. The short story that Detective Cloud produced and which you found on my laptop was deliberately created to send me here after Eliza. While here, Eliza read the first page of *The Tauxenent Strangler* before she realized what she had done and disposed of it."

"She brought me here?"

"Not intentionally, but it appears that she was responsible for this."

"Did you both get here at the same time?" Denny asked. "You carved your initials into the ground."

"I did not. Those initials were meant to stand for Eliza Benveniste, not Eliza and Badri."

Denny shook her head as if she were shaking something off.

Then she said, "Jamie said that he thought that you and Eliza were having an affair."

"When did he say this thing?"

"About a week before he died."

"Oh? What in that book of his corresponded to the truth?"

Denny sat cross-legged on the ground, exhausted. "Almost none of it. Except he mostly got the names spelled right."

"And did you give any credence to his statement?"

"Not exactly. She consulted with you an awful lot, though." At Badri's look, she said, "Her reports."

"Her meetings with me were well documented and took place merely to discuss cases of notable complexity, and this professional relationship began during the Landau case. It was through those discussions with me that we ascertained that Lonnie Dyson was the Tauxenent Strangler. In ordinary cases, she did not consult with me. As you can imagine, Detective Cloud was not a person who could be consulted with."

Denny barked out a laugh. "Sadly. I always wished she was paired up with Joe Cutter, but I kept my nose out of that. You asked Jamie to send you here. Don't you have a life back home?"

"Somewhat."

"Wife? Kids?"

"Neither of those."

"And you followed her. I'm gonna ask you again. Were you having an affair?"

"There was nothing untoward in our interactions with each other."

Denny thought for a moment. "Only one who coughed up that idea was Jamie. And his book was a font of bullshit. But you followed her here. Why?"

Badri told her.

"Wow," Denny said. "Isn't that something? Neither of you knew what the other was thinking. For five years, keeping all that close to the vest, neither of you looking at anyone else. I don't know anyone else who would have done that."

"There are love stories like that one on our home world," Wolf said.

"And now here," Badri said with a brief smile. "Eliza will be consumed with remorse that she brought you here."

"COVID mu and COVID zeta killed my family. And my husband." Denny's voice broke. "And his family. It took him two days to die. I'm an only child. My entire life was my job. I was nothing but a job."

"That book was called *Rebellion at Broken Oar*. Does the *Peregrine* really take control of this place?" Wolf asked.

"No," Denny said. "Three members of the *Peregrine* crew murder Zhan. The Kanninoin convince the village that Cody murdered Zhan and brought the plague here. There is fighting between Human and Kharkuns while the Kanninoin sit there with their thumbs up their asses. The *Peregrine* takes advantage of that. Then the *Enterprise* shows up early. The ragtag remainder of the village finally bands together to fight a common enemy. The end."

"How early?" Badri asked.

"What?"

"How early does the *Enterprise* appear?"

Still holding Malit, Eliza stood around the corner of the building. She saw a blond *Peregrine* crewmember, who looked like a female clone of the Aryan at the gate, running toward the hospital.

Eliza put Malit down.

"You didn't need to *carry* me!" he stage-whispered. "I can run as fast as—"

"Shhh!" She gently turned him and whispered, "The hospital is in front of you. Go to the tunnel!"

Malit turned and ran into the hospital. She heard a mechanical sound that reminded her of a keyless lock and realized that Malit had had the presence of mind to lock the door. Now only villagers could get inside the hospital.

Eliza drew her lasepistol and flattened against the wall.

Another crewmember took an angle and fired at her. She missed Eliza and the building entirely.

Eliza fired and hit her. *If she had a UTI, I took care of that for her.* She fired again and hit the woman on the side of her head, and she dropped and began twitching.

Another *Peregrine* crewmember ran past her, lasepistol in one hand. At first, Eliza couldn't make sense of what he was carrying in the other. Then she could. He was carrying a braid in one hand, which she realized was Kano's hair, because Kano's head kept bumping up against the crewmember's thigh.

Eliza shot the crewmember into unrecognizability.

ELIZA WALKED into the tunnel sanctuary and looked at the crowd. People were sitting in family groups, some looking wary and haunted, some treating it like a picnic. Many were crying. A group of Spiders and Kovians appeared to be having an animated debate. The Tenurians stared at everyone, making gestures. There were Marsh Ursans on the walls. The only Ursan was Belek, and he and George seemed to be in rapt discussion.

She found Malit, Badri, Wolf, and Denny.

Lita was holding Malit and repeating, "I thought you were dead!"

Suk trotted up and put her paws on Malit's shoulder, chittering.

"I went to find Suk!" Malit said. "But here she is!"

Suk approached her and put her paws on Eliza, midthigh.

"Can I pet Suk?"

"She loves having her ears scratched," Malit said.

Suk sniffed Eliza's hand with a wet nose and then said, "Scratch now."

Denny jumped.

Suk's ears were so soft. Suk purred and rubbed her face against Eliza's hand, the softness of her cheek punctuated by the prickliness of her whiskers.

Eliza relaxed. "Thank you," she said. "Take good care of Malit, little beast."

She saw that Banner and the rest of the village leadership were standing at one end of the sanctuary. "The *Enterprise* comes early," Denny told Banner without preamble. "And you look exactly like I pictured you."

"How early?" Badri demanded again.

"Krista Denbow, a.k.a. Denny!" Kelly said. She was leaning against the wall and had half a pitcher of beer between her knees. She raised a mug of beer and toasted Denny. "Holy hell. Did you read David Dove's shitty sex writing too?"

Denny turned to Badri and said, "Summer Solstice 55."

"Bathrooms are over there, in case you wanna know," Kelly said.

"Kano's dead," Eliza whispered.

Inani did not respond.

"How do you know?" Banner said.

"Because," Eliza said in despair, "they're taking heads as trophies. Ujuq's dead too. And a Tenurian."

"They shot Aphrodite too," Kelly said, slurring her words.

Wolf actually started vibrating.

"Wolf?" Eliza asked.

"She was my mother."

She stepped close to him, and, to her surprise, he leaned against her. The hairs on his abdomen were soft, and she felt his breathing against her. She thought about touching his back but didn't know if that would have been upsetting to him.

"Enkhid shot her murderer with a crossbow," Kelly said.

Inani remained with her half-smile.

"*I'd love to wipe the smile off her face*," Wolf said.

"*You and me both*," said Kovian 2.

"*Thirded*," said Eliza, furious.

"Why haven't you gotten that ship working?" Denny said. "You never did in the book. You have dispensers. They can't make fucking auto parts?"

Belek clacked his antennae.

"We never thought we would need to," Kinkead said.

"Now we need to," Gino said. "If we can avoid getting shot. How many of those cockroaches are left?"

"There are eleven left," Badri said.

"And they're all here?"

"Eight," Eliza said. "Four at the gate. I shot two in front of the hospital. Ujuq literally ripped the throat out of one. Half his face was gone." Her voice broke. "Enkhid shot one. Inani, do not say a word."

"They were standing with your friend," Inani said calmly. "She let them in."

"They had a lasepistol pointed at my head," Denny said.

"Still want to negotiate?" Eliza said with loathing.

Inani remained impassive.

Suddenly, Kinkead said, "What were they *doing*? Why hadn't they *evacuated*?"

"Who?" Banner said.

Kinkead held up a small monitor. "This is a live video feed of the entrance to the hospital. I put security cameras throughout the village. Look!"

Ten-year-old Alfred Bartmann, the Tenurian chick Eliza recognized as Keela, a juvenile Spider who Eliza recognized as one of the two playing web ball, and Jhuq were lined up against the wall of the main social hall. A *Peregrine* crewmember was pointing a lasepistol at them. Alfred was crying. The Spider was vibrating. Jhuq was staring at the shooter with contempt. The Tenurian was making what looked like warding gestures.

Meyer and Fanny started crying. Kolokh, Kyr, and Ror started for the tunnels.

"No, it's too late!" Kinkead called out. "Omigod, wait!"

The Tenurian chick's head was gone. So was the left side of her chest. Jhuq was bleeding and so was Alfred Bartmann. The crewman with the lasepistol now lay on the ground, disemboweled and screaming. Jhuq picked up the lasepistol and put it in his belt, then he picked up Alfred Bartmann. He started to turn but stopped and quickly knelt and picked something else up, then he disappeared, the Spider following behind.

"They're going toward the hospital!" Kinkead said.

"Seven," Kelly said.

Banner said, "Let's go!"

Ror was already at the weapons rack, taking two lasepistols. He handed one to Banner.

Badri took one too.

"Wait," Denny said. "Those things, when they fire, they basically are like big arrows that tell the other side where you are. Can't they shoot any other way?"

"They're harder to hit things that way," Ror said, twisting the muzzle of his. Eliza thought of a spray bottle of cleaner and almost started giggling, but she was afraid she'd never stop.

"But harder to see you that way."

"Oh, shit!" Kinkead said. *"Shitshitshitshitshit!"*

The three doctors started to leave.

"No!"

He pointed to the monitor. A large herd of Donners had

wandered in through the open gate, making a beeline for the *Peregrine* crewmembers in view.

"Where are their dogs?" Eliza whispered.

A Donner grabbed a crewmember from behind and literally bit off half of her skull. The woman started seizing, and the Donner dropped her and ripped a hole in her gut. The seizures took a long time to stop.

"Six," Kelly said.

Then four other members of the *Peregrine* crew came through the gate and into the village. One was pulling the body of a Highland calf on some sort of flatbed wagon, and Eliza wondered where they'd found the wagon. Another was carrying the body of a crewman firefighter-style, who looked like he'd been kicked and stomped. Eliza looked again. *And gored.* She hoped it was by the calf's mother. The lone female crewmember was behind them.

"Two," Kelly said.

Eliza giggled, despite herself.

"Two?" Denny said. "But—oh. Those four don't have a prayer, do they?"

"One's already dead," Eliza said. "I think."

The crewman who was carrying the gored crewman dropped him like a rock and drew his lasepistol. The crewman who had been pulling the wagon let go of it. But the wagon still had momentum, and it rolled forward, knocked that crewman over, and pinned him by one leg. He looked like he was screaming. The man who'd dropped his friend tried to shoot a Donner but ended up hitting the pinned crewman by mistake. Instead of running, he stood there and gibbered nonsense at the pinned crewman. A Donner pushed him to the ground. Several Donners squatted beside the pinned crewman and blocked Eliza's view. Another group crouched around the gored crewmember. The Donners ignored the calf.

The lone crewmember tried shooting the Donners, but there were too many of them. A Donner grabbed her by the back of the neck, yanked her to its mouth, and bit the top of her face off. The woman started grabbing for her eyes. The Donner reached through the new hole in her face. Incredibly, the woman started trying to pull away, but it was too late.

"Fuck this," Banner said. "Let's go to the hospital. And bring dogs."

Wolf stood.

"Should the Donners breach the tunnels, it will be necessary to protect those here," Badri said, looking at Wolf. Then Badri kissed Eliza.

"Be careful! Please!"

"For you, my little monkey." And Wolf sat next to Eliza.

"You two are buddies?" Denny said, who was obviously still recovering from the sight of the medical examiner kissing the homicide detective.

"Siblings," Wolf said.

"Siblings," Eliza said.

Denny shook her head in wonderment.

Eliza smiled in contentment.

Kovian 2 sat down beside her. "Siblings," he said.

Denny studied the three of them. "You three look like you fought a war together and came out alive."

Banner stared at the three of them with a look of comprehension. Then he looked at Badri and said, "Amatrazine?"

"It nearly killed her," Badri said.

"What just happened?" Denny said.

"Oh," Eliza said. "We fought a war and came out alive."

But the three doctors were already gone.

✳

Three dogs sent the Donners into a rout.

Badri shot the nearest Donner anyway, and its head exploded, its berry eyes rolling onto the bricks.

Two Donners picked up the bodies of two *Peregrine* crewmembers. A third picked up a dead Donner. They fled the village.

Badri noted with interest that the Donners remembered where the gate was.

The Highland calf was untouched.

The gate was closing.

The three doctors got to the hospital at the same time, and when they went through the double doors in the back, Badri saw Meyer standing between two gurneys that bore Jhuq and Alfred.

"He's had tranexamic acid and a unit of O neg. already," Meyer said, pointing to Alfred. "I sent Ares to the tunnels already."

Badri quickly saw that Alfred was the most critical. Upon examination, he said, "Someone did a needle decompression in the field. Was that you?" He was looking at Jhuq, who was being tended to by Ror.

"It didn't sound right in there. I used one of Keela's ribs. Alfred kept trying to scream, but he couldn't breathe in all the way." Then he said, "Blood and bubbles were coming from his mouth and nose."

Alfred had an IV line and oxygen.

"We need some nurses. And a pediatrician," Banner said, "per species."

"What is this device?" Badri asked, pointing to a machine

beside Alfred's head.

"Oh," Banner said, "the only reason that even though we don't have an anesthesiologist, Alfred is somehow not dead."

"Why were you above ground?" Badri asked Jhuq.

"Trying to get Keela to go to the tunnels," Jhuq said. "She said something about bad luck. She was our friend. She finally agreed to go, but it was too late."

Alfred was intubated, eyes glassy, his chest opened like a split pomegranate. "Alfred might just lose this lung," Banner said to Badri.

Out of the corner of Badri's eye, he saw Ror tending to Jhuq. A lasepistol blast that would have incapacitated a Human had only rendered Jhuq a little bit uncomfortable. The biggest issue for Jhuq was bleeding. Ror applied a pressure bandage to the wound and then went to assist the Humans with Alfred.

After Alfred was stabilized and given a bolus of prophylactic antibiotic, Badri and Banner went to check on Cody, who was across the hall.

Meyer had put Cody in a non-rebreather mask, which covered Cody's face. Badri went to the terminal next to Cody's bed and saw that Meyer had noted "Pt on o2 via NRB 15lpm."

"What the hell were you doing?" Banner said to Cody.

"Protecting ... the puppies."

Badri saw that Cody had a lasepistol on the tray table next to him and that there was a security monitor hanging from the ceiling. Cody would have had full view of any invaders.

"Puppies?" Badri asked.

"Kano's ... puppies." Cody spoke slowly, catching his breath.

"What? Kano doesn't have any puppies!" Banner said.

"Cloned. Here." He looked to his right.

There was a large, closed metal container that looked like a series of incubators. It had tubes going in and out.

"In this?" Banner asked.

"Looks ... better inside. Kano ... showed me."

"Kinkead *permitted this*?" Badri demanded.

"I needed oxygen. It wasn't ... portable. Kano's puppies are ... they need another fifty days."

"How many puppies?" Badri asked.

"Twenty."

Badri tried to ask him another question, but he had fallen asleep.

Suddenly, he heard a commotion and the squealing of a dog in pain. Badri ran through the double doors and saw a man carrying a dog.

"There were more crew on the *Peregrine* than we thought!" the man shouted, putting the dog on a gurney.

It was Ralph. He had been shot in the hindquarters. The man looked familiar.

"Get away from the door!" Badri ordered, flat against the wall.

The man who'd just arrived moved Ralph's gurney quickly and resumed work. Badri realized that this was Christian Dodd, the veterinarian.

"How many?" Badri demanded.

"I know that hurts, baby puppy." The man gave the dog an injection, and Ralph closed his eyes and stopped squealing. "Ten."

Badri said, "Is he—"

"He'll be okay." He intubated Ralph with one of the anesthesia bots, saying, "Couldn't Space Force have sent us an actual anesthesiologist? Ralph'll walk with a limp for a few days, then he'll be back to his same boneheaded self. The bitch who shot him isn't though. I spread her thoughts all over the brickwork."

Ralph's tongue was pulled forward and to the side. The man stroked the side of the dog's face gently. "I could shoot, couldn't I, baby puppy? Fuckers shot a *dog*! She was *aiming* for him too! He was running up to her with a ball in his mouth. She shouted and he turned around to run. Even in the middle of a battle, a dog with a ball comes up to you, you throw the damn ball!"

"Christian," Ror said, "did you alert anyone?"

"No all-clear yet on the comm-watches. Everyone's still in the tunnels. I'm Christian Dodd," he said to Badri, "the veterinarian. Uh, obviously."

"So I surmised," Badri said with a small smile. "Ralph is fortunate."

Banner brought a Hansen scanner over, and he and Christian studied the scans.

"Good. No bone damage." Christian started making a series of injections into the muscle of Ralph's flank. "Bitch couldn't aim, thank God."

"How many entrances exist to this hospital?" Badri asked.

"Just the one," Meyer said.

A Kharkun man barged in cradling a Kharkun woman. "Help her!"

Badri slammed the door shut and saw that the woman was dead. The Kharkun was distraught. He demanded that Ror treat her. Ror tried to tell him it was hopeless, but the Kharkun grabbed his upper arms.

Ror growled something at him that the translators couldn't grab, and the Kharkun let go of him.

"Meyer, do you have combat training?" Badri asked.

Meyer had a lasepistol and was holding it at low ready and

staring at the door. "Not yet." The expression in his eyes was grim.

Badri took Meyer's place wordlessly, and Meyer said, "Now what do I do with myself?"

Badri heard lasepistol fire, and the door slammed open.

Lasepistol fire narrowly missed Banner and hit the Kharkun in the side, but the Kharkun was wailing next to the woman's body and didn't seem to notice.

Two *Peregrine* crewmembers ran in. Badri shot them both in the head at the same time. *Something to tell Eliza.* He desperately hoped she was still in the tunnel. He heard the static crack of lasepistol fire, and Eliza ran into the room, breathless.

"What were you doing?" Badri demanded.

"Looking at Kinkead's monitor." She looked at the dead crewmembers and said, "I'm going back out. I love you." She kissed him and left before he could stop her.

He slammed the door shut.

THERE WERE seven more *Peregrine* crewmembers left that Eliza knew of. She flattened herself against an outside wall of the hospital.

Enkhid and Eliza had divided the village in half so they would not accidentally shoot each other. Then they had to divide the village into thirds, because Rabbi Einhorn showed up.

Now she was alone, backed up against the library.

She saw a crewman running from the hospital to the library. Looking around, he appeared to decide there was no one in the village.

Eliza moved forward and peeked around the corner of the library. The crewman looked around again, stopped, and listened. Then he walked instead of running. Then he swaggered instead of walking.

She saw the man's brown five o'clock shadow, his greasy brown hair. He was holding his lasepistol inexpertly, with no muzzle discipline. One foot went in and out of the line of fire.

Eliza looked again. He couldn't be older than twenty-one. A baby.

She took aim and fired. He dropped to the brickwork, looking wildly around.

He was breathing hard, and he pulled himself onto his elbows. He was trembling. He wasn't controlling his breathing.

To her surprise, he made no effort to take cover. Instead, he spread his thick legs wide. She took cover behind the corner of the building. Heart pounding, she waited for him to fire again, and he obliged. The corner of the library spattered rock. She could hear his heavy tactical boots getting closer. When he fired again, she started screaming.

He walked around the corner of the library with a strange expression, patches of red on his face. He saw her crouched and ready to fire and dropped the lasepistol in a panic. Frantically, he got on his knees to find the lasepistol that was right under his fingertips. She shot him through the top of his head. Belatedly, she realized that his expression was of horror, as if he realized he had actually hurt another Human being. And Star Service had brought him even though he panicked in emergencies. She felt momentary sadness until she remembered his shipmates, who'd nearly made it into the hospital.

She turned to run, but there was a *Peregrine* crewmember maybe thirty feet in front of her trying to look into windows as she walked. The woman turned around, but instead of firing at Eliza, she started screaming.

Eliza fired at her, three shots center of mass, one to the head. The woman's head exploded. Eliza turned around. A crossbow bolt was protruding from a crewman's neck and another from the back of his head. He had landed nearly on top of the crewman she had just shot.

Four left.

Someone shot at Eliza from above, and she saw a sniper on the roof of the building across from her.

In terror, she ran under the roof and flattened herself against a door, then went to her belly. It was no good. She was still effectively in the open to any crewmembers walking by.

She wondered where Enkhid and Rabbi Einhorn were.

She opened up a channel. "Guys," she said quietly.

"Busy here," Enkhid said.

"Sniper across from the library."

The rabbi didn't answer, and Eliza hoped he was busy too.

She slowed her breathing to control her panic. She wondered how long the people in Broken Oar would stay in the sanctuary before some would lose patience and come up.

Maybe she could take an angle and surprise the sniper.

No, she couldn't. He'd see her before she saw him.

If she ran up the stairs, he'd hear her. At her end, the roof of the village stopped at the gate. She couldn't get to the roof on the other side of the village. Kovian 2 was operating there.

The sniper sent a volley of lasepistol fire at the library. Then he got on his knees, but before she could react, she heard lasepistol fire, and the sniper lost his balance and landed with a sickening sound.

Eliza turned at the sound of footsteps and found herself face-to-face with a panting Rabbi Einhorn. He was covered with sweat, but he calmly said to her, "There's one more *Peregrine* corpse near the social hall."

Eliza notified Enkhid, and the three did the math. Enkhid shot the crewmember Eliza saw and two others. Eliza shot two. Rabbi Einhorn shot two.

All of the *Peregrine* crew were accounted for now. It was time to go back.

LITA AND KOLOKH were litter bearers at Zhan's head, Kyr and Enkhid at the feet. Eliza didn't know the Kharkuns who were carrying Ujuq or Mira. One of them was walking painfully.

They were escorted by four of the dogs to keep the Donners at bay. Ralph was still recuperating at the hospital.

Kelly and Kolokh walked side by side.

Badri and Banner walked with Ror.

Eliza had Malit by the hand.

Eliza saw that the rings holding Zhan's and Ujuq's topknots were stitched to the top of each sheet, which were plain Ursan cream. Beneath, all three were zipped into body bags, but Eliza still caught the scent of decay.

The group walked in total silence.

As the group wended its way down the trail in twos and threes, the dogs alongside, Eliza saw that someone had filled in her *EB* and arrow with Broken Oar brickwork. It contrasted with the orange pink of the trail. Beside it was a larger cairn made of metal "stones" soldered together, dark gray and black, but with red stones in an upward spiral pattern. Beside it was a metal replica of the spray of lichenwood. The whole was at the edge of the trail, so Eliza doubted that anyone noticed it, which made it for the moment a private communication between Wolf and herself. She felt a lump in her throat.

She was grateful that no Donners disturbed the quiet procession of Kharkuns carrying their dead and for the cold, tight grip of Malit's hand.

The bats dove in and out of the ocean, and she thought of the way Malit could hear them. The small boy walked beside her, dry-eyed but quiet.

The procession stopped at the beach. The pyre was waiting at the edge of the water.

It looked deceptively small until the mourners approached it and lifted the bodies on top. The dead were laid in a row, feet facing the ocean. Ujuq was the smallest.

The Kharkuns looked anguished, but they were dry-eyed like Malit.

Lita, Ujuq's mother Q'ulah, and the limping Kharkun lit the pyre. The group stood in a half circle, the dogs to the rear. Now the sound of the waves was punctuated by the crackle of flame. Eliza smelled burning plastic, burning fabric, and burning flesh all together.

In the nearly forty-five minutes between the time that the procession had left Broken Oar to this moment, no one had uttered a word. There were just the waves and now the crackle of the flames.

When the bodies began to burn, the Kharkuns fell to their knees, wailed, sobbed, rent their clothing, and wailed again, rocking back and forth.

The thunderheads, Eliza saw, were gathering in the distance, and the group gathered itself and walked up the trail, once again in silence.

By the time they got to Broken Oar, it had started to rain.

✳

Eliza, Wolf, Kovian 2, and a group of Spiders walked outside the village. It was overcast, and Yossi had cautioned that a storm was due in early evening. Aphrodite had been wrapped into a ball of silk, and Wolf carried her remains on his back. Eliza walked very close to him.

As the group proceeded down the trail, they shared anecdotes about Aphrodite, and now Eliza started catching bits of the telepathic conversation. Eliza got an image from Wolf of Aphrodite's feet tucked under her like a cat, then her standing up to touch one of Wolf's sculptures. She had said it was perfect.

Dr. Spider looked at Kovian 2 and said, "What about you, bald Spider?"

Kovian 2 went multicolor, and he said, "She was the first of you to call me that. She was the first person at this village to make me feel welcome."

"She was my daughter," Dr. Spider said. "What about you, monkey?"

"*I'm so sorry,*" Eliza said, crying. "*She was welcoming and kind. We were supposed to drink together. May her memory be for a blessing.*"

"*Thank you,*" Dr. Spider said, "*civilized monkey.*"

The funeral pyre was nothing but a husk now. The rest of Aphrodite's children together dug a hole in the sand beside it, which immediately filled up with water. Wolf lowered Aphrodite's remains into the hole. Impulsively, Kovian 2 gathered up some of the ashes from the pyre and dropped them on top of Aphrodite. Then he turned white. Eliza realized that this was fear. But Aphrodite's children scooped up more ashes and poured them on her remains. Eliza gathered up ashes by the handfuls.

Aphrodite's body in the silk looked pitifully small.

When Aphrodite was buried, the Spiders' shaking could be felt through the sand.

Then Aphrodite's children, Kovian 2, and Eliza walked into the surf up to their waists and dunked under the water. Eliza dove through a wave.

The group left the water and walked back to the trail.

When two Donners approached, several Spiders streamed after them and caught one. One Spider bit it. One of Aphrodite's grown children carried the Donner on her back, the Donner still convulsing within the silk.

As they passed the *EB* and the arrow, Eliza said to Wolf, "*Thank you.*"

They trooped into the village. She took her leave of the Spiders and walked into her home.

Still sopping wet, she took her medication, and then Badri took her by the hand and led her to the whirlpool tub and said, "We are going to get in this together."

They got into the tub together, and Eliza slipped into Badri's arms.

PART FOUR

PART FOUR

DENNY WALKED with Tony Polichek and Gino Accardi. Service dogs Ralph, Duncan, and Scout trotted alongside them. Ralph had healed faster than anticipated. The sky was overcast, but Denny saw the equipment they packed and noted with approval that they had learned from Baines's mistakes—including checking in with Yossi about the weather.

Tony carried the necessary ship parts in his backpack, and Denny had been surprised at how small they were when Tony had them all laid out before they departed.

"Just those itty-bitty parts to fix a great big ship?" she'd asked.

"That sounds vaguely obscene," Gino said.

"Serious question, though," Denny said. "I was expecting something the size of a chassis at least. This thing is small, like a tablet with charger cords sticking out either side."

Tony laughed. "I don't know what a charger cord is, but I get the picture. Yes, this is the component that was destroyed. You start to nuke the inner ear of a Human, they don't know which way is up, and then they have vertigo. If our ship doesn't know which way is up—or in space, where there is no 'up,' which direction it's going—it's programmed not to move."

When Denny saw the ship, she gasped. It was over three hundred feet long, with a silvery skin and *SS Kestrel* in sans serif over a blue silhouette of the bird.

"Did you know that an old name for *kestrel* was *fuckwind* or *windfucker*?" she said.

Gino laughed. "That must have been Space Force's idea of a joke."

"Space Force doesn't have a sense of humor," Tony said. "They saddled us with Glenn, Bynum, and a teenager."

"What have you got against Maura?" Gino asked.

"Sweet kid," Denny said. "I met her. I like her. She's been through hell, and this is a good place for her."

"I agree with everything you said except for the part that this is a good place for her," Tony said.

"She'll adjust eventually," Denny said, "even though the Human kids her age are from 1941. She'll teach them Dungeons and Dragons or some other role-playing game and turn some of them on to the same books she reads. Those kids have been through hell too. She'll be okay."

"Fine. But we needed an anesthesiologist, and there was no room for one on the ship," Tony said. "We needed an ethologist. Instead, we got a psychopath and butcher. And a high school sophomore. And now what the hell are we going to do if a Human gets pregnant? Are Banner or Badri going to open up an instruction manual?"

"You haven't been paying attention," Denny said. "One of the Holocaust survivors, Leon Glass, is an ob-gyn, and he's learning. By way of specialists, Christian Dodd's even learning about—about the Kharkuns' weasel pets and the—the ones belonging to the Kovians. You know, the ones who look like gigantic water bears. And Enkhid is a vet too. Everyone will catch up."

Tony relaxed.

"How do you know?" Gino said. "I didn't even know."

"I've been talking to Badri and Eliza. You haven't?"

"Yes, but those specifics didn't come up," Gino answered. "I was too horrified that she first thought your buddy had invented the village—don't worry, we worked it out. And yes, this whole situation is ass-backward for you, but the issue was a distraction."

"I understand. Both of those things. Well, I still think Maura's an asset. She can help the other Human kids adjust to this date, and they can help her. She's also even smarter than her brother, and I didn't think that was possible."

A ramp opened up below the ship. They walked in, and Denny saw that they were in a hallway. She heard the hydraulic sound of the ramp closing and wished it somehow clicked in place when it was closed, but it didn't. They started walking down a long corridor. About halfway down, the dogs stopped.

"What's going on?" Tony said, kneeling.

Tony put a leash on Ralph first and tried to lead him, but he pulled backward. Hard. Scout backed off before Gino could put a leash on her.

"That doorway leads to the room where they were kept in stasis," Tony said quietly. "They don't want to go back in. Hold on." He pulled some treats out of his pocket. Then he walked well past the room, down the hall, and called the dogs.

Ralph went bounding right to him and was rewarded with a treat. The other two followed.

Denny studied Tony. He was tall and lean, with honey-colored hair that had been cropped but was at this point growing out. He was graying at the temples, and she guessed he was her age.

The door to Engineering slid open, and Tony opened up a cabinet. He and Gino immediately started working, heads inside the cabinet, feet sprawled out behind them.

Denny sat down and leaned against another cabinet.

"So what do you think of this place?" Tony asked Denny. His voice was muffled in the close quarters of the cabinet.

"I like it. Do you notice how the people here don't seem to have a place to go back to? I had a job I loved. That was it for me."

"What do you make of Eliza and Badri?" Tony asked. "Badri's kind of a stiff, isn't he?"

"Oh? Word is, when Eliza didn't come back, he lost his mind," Gino said. "You can't be an icicle and love someone from afar for half a decade, but there those two were, just plugging along, doing their jobs, and loving each other. Denny, did you see that coming, those two?"

"No."

Ralph had crept up to her and lay down with his head on her leg, and she stroked him.

"I don't understand," Tony said. "Why couldn't they have gotten together?"

"Conflict of interest," Gino said. "Right?"

"Yes," Denny answered. "We were worried enough that when the two of them went to a conference, we asked an ME at a different office—one who wouldn't ask too many loud questions in the process—to keep tabs on the two of them. And ... nothing."

"Oh," Tony said.

"So who's going to fight the *Enterprise*?" Denny asked. "Are you all just gonna fly up there and start shooting?

What's the plan? There are three hundred people on that ship!"

"We'll show you the *Fatherland Mural* when we're done," Tony said.

"I know about the *Fatherland Mural*."

"Oh, right. Jesus," Tony said. "Well, do you want to risk the lives of the people in that village on the off chance that some of the people on the *Enterprise* aren't as homicidal as the crew of the *Peregrine*? Because I don't. We still have the *Archer* on its way too. Bonus."

"Speaking of which, where the hell *is* Bynum?" Gino asked.

Denny remembered Eliza, Kovian 2, and Wolf and got a chill. "Maybe he ran out to meet the *Peregrine* and never came back. Hell, maybe they ate him," she said. "The crew, not the Donners."

Tony looked at her sharply.

Gino said, "But—"

"Gino, don't ask, okay?" Tony said. "No one's seen him in days, and fundamentally, who cares?"

"No one went to his house to check?" Denny asked.

"Inani did," Gino said. "She didn't find him. Maybe she doesn't give a shit either."

"You sorry I'm here?" Denny asked.

Tony softened. "I'm glad you're here."

"Did you take him out?" Gino asked.

Denny bristled. "Which one of us are you asking?"

"No," Tony said. "I didn't. Whoever did? More power to 'em, and I'd prefer not to call attention to the issue."

"There you have it," Denny said. "My personal advice, as a former prosecutor, is to shut the fuck up about it."

"I don't know," Gino said uneasily.

"And yet you're preparing to blow up a ship with three hundred people on it."

"That's different."

"Different how?" Tony said. "Aaand, we're done!" He crawled back out from underneath the cabinet and closed it. Then he said to Denny, "Care to go for a ride?"

Denny did.

First, they took a detour to the mess hall. In addition to the *Fatherland Mural* and the *Little Green Man and Fruit Basket* mural, there was a mural of Humans in Space Force coveralls standing over kneeling green men, some of whom had fruit baskets in their laps, with other green men were filling them. There was another mural with felled trees and a small town, a Human in a Space Force coverall carrying the body of a green deer over its shoulders.

"Good God, that's obscene," Denny said. "How is it you all don't have that mindset?"

"I think they wanted the researchers to go first. The exploiters were next. That's my theory," Gino said.

"It's a good theory," Tony said. "Once we'd landed, we planned to paint over the murals."

"They're frightening," Denny said. Then she had an awful thought. "Is NASA gone? Where's NASA?"

"Without the trillions of dollars needed to fund this mission," Tony said. "Sadly. If the mission had been NASA's, it wouldn't have been a clusterfuck."

"Let's get out of here," Denny said. "Those are making my skin crawl."

When they got to the bridge, Denny said, "This thing is operated by two people, right? I hope you're not counting on me!"

"It can be operated by one person," Tony said. "The *Enterprise* is more complicated, and they have shuttles."

Gino looked sick. "And the shuttles have weapons too."

"So there will be two ships against an aircraft carrier and a bunch of fighter planes?"

"We plan to take out their shuttle bay," Tony said.

"*We?*" Denny said. "Who's gonna go up there?"

"I should," Gino said. He turned to Tony. "I can't fix these crates on my own. You can, and you might need to make some repairs in time to meet the *Archer*."

"What if the *Archer* had gotten here first," Denny asked, "and they'd given you the same welcome?"

"Are you a gambler?" Tony asked her. "The *Peregrine* had bioweapons."

"No. But you're talking about killing three hundred and sixteen people on guesswork."

"And?" Gino said. "The *Peregrine* had bioweapons."

The trio walked up to the bridge and Gino said, "Put your seatbelts on!"

Denny laughed. "There *are* no seatbelts. Why is that? Starships and school buses."

"What do you mean?" Tony asked. "And what are school buses?"

"Why no seatbelts?" Denny said.

"Oh, well," Tony replied, "with a sudden decel, you'd just keep going and the seat belt would cut you in half, so it really doesn't matter."

"Okay," Denny said, "but when the ship crashed—"

"I busted my nose," Gino said. "That's all. The pressure dampers worked." He went back to his old chair at the navigation console and sat down, fingers moving across the buttons so rapidly that they were nearly blurry.

Tony sat in Baines's seat, and Denny said, "Where do I sit?"

Tony pointed to the chair next to his. "Usually, that's my seat, but there's no one in it."

Denny laughed.

The ship went straight up, and then they were in orbit. It took no time at all.

Then they were in space.

Denny gasped. "This is gorgeous," she said quietly. TV and movies hadn't prepared her for this. The stars occupied her whole field of vision, an eternity of lights in the pitch black of space. "It's like I can see infinity," she whispered.

Gino banked the ship, and she saw an arm of the Milky Way galaxy. It was both impossibly far away and as if she was walking around the middle of it. Stars and splashes of white.

Tony grabbed her forearm and whispered, "It really is amazing, isn't it? This is one of the reasons we're here."

"I was never gonna see this," Denny said softly. "Not ever."

"You never thought we'd make it here?" Tony asked.

"I thought Humankind was gonna turn the Earth into a flaming ball of shit. But I'm pushing forty now, and I wasn't going to be north of the ground if we ever did."

Tony laughed. "And now you're here."

"I don't want to take this thing too far away from Ursinus b," Gino said. "There've been too many mishaps." Instead, he took the ship through various maneuvers, turning, banking suddenly, climbing "up" and diving "down."

"The *Kestrel*'s more agile than the *Enterprise* will be. The *Peregrine* and the *Kestrel* will run circles around it," Tony said. "I'm going to take some data on life signs and do a spin around the planet before we go back."

"You're not gonna get lost?"

"No, that's Baines's trick," Gino said. "We almost did on

the way to the wormhole when we had to do a U-turn to get away from a notable astronomical event. All because she wanted to go exploring."

"Holy shit," Denny said. "That woman's a menace!"

"And you wonder why we're afraid of the *Enterprise* and the *Archer*?" Tony said.

Denny saw that the ocean at Broken Oar was huge, bigger than the Pacific, but broken up with archipelagoes of what looked like volcanoes. The reed forest turned into scrubland, then forest, then steppes. There were foothills, then mountains.

"That's a lot of plate tectonics going on right there," Gino said, looking at the viewscreen. "I keep seeing what looks like volcanoes. I wonder if there are earthquakes."

"We'll ask Yossi to set up a seismometer." Tony said.

The ship landed.

Tony pushed a button on his chair. "I'm transmitting this data to our computers at the village while this ship is still whole."

Denny froze.

"Still whole," Gino said, pale.

"Let's go," Tony said.

He had to walk past the dogs' stasis room and drop treats on the other side before the dogs would pass the door.

In front of the ship, he said, "This is one thing I wish Space Force knew about—how this traumatized the dogs." Tony knelt and soothed and petted each dog, then gave them each a treat.

"Star Service probably wouldn't care," Gino said.

Denny hesitated. "I'd like to meet the dickweeds."

"One of these days, we'll all know the same things at the same time," Gino said.

Denny didn't realize how close the creatures were to the ship.

The *Macrodactylus* had telescoped upward and their— Denny thought there was only one word for what those were— their tongues came out, flicked the air, and then returned. She counted almost fifty of them, all lining the washes and the pond at the bottom.

"You say they're everywhere?" she asked.

"Only next to bodies of freshwater, or the washes," Tony said. "There are some of their smaller cousins in the streams on the other side of the reed forest and some in the marshes down the beach. Some of them are entirely aquatic, and Cody says that the ones in the water are carnivores."

Ralph galumphed over to one of them, lifted his leg, and peed on it, and Tony whispered, "Oh, no."

And Ralph trotted back to Tony, looking proud of himself.

"I'd've called him," Gino said, "but it—"

"You must know what happened to Jennifer," Tony said to Denny.

"I do. What's the difference between them and the dogs?"

"She's another one who should have been left behind," Gino said. "She was trying to take a fucking *core sample* of one of those guys. It's that one, right there." Gino pointed at one two down from the one Ralph had peed on. "Cody told her she was about to wound an animal, not kill a plant, and not to do it. He yelled 'stop,' she blew him off. Duncan had just peed on it, so she assumed it was safe. As soon as her instrument touched the side of it, it threw up. She never had a chance."

"How do you feel about that?" Denny asked.

"She tried to vivisect an animal. Scared the shit out of me," Gino responded. "One more sociopath. The *Peregrine* was crewed by maniacs. You still having second thoughts about the *Enterprise*?"

On the way back, the trio heard noises in the reeds. "Those aren't Donners," Gino said. "I wonder what they are."

"Well, we have the data now," Tony said.

On the trail, just as they passed the *EB*, Tony took Denny's hand.

By the time they got to the gate, it had started raining.

Banner called Eliza and asked her to come to the hospital alone and speak with him.

When she walked through the door, he took her beyond the double doors and sat her in a room that was obviously used for surgery. Then he slid the glass door shut and sat on a stool. Eliza looked around for another chair, and he motioned her to another stool.

"I think I've figured out a way to get you straightened out," Banner said.

"I need straightening out?"

"You're not going to stop talking telepathically to Kovian 2 or Wolf, and who can blame you? I'm a little jealous of that ability, to be honest. But every time you do it for very long, you're in a ball on the floor puking your guts out, and then you have a migraine. And you do it for a real, real long time, the headache knocks you out and you lose a day." He took a long breath, then let it out. "One of those days, you're *really* gonna have to take that amatrazine, and it's not a risk-free medication by any means."

Eliza sent up a prayer of thanks for her poker face. But

when she looked him in the eye, she saw compassion and concern.

"You look like you've been to hell," he said, "and you haven't come all the way back. You get to feeling like you did the other night, you come and find me. I'm not a psychiatrist, but I did a rotation, and it's going to have to do."

Eliza took a breath.

"It's confidential. Whatever happened that night, it took a bite out of Badri too. You understand?"

She was afraid to answer him. She didn't know what he knew. She also hadn't said a word to Badri about the additional cast member in her nightmares. "The pilots who take out the *Enterprise*, and probably the *Archer* ..."

"They're going to need a support group when they come home. You join them."

She looked at him.

"The *Peregrine* crew murdered Zhan and turned him and Cody into bioweapons. You killed Bynum with the weapon you had, not the weapon you wish you had."

Eliza started sobbing.

Banner sighed. "This place really is a backwater, thank God. Four ships go out, none come back, you think anyone's gonna spend a dime going after them? We've been here a month, and the only violence came from outside the house."

"Not all of it," Eliza said tearfully.

Banner handed her a tissue. After she calmed down, Banner said, "That night's gonna live with you for the rest of your life, I'm not gonna lie. I can only guess how it happened, but based on the three of you, I know it was ugly or it wouldn't have worked."

Eliza started sobbing again. Through her tears, she said,

"He was terrified, and he died in agony, and when I went to put him out of his misery, his blood ... his blood was in my hair."

"And I'd be a hypocrite if I judged you. I went out looking for him with something that would have killed him fast. But getting right up close to him like that, it's possible that he could have gotten the upper hand, and this hospital would have turned into a lab. I could have gotten us all killed. When you start having the same feelings you did that night, I want you to come find me."

"I will. If I ever do again."

"Hell, I briefly had those thoughts, and I *didn't* find him. The other reason I brought you here was to see if we couldn't mitigate your post-telepathy symptoms. I was trying to figure out exactly what was going on. I could put you in the Hansen scanner and get a complete picture, but Kovian 2 and Wolf both said no."

"Why?"

"They're afraid that the Hansen scan could affect your abilities. I don't have the same concerns, but since they both said no, it's moot. So I have to do what I can with what I have. The first thing I noticed is that periodically, your eyes move rapidly."

"You think I'm dreaming?" Eliza said in horror. "Really?"

"No, you're not dreaming. But something is going on neurologically, and you sometimes have rapid eye movements. I think the vertigo is related to inflammation of the muscles of the eye and the optic nerve, because it's connected to the vestibular system. Telepathy also affects your neurotransmitters, causing a migraine to come on afterward. I'm surprised you aren't showing mood symptoms as a result too. We now have a medication for migraines that works more consistently and effectively than the triptan medications you probably used at home, with fewer side effects."

"Wow!" Eliza said. "And the vertigo?"

"Is it getting worse or better now after each exercise of telepathy?"

Eliza considered. "The night we—we murdered Bynum, it was really bad ... but after that night, the vertigo wasn't as bad. The headaches are worse."

"I thought that would be the case. Whatever's going on is making your brain plastic enough to adjust. Just not to whatever's causing the migraines. The migraine medication is an implant. If you ever intend to become pregnant, it'll have to come out before you go into labor, or you'll need a C-section."

Eliza nodded.

The group that Eliza was beginning to think of as a council met in the hospital. She and Banner were already waiting in the infirmary. This time, someone had set up chairs for the humanoids. Also present were Tony and Christian Dodd, looking stone-faced. Kinkead was staring into the middle distance.

The mood was bleak. Eliza noticed that Inani was not present and that Johalo had taken her place.

"Where is Inani?" Badri asked.

"We asked Inani to move out," Johalo said impassively.

"Tony, what's wrong?" Eliza asked.

"The *Peregrine* never woke up their dogs," he said, "so we did. They were Belgian Malinois. It was almost too late. Putting the dogs under isn't as benign as we thought. They were disoriented and terrified. One of them pancaked himself on the ground and wouldn't move. I—"

"Tony had me examine them," Christian said, shaking with fury. "They had explosive devices in their abdomens."

There was a moment of chaos in the room.

"We don't have a bomb squad here," Kinkead said. "But I … I was the next best thing. The devices had a remote-control sensor. Operable with a comm-watch. Each dog could have killed everyone within fifty feet and reduced the dog to a pink mist. Fortunately, a Hansen scanner didn't detonate them."

"It was tricky," Christian said, his arms now around himself. "But the dogs are stable, and one of them wagged her tail when I went to check on her."

"Where will they live?" Badri asked.

"With me," Christian said. "Belgian Malinois need five hours of training a day, or they'll go mad."

"Thank you again, Kinkead," Eliza said. "You all notice that Kinkead takes care of problems before it all goes to hell? What would we have done without the security cameras while we were in the tunnels? And now he saved the dogs and us. Again."

Everyone said thank you, some of them shamefacedly.

Badri said, "Who is going to staff the *Peregrine* and the *Kestrel*?"

"I'm going up on the *Kestrel*," Gino said. "I know the ship and how it behaves."

"I'm going with Gino," Tony said.

"No," Baines said. "It's a waste of manpower. Lieutenant Accardi will staff the mission alone."

"What kind of bullsh—"

"Remember your rank, Lieutenant. There will be no—"

"Yes, there will be a copilot," Tony said firmly.

"Lieutenant Accardi flies alone!" Baines said. "That's an *order*!" A vein appeared on her forehead.

"When you first landed," Eliza asked her, "who was it who told you that you should send drones first? Was it Gino?"

"It was Gino," Gino said. "And Tony. Gino also told you not to take us off course before we got to the wormhole, and so did Tony. Both of us did. You gave the order anyway. We almost got shagged by a supernova. Our route had been plotted to avoid hazards like that, including the massive EMP pulse from a solar flare you narrowly missed taking us through. We didn't learn a damn thing other than that you were an idiot—"

"I didn't even learn anything from that," said Kinkead quietly.

"You barreled into the reed forest without a thought for your crew," Kelly said. "And Chloe died."

"This mission has risks," Baines said. "If you didn't want to take any, you should have stayed home taking beatings from Glenn!"

More chaos broke out in the room.

Kelly recoiled from her. "Omigod."

"Get *out*!" Badri yelled, taking a step toward Baines.

"It's mutiny!"

Some people laughed.

"You're insane," Rabbi Einhorn said.

Baines stalked out of the room and slammed the door.

"Is she gonna turn into another Bynum?" Kovian 2 asked, turning blood red, his gills rippling.

"No," Kelly said. "A lot of captains would have ordered us to start cutting down the reed forest, shooting the wildlife— she didn't even shoot the *Macrodactylus* that killed Jennifer Simms. She knows that Star Service would be slaughtering the wildlife and offering Highland steaks, especially after those assholes on the *Peregrine* showed up with the dead Highland calf. She ordered it buried, remember? She'd never risk that just because she's angry at us."

"Fair point," Gino said. "Who's going to fly the other ship?"

"I believe I'm the only other pilot in the village, am I not?" Kyr said.

"What are the copilots there for?" Fanny asked.

"Firing weapons," Tony said. "Someone has to steer while the other one shoots. Someone could do both, but sometimes that causes problems with divided attention. The damage those plasma waves can do to those ships, I can't fix, no matter how many auto parts the dispensers can make."

"Auto parts?" Wolf asked.

Kyr said, "I don't need a copilot."

"Kharkuns don't have the same issues with divided attention that Humans have," Ror said. "There's no one else to send with him in any case."

"We think faster than you Humans do," Kolokh said.

"The sun is the sun," Eliza said.

"You want to figure out what each button does in the middle of a firefight?" Gino asked Kyr.

"No, I'll acquaint myself with your console beforehand. But I agree that in a mission with stakes as high as these, it is best to have a copilot."

"Well, I'm watching the skies," Kinkead said. "We'll have a two-hour head start, so none of you better get hurt until then. And I'm going with Kyr."

Kovian 2 went multicolor.

"I don't need you to fight," Kyr said, "and you can't fly the ship."

"I can fly the ship, and it's an Earth ship. Tony, tell him."

Tony sighed. "He's almost as good as Gino. No one is *as* good as Gino."

Kyr, smiling a little, said, "Thank you, Kinkead."

"Then who will watch the skies if Kinkead is flying the ship?" Rabbi Einhorn asked.

"Yossi," Kinkead said.

"Two hours is not a lot of time, is it?" Kovian 2 asked.

"And it takes an hour to get to the *Kestrel* from here," Kelly said.

"*Rebellion at Broken Oar* hasn't gotten much right," Eliza said. "What if they show up earlier?"

"We're leaving on Summer Solstice 36," Tony said. "Two weeks early."

"I'm okay with getting there on the thirty-sixth," Gino said. "The thirty-sixth. The fiftieth. People talked like that in the 2020s, but only as a joke."

"You can show me how the ship runs in case I have to switch from firing weapons to piloting," Kyr said.

"I don't want to take them up before they get there," Tony said. "If they're within sensor range but far off enough, they might be on to us, because both ships were supposed to have landed. But I agree that at least helping you understand the controls is best."

Badri said, "We must prepare ourselves for the shuttles."

"I thought we were blowing up the shuttles," Gino said. "It's on my to-do list."

"Unexpected events are the essence of any undertaking," Badri said, but he looked briefly at Eliza, "or of no undertaking."

"Good point," Gino said. "But, Jesus, can we keep the Kanninoin off the turrets? No disrespect."

"We will staff the tunnel's sanctuary," Johalo said, "regardless of what Inani directs."

"She doesn't own the village," Eliza said coldly. "There are thirty-five Kovians and forty Spiders here. There are only thirty of you. Why do you think you decide who staffs what?"

"And there are forty-seven Humans. What of it?"

"And we have done a fuck-all job of running anything," Eliza said. "So we're not."

"Forty-six, probably," Gino said.

There was an uncomfortable silence.

Quickly, Eliza said, "We have a council here for a reason. Inani might be *your* boss, but she's not ours. We need *real* fighters on those turrets, and we need fighters at the entrance of the gates."

"I didn't mean that Inani made the decision," Johalo said. "I mean that no one made a decision."

"We need to run simulations," Kelly said.

"Every day," Tony said.

"We need fighters in the tunnels too, in case somehow—"

CHAPTER
FORTY-EIGHT

ELIZA SAT in Denny's apartment over lunch. Denny had a sampler of Kharkun food and Kovian mollusks.

Denny pointed to a pale object that looked like a cross between a potato and a carrot and said, "This isn't bad. You expect it to be savory and it's all melty and sweet. Veggie ice cream."

Eliza took a forkful. "Hey, this is good."

Denny had a bowl of the red liquid that smelled and looked to Eliza to be the same substance that Lita and Malit had been drinking. Denny took a sip and cursed. She got up, ran to the sink, and spat it out. "Slimy and bitter."

Eliza handed Denny a mug of naiya and tried the red liquid herself. "Congealed tomato soup with rust. It's definitely made of blood. I wonder how it doesn't clot."

"Oh my God," Denny said. "I need to bleach my mind now." She raised the mug of naiya to her lips and drank. "Ohh, this is good. What is it?"

"Naiya. It's Kanninoin. It's a stimulant too. Don't drink it at night. And this stuff?" Eliza said, pointing at a bowl. "It's probably good for you, or Lita wouldn't have given it to Malit." She took another sip. "It's not ... not terrible. Like liquid steak. I'll bet it's nutritious as hell, and it wouldn't be bad in a pinch."

"It's all yours," Denny said laughing. "The naiya is fantastic."

They practically inhaled the Kovian food.

They then tried Q'a'ta fat and strips of flank, which were, as Eliza expected, raw.

Eliza tasted the meat. "Good God, this is amazing," she said. "Tender enough to melt in your mouth, buttery finish."

Denny nodded. "It's fantastic!"

Eliza tried the Q'a'ta fat. "Rubbery," she said, "but also melty."

Denny took one. Mouth full, she gave it a thumbs-up.

The red broth had cooked leaves and balls the size of chicken eggs of what looked like a root vegetable but tasted like apricot. The bitterness of the leaf played against the sweetness.

"It's close enough to tzimmes that it's not bad. What's this?" Eliza pointed to drinking bowls of something white that bubbled. She remembered that Ror had been drinking it when she'd first met him.

"Fermented milk. I can't remember from what animal." Denny took a sip. "Buttermilk. Or maybe cream. With bubbles. I don't know. Also Kharkun. The Kanninoin food is all bland and flavorless—"

"Or terrible. Did you have the plaster of Paris school glue breakfast yet?"

Denny laughed. "I missed that. What I tried tastes like flour except when it tastes like flour paste, except when it tastes like naiya or like lightly salted water with flour. There was also a bowl of small red berries that were so spicy and bitter that my eyes watered, and I love eating ghost peppers."

Eliza laughed. "I'll take your word for it." Then she looked at the white beverage. "I wonder if it's alcoholic." After she tasted it, she said, "Oh, it's good. Definitely alcoholic. But enough food field trip," Eliza said. She went to the dispenser and came back with two plates of goose ham and pilaf. Then she brought a dish of olives and a bowl of Israeli salad. "I made an executive decision."

Denny had already set a pitcher of water on the table and came back with a bottle of wine. She poured Eliza a glass of wine.

"I like your executive decisions," Denny said taking a bite of the goose ham. "And if you really brought me here, I'm fine with it. Other than the job, there was zip. Holidays sucked. I thought about taking leave after the Dyson case, because it wrecked me, but then I would've been alone. And I had no balance in my life."

"Me too. And I still have flashbacks about Dyson. It wrecked so many in my department—"

"A couple were drinking themselves to death. I was a little worried about you, to be honest."

"When Dyson was murdered, it was just ... over. I was afraid I was going to go home and do what Randall did."

"What changed?"

"I don't know. Going back to work, the next murder was a stabbing."

"I remember."

"He walked out of the bar, got into it with someone, and then someone walked over, stabbed him overhand, and the dude took ten steps and died on his feet. He acted like a guy would act who'd taken a punch, because that's what it can feel like. No suffering. Nothing twisted. I don't mean I didn't care about the case, but after Dyson ..."

"But then there was Chloe Jackman."

"And no videos." Eliza started sobbing. "Good God! Those videos!"

Denny hugged her, and Eliza cried.

Soon, Eliza said, "I'm okay now."

"See, that about you. Emotion pops out, and then you change the subject. On and off like a faucet. I worry most about the people who can't just sit with it."

"What we needed was EMDR, but that's a couple hundred a week."

Denny said quietly, "Jamie shot himself."

"I know. He did it in front of Badri. That fucking book. If he'd just dropped the book on my lap when Glenn died, he would have been okay." Eliza's eyes welled up. "What did the PIO say?"

"Oh," Denny said, "'Can't comment on a pending investigation.'"

"About what I thought, then."

"Do you think they'll solve the case?"

"No." Then Eliza had a terrible thought. "Glenn and Kelly had parents, and Glenn had a sister and brother, then just Maura and Cody. But we didn't see Glenn's parents. Jennifer Simms had no one. Neither did Chloe. Rafaella knew nothing about Chloe's past at all. Do you think—"

"Who the hell knows? If I think about it too long, I'll start hemorrhaging from my eyes."

Eliza dropped her glass, shattering it and spilling iced tea all over the floor. Then she reached for her hair. "Omigod! Let me get that—right, rags are in the textiles dispenser."

As they cleaned up, Eliza reached to pick up a shard of glass, and Denny grabbed her wrist. "They did leave us a broom. Let me get this. You don't look good."

As Eliza sat down, shaken, Denny leaned on the breakfast bar. She studied Eliza. She got up and came back with a mug of something that smelled of jasmine. It was thick. As she handed the mug to Eliza, she said, "You've done a lot of killing since you got here."

"What's this?"

"I asked the dispenser for something hot to calm you down. This popped out. I don't know."

Eliza took a sip, then a deeper drink. "It's—it's good! Tastes like jasmine, but a little bit sweet ... something almost like cranberry juice and ..." She suddenly felt calm, but not sedated. "When the *Archer* gets here, there will be more bloodshed. And soon, four of our people will be off to blow up a ship with three hundred people on it."

"I never would have thought you'd had it in you."

"Me neither."

Denny took a drink of wine. Then she said, "That was the three of you."

"He would have let them in. He would have let sixteen mass shooters in."

"Instead, I let them in."

"You were a hostage. And no one could have predicted that you would show up, let alone just that moment. But I wish—"

"You always did think in black and white. This is a war zone, not Tauxenent County."

"But—" Eliza finished off what she had in her mug.

"And days ago, children buried their parents, and parents buried their children."

"I know. We had no choice. We're lucky there were only

two monsters on the *Kestrel*. With the *Enterprise* and the *Archer*, we can't know." Eliza took another sip of the Kharkun white fermented drink. "We can't let three hundred unknowns onto this planet! What if they bring more bioweapons? What if the *Enterprise* can see the tunnels? Maybe they can nuke the translators so we can't even talk to each other! Denny, if we lay down our arms, there will be no Broken Oar."

"What about the Ursans? Wasn't this their village?"

"No. They say it just showed up here. The Ursans can't say when. That time-blindness. According to Cody, Belek thinks this village is a mud hut. He's the only one who lives here, and he ... acts like he's studying us. Like an anthropologist or something. They think we're all pretty backward. And they never lived here. Belek told Cody about their underground cities."

Denny took a drink of the Kharkun fermented drink and said, "So the Kharkuns had a funeral, the Spiders had a funeral, what about the Tenurians and the Kanninoin? There wasn't one for either, was there?"

"The Tenurians ate their dead. Given that the Tenurian chicks normally eat their mothers, that's no surprise. The Kanninoin are very practical. They took the remains of their dead out to the edge of the reed forest and then came back, but R'ani and Sha'in haven't eaten since Kano's death. Johalo says this is typical and that one or both of them might actually die."

"This really is another world, isn't it?"

"That it is. And another thing. Remember *Painted Walls*?"

"I do."

"Puppies."

"What about—why do they need artificial uteruses for puppies?"

"All five of the dogs here are neutered. The Kanninoin can

make gametes out of stem cells. There are twenty puppies who will be here in a month and a half or so." Then she rolled her eyes. "The Malinois weren't spayed or neutered."

Denny shook her head in bewilderment. Then she said, "I wonder whether they'll let me adopt one."

"You could ask."

BAINES HAD MOVED in with Inani, and they refused to participate.

Kyr, Kinkead, Tony, and Gino walked to the gate, fully equipped with provisions. No one wanted to live only on ship rations. Almost the entire colony was there to send them off, cheering and applauding. The Tenurians kept to themselves, but George clung to Belek's back.

Gino and Tony were escorted by Kelly, Denny, and Ralph. Kyr and Kinkead traveled with Eris and Enkhid. They carried their provisions on gurneys.

"Y'all don't have any sort of motor vehicle?" Denny asked as they walked past the lichenwood.

"Nope, and we're not going to," Gino said. "To drive it, we have to make roads. To make roads, we have to kill stuff."

Denny noticed the Highland cattle on her left. "They look so sweet! Deadly, but adorable."

"They are that," Tony said. "Oh, shit, no—Ralph!"

Ralph had run after what looked to Denny like mutant wolves.

Gino grabbed Tony from behind. "Stay!" he said to Tony.

"Look!" Denny whispered.

Ralph had gone into a play bow with one of the wolves. The wolves were easily twice Ralph's size.

"Ralph, you idiot!" Tony said, anguished.

But the wolves were playing with Ralph. At one point, Ralph squealed in pain, but the wolf he was playing with backed off, and the wolf and Ralph went right back into another play bow, and the two were off again.

After about five minutes, Ralph trotted back to the group, proud of himself again.

"Well, what do you know!" Gino said.

Tony leashed Ralph, saying, "You almost gave me a heart attack, you furry idiot!" He kissed Ralph on the muzzle and said, "Let's get out of here before this goofball does something else!"

Denny saw that Tony was shaking a little, and she slipped her arm around his waist.

After the ships had been loaded with provisions, and as the council had agreed, Kinkead did another test run of the notification system.

Kinkead held up his comm-watch.

It said, *Received*.

"Well, I don't know about you all, but I installed a seat belt," Kinkead said. "I don't need to get knocked out of my seat when I'm flying."

Kelly looked at Gino.

"Kinkead," Gino said, "not a good idea."

But thunderheads loomed in the distance.

Kelly looked at the sky and said, "Time to leave! Kinkead, you're an idiot!"

"Noted! I don't trust those pressure dampers on the console."

Gino said, "Those seatbelts are a bad—"

"Gino, trust me."

The group turned to leave the pilots.

Denny lagged behind.

Tony kissed her. "I'll be back, I promise." Then he went into the *Kestrel* and the ramp closed.

CHAPTER
FIFTY
SUMMER SOLSTICE 41

ROR SENT OUT THE WARNING. The *Enterprise* was two hours away.

Gino's communications console lit up.

"You see it?" Banner asked.

"That's affirmative," Gino said. "Want me to bring you something from the store?"

Banner laughed. Then he said, "God be with you."

"Received," Gino said.

Gino and Kinkead took the ships into orbit.

The *Enterprise* was within hailing distance. It gleamed orange in the sunlight, all three hundred meters of it. It was triple the size of the *Peregrine* and the *Kestrel*.

Gino's blood filled with ice.

The *Enterprise* was shaped like a submarine, except for a visible bridge near the nose. At the rear, there were four smaller arms. The top arms curved upward. With their multiple windows, they looked like skyscrapers, only taller. Between those arms was the shuttle bay.

The *Peregrine* was the *Kestrel*'s twin—shaped like an old

C-17 military transport plane but twice the size, white, with sans serif writing on the side that was visible in the light of Ursinus.

"If the *Enterprise* drops those shuttles, we're fucked," Kinkead said via ship-to-ship comms.

"That's an affirmative," Gino said. He moved the *Kestrel* until it faced the *Enterprise* broadside.

"How do you like that?" Tony said.

On the viewscreen was a close-up of *Enterprise*'s hull. The name "*SS Enterprise*" was written in sans serif across a black, red-eyed kraken.

"Heartwarming." Then Gino hailed the *Enterprise*. "How are you doing, *Enterprise*?"

A face showed up on the viewscreen. "*Kestrel*, why is there an alien on the *Peregrine*?"

"Nice to see you too!" Gino said. "To whom do I have the pleasure of speaking at?"

"Captain Peter Q. Runhede of the SS *Enterprise*. I'll ask you again, why is there an alien on the *Peregrine*, and why are you in space?"

Gino muted the comms. "Thank God he told us what ship he was of." Then he unmuted. "We're the welcoming commit-tee. You're here early. How's the *Archer*?"

"Supernova. We're here to clean up your mess. I ask you again, why have you permitted an alien to take over an Earth ship?"

"The *Archer* is gone?" Gino asked.

"Our instruments are state of the art. We saw it. I'll only ask one more time. Why have you permitted an alien at the helm of the *Peregrine*? You're given it classified information to *use against us!*"

"Use what?" Gino said. "The ships of Kyr's people are more advanced than ours. To him this is like driving a crotch rocket and not a starship. He just wanted a chance to try one. He's doing a good job, isn't he?"

Gino muted comms again, then announced over the Broken Oar channel, "The *Archer* is gone."

"Received. Good news," Banner said.

"Tell him to land it and disembark. We'll be sending our people down to take control," Captain Peter Q. Runhede of the SS *Enterprise* said.

"Why are you powering up weapons?" Gino asked, noting with satisfaction that Kinkead was maneuvering the *Peregrine* aft to the *Enterprise* shuttle bay.

"He is trespassing on one of our ships over an Earth colony."

The viewscreen went dark at the same time the *Enterprise* fired on the *Peregrine*, the white blobs narrowly missing her hull in the distance of space.

"You want to go to war with the Kharkuns, *Enterprise*?" Gino said as Tony returned fire. He muted the comms again. "Those aren't waves. They're—plasma *balls*."

Tony fired again, scraping the top of the *Enterprise*. "I don't know."

The *Enterprise* fired at the *Peregrine* again.

The *Peregrine* dropped. It was close enough that the *Peregrine* shuddered, but she returned fire, narrowly missing an upper arm at the stern. Gino wondered if the crew in it was watching the battle.

"*Enterprise*! What the fuck?" Gino asked.

The *Peregrine* disappeared behind the *Enterprise*.

From the *Enterprise*'s starboard, Tony fired on the

Enterprise and ripped an ugly gash down the hull, yielding a lightning show of blue sparks. He fired another volley, but it hit only empty space.

"Gino, take us around to the bow until Ursinus is shining right into their bridge's viewscreen!"

But Gino had already planned for this, and he swung the ship around. The orange light of Ursinus flashed off of the *Enterprise*.

The *Enterprise* fired, but the shot went wide. Tony fired back and scoured the kraken off. "Dammit! Not close enough!" He fired again and took out a chunk of hull behind the bridge. The sparks crossed the line of sight of the viewscreen.

"I hope they're shitting bricks!" Tony said, and he fired again, but the *Enterprise* had dropped, turned, and fired on the *Peregrine*, the blobs reflecting light off the hull and moving into space.

"That thing moves faster than anticipated," Kinkead said ship to ship.

Suddenly, Gino got a transmission. It was faint. "*Kestrel* and *Peregrine*, hold your fire! There are fifty-three of us trapped on the ship! I'm Sergeant Caro Dean!"

"And?" Gino asked. "Your captain is trying to murder us. This is the *Kestrel*."

"He's not our captain! There was a mutiny. Forty-seven people control the ship. There are fifty-three of us. Runhede murdered the rest."

"Runhede murdered *two hundred people*?"

"That's affirmative, *Kestrel*. Please hold your fire!"

The *Enterprise* fired on the *Kestrel*.

The *Kestrel* dove, fired, and breached the hull plating in the belly of the *Enterprise*, taking people and cargo with it.

"Little busy right now evading your ship's weapons! Can you get to the shuttle bay, Sergeant?"

"That's a negative. We're trapped in D-20! That's the twentieth floor of the upper starboard arm. One of you took out the power back here. We're stuck."

Tony hit comms. "*Enterprise*, hold your fire! Hold your fire!"

Instead, the *Enterprise* fired on the *Peregrine* again, sending multiple volleys. In the process of firing at the *Peregrine*, it nearly took out a portion of its own hull. Then it fired on the *Kestrel*.

Gino lurched the *Kestrel* upward.

"Friends don't let friends drive drunk!" Kinkead said ship to ship.

But the *Kestrel* took a hit, knocking Gino out of his seat and frying an instrument panel.

"What'd we lose, Gino?"

"Environmentals! We've got an hour's worth of air, max!"

"We won't be here an hour!" Tony fired again. "Where's the *Peregrine*?"

Gino saw space debris, and his stomach lurched. The smell of burning electronics coming from the instrument panel gave him a chill.

But it was *Enterprise* debris. Gino relaxed. Tony was firing at the *Enterprise* again, cracking the belly of the hull.

The *Enterprise* fired once more, and a plasma ball lit up the smaller moon, revealing what looked like metal debris.

"*You idiot!*" Captain Runhede screamed. "*You blow up that moon and God knows what happens to the climate!*"

It lit up again when the *Kestrel* returned fire.

"Nice of the *Enterprise* to keep their hand on the intercom!" Kinkead said ship to ship, coming back around from the rear of the *Enterprise*.

Gino saw a geyser of light.

"Shuttle bay's gone," Kinkead said to the *Kestrel*.

The *Enterprise* fired on the *Peregrine* again and missed. And missed again.

Gino watched the plasma balls' reflection on the *Peregrine*'s hull, like flashlights in the woods.

"*Enterprise*! Your crew's gonna have to walk to the surface from outer space!" Gino said. "Hold your fire!"

"Oh, shit, look at that," Kyr said.

A shuttle flew past, a small parallelogram with runners.

"*Kestrel* to Broken Oar," Gino said. "A shuttle's on the way."

"Received. Welcoming committee in place," Ror said.

Tony fired on it and missed.

"It's too small! We'll waste time!" Kyr said on ship comms.

Gino took the *Kestrel* behind the second moon, closer in size to Earth's, waiting for the *Peregrine* to get out of the line of fire. The moon was a red-gray ball, tidally locked with Ursinus b, and the *Kestrel* was in the terminus.

"Kinkead, move out of the way!" Gino said, then he said to Tony, "He's getting flustered."

"Kyr should have piloted. Kinkead could shoot okay."

The *Peregrine* took a hit. Tony fired on the *Enterprise*, and then Gino's stomach lurched. The back quarter of the *Peregrine* was gone.

"We're okay, *Kestrel*, but our Christmas presents were in the back." Gino heard the fear in Kinkead's voice.

Gino brought the *Kestrel* above the *Enterprise*, and Tony fired. He missed the bridge again, but he tore another ragged piece out of the hull and, with satisfaction, Gino saw Human bodies flying out into space, some getting caught up in the laser pulse around the edges like insects in an electric zapper. He grinned wolfishly.

Tony fired again.

"*Enterprise*," Gino said, "you overgrown dildo! Disengage!"

"Disengage, *Kestrel*! *Please!*" Sergeant Dean begged.

Somehow, the *Enterprise* fired and lurched in the opposite direction. The *Kestrel* took a hit.

Gino almost fell out of his chair. "How're we doing, Tony?"

"Pressure dampers holding, but they ask that the *Enterprise* not do that again. What the hell are they firing? Those aren't plasma waves!"

"Who the hell knows?"

From below, the *Peregrine* fired and cut a hole in the side of the *Enterprise*, which fired more plasma balls, missing the *Peregrine*. Then the *Enterprise* lurched backward again, and the *Peregrine* took a hit.

"Fuck me," Kinkead said ship to ship as the *Peregrine* glanced off the larger moon.

Gino knew that the impact would've bounced Kyr off the console in front of him, saved from worse injury by the pressure dampers, but the decel would've sent Kinkead's body flying forward against his seat belt, and the forces would rip him in half, spraying blood everywhere.

Gino heard it, because Kinkead had his hand on the comms.

Kinkead said, "I'm dying, Kyr!"

"You'll meet your ancestors in the sky," Kyr said gently.

"What the hell was that, *Peregrine*?" Tony demanded.

"Disengage," Runhede said. "Or we'll move into orbit and

fire on that nest of aliens." The *Enterprise* fired on the *Kestrel* again. "Prepare to be boarded!"

"*Kestrel*, hold your fire!" Sergeant Dean pleaded.

"With what, asshole?" Gino asked Runhede. "Your shuttles are space dust!"

Tony went ship to ship with the *Peregrine*. "You two catch that?"

"Kinkead is dead," Kyr said over the comms.

At Tony's look, Gino saw red, and Tony let go a volley of fire at the *Enterprise*. In the distance of space, most of them missed, but one blew off the top of one of the ship's arms.

"Somewhere, he's still holding forth," Tony said.

"Affirmative," Kyr said.

The *Peregrine* aimed for the *Enterprise*'s belly but missed again.

"Disengage and prepare to be boarded!" Runhede shouted.

"That's a long walk, asshole," Gino said.

But the *Enterprise* started moving into orbit.

On ship comms, Kyr asked, "What happens if the *Peregrine* collides with them?"

Full of dread, Gino said, "You'll turn the *Enterprise* and the *Peregrine* into a fireball."

"Gino, the damage to the *Peregrine* is too great. I won't survive reentry, and you know it."

Gino knew it.

The *Enterprise* continued moving into orbit.

They had minutes.

Desperately, the *Peregrine* and the *Kestrel* fired on the *Enterprise* in unison. They cut more holes in the hull, but the *Enterprise* wasn't stopping.

"Stop, *Kestrel*, please!" Dean was sobbing now.

The *Peregrine* backed off, and Tony said, "What the hell are you doing?"

Ship to ship, Kyr said, "We have no choice. Back off."

Despairing, Gino took the ship behind the larger moon.

Then the *Peregrine* rammed into the *Enterprise*.

Gino saw a flash of light and then nothing but space.

"Let's go home and take out the garbage," Tony said, voice shaking.

ELIZA STOOD on a turret armed with a laser rifle. She was flanked by Kovian 2 and the *Kestrel* botanist, Shannon Rodgers.

Eliza saw a flash in the sky. "Pray that's the *Enterprise*," she said in horror.

A moment later, she could make out a small shuttle heading straight for the village, and Eliza felt panic rising. "Fuck you, *Enterprise* shuttle!" she yelled, and felt better.

Kovian 2 opened fire, and Shannon followed with a single burst.

Eliza aimed her rifle at it again, but then paused, whispering, "What's it doing?"

The shuttle wasn't returning fire at all. It tried to land inside the village, but as it hovered, it took laser cannon fire, so it retreated and landed in front of the gate. Only Eliza's turret and the Spiders' turret had the shuttle in their line of sight.

"It must not have weapons!" Eliza said, and her relief was visceral. She opened comms with Badri on her comm-watch. "The shuttle has no weapons, Badri!"

"Then get out of there!"

"No—"

Badri disconnected.

Ten crewmembers poured out of the shuttle, lasepistols already drawn. One was obviously a teenager, and he held back near the shuttle door. The rest of crewmembers ran behind the shuttle, then appeared to figure out that the shuttle was too tall for them to take cover there and see what they were aiming at, both at the same time. The teenager crouched behind the nose of the shuttle.

The crewmembers in the rear all threw themselves on the ground, except one, who knelt.

The one who knelt was a very pregnant woman.

Eliza's stomach lurched.

"Open the gates!" the pregnant woman yelled. "Or we'll blow them open and kill you all!"

"Go fuck yourself!" came from the Spiders' turret.

The pregnant woman crouched at the rear corner of the shuttle and took aim—right at Eliza's turret. Eliza took cover, but the shot came up short and she heard stony debris skittering down the side of the wall below her.

Eliza knew that the walls were nearly impervious, but she still shouted, "You bitch!" and fired at her. The pink gravel turned purple and melted into globs of glass.

"You'd shoot at a pregnant woman?" she shouted at Eliza's turret, enraged.

"You're shooting at us!" one of the Spiders said.

The Spiders, Kovian 2, and Eliza fired a volley at the woman, but she had withdrawn behind the shuttle.

Eliza was relieved they'd treated the lichenwood with flame retardant before the battle.

The pregnant woman suddenly emerged and fired again,

killing one of the Spiders in the turret. Eliza could see the blood spray.

To Eliza's left, Shannon started to cry.

"Don't cry! You can't aim if you cry!" Eliza said.

Shannon was panicking, firing at random, and she hit the shuttle. Then she stood up, probably to get a better view.

Eliza ran over and pulled her down, saying between gritted teeth, "Take. *Cover.*"

Shannon, weeping, said, "They killed Eris!"

"They'll kill you too if you don't keep your fucking head down."

But Shannon stood up again, fired on a crewmember, and missed.

Shannon's head exploded, spraying Eliza's face and shoulder with blood. Eliza smelled ozone, iron, and blood and felt sick. She felt Bynum's shade in the turret for a moment, and she broke out in goosebumps.

Then she took a breath and aimed at a crewman. He too was firing wildly, nearly winging the woman next to him. Eliza blew him in half. She singed the woman with her next shot.

The woman ran, and Eliza fired again but missed. The woman flattened herself against the wall and tried to open the gate.

"They're wearing a patch with a black kraken on a red field," Kovian 2 said. "Under their Star Service insignia."

Eliza's stomach filled with ice water. She remembered Glenn's tattoo—and Jamie's horror.

Suddenly, the teenager fired on the woman near the gate, and she dropped.

"*You catch that?*" Eliza asked Kovian.

"*Fuck yeah!*"

None of the other shuttle crew appeared to notice where

that last shot had come from because their attention remained on the turrets.

The Spiders in their turret shot and killed a crewmember, their volley of fire reducing her to body parts.

Eliza saw that the shuttle was marked with a black kraken with red eyes. *Glenn's tattoo.*

From beneath the aft of the shuttle, a crewman was eyeing Eliza's turret. The Spiders kept firing at him, but he took cover behind the shuttle again. His broad face was expressionless. He took aim at Eliza's turret, standing up in the process, and she literally shot him in half. The lower half was twitching, and the crewmember was gasping and clawing at the dirt.

"We're gonna have to call in the Donners as a cleaning crew," she said aloud to Kovian 2.

"*Why isn't the kid going inside the shuttle?*" Kovian 2 asked.

Two crewmembers fired at the turrets again, one each. Eliza took cover.

Kovian 2 shot a crewman, whose head exploded. The pregnant woman let out a keening wail. She was beside herself, and started firing expertly at the Spiders' turret, taking a foreleg off one of them. Grotesquely, it fell to the ground.

Eliza heard cursing coming from the turret.

The teenager shot another crewmember, taking out one of his legs. The wounded man started screaming and tried to crawl under the shuttle. The teenager shot his head off.

One of the crew looked at his decapitated shipmate in shock and dove beneath the shuttle, lay on his belly, and fired at the Spiders' turret.

Eliza shouted, "Fuck you!" Then she said, "*How doesn't he notice that the kid's killing their own?*"

"*Tunnel vision,*" Kovian 2 said. "*Stress.*"

The teenager fired on the crewmember beneath the shuttle,

turning the man's neck into a stump. The Spiders fired all at once, but the crew had taken cover. Black streaks appeared on the skin of the shuttle. The teenager shot another crewmember, who dropped.

Eliza didn't trust the teenager to stay put, so she was afraid to fire on anyone close to him in case she shot him by mistake.

Kovian 2 telegraphed her an image of Cody, and she replied, "*Yeah, he reminds me of him too.*"

The teenager shot at the last two crewmembers, but they kept changing position, so he missed.

The man looked at the teenager and shouted, "What the hell are you doing?"

Eliza realized that in the heat of combat, the pregnant woman hadn't figured out that the teenager was shooting his own people.

Finally, the light went on for the pregnant woman, and the teenager was flanked.

Thinking of Maura, Eliza said, "Oh no you don't, fuckers —get out. Of the line. Of fire!" she said to the teenager, who she knew couldn't hear her. "Get out of the way! Get out of the line of fire!" she shouted at him. To her relief, the kid ducked beneath the shuttle, and she and Kovian 2 fired on the remaining two crewmembers.

The pregnant woman, from the nose of the shuttle, began firing on the gate.

The village had drilled for this scenario, and what happened was what Kinkead had said would happen.

Rebound.

One of the woman's shots ricocheted off the gate and hit her. There was blood everywhere. When the dust settled, a well-developed fetus lay on the ground in their mother's blood and globs of glass. The baby started crying. The kid dove for the child, nearly taking a hit from the lone crewmember, and retreated with the baby, taking cover beneath the shuttle.

The remaining crewmember was still out in the open, and the volley from both turrets blew him into hamburger.

The teenager was tying a knot in the baby's umbilical cord.

He looked around. Eliza knew that his shipmates were dead. So, obviously, did the teenager.

He laid down his lasepistol, crawled out from under the shuttle, then dropped to his knees, put the baby in front of him, and put his hands on his head.

GINO AND TONY hadn't notified the village of their return because they wanted to do so in person. The walk from the shuttle was excruciating, and the men were silent. As soon as they saw the village in the distance, they held their lasepistols at low ready.

They walked past the shuttle and the carnage at the gate. Tony started quietly counting bodies, then he relaxed. Gino pointed to the base of a turret. There was a Spider's leg.

The two men traded looks, then walked through the gate.

Broken Oar looked like a ghost town.

They walked into the hospital, past Ror, and sat beside each other on a gurney.

Ror followed.

Eliza's hair was wet, and she was drying it with a cream-colored towel.

"Where are the others?" Ror asked Tony. *"Where?"*

"They rammed the *Enterprise*," Gino said in a guttural voice.

"Why?" Kelly asked, shaking.

"The *Enterprise* blew the back off the *Peregrine*," Gino

said. "No one on board would have survived reentry." Then he took a breath. "Kinkead was already dead. His fucking seat belt."

"The *Enterprise* was going into orbit to destroy Broken Oar," Tony said, hollow-eyed. "There were fifty-three innocents on the *Enterprise*."

He started sobbing, and Denny walked over and put her arms around him.

"Sergeant Caro Dean!" Tony said. "He kept begging us to hold our fire! But the *Enterprise* wouldn't stop shooting! Their captain said they were going to destroy the whole village! What could we have done? Caro Dean begged us to disengage!" Abruptly, he pulled back from Denny and stood up. "I've got to go get some air." He started for the door.

Banner took him by the arm. "Tony, you gonna be okay? You're making me nervous."

"Yeah, I'm fine. I ... I need to get out of here. I just need to take a walk!"

"Strolling among the corpses?" Gino said. "Yeah, okay."

Tony stopped in his tracks.

"Caro Dean wouldn't have wanted the *Enterprise* to turn the village into a crater," Gino said, "and after it landed, his life expectancy would've been what, exactly, if someone was monitoring the comms?"

"We're going to keep you here tonight," Banner said, "if that's okay."

"That's okay, Tony, right?" Denny said. "Please!"

But Tony started crying again. "I'm sorry! I killed Caro Dean! I killed fifty-three people who shouldn't have died!"

Badri quietly walked up to Tony and took his lasepistol.

"*We* did, buddy," Gino said.

"Tony," Banner said, "I'd like to give you something to

help." He handed Tony two pills. "This is kelazine. It's gonna make you sleepy and take the edge off."

Denny handed him a glass of water. "Tony," she said softly, "I'll be here for you when it's time for you to go home. Please do this."

Tony took the medication and stared at it. Then he put it in his mouth and swallowed it.

Everyone in the room relaxed.

"If you have to take this for a while," Banner said, "that's okay. We'll give you a quarter of that dose. It's gonna make you drowsy, so you'll take it at night."

Tony nodded. Denny and Banner led him through the double doors.

When Banner and Denny came back, Banner said, "He'll be out for the night. We'll notify you when he wakes up. If he's safe to go home, then—"

"Then he'll come home with me," Denny said.

"If he's not," Banner said, "he'll have to stay."

Denny nodded.

"Also," Banner said, "I've been doing some reading about cognitive behavioral therapy and EMDR. A trained therapist should be doing this, but we're stuck out here. Gino, I expect you to show up for group. You too, Eliza."

"Do you treat Spiders, Banner?" Wolf asked. "Because my mother ..."

"I can try."

"Who the hell is that?" Gino asked.

Meyer had just walked out of the double doors with a blond teenager with eyes almost as light as Kelly's.

"Who is that little punk?" Gino demanded. "Was he on *the shuttle*?"

Gino stood up, and Badri and Banner held him back.

"*Sit down!*" Badri said, shoving him back into his seat.

Gino sat.

The boy was slightly built and reminded Gino of Cody. He was feeding formula to a newborn through a bottle. The boy sat in a chair, still holding the baby.

"This is Annelise Bauer's daughter," he said to no one in particular. "I'm Keenan Runhede. *That* Runhede. My father was a piece of shit. He wasn't even the real captain. There was a mutiny. Forty-seven of the crew took over. They were going to wipe the planet clean of sentient life and make as many babies as possible." He didn't seem even the least bit fazed by Wolf. Or Kovian 2. Or Kolokh.

"Tony and I know about the mutiny," Gino said, softly. "Caro Dean told us."

"The rest of the crew," Keenan went on as if Gino hadn't spoken, "thought we were a research mission. Except me. I'm thirteen. My dad told his friends to take the people who fought the mutiny to the shuttle bay and opened up the airlocks. Including my mom." At this point, Keenan was crying and talking at the same time. "My father—Peter Runhede—made everyone swear a loyalty oath. They sent the ones who wouldn't out into the shuttle bay. Anyone who said anything Runhede didn't like, he'd have his guards pull them out of their quarters and then make an announcement. Then he'd take them to the shuttle bay. Runhede was going to make *me* do it this time. There were barely a hundred of us left. Some of us made it to the shuttle. We were supposed to ask to be taken in when we landed, but on the way, they decided they could shoot their way in and impress Runhede. Get on his good side. Especially Annelise Bauer. Please just call me Keenan. I don't want to use my last name ever again." Then he said, "Caro Dean was a good guy."

The group remained silent, except for Kelly and Kolokh, who had been whispering.

Finally, Kolokh said to Keenan, "You and the little one will live with us."

"The two of you have a sister and a brother," Kelly said, "whose father was also a piece of shit."

Keenan wiped tears away with one wrist. Meyer gently took the baby, whispering something to Keenan, then nodding.

"What's the Q stand for? Your—Peter's middle initial?" Gino asked.

"If he had been a girl, he would have been Petra Runhede, after one of our ancestors. She ran a place where they harvested people's organs when they're over fifty or something. We haven't had those laws in a long time. The Q? He wouldn't tell anyone."

"*Omigod!*" Meyer said at the same time Gino said, "Ding-dong the witch is dead."

When Kolokh embraced Keenan, his shirt slipped up, and his back was covered with bruises.

Kelly collapsed, throwing up.

"Did I do that?" Keenan asked.

"No," Kelly said from the floor.

Ror and Kolokh lifted Kelly onto a gurney, then Kolokh started wheeling her behind the nearest curtain.

Meyer looked at Kelly knowingly and said to Ror, "Will a Hansen scan hurt a fetus?"

After a moment, Kelly called from behind the curtain, "His name will be Kyr."

Ror said, "We need to tell Lita and Malit."

"We need to send those probes to Earth," Gino said.

THE DAY AFTER THE BATTLE, practically all of the residents of Broken Oar stood in the central plaza. A makeshift stage had been built. Everyone in Broken Oar who had helped preserve the village stood closest to the dais. Ror, Da'in, Wolf, Belek—with George clinging to his back—Kovian 2, and Banner. Someone had hauled forward the reluctant Eliza and Badri. Tony stood on it with Denny. He still looked hollow-eyed, but calm. Ralph was sitting on his feet, sidesaddle, and Scout was leaning against him. Gino stood beside him.

By agreement, Keenan stood in front too, looking self-conscious and shifting from foot to foot. Impulsively, Jhuq and Channa joined him. Jhuq put his hand on Keenan's shoulder, and Channa put her arm around Keenan's waist.

Also on the stage hovered the two probes, each the size of a mini-compact car but shaped like computer mice. They were sleek, silver, and labeled *Kestrel Alpha* and *Kestrel Beta*.

Tony and Gino walked up to a microphone together.

Gino said, "These probes will tell Earth that Ursinus b— basically, I told them they'd be trying to land on what amounts to our planet Venus. Too hot, too corrosive, impossible atmospheric pressure, methane atmosphere, don't come here, you'll die. I told them that Ursinus c was like our dwarf planet Pluto. Too cold to sustain life, almost no atmosphere, no magnetic field, don't go there, you'll die. None of the moons support life either. Sorry. We tried to retool the ship to return to Earth but were unsuccessful. The *Peregrine* lost atmosphere due to a malfunction. We tried to warn the *Enterprise*, but we received a distress call that something disabled their ship and zapped their environmentals. Don't bother coming here. We're dead. The end."

"Will they believe you?" Enkhid asked.

"It took an obscene amount of time and money to build those ships," Gino replied. "No one's gonna sink another dime into that project. They'll keep trying to build ships that go faster than ST-9, maybe try to put everyone under and send the ships out randomly, but if anyone tries to get here, it won't be Humans. Tony, will you light the birthday candles?"

Tony knelt, opened a side panel on *Kestrel Alpha*, typed even more rapidly than Gino, then closed the panel. He repeated the process with *Kestrel Beta*. "The panels will seal up now."

The villagers watched the two probes take off until they were too far to be seen even by the Kharkuns.

The Humans and, to Eliza's shock, the Kharkuns applauded. *They applaud? Huh.*

From the stage, she saw Inani looking at her with cold speculation. Standing next to Inani, Baines was looking at Kelly like she wanted to rip her throat out.

As she left the stage, Eliza told the other adults what she saw.

Then she and Badri walked back to their home together.

ACKNOWLEDGMENTS

First and foremost, I would like to thank the Cops and Writers Facebook page, because even though I am a former prosecutor, that does not make me a cop, and their wisdom and selfless assistance helped me get it right. I'm also so very grateful to Danny Plott, retired from the Virginia State Police Bureau of Criminal Investigation, for fact-checking the interrogation scenes and police work.

It's a foregone conclusion that even editors need editors, so I would also like to thank the following: copyeditor John David Kudrick for finding discontinuities and pointing out issues with clarity, because in retrospect, they make me cringe; proofreader and book designer Katherine Kirk who helped make my book shine; and cover designer at AuthorsHQ.

I wish I could thank by name the chief instructor, lead instructors, instructors, and my fellow students at my martial arts training center for teaching me on an ongoing basis how to defend myself using street fighting techniques. Because of them, my fight scenes are realistic. I would name them and my school, but don't ever broadcast to strangers how to find you.

I thank Guy, for listening to me go on and on about this book; my dear friend/Guy's cousin Laura, for being a listening ear; Joey, cat extraordinaire, who posts himself at my side on the couch and reminds me when it's time to take a break by reaching up and pulling my glasses off my face; and my gigantic, hypervigilant potato dog Frederick, for sometimes making room for me on the couch.

I'm grateful for the bears. (*Ursinus* means *bear* or *bearlike* in Latin.) This book was conceived of long before the man vs bear idea emerged on social media and has nothing to do with that question. (Choose the bear.) You will see more bears in Book 2, *Sick Puppies*.

I apologize to the hours between 6 a.m. and noon. As a result of my work on *A Million Monkeys*, I haven't seen you in a while. Since I'm now working on *Sick Puppies*, let's plan to get together some time in the future. Really. I promise.

ABOUT THE AUTHOR

Karin Horwatt Cather is a former prosecutor and child welfare attorney, martial artist, and editor of detective fiction, science fiction, forensic psychological/psychiatric reports, and memoirs of first responders. She lives in the Phoenix, Arizona, metro area with her dog, Frederick, and her cat, Joey. She grew up in Reston, Virginia, a  planned community, and moved to Arizona with her two children in 2007. She switched from the practice of law to editing to take care of a sick family member and wished she switched sooner. As a nonpracticing attorney licensed in two states, she does not miss the eternal conflict, the paperwork, the dry cleaning bills, and the commute.